Herough
Herough

Herough
Herough

A NOVEL

GARTH BEYER

Herough Herough
by Garth Beyer
First Edition

ISBN 979-8-9985620-0-6

This is a work of fiction. Names, characters, places, and incidents are either products of the author's imagination or are used fictitiously. Any resemblance to actual events, locales, or persons— living or dead—is entirely coincidental.

"If you're the kind of person who reads the copyright page,
email me with the subject line: 'The oyster is awake.'"
thegarthbox@gmail.com

Cover design by professionals at Damonza
Edited by professionals at Kirkus, Reedsy, and Upwork

Published by GarthBox
www.garthbox.com
Madison, Wisconsin

Printed in the United States of America
First Printing

A special dedication to Tom, Kurt, Seth, Kodaline, and Sweet Cheeks.

"A book I would like to see made into a movie. *Herough Herough Herough*. Good luck."

Herough Herough is a novel by Garth Beyer, concerning the battle for business between two competing seafood restaurant owners. The story encompasses a broad range of topics including Cambodian spies, women with freckles, consumerism, personal libraries, hot sauce, hot romance, not-hot rap artists, umbrellas, and a few empty containers of chocolate milk. The novel continuously addresses the question of "How do I keep moving forward?" and some might call it a "post-modern daydream."

≥ I ≤

"There's a leak in the boat!"

Jim Herough Bois, with a seething but sleepy "*zzz*" at the end due to his Idahoan ancestry, was a joker, a jester, a jubilee of hahas. He would carry a leek—a vegetable grown in abundance in the otherwise tiny community garden beside his apartment complex in New York City—and place it somewhere that would be detrimental, a nightmare, a panic attack awaiting anyone who found an actual leak there. "There's a leak in the"— here is where JimBo inserts a place or an object that could have a leak—"boat, toilet, stomach!" he would shout. Few found this joke humorous. Jim didn't care. If it made him laugh, it was funny. And it always made him laugh.

Jim owned a restaurant called Herough. Customers attributed it to his middle name. Jim attributed it to the number of Asian jokes at his disposal, which he was proud to tell at informal, and sometimes (to the host's dismay and chagrin) formal, tasting parties. In fact, whenever a patron would arrive, Jim would greet them with a bellowed "Herough!"

Funnily enough, his laugh rings to the same sing-song sound as his middle name: *Herough Herough Herough*. At most tasting events—not that Jim made an abundance of time for them—his laughter, his middle name, and the way he'd greet people all bled together, like a massacre for comedians.

Jokes aside, Jim wasn't the greatest businessman, but he had one thing going for him: He knew that the businesses that would be a success in five years would be the businesses that would be a success in five years. There was no doubt in his mind about that.

If you think about it, not many of the most successful people in life are the greatest businesspeople. Not at first, anyway. Jim would be. One day. Perhaps by the end of this story.

Perhaps...

Anyway, in addition to a particular sense of humor, Jim had something most others didn't: a passion for food. A real passion. Not the kind of I'm-a-foodie mentality. Not the kind that prompts someone to take a photo of the food, the drinks, the plates, the silverware, the napkin, and anything else that's on the table in front of them.

Jim cooked. And when Jim cooked, he *cooked*. He might be a daily amusement, but he put the *muse* in *amusement* when he cooked. Cooking was his craft. In the kitchen, he was the captain. A culinary maestro. The Picasso of the palate and the sultan of sauté. Jim could take mundane ingredients and turn them into edible symphonies. And he was an artist: In his kitchen, measurements were mere suggestions and recipes were but guidelines. Precision? That was for amateurs. Jim scoffed at the notion of measuring cups. He didn't even own one.

Using his imagination, his inherent humorous charm, or the fork in hand, Ol' Jim, or rather *youngin'* Jim, loved to laugh. His laugh would shake martinis. His laugh would make the air that didn't carry it jealous. His laugh would echo in your head, for better or for worse. *Herough Herough Herough.* Even if Jim laughed for just a short second, it would ripple through the air like a melody written by joy itself. There was a contagious quality to it, an infectious rhythm of sorts; a cozy blanket for the ears of passersby.

Very few laughed harder at Jim's jokes than his friend Lemon Fraser. Lemon laughed harder than a hyena on a comedy club tour.

Believe this: Jim's best friend was a natural public speaker. Just as Jim excelled with food, Lemon could squeeze an assortment of letters together to get a standing ovation. All while coping with a disability of sorts. Lemon had an unusual form of what seemed like Tourette's, and people loved him for it; so much so that Jim wished society would quit trying to cure it and start trying to leverage the power to make it like Fraser's.

That's Jim for you, though, always making a positive out of a negative. Deep down, at the core of it, Lemon and Jim both believed the world needed more people who spoke up and said what was on their mind—in fact, repeating it a few times to drive the point home never hurt. Along with an expletive or two to make the statement permanent in the brain. Maybe Lemon didn't have Tourette's after all. Maybe his parents simply forgot to install a filter for him after he was born. Speaking up; that's what Fraser did. He spoke up. Turns out, speaking up comes out more elegantly than what our lizard brains lead us to believe when we lean into it with focus and intention and, like a good ad about syrup—or any consumer good, really—... repetition. Repetition. Repetition.

Fraser recited a poem a few times at a party Jimmy held. And be it because of his speech condition or not, he reiterated it a few times through the night. Some were grateful to hear his poetic monologue of less than twenty words, regardless of whether it was the fourth or fourteenth time they heard it that night. The moon may have disagreed, however. But again, that's Fraser for you.

After giving it a shot the first time and hearing Jim's laugh, Fraser just had to repeat it. It gave people a second chance—maybe a dozen—to understand his points before the punchline. Their brains needed to air the words like a glass of cabernet or make some up where there were none. Fraser's mini-monologue gave people the one thing they craved most about attending a wedding: an escape from the real world. That was one of Lemon's party tricks—he let others find a void. Sometimes he'd stop mid-sentence just to see how long it would be until someone chimed in to ask if he was going to finish. It helped him ascertain if people were paying attention or not.

As skilled as Fraser was in letting someone lose themselves in their own abyss, he had the creative mindset to get them back.

No one could spin a cliché on its head and still gather enough street money to pay for rent like Fraser could.

More on Fraser later, though; right now we find our barley-built protagonist hopping around his SoHo pad. It's been three months since the doors opened at Herough. Ninety-one days. 2,184 hours. And some amount of minutes. But Jim's not tracking *that* closely.

The three months hold their own special story. For now, the time is today. The person is Jim. And Jim? Jim's bored.

Bored is when you look in the fridge when you're not even hungry. Bored is when you can hear your own heartbeat because the world around you doesn't have your attention. Bored is when your thumbs don't even want to twiddle. Jim was peering in the back of the fridge trying to find the raspberry jam he canned a year ago. He'd picked the raspberries himself. Rather, he stole them. Jim had only ever stolen two things in his life: raspberries, and a Mac computer from a friend who had it coming. If you ask him about it, he says he went raspberry and apple picking. The punchline would be followed with the ever-natural *Herough Herough Herough* when he'd tell the story to guests at his restaurant.

He found the jam next to some expired eggnog. Jim took the jam and left the eggnog. *I'll find something to make with it,* he thought to himself as the refrigerator door shut on its own, albeit slowly and loudly due to rusty hinges. Jim didn't necessarily believe in best-by dates. But it wasn't that he was ignoring the dates. If anything, he knew he would stretch his artistic capabilities by using something that was well past its best-by date. No one else would. Isn't that the core quality of the avant-garde, of the remarkable, of the heroes we admire in our lives? They embody the opposite of status quo and expectations. Best-by to Jim could be someone else's best buy.

Jim was squinting, trying to see in his apartment using what little light was seeping through the porous blinds that came stock with the space. Jim set down the jam on the counter and clapped twice to turn the lights on. He squinted tighter now, trying to let his pupils adjust. He reached for a dirty—and at that moment blurry—knife in the sink and then pulled out two slices of bread that had white fuzz on them from the cabinet. It was probably mold. He told himself it was flour. *Au naturale.*

A questionable few will tell you that when you start a business with your passion, you tend not to want to put as much energy into that passion at home. Homebrewers-turned-brewers stop brewing at home. Chefs stop cooking for their family. Cleaners stop cleaning in their apartments. Have you ever heard of a prostitute working in their own home? So it goes.

As successful as Jim's restaurant business has become in a few months, defying every prediction of the bank loan officers who denied him a loan to get it started, it's odd how he takes such poor care of his own diet. It's as if you went to the doctor and the doctor was a fat Santa, or learned that your accountant, who has been in business for twenty solid profitable years, is actually in debt himself.

The food at JimBo's home? Not that delightful. The food at Herough? Well, it's tastier than unicorn tongue, tastier than your grandmother's sauerkraut and dumplings, tastier than the gumball you begged your mom to get you while you waited in JCPenney for her to finish her last-minute Christmas shopping. Yea, *that* good.

All the food at Herough is made from Jim's own recipe book. From the crab fly cakes to the cricket crustacean casserole to the decadent chocolate oyster mousse to the candy corn crawfish iscream. (That is how Jim has always spelled ice cream. Brace yourself: Jim likes to do things his own way. These are not typos, my dear reader.)

But not at home. Home had no recipe book. Home was an improv session with expired ingredients put together in a reality-TV-show-level dare.

While Jim slathered the raspberry jam on, nearly blocking any view of the white "flour" on each piece, the lights turned off.

Someone had knocked twice on his door.

After sticking the knife deep in the jam, swaddling it with raspberry seeds, Jim clapped twice to turn the lights back on and walked to the door. On the other side was a man from St. Louis.

Now let me tell you about *this* man. He had an odd Cajun accent. Maybe it was Southern. Or maybe he had a lisp. Or maybe it was just his lack of teeth. Or maybe it was due to the chew he always had in his mouth. Chances are good that you've never seen a man who would chew and smoke a ciggy at the same time, but go ahead and visualize it. That's the reality here outside Jim's door. This man was as rustic as John Wayne's spur in *El Dorado*. His name was Gus Harris, and boy did he have some juicy news.

"Buddy, buddy, you hurr dare opening a [inaudible] restaurant nest to yurrs?"

Jim laughed. "*Herough. Herough.* What were the other options?"

"It isth kinda funny, in't it?"

"Gus, if it weren't funny, I would shoot you in the foot."

They brother-hugged and both walked into the main room and sat on the couch. The floral pattern of it was comforting to Jim. It reminded him of the days when he was little and would knock all the pillows off his grandmother's couch, just to rustle her jimmies. His grandma's couch had similar flower patterns. They were more faded in color than his own, but not by much. That's because Jim got his from someone else's grandma who passed away.

"I downright hate dis couch, Jim, you know that. I have no clue in mah mind why you hang on-tuh it."

"Sentimental value, my friend."

"Yea, while sometimes declutterin' is the punch line ur life needs."

"Yea, I know, I know. When you're right, you're right. But enough about the couch, anyway. About this new restaurant opening. I'm not too concerned about the competition. Sure, I've only been open for three months and the newness is sure to wear off, but I've built my business in a way that can't be replicated, let alone beat. Perhaps I'll phone Frank tomorrow and he can set up a meeting for me with the owner of the new restaurant. You know what they say about a rising tide."

"All ships rise, unless yur one of a thousand in a small bay of the ocean, Jim. But yea, call Frank. That sounds like a splendid idea, Jim. I jus wanted to fill you in on the news. Take curr now, I'll be off. Is late anywho, and I can't take another second ah' lookin' at that couch."

With that, Gus was out of Jim's pad and Jim was back working with his jam, thinking about what he'd say to this new... what did Gus call him? "Competitor."

Whatever you think of Gus, whatever stereotype you're labeling him with, drop it. Sure, Gus is one of those types that—after taking a look at him, or after listening to his voice—you wouldn't dare lend a wad of money to, but Gus is one of Jim's "ins," if you can call it that. Gus's the insider at the restaurant association of SoHo, TriBeCa, and NYC at large. He's the ringer.

Gus found Jim when he was at Ralphie's restaurant, impersonating a cook and doing a hell of a job at it. Gus knows every restaurant owner, cook, server, and hostess by name, even if he may not be able to pronounce them right. Jim has been connected with Gus for a number of years, if only seeing him a few times a year here and there.

That's the thing with headhunters like Gus: As soon as one job is done, it's onto the next.

The Jimster finished his heavily jammed sandwich, flipped on his sound machine, which played the sound of insects from different countries, and leaped into his bed, fully clothed. He saw no use in pajamas. To him, you oughta feel so comfortable in what you wear during the day that you could sleep in the same clothes at night. Plus, you save plenty of space for laundry that way. As each insect joined another in shrill nocturnal harmony, Jim fell further and further asleep, and his imagination began to cricket in. Jim had been doing his thing all day. It was his brain's turn.

Now, JimBo had an odd sleeping condition. He was a hallucinogenic sleeper, a hypnagogic napper, a philosophic (or psychopathic, depending upon which foot you step forward with first when you're pushed) snoozer. With a notebook by his side, he would scribble, scrawl, and sometimes scrape on the pages during the night. He jotted stories his brain produced while half-asleep, in another dimension. He always thought he had it better than any Buddhist. "Don't confuse anxiety with fear," Jim Bois would say to himself as a mantra before going to bed. "You'll make a lot of enemies by doing so." It was as if the sound machine Jim had by his bedside filled the air with shrooms as he went to sleep. Gentle Jim clapped his hands—lights off—and closed his eyes. Within minutes his foot was off the side of the bed. His leg fell asleep while the rest of his body tingled. His brain punched in and got to work. There were many rows for it to hoe.

Jim woke up a couple of hours later and wrote about what he'd dreamed in his tableside notebook, the cover of which showed a city line like a heartbeat monitor. NYC, baby. The Big Apple. The one he longed to steal but knew he never could.

There were already a few notes about beignets and WWII Spam, but now he wrote about how The Molasses

Gang of the Seventies was at it again. They would force a shopkeeper to fill a hat with molasses and then slap it over his head—with a gun pointed at you, what wouldn't you do?—and then they'd run off with the shop's cash register. This time was different, though. This time the shopkeeper ran out after them, molasses sliding down his face and a gun in hand. He shot. The bullet clipped the hand of the Molasses Gang member who was carrying the container of cash. It hit the ground, popped open, and the money flew out. The wind took the money and blew it toward the shopkeeper. The Molasses Gang kept running, helping the wounded member along with them. Adrenaline rushed through the shopkeeper's body and his brain registered that they were leaving an index finger behind. Money stuck to the shopkeeper's molasses-pasted face. He managed to get most of his money back; however, who would choose to accept his cash in such a state of dirt and molasses? Nobody, that's who. What a waste of giving the undeserving attention. But hey, at least now the shopkeeper had a sticky story for why his money was covered in molasses—and a severed finger as proof that crime doesn't pay... in cash, anyway.

≽ II ≼

Jim woke up to his alarm at 6:00 a.m. on. the. double. dot. He shut it off, hitting it a bit more aggressively than necessary, but there was still a buzz in his street-art-filled room even after the alarm went silent. A bee had evidently found its way through a hole in the screen window and landed on his bedside. Jim gave the bee a menacing look and it flew away. Jim had the same effect on people he didn't care for. Fortunately for people—less for bees, to which he was allergic—Jim had a pretty open heart. He saved the hard stares for the black-and-yellow-winged annoyances.

He didn't care what kind of bee it was. It wasn't like the doctor gave Jim's mom a chart of all the different bees in the world and which ones Jim was allergic to. He pumped Jim with some Benadryl and that was that. Jim and bees? *No bueno.* The world saw black and yellow. Jim saw red and dead.

He first learned of his menacing power in college. In a philosophy class, as it happens. Another student raised his hand and asked a dumb question about Plato's cave. It had something to do with the man not watching the shadows but watching the light. Because the man has always stared at the cave wall, there's no way of knowing that the darkness that moves on it is actually a result of what's happening behind him; that the lightness on the wall is what's really moving. Yes, his question was this dumb and unclear. The look this boy received from Jim petrified him. After three inquiries by the professor and a prod in the ribs from a student sitting behind him, the boy finally came back to reality. Shook his head, apologized, and never spoke in the class again. Funnily enough, Jim wasn't actually paying attention to the student himself. There had been a bee hovering right behind him. The unlucky student was simply caught by friendly fire.

Since learning of his talent, Jim has used it plenty of times to his advantage. He's given it to a few guys at bars so he could make a move on a lady. He's given it to his greedy, constantly begging cousin-in-law who—as is typical of any drug-addicted person—only shows up when he needs something. Jim even used it on an ex-girlfriend a few times when she wouldn't quit pestering him while he was running food orders at a local diner and trying to learn the practices of the talented and underappreciated chef in the back (whom he would eventually impersonate in order to get some more "hands on experience"). Again, he used the power sparingly, though a bit more often on Halloween. Bzzz.

Around Jim's apartment, aside from the street art, you'll see an out-of-place rustic—vintage, maybe, or retro, depending on the generation you grew up in—chandelier from a 1950s restaurant that Jim's grandmother opened. Jim is a keeper of both family memorabilia and art. Though, if you ask him, art is merely a form of memorabilia. He scoffs at those who wish for the superpower of teleportation to see the wonders of the world when art is already all around them. Anyway, on nearly every inch of his walls, a photo of street art hangs. Jim would get into bidding wars to buy a piece of street art that spoke to him. Back in the diner days, he'd take his tip money and walk the back alleys to purchase what spoke to him. He'd walk by, and it would be as if the seller was a ventriloquist, the way the art coerced him. Oddly enough, Jim doesn't dabble in art himself. In fact, his fingers have never pressed down on the top of a spray paint canister or touched a paintbrush, unless you call squid ink an artistic tool or a grill brush an artistic accessory. All in the eyes of the beer holder, they say.

Jim threw off the covers, walked over to the only window in his apartment that opened, grabbed his robe off the sill—he set things there to warm up from the natural sunlight (robe, lotion, chocolate chip cookies, you know)—and then he closed the window so no other bees could come in, lest he need to give them "the look" again. He may still have been in his street clothes, but the robe gave him comfort and put a bit of gumption into his step.

Like most mornings, business first.

Jim tied his robe tight and grabbed his phone, sifted through the recent messages he'd sent, found Frank's name, tapped it and selected the call icon. Frank was on speed dial, but who uses that? Jim poured a cup of coffee while he listened to the ringtone of Beethoven 5. It was always frustrating calling Frank because as soon as the high notes of Beethoven would begin, he would pick up and you'd be left wanting to hear the rest of it. It was as if Frank waited for that moment every time. No wonder he thought Beethoven 5 was a joke. It was. But only to him.

"Hey there, chap. It's been a while." (It had only been three days.) "Fair to say you're calling about your new streetmate?"

"Funny, Frank. You know how it goes. Straight to business on any call before ten a.m. You-know-who let me in on the news someone is moving in a few doors down from me. Could you tell me who? Have any contact info for me? Spill the beans."

"I see Gus wasted no time in getting to you. I'm actually surprised you waited until morning to ring me. I expected you to wake me from my beauty sleep."

"You know Gus. Well, was my delay a good enough deed to earn the details? God knows you could use more beauty. Your eyes have drooped lower than the tits of a retired stripper since I met you."

"Oh shut it. His name is Phil Hamilton and damn is he gung-ho about it all. Got backers too. He's wired over thirty-six months of lease payments already. He has men working to shape up the place his way, day and night; they were working this morning while you were busy with *your* beauty sleep... I'm assuming he would be there now if you wanted to meet him. He's the kind of guy that says it's his way or the highway, though, so I'm sure he's there micromanaging, making sure everything is up to his kind of snuff."

"Vroom vroom. Frank, do you think I have any need to worry?"

"Well, his family's a group of successful trout fishermen. Have been for two hundred years. Money talks."

"Thanks, Frank. Money talks, but not everyone listens. Anything else?"

"You're talking like a porn star. But actually there is something else. One thing. Don't start any trouble, JimBo. I'm assuming Gus already told you, but Phil isn't one to push, unless you want to be pushed back ten times harder. It's rumored he burned down a neighboring restaurant in Boston. And the place kitty-corner to his place in Austin had a pipe burst... last August. His family is rough. Scrawny. But rough."

"Gus didn't mention that. Thanks, Frank. I'll stop by after I get to the restaurant and meet Phil. Take it easy."

"You too, Jimster. Seriously. No need to go looking for trouble lest you find it."

Jim hung up with a new determination, but somehow, looking at him, you could see the worry beneath. Jim quickly put layers of gumption over it all like a winter coat. No matter how much of a bite Phil may have, Jim wasn't going to be pushed around. He'd worked years to own his own restaurant and he wasn't going to let some pesky pompous man named Phil trump his life's work. Anyway, Jim got to where he was because he abided by the mantra, if you can't take the heat, get out of the kitchen. Jim could take a third-degree verbal burn no problem. Hell, it's a rite of passage for a sous chef.

⇒III⇐

While Jim was a man of routine, something about his talk with Frank made him want to do things differently today.

He tossed his robe off and onto the floor of his medicine cabinet–sized closet. Instead of his typical parfait of overnight oats, raspberries, stem and all, and Greek yogurt, he made himself eggs, scrambled, with equal parts salt, pepper, and a dash of cheese, aged, whether it was supposed to be or not.

After licking the plate clean like a dog that has only stared at the bottom of an empty bowl for three days, he dressed in a tie, as opposed to his typical button-up look which left the top two buttons unbuttoned so some of his chest hair poked out. The hair? Yeah, it's just like you see in movies. And, yes, it did make him feel macho. How you appear on the outside influences how you feel on the inside. That said, he did believe there was a limit to the idea that you can never be overdressed or overeducated. He spent an hour reading Tolstoy instead of the wining and dining food critic section of his neighborhood magazine before heading out the door to pay his visit to Phil. He also performed twenty pushups and thirty dips. I say *performed* because Jim hadn't worked out in six years, since he tried picking up ladies at his college gym using lines like, "My name is Jim, want to work out at my place?" He attempted to make a play off his name but was ultimately unsuccessful. He gave that up, along with working out, after the fourteenth girl in a row turned him down. And she was just that, fourteenth out of fourteen in the lineup of looks. Jim saw the fifteenth and knew it was time to call it quits. This time, though, Jim nearly blew a tricep to get his muscles showing more than normal. If there was one thing he took to knowing about business, it was to fake it to make it. He would play the part of a macho man, a tough guy, a man not to be taken lightly, when he visited Phil. But in all actuality, Jim never needed to put on a show; he merely needed to show what rested on his hip: a .44 Glock. His dad handed it down to him when he was twenty-two. Matte black. As if it was designed to fit Jim's grip. Jim takes the fake-it-to-make-it plan seriously, though. There are no bullets in the Glock.

Though this particular gun was not loaded, Jim had been shooting guns since he was old enough to say, "Pew." Of course, not real guns at that age, but his dad always acted as if they were. Any chance you wondered why there was a hole in Jim's apartment window screen for that bee to fly in? Hmmm...

JimmyBean took his father's role-playing to heart and even trained their golden retriever to play dead when Jim pointed his fingers at it and shouted, "Pew, pew!" Classic.

In all, Jim has shot fifteen sparrows, eighteen doves, seven geese, one turkey, six possums, twelve groundhogs—all in one day!—and twenty-eight other bird species he never looked up in a bird book to find out about. Jim's father was never intentionally watchful. Obviously. Once he taught his son how to shoot, the rest was on JimBo. The DNR has had to talk to him a few times, to say the least, but the cops just once.

On his way south into the city, a two-mile walk from his apartment to the restaurant, Jim stopped in a store to get Phil a restaurant-warming gift, as was tradition at the square his restaurant was located on, or at least that's what the restaurateur before him had said as he handed Jim a basket of week-old avocados. After all, you could be tough while being considerate. That may just be the mark of a true leader, or so Jim figured.

He had a tough time deciding what to get Phil. Jim had to consider the situation fully. He had to stay on Phil's good side per Frank's recommendation, but he also had to make a statement per his own idea for an intimidation tactic as his muscle swell had already disappeared like the tide, along with the fog that had been burned off by the morning sun.

Jim settled on a case of Fitzgerald's Amber, his go-to beer for gifts and for himself on nights he felt inspired to cook his own meal at home. It took a little inebriation to get him to care about himself. There's nothing he'd rather have by his side at the dinner table, anyway. No bottle of cabernet. No bourbon aged in who knew what served in a glass that could dock a cube disco ball of ice like a *Deadliest Catch* boat coming back at season's end. It was Fitzgerald's Amber

or bust. It's a perfectly fine beverage, but you look like a tool
drinking it out in public, especially in NYC, where there's
no shortage of better drinks within arm's reach. This wasn't
a poor man's beer, per se, but it was the beer of a burnout;
present company excluded, of course. Jim was just getting
going.

At the checkout line, Jim contemplated what he would
say to Phil. Would he go on the offensive? Try to make
partners?

Stupidly, but not surprisingly, he'd neglected to ask
Frank or Gus what kind of restaurant Phil had. Jim was,
after all, a run-and-gun, move-forward-fast guy. His ratio-
nale was that he could get more done faster, despite some
hiccups, than those who went slow and achieved work closer to perfection. Coincidentally, I've forgotten to tell you
about Jim's restaurant and how it runs in the family. I'll do
that now.

Jim's family has been in the restaurant business for decades, generations, leaps of time; whatever way you want
to slice the clock cake, it was a long while. However, though
it's a family industry, it's not a family business Jim inherited.
Recall his restaurant memorabilia from his grandmother.
His grandmother owned a diner she was able to expand on
each year. According to his grandmother, his great-grandmother had a house that she practically ran like a restaurant. The moment each of her kids—there were seven—got
old enough and moved out, their rooms were converted
into dining rooms. There were always guests coming in for
breakfast, lunch, dinner, and a late-night snack. There was
no menu, but there was always something new on the table
that even those with the pickiest of appetites who enjoyed
the stingiest or strictest of flavors could appreciate. There
was no register, either. People left whatever they wanted
under their dinner plates as a surprise gift of gratitude.

The diner Jim's grandmother started was actually from
the profits his great-grandmother made from her home.

She left it to Jim's grandmother after she choked to death on a fishbone. Both his great-grandmother and grandmother had odd sales points, actions of distinction they took. His great-grandmother's was the homestyle layout and the lack of formality and structure. She simply had an open door and an always-on oven. Then there was Jim's mother.

Taking a different tack, Jim's mother was a musical artist as well as a food artist. Every week at her diner there would be a new musical theme. Everything was a jukebox. Most of the expansions were intended to attract more people, but actually prevented fitting more people inside. Her place was always crammed, but to add another jukebox or self-running musical instrument, that wasn't even an argument or pros-cons list; it was a calling she had to answer.

The menus were jukebox-shaped, and all the platters were named after songs on the jukebox. Her happy hour was if a particular song was playing at the time of her taking your order. One day it was *Ring of Fire* by Johnny Cash, and your meal would be half price. The next day it may be *Little Red Corvette* by Prince. She, too, didn't have much of a structure and didn't have much money to hand down to Jim; it had to be Jim since his mother never had a daughter. She so resented having a boy that she considered naming him Sue, after the Johnny Cash song. She got over it after Jim took up practicing guitar as a kid.

And that all brings us to Jim and his restaurant endeavor. Now, brace yourself, because Jim's style is probably the most unique of the Bois family.

Jim opened his restaurant, Herough, on Spring Street in Lower Manhattan. It's rustic around the edges and naturesque at the walls, cypress wood lining them with branches of art. The centerpieces, especially the bar, are street-styled with copies of art he has in his SoHo pad. His unique selling point, you may be wondering?

You know how some restaurants have buffet-style lines for salads or pizzas?

The east wall of Jim's restaurant has a line of basins filled with insects. Crickets, grasshoppers (covered in chocolate, of course), caterpillars, ants, centipedes, water beetles, and his personal favorite, scorpions. He's a sea-food-first restaurant, but the cherry on the top of his eel cake is an insect.

When Jim's mother told him about his grandmother choking on a fishbone, he knew he wanted to be in the sea-food business. It was his fuck-you to the sea world.

Jim, as a kid, was known for eating whatever any other neighborhood brat dared him to. Jim was, and still is, fearless when it comes to food. Surprisingly, a lot of people in New York are just as daring, or so the success of his restaurant suggests. I suppose that's the vibe of NYC, and why Phil chose Spring Street as the location of *his* restaurant. It's infested with the most adventurous of neighbors. The street has come to be known as the street where you go to try menu items you've never had before.

As you stroll down Spring Street, your senses are tantalized by the aroma of sizzling octopus tacos and fragrant bowls of Vietnamese *pho* with a twist of lemongrass. Scandinavian French toast with sweet fried plantain for breakfast. Triple smash bison burgers with mango habanero sauce for lunch. And while there were no Michelin star restaurants on the street, anywhere you wanted dinner would result in some form of remarkability. And don't get me started on the drinking situations.

Jim walked past his own restaurant and turned at the intersection onto Howard Avenue. It was obvious which location was soon to be the home of Phil's restaurant. A sign read "Lip's Esquire Club" beside a giant photo of, according to the name below the photo, Phil Hamilton. Above both the sign and the photo was a banner that read, "Opening This Weekend."

That was fast.

Although Jim doesn't typically walk past Howard Avenue, he'd walked by it just a couple of weeks ago to buy a bouquet of flowers for a friend and hadn't noticed any remodeling happening then. The windows in the space had been papered, the same as they had been for the last couple of years. Jim scoffed at Phil's ninjalike ability to turn a vacant space into a restaurant right under Jim's nose. That is, though, something few are told about starting your own business, let alone a restaurant. The rest of the world, whether it's a thousand miles away or a thousand feet, becomes less visible.

Nearing the restaurant now, Jimster could smell a smell he was all too familiar with... trout. His father had been a trout fisherman, always out on the water, never home for dinner and if he was, he was late. Jim's mother cooked trout once a week for fourteen years until his dad had to retire early after a freak accident on the boat that left his leg chopped up, mostly intact but out of commission for future charters.

Their freezers were filled with trout. Lures lined the garage. And the laundry—that's the best part about Jim living on his own now. As a boy, his clothes would always smell like trout because his mother would wash them with his father's. Just one wash together would ruin his clothes, permanently staining them with the stench of a streamlined, speckled, edible torpedo.

The memories flooded Jim's brain as he rounded the backside of the building, where the alley was all but blocked with trucks: delivery, maintenance, and runners. Jim squeezed behind a corkboard door at the back of the building that read "Employees Only" while hoping to himself that the lack of a legitimate door was a sign that there was much more work to be done inside prior to opening. The "Opening This Weekend" sign must be out for a test run, is all. More hope than an honest commitment.

A few steps into the restaurant's back hall and Jim could see nearly the whole shop. Men and women were hard at work with touch-ups, polish, and last-minute elbow grease. It was dismayingly clear the inside was nearly finished. The restaurant already had a vintage, barlike, aquariumesque feel, but something felt off. It had to be the trout smell, but where was it coming from?

"What the hell, Nathaniel! You know better than to lean things against the aquarium glass!"

"Sorry, Boss."

If Jim had the look, Phil had the voice. Jim walked to the person who Nathaniel referred to as Boss, clearly Phil. His image was nearly the same as the one outside. No touch-ups needed. He had a strong jaw, which only accentuated the power of his voice. His eyebrows looked heavy and though he had a nose like a clown, Jim guessed it wasn't one anyone chose to laugh at, and certainly no one would dare honk it.

Jim pulled his shoulders back and walked a bit straighter, catching Phil's glance.

"Jim, I suppose, right? Frank dropped the word you might be stopping by sometime today. Like what you see?"

Not expecting Phil to recognize him, he forgot to hold his shoulders back and they fell forward to their tall-boy slouch position, slackerlike, as if he'd just asked his college crush out and she'd informed him she already had a boyfriend. The kind of slouch one wears in defeat.

"Why, yes, it is. Did Frank mention I would be bringing a gift?" Holding up the case of beer for Phil to see.

Even Jim wondered why he was talking the way he was. His words following the loopity-loop of his brain. Speak defiantly? Defensively? Confidently? Uncertainly?

The space between Jim and Phil was like a battlefield for status. Both were armed and ready. Nathaniel recognized the tension and left the no-man's land without a peep.

"Pleased to meet you," Phil said.

"Likewise."

"Let's take the beer to the kitchen. I'll give you a tour from there; that's where the magic happens, anyway."

Something about Phil's persona was off. Although Phil didn't lead to it, Jim felt he had some thick ice to break.

"Sounds like a plan," Jim said as he followed Phil toward the back of the restaurant. Taking it all in, though his internalization was interrupted before his jaw could do what his shoulders did and droop.

"I heard you tell some great Asian jokes," Phil said.

"I sure do, but the setting has to be right; perhaps if you stop into my restaurant—"

"We'll see," Phil cut in.

It was clear that Phil would never hear an Asian joke from Jim, nor would he hear his laugh or understand the symbolism of his restaurant being named Herough. He had more important things to do.

In the kitchen, Phil pointed out how it was unfinished, indicating that he would be knocking out the walls so attendees could see the cooks handle their food. It was a win-win situation, he said.

"People want a real experience. They want to watch the magician perform his tricks and they want to know how he does it. There's nothing to hide here."

Nobody says that without something to hide.

"Now there will always be someone watching the cooks to make sure they're doing their jobs right and the attendees won't have to worry about the mishandling of their food. People love seeing how things are made. The delivery matters here at Lip's Esquire Club."

Phil spread his arms out, gesturing at the rest of the venue like he was showing off Niagara Falls to a tourist from Mumbai.

"Apologies about the smell, by the way; we just had a practice trout-cooking show for our opening weekend and we're adjusting the ventilation to accommodate the show."

Show? Jim thought. What was this, some circus? Magicians. Aquarium tanks. Jim looked up to make sure there were no trapeze bars hanging from the ceiling. He'd been to a beverage trade show once that had a woman dangling from the ceiling pouring shots to the attendees. After seeing what had been put in place already, Jim wouldn't have been surprised if it was something Phil had considered.

"I love the concept and must agree that delivery matters. How did you come up with the name?"

Jim was still in processing mode. Information intake. Market research, if you will.

"It's called Lip's Esquire Club because although my name is Phillip, no one ever calls me that. I have this thing about full names; I always use them and don't understand how people could call me Phil without me giving it the okay. I figured I'd use the second half of my name which everyone fails to use. If nothing else, it's a reminder for me and my team to respect everyone who enters.

"Anyway, this is where the food is prepared in a showcase, spotlight, circus-style. To the right here is where the aquarium starts. It will run all around the top half of the walls. They're just installing the last of the glass today. Follow me."

Jim was right. This was a circus. Phil, its ringmaster.

Jim couldn't believe the amount of detail he was beginning to see. From the kitchen design to the fishing theme. It finally hit him. This wasn't a circus, it was a seafood restaurant. How had he not picked that up from the smell? He was letting his concern for competition dull his senses.

Jim and Phil stopped in front of one of the seats, which looked like a replica of the seats on *Carol Stream*, a boat Jim's dad had owned and had framed in a photo, one Jim still has on his wall, though it clashes with the graffiti art. The resemblance was uncanny. Jim spaced out on what Phil was saying entirely.

"The tip is written into the price of the food," Phil was saying. "So waiters and waitresses don't have to put on a show to get extra money. Tipping will be highly discouraged. I want people to be able to come in here and chat in private and eat in private, like a getaway from their busy days and shamingly public lives. They can acquire a reasonably priced meal given the atmosphere I'm providing. To allow for further privacy, there are these boat lights, like the ones you see on the top back of boats. Beacons of light, if you will. If a customer wishes to speak to his or her waiter or waitress, they merely need to flip the switch to turn the light on and the waiter will be there in seconds. I considered removing the waiters from the picture except to deliver the meals, letting customers order what they wanted on an electric device, but I thought this neighborhood would still want the social aspect of being waited on, of having a person serving them. It's one thing to order a hot dog from a machine, another to order octopus legs."

Jim was taken aback. Phil seemed equally considerate and outright elitist. *He's a walking oxymoron, but he's walking, and this feels like it might work.*

"Who are you appealing to, marketing to?" Jim prodded, buying his brain more time to process.

The glass installers came in and interrupted them. A machine was whirring right outside, likely to bring the last bit of glass case in.

"Let's go out in front and chat, away from the hubbub. I'm gonna pull my hair out if I've gotta watch Nathaniel coordinate this last glass insert."

They passed two workers lugging a life-sized great white shark toward the accent wall that didn't have the fish tank on it.

"Is that a real shark?" Jim inquired.

"Sure is. Caught it two years ago on the coast of Texas. Water cattle, in my mind." Phil pushed the front doors, which were *not* cork but were covered to prevent peeping

Toms, Terris, and Teresas from seeing how the sausage was getting made. Ironic, given Phil's philosophy on transparency in the kitchen. Oxymoronic, yet again. A man of contradictions.

"I'll have you know outright, Jim. I've had my guys do the research on this area of town, and I plan to buy out your business before long. I'd offer you a check now, but I know I'll be able to offer you something you can't refuse once I get the Esquire Club going."

Phil pulled out a box of matches and lit a cigarette he had tucked behind his ear, which his hair had covered. Jim grimaced and reassessed Phil's culinary acumen. There's no worse palate-killer than smoke. Phil took a puff and continued.

"I'm a very forward man. I hope you'll keep the option open for me. I have a couple of competitors that may try to reach you before I do so they can keep me from expanding my business network. My old man wasn't good at making friends when he first started his seafood restaurant on the West Coast, either. That's not news, but it's a reality I face. And I face it well. Face on."

Well, at least we know where Phil got the inability to make friends from. Jim may have been taken aback by everything, but he was quick-footed. He had to be. He was a businessman in New York. Like a light inside Lip's Esquire Club, something flipped inside Jim.

"It's just as well. I can be quite forward, too."

Jim started to furrow his eyebrows, his face getting eerily close to the look he'd given the bee that morning.

"I have no plan to sell my restaurant, no plan to move, no plan to leave it. I'll have you know outright, Phil. I've had guys make me offers already and I've denied each and every one. It was a hell of a fight to get the location, build the connection with the neighborhood and the vendors I wanted, and I won't be letting it go anytime soon."

There was silence. Jim's glare was in full force. Phil puffed out smoke, real *and* metaphorical.

"We'll see about that," Phil said, meeting Jim's force with his own: his voice. "Take care," he said as he flicked his cigarette toward the curb, turned on his heel and let the front doors close gently behind him. Take care? In actuality, he meant the complete opposite. The tone and tenor told it all.

Jim shook his head and took off up the street, so distracted that he was going the wrong way. Jim's fists were clenched in his pockets. It wasn't until he'd walked two blocks that he began to relax. Phil was a goon. And if Jim knew one thing about goons, it was that they always led themselves to their own demise, but, *but,* most of the time it doesn't hurt to speed up that demise. Jim was already thinking of how to challenge Phil without the restaurant association knowing or the neighborhood caring, without putting his own business at risk. It was clear as day that Jim had to act fast. Frank had been right about Phil.

Rest assured, my benevolent reader, no matter what path Jim might take, he knew there would be fire.

First, though, he would pay a visit to Fraser and then to Frank, if he could get ahold of the damned wit.

≫IV≪

Back at Lip's Esquire Club, Phil was mumbling something about submission not being an option while he put the beer Jim gave him in the fridge, which, unbeknownst to him despite his micromanagement, was not plugged in. A bummer for the workers, who would be the ones to drink it at the end of the day. Alas. Beer is beer to them. Room temp or not.

Phil—and yes, we'll keep calling him Phil rather than his preference of Phillip, as an act of your author's creative

defiance and alignment with Jim—walked to his office, the
first completed room in the club, which had been one of
Phil's many demands. He hovered behind the stand-up
desk and pressed a key on his laptop to wake it up.

On the shelves hung around the office you'll see photos of Phil standing tall. Phil holding a trophy and a giant
walleye. Phil holding up a certificate recognizing his business administration talents. Phil holding up a court order
from a Boston business. It was a trial against him alleging
he'd burned another business's building. He'd won his case
and no charges were seen through.

The left-hand drawer of his desk held boxes and boxes
of matches. He was old-fashioned like that. Phil loved the
smell of lit matches almost more than that of cigarettes.
Phil loved the smell of fire in general. The nuances of it,
charcoal or wood, the fact that it tangoed with other aromas but was always the one leading, one charred step after
another.

On one wall adjacent to the entryway hung a huge
map of New York with red pins—again, how old school, yet
again—sticking out of points that marked restaurants Phil
had already acquired or basically controlled indirectly.
The yellow pins marked those he would focus on acquiring
next. Currently there was only one yellow pin. It was on the
corner of Spring Street. Herough.

Behind his desk, Phil was furiously typing. So furiously that two of the keys popped out of his keyboard. This
wasn't the first time this had happened. Phil had a bit of an
anger problem, but he had it under control. Or at least he
had bought a keyboard with easily reattachable keys, if you
call that control.

He got up and walked to the back of his office, where
he opened the door of his personal fridge, which unlike the
other one was plugged in. Lo and behold, it was stocked with
Fitzgerald's Amber. Yup. The exact same beer Jim had given
him. It was meant to calm his nerves, but its deliciousness

made him angrier. How dare Jim give him such a great gift, which all but ruined the personal supply he would imbibe after a long day managing folks like Nathaniel?

Phil finished the bottle while standing in front of the fridge with its door still open. The coolness leapt from the bottles to Phil himself. He grabbed one more and brought it back to his desk. He closed his laptop and took out a sheet of paper to write on instead, wisely choosing to use a pen rather than a pencil. The pressure he'd put on it would just break it, and that would piss him off even more. It's a pen or bust for Phil. It has been ever since second grade, when he punched a classmate for offering him a pencil after he'd already broken off the tips of all his own. With pen in hand now, Phil was writing his worst-case scenario for taking over Jim's restaurant. He couldn't do anything to Herough, he couldn't hurt its image, couldn't poison the food, couldn't set it on fire either. Phil had been in Herough a few times in disguise and fallen in love with the design. Phil isn't really an evil mastermind wishing to take over New York; he's merely an overly enthused restaurateur who can sometimes act aggressively to acquire what he longs for. He has good taste: in fashion, in food, in felines and females. Heck, you may just call him a bit of a business addict.

Currently, Phil was looking at the two storefronts next to Herough's as an option. He could bribe them to cause a ruckus, so while the restaurant's attendees would complain, they wouldn't be complaining about the restaurant itself, and once Phil bought out Jim, he could resolve the issue and be seen as the hero who brought Herough back to its friendly neighborhood prime. Still, concern over doing any damage to the place, even reputational, bugged Phil. He picked up his phone, dialed, and set up a meeting with an unnamed adviser.

We will have to keep a close eye on Phil, you and I.

While it is early in the story, I would like to talk a bit about Jim's heart. While Jim was usually an unknown in his high school, and even college, his dating history was marked by two unique traits. The first is that he would date girls of different color, accent, language, culture, and personality: overly attached, clean freaks, depressed, girls with other social disorders, and so on.

Jim wasn't known for what he did, but for who he dated.

The other unique aspect was that these girls only dated Jim for his cooking. These famished females loved trying new foods, loved a man who could cook food from their own culture or from their upbringing when their mothers had cooked for them, because they had daddy issues. Although it might sound like Jim was a player and had a Rolodex of women, he didn't. The relationships he entered into, he took seriously, and he stayed in each of them for as long as he could. The same problem ended every one of those relationships, though. Once the honeymoon phase was over and Jim began devoting more time to planning a business rather than cooking, the ladies left him. It's quite depressing really, to only be loved for your food. And they say the quickest way to a man's heart is through his stomach. How sexist.

Two months before Jim was to graduate from college, when he was in top gear learning how to start his restaurant business, his Asian girlfriend left him because Jim stopped cooking for her on weekends. One month later, only a mere three weeks before graduation, Jim met another woman at a sauce and wine pairing event; what was the sauce on, you may (or probably may not) wonder? Insects. It was love at first crunch. Between the dung beetles and the ant balls, they kicked it off talking about their preference for beer over wine, that there were so many other insects out there that could be eaten for nourishment or simply for pleasure, and, most importantly, that they both loved to cook.

That last connection was what solidified the relationship between the two. The conversation got increasingly personal, and she began divulging to Jim that she had broken up with all her boyfriends because, while she loved to cook, she wanted a break now and then, be it just to relax or to do research of her own, undoubtedly making something incredible by pushing the ingredient boundaries too much. She wanted to be pampered at times too. Jim smiled, bellowed his Herough of a laugh, and said, "Would you like to split a scorpion?" The tail of that scorpion is, to this day, sealed in an Aztec Herough laugh, hand-molded canister and displayed atop the spice cabinet in his apartment.

The following months of their relationship were remarkable. Jim even postponed starting his restaurant to travel with the damsel. They would switch off which one decided where they would head next. It was a fast-paced travel experience during which they visited every continent and tried food from more than forty-six different cultures, where culture is defined as a group of people who cause a culture shock.

When it was Jim's turn to decide where to go, he would always choose someplace warm. The reason Jim always suggested some warm place?

Because seeing this woman in a scant few pieces of clothing was the best sight in the world to him. She had average-length legs but always wore wedges or heels to accentuate them. Although pale by nature, the tan she would acquire would color her the hue of a delicious *stroopwafel*. The ends of her hips were fourteen inches from end to end, the perfect birthing length according to experts in the field, but also the perfect width to emphasize what she had behind her, according to self-identified experts in the field. As for her stomach, she had conveniently started working out the same day Jim's last girlfriend broke up with him. By the time they met at the pairing event, she had worked off her extra weight, and there hadn't been much to get rid of to begin with, as is the reality with most women who feel the need to lose weight. She wore a cup size B when she did wear a bra. When given the option during their travels, she didn't. Jim never complained.

Jim would agree with me, though, that nothing was as special as her face. Her nose angled in the same way her firm breasts did. Her eyes the color of a sand crystal, her eyebrows bold but petite. Her ears just petite. Her lips inviting, the rosiness of them never requiring her to apply lip gloss or lipstick. Her long dark hair always looked styled, whether she'd just gotten out of a shower with elephants, pulled it out of a bun... straightened... curly... you name it, she made it work.

Now I must let you down slightly, because this female won't show up again. She's off dancing in another novel, on a research assignment in Timbuktu, chasing down a new species of insect. Disappointed?

Imagine how Jim felt when she turned down his proposal a month after settling into the apartment Jim's still in today. All to say, love has a similar sting to that of a scorpion tail. Between you and I, reader, I'm not sure Jim ever got the poison from the sting out.

⇒VI⇐

"All the business plans you can Google, all the methods rap artists use, all the daily routines of famous writers are wrong. All the business plans you can Google, all the methods rap artists use, all the daily routines of famous writers are wrong. Why are they wrong? Because it's not your method, not your plan, not your routine or formula."

Jim was on the phone with Lemon Fraser, his artistically lingual best man (that's how you spin a negative into a positive), his go-to fellow for advice, inspiration, and just a good bud to talk to. Lemony Snicket was in the middle of reminding Jim of how he'd built his restaurant.

"You've always had your own method, mate. You've done things your own way and they've always worked out. One competitor can't get you down, especially after all you've gone through to get where you are now. You've put too much into your business to let someone else burn you out."

Lemon continued in this vein for the next five minutes, inspiring Jim. I've cut out a lot of what he said because it was repeated multiple times, in true Fraser style, but you'll get the gist of it.

"Stay focused on what your mission is...

"Don't let others deter your attention...

"When you give people like Phil the time of day, you give them the power...

"Failure isn't an option. You've always said that. You'll make it through. When the going gets tough, the tough get going."

And here is when Lemon got a bit sour.

"That being said about you... *He's* a whiny, ungrateful dickhead who has had everything come easy for him. He probably had parents who pushed him this way, gave him money, forced him into this state of mind. Some say there is niceness behind a person's curtain; I think that's bullshit for this guy. He's the type of guy who always had a car at the door, a taxi waiting. I just don't see the point of him wanting your location when there are dozens, hundreds, thousands of other possibilities. I'm sure you would agree that some are even better than the location you have now. He wants what you've built. It doesn't matter. Some people are just assholes, and there is no reasoning with them."

This made Jim feel a thousand and four times better, though a touch confused by the ending remarks. He shrugged those off. You need to take what you want and discard the rest. So it goes. A resurgence of confidence and composure swept over him. And as if on cue...

"All you need to do is remain confident, Jim. You may not be able to get Phil to like you or appreciate your confidence, but everyone else looks up to you. If you break because of Phil, well, perhaps you may not be fit for this kind of role in life after all. But if you stay confident, you'll prove him wrong and yourself right. Stick to your guns, JimBo. You wield them well."

JimBo's shoulders were more pulled back, he regained the steadiness of his stance, and his chin rose to its usual upward position. After getting what he needed from Lemon Fraser, they hung up and Jim settled down in a nook to write to his mother. She loved when he sent handwritten letters. Jim wrote merely twelve words, licked the envelope, and left it in the outbox for the postal service to carry to its destination as he headed to Gendrick's Gin to find Frank. It was just past three, so he figured Frank would be there, as he always was.

When Jimster walked out the door it was already dark outside. Heavy cloud cover made it seem as if it were the middle of the night. From the doorway, Jim couldn't actually see that it was raining, but looking up at the streetlight he could see white specks in front of it. Mini strobe lights from the light waves refracting off each drop from the sky.

Jim began walking the seventeen blocks to Gendrick's Gin. He didn't own an umbrella. He didn't believe in them. The raindrops kissed him on his walk. Mother Nature's way of expressing her love.

Ten more blocks provided enough time for Jim to let his mind wander off on its own, like a happy-go-lucky preteen. He remembered a time as a kid when he ran through flowers without taking the time to smell them. He was interested in what was on the other side of the field. In this case, it had been a hill, and atop that was a swing set. It was completely picturesque. You rarely ever see swing sets on top of hills by themselves. Not in real life. Not even in movies. Typically, you only read about them in books, just like this one. So it goes. There were three swings on the set until Jim broke the third one down so that another boy from school would leave him and Stephanie, the schoolgirl he had a crush on, alone to swing together. When there were three swings the boy would cockblock Jim, even though that term didn't exist for a sixth grader; you get the point.

Then his mind wandered to a time when he had been out hiking with some friends during a day when they skipped high school. Jim was the experimenter of the group—still is—and on the hike had tried eating numerous varieties of insects. Basically any insect his buddies could find, they'd dare him to eat. And when they stopped daring him, he kept going. In particular, there had been a centipede they'd caught by getting all four boys to form a circle and dig together so as not to let it escape; well, that centipede had left Jim's tongue numb for four days. His tongue started to tingle with the memory here and now.

Before another memory arose, and for the thousandth time since hunkering down in New York, he arrived at Gendrick's Gin. To the right of the restaurant was a printing company that did the menu work for Gendrick's and numerous other restaurants in NYC, Seattle and even so far afield as a few zesty Asian restaurants in Hawaii. The publisher's building itself had had its windows broken fourteen times in the last year. It would have been more, but it took the publishing company time to repair the windows each time, which only allowed the vandals to break the windows an average of slightly more than once per month. The reason for the vandals always breaking the glass was due to the questionable activities of the publishing company. Its CEO, Thomas Friedland, was prone to gamble and often held illegal events in the back of the publishing house. That wasn't all, though. As you could presume, any chump who has a passion for gambling so much as to house the activity on a large scale within the four walls of their own business also, quite likely, has other issues.

Now, dear reader, if you begin to pan *to the left* of Gendrick's Gin, you'll find a boutique bakery that serves creamy chocolate delights along with not-so-spectacular items such as sweetened hot dog buns, crescents the shape of ears of corn, and some special fruit that they have learned how to grow without the pit, so they can fill it with yet another special kind of sweet gypsum. New York has gotten weird, I'm telling you. Might as well call it the Big Candied Apple.

Jim opened the doors of Gendrick's Gin, which had knobs like the face of a pitbull, and his eyes took a moment to adjust to the heavy glow from a sea of Edison lights. If you wanted a dive bar, you've got one. Cash only. It was so divey, you'd practically be in a submarine out in the middle of the Pacific Ocean. Mermaids galore.

A sign indoors said, "We know how important water is… especially after ten shots." But Gendrick's Gin knew not only gin, but food, too, which is why Frank went there. He said the reason he loved Gendrick's Gin is that he could go there and not drink and people would still talk to him and not judge him. Anywhere else, if you don't order a drink, you feel out of place. It's an odd phenomenon at Gendrick's Gin, but then again, Frank is a bit odd, too. Jim saw Frank in his regular seat, talking to another fellow. Frank had already spotted Jim, and he nodded his acknowledgment and held up his hand in a gesture to indicate he would be another five minutes. Jim walked to the bar and ordered a Flying Wallenda.

"Crisp or dry?" the bartender asked.

"Surprise me."

He started making the drink and asked Jim, "Are you waiting for Frank?"

"Indeed I am."

"Be sure to remind him to pay off his tab. It's getting a bit behind. I've reminded him a couple of times, but I'm assuming you know how he is; he's always chatting with someone, so I can only assume he's forgetful of what must be lesser matters on his mind." The bartender took a breath and looked back at Frank. "That is me giving him the benefit of the doubt, of course." The bartender looked at Jim as if hoping for a conversational response.

"Sure thing," Jim said shortly, clearly able to tell that if he responded with any more than five words, the bartender would keep talking to him, and right now, although there wasn't much to do until Frank was finished with his conversation, Jim was not ready to chat casually. He was still there on business.

After a few sips of his drink, the coriander hitting a little differently this time than usual, the gentleman sitting with Frank began to get up and put his overcoat on. As he passed by Jim on his way to exit, Jim let him know it was raining dogs and frogs out there.

Having no umbrella, the fella took it as a warning. Jim meant it as the opposite.

➤ VII ⥸

It was all business.

Jim had been sitting with Frank for over an hour now, a few deep in—Jim, with Flying Wallendas and Frank with the cottage cheese-stuffed fig plate—and as much business as they'd discussed, Jim'd gotten nowhere. No solution for overcoming Phillip or whatever the fuck his name was, no way to appropriately tweak his menu to pull from the other business. They considered leaning on the restaurant association, hiring a detective to point out the dirty work Phil had to have going on, and even pulling some strings with the World Wildlife Fund.

The WWF or, as Jim liked to call it, the "wwwwofff"—you know, like the sound you make when you stand on a scale after a summer of eating and drinking like there's not another summer around the corner—was an organization Jim had volunteered with one summer of college.

At first, he was running papers, printing fliers, and helping run events for his city's zoo as a way to make some extra cash. One night, he was smoking a joint outside the zoo when he saw some folks smuggling animals out. Thinking it was an illusion, just some kids getting into trouble, Jim approached the crew, which proved to be much older than a batch of children, and ultimately resulted in an ultimatum: Either Jim joined in helping them or he was going to be forced into the same cage as the lion. As much as Jim thought about death and the twenty-three ways he'd written down how he would be okay dying, in a cage with a lion was not on that list.

It wasn't until they arrived at a small airport about two hours from the zoo that he learned that the WWF had coordinated a massive capture and return initiative with multiple zoos in and around the city. While none of the vans, trucks, or trailers hauling the animals had any logos on them, the plane was actually one giant panda, reflective of the organization's logo and branding. Wherever they were taking them, they had no problem with an audience knowing it was the WWF flying.

Over the next two summers, Jim became a stealth animal capturer for the WWF. In all, his interactions both in the country and out were where he learned about how cultures made the most out of what they had: ants, crickets, dragonflies, et cetera, and how to cook 'em. And, admittedly, the harsh truth of returning animals to their original environments was that some were quickly poached or, because they had been in captivity for so long, fell prey to the circle of life faster than the flight that had brought them "home."

Suffice it to say, Jimbean got to taste no shortage of proteins: tiger, elephant, capybara, and more. Though some cultures made a mean meat pie out of some of the animals, Jim had an affinity for the insects. All the while he was trapping for the WWF, he set out insect traps of his own. By the second summer of trapping for the WWF, he had the equivalent of an MBA, but in entomophagy.

That trip down memory lane triggered something in Jim. It sparked an idea. It ignited a challenge. His brain had been fishing for a while, and now a neuron bit the bait.

Without a word to Frank, Jim sat up, kicked back his fourth Flying Wallenda, and escorted himself out of the bar. His chin was down, but not in sorrow or defeat as it had been when he entered the bar; this time it was at an obtuse angle of determination.

The Flying Wallenda had that effect on people at Gendrick's Gin. Liquid courage, they call it. Something about the lavender and star of anise flavors, the sneaky 80 proof sake added to the cocktail. Or, you know, the fact that he'd had four of them.

Frank hailed a waiter over and ordered his one Wallenda for the evening. He'd seen this look on Jim's face before. Unspoken determination.

Before Phil would know it, Jim would have him in handcuffs, eating a roasted mockingbird, and begging him to be kind to his staff. Maybe.

⇒ VIII ⇐

It's hard to call Phil's restaurants a monopoly. It's no KFC or Tim Hortons; each restaurant is different, like a coalition, an enterprise or a union of disparate but connected restaurants; no two are the same, but at the same time he

plays business like a game of Monopoly, pissing off everyone he plays with.

The anger, passion, and gusto for the business came
only after nearly breaking his back in the mountains. He
had been climbing in the Alps alone.

See, Phil wasn't always the get-what-you-want-and-
don't-stop-until-you-do bastard he is now. He used to meditate, play solitaire, and—to put it bluntly—simply not give
much of a damn about life. It takes a special kind of person
not to. Phil was that kind of special. At least, he had been.

Not in the way of letting himself go, ruining his life.
No, sir. This is no life-hit-rock-bottom-and-bounced-back-
up kind of story either. Those are blown all out of propor-
tion and are simply a sad excuse for those who make more
poor choices in their life, because, after all, the harder you
fall, the higher you bounce, right? A truth not worth seeing
to its fruition. It's simply bullshit, and Phil knew that. He
made a steady run at floating from restaurant to diner and
diner to iscream shop and iscream shop to bar and bar to
strip club and strip club to supper club. While Phil's dad
wasn't around much, busy operating his trout fishing business, he had connections at all the restaurants Phil jumped
from. (Ever tasted Mint Chocolate Chip Trout ice cream?
That's Phil's father's doing.)

Anyway, of that list of locations, only at one of those
places did he play more of the role of customer than work-
er. It was there that a fine young performer, if you will,
whispered the words Phil had never known he always
wanted to hear until he did.

"Head to the Alps."

Climbing the mountains, the wind blew his leg hair in
an odd direction. Phil always wore shorts, and not those
cargo ones with extra pockets either. Phil wasn't one to
need pockets or storage or any kind of space; it was why

he found such a quaint hut in the Alps and only brought along a single grocery bag of necessities. You know, a razor, a notebook, a paint swatch that reminded him of the Eiffel Tower, tube socks, and a few changes of shirts and zip-ups, fully intending to make the most of his single pair of hiking shorts.

The wind almost tickled, like a spider or some sort of Alpine bug was crawling up his leg, using his hairs as grapple hooks. For some reason, the wind, the air, and the tickle all reminded him of war stories his grandfather would tell him when he was a child. In truth, there were only four war stories. Four war stories that could have happened and likely did.

Anyway, to enjoy anything in life, one merely needs to be open-minded enough to believe these four stories and enlightened enough to know how ruthless, scary, and polar war can make one become.

For the sake of keeping this short, as this is just intended for you to become more acquainted with Phil while he's in the Alps:

One day Senior Hamilton (Phil's father's father) found himself on the sandbanks of Toujane, Tunisia. Sandbanks might not actually be the right word. Sandbags is closer to the truth. Oh, the irony of bags of sand being placed on banks of sand, yet there Sergeant Senior Hamilton found himself. Dust flying across his face like a freshly smacked open pack of flour and piercing its way through his cloth face covering like a swarm of wasps flying pointy-end first. *Better sand than bullets*, he thought. Then a sand block hit him in the eyes, causing them to bring water to the land that was dry of it. Perhaps bullets would be better after all. Senior didn't need to wait long for his wish to be granted. He could hear his group in action around an embankment on the

East run. He had to get to them if they were going to be led to any sort of minute victory in the moment. He had three options: Go the long way through trenches and houses, attempt to go rooftop to rooftop to get there, or bolt faster than the sand blowing across no-man's-land. No-woman's-land. No land. It was all sand. And running in sand is tougher than trying to pull out a sliver with the Jaws of Life. However, he chose the latter because at least he knew what he could expect from the run, whereas he had no clue what lay in the homes, streets, and rooftops above to get to his troops. And when you know what to expect, time moves faster; you move faster. It was time for him to bite the bee and start running. At this point, Phil thought, the sand on his grandfather's legs must have felt like what he was feeling now. Senior Hamilton bolted and hoped the dust, debris, and taciturn desert leaves would keep him covered. They did. He arrived at his squad, knocking a few Germans from behind on his arrival. The platoon was so grateful they shot a few additional rounds in joy. Turns out the path through hell is a direct one, nine circles be damned. Those aren't bullets of sorrow; those are bullet sounds of joy.

The second story is about when Senior Hamilton had to play the role of sniper because *his* sniper was picked off, leaving only the blood of a shot missed and the gun waiting to have its next round cocked. Senior Hamilton crawled toward it, loaded the next bullet in the chamber, and poked its scope out beneath a drapery that held a hole in it not six inches away from his head. Upon scanning the land, the tonstein bricks, the unpaved pathways, the graffiti, and the pots with now-deceased plants in them, he found windows. Windows with life behind them rather than death. People cooking, sharing meals, kissing. He kept looking until he found what he was looking for. Senior Hamilton always said it wasn't the moment of any kill that he remembered strongly, it was the moments, the milliseconds, the few thump-thump-thumps of his heartbeat leading up to it. The things you saw, the smells you smelled, and the sounds you heard just beforehand. They are more of a trigger than the one he pulled with his finger.

The third story is one about food. It's the story behind one of Phil's most central values: Never dine with anything but delicacy. Senior Hamilton was at El Alamein in Egypt, providing information to the Brits and sick of carrying canned corned beef and hardtack biscuits; meals then were monotonous and heavy to carry into combat on foot. Though they were undoubtedly better-tasting than food from previous wars, Senior Hamilton ranted endlessly about how lackluster the flavor was, how they were encouraged to heat it up but never had a source, a time, or a safe enough environment to do so. Anyway, everything tasted like sand, gunpowder, and bloody barbed wire. Not that anyone went licking the damn metal, but according to Senior Hamilton, when you spend as much time around something as he had barbed wire, everything begins to look, smell, feel, and taste more like it. One of the last meals Senior Hamilton ever actually enjoyed was one that Phil had made in his youth. A simple homemade clam and crawfish chowder, heated to a perfect 102 degrees and garnished with shards of garlic and onion petals. As a side, he shared sourdough bread he made on his mother's stove from yeast he'd stolen from a baker. Of course, he didn't share that fact with Senior Hamilton, but even if he had, the bread and chowder was so delectable that Senior Hamilton would have waved it off or forgotten entirely after the spoon touched his lips. That was the first moment after retiring from the military that Senior Hamilton tasted something other than metal.

The fourth story was about a landmine and always ended with this advice: *You need to know where you're walking. Either you'll get your leg blown off or you'll be the one to catch the blown-off leg. Either way, you need to be ready for it and unphased when it arrives.* Senior Hamilton said it so many times to Phil when he was a kid, you might have thought he had a tick just like Lemon Fraser. Alas, he said it with such distinction that it came off as sound advice Phil has never forgotten.

As Phil climbed the mountainside, the wind at his back, he saw smoke ahead. It was no ordinary fire causing it; it was the combination of a crimson and a green glow emanating from a cave. Having no clue what to expect, he walked toward the light, like a moth to a candle flame, only Phil would discover a new life rather than meet his demise. He'd come out with wings.

This cave was no shaman's holy dwelling. Inside Phil discovered an alpine crime scene of sorts, deducing that the body of the man he was now looking at had sought temporary refuge or, at minimum, become lost. He was wearing a two-piece suit, though his shoes and cuff links were missing. A journey bag that could pass for a briefcase lay near him, with the remnants of the bag's contents scattered across the floor. Phil didn't need to be a detective to see that this man had been beaten and robbed. The culprit was no doubt long gone now, judging by the dwindling of the fire he or she had tried to pat out with the businessman's belongings. The leather smothered the flames but made more smoke, which was what had caught Phil's eye, but it was what was next to the fire that had Phil's attention now. A luminescent vial of green liquid lay nearly empty near the fire. That explained the green flash. Phil quickly swiped the vial and exited the cave before the smoke got to his lungs.

Outside the cave, he held the vial up to the light and inspected what little liquid remained. As per human nature, Phil smelled it. It smelled like tangerine, dandelion, and the pages of *Siddhartha*, the book his grandfather had given him before passing.

Passing the sniff test, he poured the remaining few drops from the vial onto his tongue.

Needless to say, it was the inspiration he needed to have a goal in life: to pursue a flavor like the one he had just experienced.

≽IX≼

All that has been happening to Jim has been winding him up like a toy, if a toy were a rhinoceros—the kind with two horns rather than one—and when you set him down, he'd be the most dangerous animal you could ever cross paths with.

Not but two nights after peeling himself from Gendrick's, he'd perfected three new recipes with different color injections of mussels, seaweed sprouts, and edible harpoons. Alongside the dirty dishes, the test batches and non-edible harpoons waited for their turn at the table. Beside them was his nighttime notebook. He'd scribbled

down his plan to beat Phil to the punch, lunch, and the upcoming restaurant association award ceremony.

All you, the reader, can hope for is that he can read
his plan and execute it to perfection. You see, Jim didn't
have the greatest handwriting, and by that I mean even he
had trouble reading what he had written. Jim's philosophy
was that if it was important enough, he would remember
it. That philosophy had hurt him a few times, with girls in
bed, with family birthdays, and with friends who got him
high, but never, never did it impact him when it came to
food. The intention was to write this plan more neatly, but
this is also one he wouldn't need to revisit, not after the first
few steps, anyway. You know what they say about plans.

After forty-eight hours without sleep, Jim crashed. He remembered falling asleep on the sofa but waking up in bed.
At least the oven was off, but there was now a gelatinized,
purple concoction on the stovetop.

Jim couldn't remember what he'd made.

"Damnit, Jim. What in the hell have I had to clean up here?
Get your ass up already would you, Jim? It's nearly three
thirty in the afternoon."

The words were a bit sour. Less than an hour ago Lemon Fraser had knocked on Jim's door. He knew Jim was in
there because he could smell the cooked mussels. (Was
that a seaweed-root-infused mussel he smelled? Maybe ube
extract, too?). Part curiosity and part concern for his friend
drove Lemon to break down the door after his knocks continued unanswered, which didn't require much energy. Ever
since Lemon was a child, he'd put on the pounds. Throwing
his weight around town wasn't just an expression, he did it
literally. Despite diets prescribed by his mother, workout
regimens assigned by both his football and shotput coach,

and one brief period when Jim meal-prepped for him for a week (although Lemon cleaned out the Tupperware in a day and a half), he had always been a heavy guy. All that, and wouldn't you know it, the door wasn't locked, anyway.

Mr. Fraser loved all sorts of food. It was what got him in the industry in the first place. While other kids were trading porn mags and poorly rolled joints, he was doing homework for lunches and blackmailing those trouble-makers for their midday snacks. Which sucked for them, because they had nothing to eat once they got the munchies or cleaned their hands of pubescent cum before their parents got home from work.

Why Lemon never became a cook, we'll never know. He must have been too positive for it, or was simply turned off by the industry's inability to retain sous chefs, or possibly he realized the food always tasted better when someone else made it for him than when he made it for himself. So, he decided to manage relationships within the industry, to become an insider without working in the kitchen. That's the best thing Lemon has been called; the most accurate, anyway. Information for edible assets. A transaction more profitable than any Warren Buffet has ever made.

"I tasted your mussels, Jimster. They're quite something. Even if I didn't give two shits about you, I'd still have broken down the door to get what I smelled was inside. It's that good, Jim. That good."

"I'll have your ass if you go around telling people about it yet, Lemon. I finally have something Phil doesn't have the experience or the guts or the time to try."

JimBo spoke the words, but his brain was egging him on with intrusive thoughts that he could and should do better. *There's always room for improvement.*

And that was the calling for his ol' mental friend, Doubt, to show up. *It's good, but still not good enough to overcome the competition from Phil. There's still something missing,* Doubt whispered.

"Ya sure do, Jim. Ya sure do. Are you ready to try it out at the restaurant?"

"You know cooking isn't about what I want, it's about the guest. Let's head over there and see if I can replicate it. My notes are a little hard to read and... I confess I don't remember making it."

Lemon looked at Jim quizzically as Jim grabbed a jacket and slipped on his laceless shoes while Lemon used his body weight to adjust the door back into position so that it could be opened, closed, locked and unlocked again. A bit of damage to the wall and frame, but nowhere near the extremes the landlord of the apartment complex has seen elsewhere.

Jim and Lemon walked down the apartment steps and out to the sidewalk. They were only a handful of blocks away from Herough.

"If you're up for ruining your appetite a bit, I recently got my hands on a chocolate bar made from the rarest Criollo beans. It's the perfect complexity of flavors, from sweet blueberry to charred mallow. The hazelnut character is to die for. To die for. To die for."

"Shoot me now then," Jim said, thinking he was playing off Lemon's words, but as he said them, he made eye contact with Phil crossing his side of the street.

"How fortunate am I?" Phil said with swagger sweating in every syllable. "Just who I was going to see and, better still, someone respectable to pay witness to."

Lemon nodded with respect while Jim merely gave a dead-panned stare in return. Lemon had a Switzerland-like reputation to maintain. Jim, not so much.

"It'll have to be another time. We have business to take care of," Jim snapped.

Undeterred, Phil pushed on. "Business is exactly what I'm here to offer. A business proposal, specifically. I've done some thinking and believe it to be incredibly fair."

"I've already told you, I'm not selling Herough and have no interest in having you be any part of it."

"And I've already told you, I'm not going to offer you money or a partnership."

Phil's lips started to curl, in what was apparently supposed to be a grin.

"I'm here to propose a challenge. The National Restaurant Association's annual banquet is coming up. The challenge is simple. Win, and I'll close up my shop and leave you and Herough alone."

Lemon was unfazed by the offer. He was used to hearing ones like this, chefs treating their shops like they were race cars. Pink slip for pink slip.

Jim, however, was fazed by the offer. That said, he liked the words he was hearing, and before he was able to ask what the catch was, Phil carried on.

"Butttttt," letting the "t" repeat like he was rolling an "r". "When I win, you forfeit Herough entirely to me."

Lemon was stoic and solid as a statue, namely because he wasn't sure who had more to gain, or which was more likely to gain from it.

"Deal," Jim responded, as if he'd been waiting for this exchange. It helped to have the confidence in the mussels he had just made. Jim was habitually a yes man, too. More so in the sense that he'd try new things. If you don't try, you fail, was a motto he lived by.

Though Jim would be lying if he said he wasn't nervous about the word he'd just responded with. That little voice of doubt in his head about his capabilities? It caught sight of this new shiny object and started telling Jim that there's no way he'll win, he's not good enough, he just made a grave mistake.

To date, Jim has participated in the National Restaurant Association's competition fewer than ten times and he's never won, though he came in second, once.

"Then we'll shake on it, with Lemon here as witness." Phil interrupted Jim's churning thoughts and stuck his hand out to Jim. Jim hesitated for a second; long enough for Phil to notice, which only made his grin do some yoga and stretch wider.

"A gentleman's bet it is. A gentleman's bet it is. A gentleman's bet it is."

Lemon was a bag of mixed emotions. Excited. Scared. And a little turned on.

Jim moved beyond the doubt and hesitation and accepted Phil's deal with a handshake.

$$\gg X \ll$$

Each year, the National Restaurant Association puts on a large banquet for people to get their bellies shit-faced, give their palates a mouthgasm, and put their small intestine through a CrossFit bootcamp. Chefs bring out their biggest dishes, breweries their biggest beers, and people their biggest appetites. You'd think the guests at the banquet had been starving for weeks on end when all of a sudden crates of the most delectable foods and beverages are air-dropped to them, and rather than rationing it they go hog-wild. One year a woman was stabbed with a fork because she took the last of "the pigs in blankets in more blankets" dish that Leroy Baggins of the Baggins Family Farms dished up. They were the first provider to run out of food.

Rather than increase their insurance coverage, the banquet designated a Golden Fork award that goes to whichever restaurant or chef that runs out of food first. It was more of a joke than anything, because the woman who was stabbed by the first fork the year prior then started working for the Baggins family and was present this year, serving the dish that got her stabbed.

We've fast-forwarded a bit in time, and here we are at the thirty-sixth annual banquet, no stabbings reported... yet.

In one corner of the banquet, you have Phil. High and mighty, literally and figuratively. Phil always took a puff before events like this, and he seemed to be bulkier than Jim had remembered him. After all, Jim hadn't seen Phil since his "introduction" at Lip's and the agreement they'd made only a few days after. It's not because Phil didn't try to use some scare tactics on Jim leading up to the competition; rather it's because Jim took off to explore Cambodia for the knowledge he needed to finish his recipe. More on that in a moment.

Phil was setting up his station when Gus swung by to investigate. Gus was an old family acquaintance of Phil's, and he just so happened to be the president of the neighborhood association that covered Spring Street.

"Quite the setup ya got goin' durr, Phil. You're bringing your A, A+ and A++ game today, aren't yeh?"

"Come on, Gus, you know how important this year is. Jim and I made a deal, and I will *not* be closing. You know as well as I that Jim might be good, but he's not elite. By this time tomorrow, as the result of my winning best in show today, Jim will be announcing the closure of Herough. At this point I'd be surprised if he even shows his face here, since I haven't seen him around since we shook on our agreement."

"And *you* know Jim went to Cambodia, right? I just heard word of it myself, from last year's Golden Fork winner of all people. No clue how she knew, but I was wondering what put the pep in Jim's step this afternoon despite what looked like ten-pound weights under his eyes and what appeared to be a piss stain on his pants, but I digress."

Gus was staring at the floor as he talked, almost having two conversations. One with Phil and one with himself, trying to imagine why Cambodia, why the pep, and how he hoped the show would be more entertaining than someone getting stabbed with a fork again.

Had Gus been looking at Phil, however, he would have noticed sweat all of a sudden beading on Phil's fivehead, pupils dilating, and hands squeezing his beautiful *yanagiba* in front of him, a single-edged Japanese fish knife, like it was a murder weapon.

⇒ XI ⇐

Let's set things straight for a moment. Jim wasn't a wealthy man of leisure. He didn't just fly off on private jets to countries halfway across the world. At least not since his last relationship sort of killed that travel bug. Remove those co-op traveling experiences, and the only trips he had taken *sans* parent or partner were two visits to two adjacent states (Pennsylvania and Vermont). And from New York, Pennsylvania hardly counts.

His journey to Pennsylvania had been to steal grape vines for a recipe he was making. He'd read up on the natural properties, earthy base and rich bacterial notes of grape vines in Pennsylvania and simply had to have them. To be blunt, calling it stealing isn't quite accurate. He intended to steal them, but during his attempt, he was met by a man named Trace who, rather than grabbing a shotgun to chase the would-be-burglar off his vineyard as one would expect, beckoned Jim to him and asked the most defining, most connecting, most valuable question in this world: Why?

Jim answered truthfully, so truthfully that it ignited intrigue in Trace, and Jim agreed to overnight a sample of his creation to Trace if Trace would cover the shipping cost. It was an odd way to start a friendship, but without it, Jim might not have ever opened Herough. More on that later.

The other trip was to a maple tree deep in the woodlands of Vermont that he had to extract sap from. He had heard whispers of this tree from Gus. Four hundred years old, with syrup that tasted like candied belt leather. Both trips were there-and-back ordeals. Jim made no time for sightseeing. He always did things fast. So while getting up and flying to another country was a little scary, the haste of it wasn't all that off-putting. For anyone else, you might say it would be putting them outside of their comfort zone, but Jim was on a mission, and comfort didn't matter. For him, the pain of staying the same was greater than the pain of change.

After an eighteen-hour flight of staring at a baby drool two rows ahead of him and to the left, playing his favorite game of wondering what the child could be thinking, and being jealous of being in such a state to drool so much, without being black-out drunk, of course, he got off the plane, made his way to a *truck* outside, and told the driver to take him to the Fancy Hotel.

The air was different there. Not fresher, by any means, but it filled Jim's lungs up with more confidence. Confidence that he was making the right decision being here, confidence that he'd get what he needed in the time he needed it. Confidence surged through him like a hydrant hose in the mouth of a snake; it was only a matter of time before it would either balloon him or come shooting out the other end.

To his left and right the world was spinning with lights and smells. Jim thought it must be the bug that bit him outside the airport that was making him hallucinate a bit. After all, it was a nasty little bug that looked like a cross between a centipede and a barn fly. It felt good to be in a new geography with new-to-Jim insects again. Jim promised himself that if he could get all of this Phil nonsense behind him, he would travel more again. *Herough could still be better, but if I only work with what I know today, it's as good as it's going to get,* Jim thought.

As distant as Cambodia was from New York, there were a lot more connections between the two places than you might think. The heart symbol, for instance, is on shirts all over. It's not hard to find New York Yankees or New York Giants championship shirts for a championship they never won. Because the dollar was worth so much in Cambodia—the price of a three-course meal in New York can pay for a month of dining out for breakfast, lunch, dinner and drinks in Cambodia—there was a lot of business done on behalf of New Yorkers here. And wherever business is done, there are secrets. Secrets to happiness, secrets to stocks, secrets to the edge of any industry—including, say, the restaurant one.

And where there are secrets, there are bound to be spies.

Oo la la.

≫XII≪

Jim sat in the back of a dusty pickup truck that had just dropped off blocks of ice at the airport, his backpack serving as a makeshift cushion against the jolts of the uneven road and a barrier between himself and the wet truck bed. As the vehicle rumbled toward his hotel in Phnom Penh, he was instantly enveloped by the vibrant tapestry of Cambodia's capital. The air was thick with memory-evoking and saliva-producing aromas of street food—grilled meats mingling with the sweetness of tropical fruits and the tang of spices that Jim couldn't name. Yet.

Leaning over the edge of the truck, he watched as vendors hawked skewers of marinated chicken and beef—beef from what, they never did say—their charcoal grills sending up curls of smoke that seemed to dance before disappearing into the bustling chaos of the city. The scent of fresh herbs and lime wafted from bowls of noodle soup served at roadside stalls, each inhalation a burst of culinary discovery. All of these fumes hit Jim's face as the truck moved in the stop-and-go-and-stop-and-go traffic, his tongue lolling like a dog with its head sticking out a window.

Everyone who was on foot and who he made eye contact with waved. Their smiles, wide and genuine, were as warm as the Cambodian sun. Children chased one another around the streets, and adults navigated skillfully between scooters and *tuk tuks*, all while laughing and chatting, their joy infectious. Despite all his travels, this was the first time that Jim felt any sense of "home" outside of New York.

As the truck wove through the crowded streets and waves of imitation *wagyu*, Jim couldn't help but notice how much of a health risk the eclectic lineup of food stands looked like they posed. Back home everything was regulated. Jim couldn't help but think of how much that held America back. Here, it seemed like, with less stringent public health systems, food not only survived, it thrived. And clearly the people thrived along with it.

The thought lingered in his mind as he watched a vendor expertly toss ingredients into a wok with a practiced flick of the wrist, flames licking the sides with each movement. Jim's stomach rumbled in anticipation. The raw authenticity of Cambodian cooking, unmarred by the constraints he was used to, promised an adventure not just for his palate but for his soul. As the truck finally rattled up to his hotel, Jim was already planning his first meal, eager to dive headfirst into the flavors of Cambodia, forgetting for a moment why he was there in the first place.

On the thirteenth floor of the Fancy Hotel, Jim was having breakfast with a woman. Her hair was long and black like a silk scarf, and she wore it as if it were truly part of her ensemble. If you looked at her smile, you'd see a couple of creases in her cheeks near the edge of her lips. *Sweet Cheeks*, Jim thought. See, Jim had run into Nora coming out of the elevator the night before, on his way to enjoy a dish of fish *amok* for one, and without allowing that ol' lizard brain of his to stun him from speaking and stop him with fear, he apologized for his haste and offered to make her breakfast the following morning.

Licensed by intrigue, clueless but curious, she agreed.

The moment of indecision didn't deflate Jim. He was already thinking of what he'd get from the market to cook her. You know when you can just feel that a day is going to be good? It vibrates your bones, it sloshes through your intestinal system, it pulsates your temples, and for some reason everything in the morning comes easy, from feeling good in the clothes you choose to wear; the toothpaste is the perfect amount on the brush; the morning wood isn't a bother, rather it's some sort of erected temple of good fortune—the little things are all good. Just good. That's what Jim was feeling about tomorrow with Nora. Of course, any time you bake a little before going out (a half-smoked joint from an off-the-clock Cambodian doorman of the hotel when he first checked in), the hours that follow tend to go in a good direction. All was good. Good. Good. Good.

Jim and Nora exchanged a few words outside that elevator, including their names, and made promises as two strangers, now acquaintances, who were staying at the same hotel, and trusted fate, as you should anywhere outside of New York.

As Jim looked back at Nora going up the elevator while he was on his way out, he could picture what perked beneath her romper, his gaze lingering on the playful curves. But his blinders were on for only a moment before his gaze was pulled back to her sweet cheeks as she looked back at him and sent a smile. He thought about her lips, which were warmed red with lipstick. His eyes traced her body down to the legs, which could clearly handle a pair of four-inch heels with grace. Jim already had ideas for a worthy breakfast that would cater to her desires—something decadent yet playful, perfectly matching her alluring complexity.

He was night market=bound and drooling already.

⮞XIII⮜

Jim first read about the Siem Riep market from a book he grabbed out of a one-night-stand's nightstand. The nightstand was more of a miniature personal library. He got a chance to browse it while breaking into her home with a few friends, an adventure he initiated when she ghosted him after their third date. Admittedly, it was, of course, Jim's fault for being late each time, having gotten lost each time in some effort and task required to be able to launch Herough.

Don't worry—the room wasn't inhabited when they broke in. Ironically, she was on a date at the local arcade.

Jim and crew split up, like any good cartoon team you'd watch on a Saturday morning. The crew nabbed a few meaningless items like a new bottle of shampoo and a throw pillow that had "The key to happiness" sewn into it while stirring up a bit of a ruckus by emptying drawers along the way.

Jim found himself in her room with her personal library. Such an overwhelming name for something so distasteful. Jim stood in awe at all the books that others could be reading if given the chance. Jim knows, I know, and you know that books are better off in hands than on shelves. We simply can't rely on people to break into partially vacated homes to source literature, and if Jim had half a mind at the time, he would have flung every book he could get his hands on out the window and into the street for someone, anyone(!) to pick up and read. But as he stood there, detesting the girl for this new reason which upset him more than the fact that she was ghosting him, something stood out. It wasn't the *Handbook For Mechanical Innovation Volume 4*, nor *What Mrs. Klaus Doesn't Know Can't Hurt The World* or the *Blowjobs and Flowers; What Men Really Want*—which happened to appear as the thinnest book of them all—no, it was a book that had an "S" and an "R" stamped on the spine along with a series of seafood icons. We're talking shark tooth, shell, and a ring that Jim—in his seafood-wasted heart—knew was an Octopus suction cup—a Vulgaris Octopus.

He opened the book to find endless pages about Siem Reap. The happy people. The culture of imported seafood, how to eat it, how to serve it, and who to share it with. The pictures, in vivid color, imprinted themselves on Jim's mind. But it was the Bai Sai Chrouk, made with pork slices marinated in coconut milk grilled over charcoal and served with honeyed rice, pickled red onions, and fried egg with fresh tomatoes, cucumbers, and carrots on top, with an assortment of sides from sea frog squares, scorpion-on-a-stick, and red tree ants that sold Jim on creating a spring on the seafood-only idea he had for Herough. Yes, dear reader, Jim has that one-night stand to thank for his success in serving seafood delicacies at Herough with an added insectile twist.

Since that day, Jim had read all he could about Siem Reap, the real, the raw, and the magical.

For this moment in time, Jim was in the market for the magical. It was at this market that he could meet the woman who strung magic from her fingers, weaved it with her womb, and sang it into appearance. Some call her the magical sea swan; others call her Bethel; others Queen

Pinmekalah. Only a secretive few know her true name. Jim wouldn't be one to find it out, but he would find her.

⇒XIV⇐

At the fourteenth stand from the entrance—or is it the exit? That's the thing about markets. They're like worms. You don't know where they start or where they end unless you throw powder over them and wait for them to fart. Whatever the directionality, Jim spotted a stand different from the others.

It didn't feature a frazzled Cambodian, cooking as if he was feeding an army; no meat just sitting there, basking in the sun; no flames to draw attention to the hundreds of tourists oohing and ahhing. It was a simple table with a mat laid atop it, likely taken from the clothes in the purveyor's grandmother's closet. So much so that if you smacked it, it would fly away like Aladdin's carpet. A peculiar pattern ran along the edges. The same pattern of the spine of the book Jim had read, except this pattern seemed to shift and change.

Were Jim's eyes playing tricks on him again?

No, certainly not. The pattern was dancing along the edge of the mat like a NASCAR race filled with drivers over the age of eighty, still hanging on to life, going in circles, but now driving slow as molasses or drying mud or the slow burn moonshine has on a sick man's throat. *Do they even know they're on a repeating track?* Jim wondered, sensing life in the linework of the mat.

Atop the mat there were only a handful of spices, with names Jim had never heard of before, not even in the book that had got him here. While the bottles were a rainbow of colors, there weren't all that many. So few that a passerby might simply write the table off as being from someone new, trying to break into the market. They'd wait a few years before giving it any sort of attention. Regulars have long since learned their lesson when it comes to markets: Don't fall in love with a vendor, because chances are they won't be there the next rotation around the sun.

That written, it's very much not the case for Queen Pinmekalah, who has had her booth for more years than you learn how to say in college-level language classes.

The woman remained silent behind the table, the mat, and her spices, as Jim stood before her, staring.

"Excuse me. Queen Pinmekalah?" Jim bent forward to get his eyes closer to her line of sight. "Heerrrooughh?"

No response.

"My name is Jim. I'm the owner of Herough."

The lady looked on in the hustle and bustle of the market, avoiding Jim's gaze, not even blinking. Jim realized neither the name of his restaurant nor his own name would mean anything to her. Clearly the Queen could care less about Jim, anyway. Or maybe she didn't speak English?

One would guess that Queen Pinmekalah hadn't so much as breathed a molecule of air more than 500 yards from where she now stood, let alone established any sort of ties to small businesses in a city with more turnover than the baked goods booth beside hers after a morning rush. She didn't need to go much beyond her bubble. She was in the heart of the world's most remarkable market. People could bring her all she needed for her spices and her survival, the internet gave her all the information she needed, and the people gave her all the connections she could ask for.

Such is an extraordinary life, and oxymoronic when it needn't be lived to be lived well enough.

The longer Jim stood, unfazed by the Queen's neglect, the more he noticed some funky energy around Queen Pinmekalah, now more than the table itself.

Having been satisfied with her evaluation of her surroundings, she sat there pouring some spice or other into an empty container and then back to the container in which it was stored. Again and again. Like some child fascinated with a completely invaluable action like flicking the door stopper or being thrown in the air. *Again. Again.* Jim stood and watched and guessed how many hours she'd spent of her life doing this. Had he really come all this way to be let down by someone as senile as the Queen appeared to be? Had the book led him astray?

It had been several years since he'd read about the Queen; like the season, like the Super Bowl champions, like the color of a newborn's desires, things change, people change.

Jim decided to do a lap around the market, stretch his legs and his mind. It was clear Pinmekalah wasn't going anywhere, anyway. Jim used the break to think about what he may have missed in his reading and what he might say to the Queen when he made his round back to her that would get her attention. But reality began to sink in. The reality of the contest, the bet he'd made with Phil, the reality of how much was at stake with this trip, the reality of not having much time, the reality of how out of place Jim felt, halfway across the world in a country he had only read about and imagined. With every step through the market of squids and squidettes, clam and clam chowder, "same, same, but different," a puddle of confidence leaked away behind him, mixing with the gestation of a market that never quite sleeps and merely layers its oils, cleaners, grease, and sweat upon themselves. Layer after layer. Just what Doubt is up to in Jim's head.

Jim paused between a shop that looked to contain more than a thousand shirts and a wood shop with hand-crafted wooden objects (duh!) hanging from thin metal twist-ties. The likelihood of normal-sized hands crafting the objects seemed questionable. Reality. It's an incredible thing... reality vs. perception.

Consider the reality that Jim could be inherently satisfied with an upcoming meal with someone that makes his
pole rise, hair on the front of his waist stand up, adrenaline
course through his legs and warmth tingle to the tips of his
fingers like an electrical circuit in a weighted blanket. The
reality of not knowing who she honestly is, what she does,
or why she's here—and not caring about any of that right
now.

Consider the reality of everything around him. People
are all happy as clouds on a sunny day parade. A barter
is taking place on Jim's side. "It's for my wife," the tourist
pleads. As if the Cambodian seller cares who it's for. All the
Cambodian sees is the owner of a shop ten feet over, selling
the same shirts, eyeing and listening for the opportunity
to inject herself with a lower offer or to find the right size
shirt more quickly or the color the buyer would prefer.

That was all reality. Yet here Jim was. Spinning on his
heels to go against the grain and walk back to Queen Pinmekalah. He began preparing a speech in his head, every
step producing ten words and building energy. Had he actually given his speech to Pinmekalah, it would have gone
something like the following:

"Pinmekalah. Bethel. Queen. I'm not aiming to please
everyone, but there are some who pick up flaws where there
are none. They've resolved to destroy my credibility. I've
been broken, I've been repaired, I've seen life and death,
I've been digitized and unplugged, I've climbed a tree that
I've cut down, swam with sharks that I ate that evening.
I've watched businesses fail and others rise high enough to
become the villain of the neighborhood they once sought
to solely serve. I've gambled and bargained, losing terribly
at times and winning tremendously at others. I'm a man on
a mission without an option for submission. I've been over
the hill and under the water and through the woods, I've
followed the yellow brick road, the red, the green, the blue,
the Day-Glo, and made my own, too. I'm now at a crossroad

and bound to fail unless I have your help. I've flown thousands of miles and need to return for a competition that will either break or benefit my existence."

That's what Jim would have said—rambly but inspirational. Raw thoughts and emotions. Instead, he paused in front of Queen Pinmekalah's table once more, having lost all the words he'd thought of, dribbled away in a trail behind him and mixed into the sand and sewage of the market floor.

Still avoiding his gaze, Pinmekalah was also still pouring the spice from one container to the next and back again. Jim knew what it meant when someone was doing the same thing and expecting different results. There was no point in a plea to Queen Pinmekalah. Jim sighed and resigned himself to heading back to his hotel without making an ornate plea to the Queen. Jim pivoted on his heels and began to make his way back to the Fancy Hotel.

"Your shoes."

Jim spun around. He heard her words, ever so faintly. They took a flight on a breeze and clearly caught some 'z's on the ride over to Jim. But he heard them all the same.

Jim stepped back in front of Queen Pinmekalah's stand.

"What?"

"Your shoes," Queen Pinmekalah said.

Jim looked down at his Ecco sneakers. Green stitches on gray leather. Sun's out, shoe's tongue out. Black abyss laces with ends that Jim had burned to blend himself after tossing the commercialized plastic wrap that caps most shoelaces these days. From where Jim stood right in front of the stand, the sun cut through the crud in the air—hitting Pinmekhala's words, too—and revealed an assortment of sneakers under the skirt of her table. Jim could spot Nike Frees and old school Jordans. He saw business shoes that could have walked themselves here and bought the market.

Jim stood in a bit of hobbled confusion, both because of the Queen's request and for being puzzled on how he'd missed the glimpse of shoes beneath the table. A booth with spices and shoes. If that's not a third-country market-place classic, I'm not sure what is.

"Your shoes... please."

Jim could tell the Queen was getting annoyed and straining to be considerate. No one likes repeating themselves twice, let alone three times. Except advertisers for Ecco, that is. They're allowed. The Danish are a persistent people.

Jim looked to his right and his left. It was as if no one noticed him or cared that he was untying his bunny ears, patting them down into the newly vacated caverns of his shoes. He put them on the Queen's counter.

"You can tell everything about a person by the bottom of their shoes," she said, still avoiding direct eye contact with Jim.

Jim had no clue how to respond. He just stood there like a scarecrow, except every Cambodian continued to graze the market stands all around him rather than be turned off by his presence. Actually, that was just like a scarecrow, because crows didn't pay them any mind so far as he could tell.

Pinmekalah set down her spice containers and took his shoes. She studied them with a practiced eye as if she could see into Jim's soul. She could tell he moved forward a lot by the way the rubber curved toward the front of the shoe, implying a busy lifestyle in a service industry, but then she caught notes of dimples in the heels, as if he frequently pivoted. Beneath the dust and dumpster juice of the market that had taken refuge in the creases of his shoes, Pinmekalah could detect the remnants of dried salt water, oxy cleaner, and black licorice made from scratch, obviously. Pinmekhala's read online about black licorice, and none contained the particular careless blend of spice that she was noting. Was that some seawood variant she detected, too?

Now the tops of his shoes were impressive. The signs of age on the leather were there, but the stitches were still lime green—not tainted with discolor or browned by the fecal imprint of life. It was clear this man took care of that which got him forward. These were the kind of shoes worn by someone who wished to be the accent of life; not the spotlight.

Pinmekalah looked at Jim for the first time. Skeptical of the situation but open to it. Her hard shell had been cracked—and to think, by a shoe. She sighed deeply.

"I assume you're here for the spice."

She stated it rather than asked it, but Jim treated it like a question the same way he treats a "no" as a "not right now."

"I'm here for the magic I've read about."

Jim knew full well he meant the spice, but in his line of work, you ask for exactly what you want; otherwise you wind up with either an imitation, a regret, or a distasteful stew of the two. He damn well didn't want to leave with nothing more than some simple cinnamon.

Pinmekalah disappeared behind the clerks and clerkettes who surrounded her booth. Jim was able to trace her progress through a curtained doorway behind a barter taking place. This for that. A handwoven basket for some baby spoons. Not the ones actually meant for babies, but ones that grandmas collect and show off, and once they pass, so do these spoons to the next generation. No trade-in value. It's not the only pointless exchange taking place in the market. Truly good deals are like diamonds in the rough.

Clearly none of the spices in plain sight were the ones Jim wanted. Jim's spice—or what was about to be Jim's spice—is magic. It's two parts potion and one part persuasion. No MSG or 8x the daily advised amount of potassium. This spice was meant to inspire dissertations on why you should only put good things in your body. The spice is like a night with your partner where you both try something new in bed, something you hadn't dreamed of, but the moment was right, and the orgasm was real and out of this world. Some might say this spice that Jim was asking for is the Spice of Life.

Pinmekalah came back with what looked like a Sunny-ville Farm bottle of chocolate milk.

What the frick?

Jim wondered if this lady was off her rocker, or if he was, for coming here based on something he'd read in a sketchy book. (Quite literally; most of the images in the book had been sketched.)

It *was* a Sunnyville Farm bottle of chocolate milk. Yup. Grade 5 plastic, microwave ready, label worn but legible, empty of liquid but surprisingly capped with what looked like a one-off seal; definitely not the original. The contents, while a similar shade of the nectar-made-better from cows, were particles though, stardust, flavored sand perfectly mixed—better than any sand wedding ceremony—edible, and... radiating?

Jim could see it and feel it. Who would have guessed that plastic, the bane of the world's existence, the harper of landfills, the king and queen of crud, would be the element used to contain magic? Not a crate or glass container, not a chest or gold-inlaid urn, but a repurposed plastic bottle of chocolate milk.

"So, the book was right." Jim mumbled it more than outright asked, but Pinmekalah served up some of Jim's same personality.

"I don't know where you found it, but yes, it was and is true."

"What do I owe you?"

"You read the book. You know."

Pinmekalah sat back down and resumed the same pose and work she had been doing when Jim walked by the first time. As if the water of her life was turned off and now back on. Steadily streaming. All was right with the world. Pouring contents from one container to the next. Back and forth. Fill and empty. Fill and empty. Fill and empty.

Jim stood in a microbubble of discomfort. The pain of what he had to trade settled into his soul like a needle in a haystack some teenagers were jumping into from the roof of a barn. There was part of him that had figured the story he read about in the book was just that: a story, a hoax, something your talented author may have written as a short story in middle school or that the kids lied about with the haystack to see if the younger lad would make the jump or not; if he deserved their trust or not. Alas. Jim pushed the discomfort aside and asked the cells in his heels to vibrate in such a way it could move him forward. His shoes, left behind, piled under the counter of the Queen as part one of his offering. He had asked the Queen for enough already. Anyway, he was in a market, after all; he'd find shoes in no time.

And before no time could show up, Jim was in front of another shop with a pair of Nieke shoes in his hands. And no, that's not a misspelling. Well, technically it is, but it's an accurate typing of the name sewn on the shoes—halfassedly, like a child did it for the first time. Oof. No bartering took place in the moment, not with convenience and need pressing their smug faces on the window of Jim's life. He also purchased a blue shirt with the writing "same same" stamped on it—not to wear but to wipe off his feet before slipping on his new Nieke shoes. Sure, "same same."

With his new kicks, he approached Queen Pinemeka-lah again. Ready for his shoes to write a new story.

XV

W hen Phil was a boy, he had three life-changing experiences. No more. No less. Exactly three.

The first was a dream he had about a time when mental pictures could be painted: What you saw in your mind got translated to a photo. Have an abstract vision that out-Pollocks Pollock, put on the headset, close your eyes, and hit "print." One day Phil dreamed up the most beautiful woman and swore he would find her one day. His hope was that he could print out a photo of her based on how he's etched the image in his memory like a permanent sandcastle, and then he'd lead an excursion across the world to find her. Phil still thinks of her to this day. There's not a pair of feet that walks into his restaurants that doesn't make him wonder if it's the one he saw in his dream. If she is real. It keeps Phil on the edge of his end-of-the-twenty-first-century seat. It's the reason why he maintains his looks, his money, his status. One day that piece of art will show up in his life and he'll be ready to whisk it away into the reality of his dreams. See, Phil isn't completely heartless...

The second moment was when he was bullied and he decreed that bullying, like smiling, cooties, and bird flu was contagious. He understood the chain of bullying, and though it felt uncomfortable to act as a bully, the results of it were there, consistently and in tip-top shape. Bullies are more than squeaky wheels; they're the whole damn bike. Who needs grease when you can bend the wheel back in shape or toss it altogether? You either die a hero or live long enough to see yourself become a bully, so they say. So Phil says, anyway. And Phil saw himself as one early on and often since. Such is life and such is a story that makes him the perfect antagonist. Simply put, if you asked him about being a bully, Phil would say it's in his blood.

The real nail in the coffin of Phil's personality was, of course, heartbreak—and from a woman with freckles no less. Those are women you have to be careful with. They sunburn easily, they play music with your heartstrings that would put Satan to sleep, and they have a proclivity to be stubborn, more so than a hippie tied to a tree that's not even endangered, the kind of hippie that does damage by being stubborn *and* doing damage for having been stubborn. She was the Now and Later candy of stubbornness. The Jaw Breaker of a heart's palate. Another novel could be written solely on the love story that persists to this day, but the short version is that Phil is in a constant state of attempting to fill the void in his life. And it only added to his hope that the other woman of his art-printed dream would be real. For every freckle that she had, there's been a hole in Phil's life ever since. Holes made of what-ifs and wish-I-wouldas, and why-didn't-Is. That's not to say this gives us reason to like Phil any more than we already don't, but there's always an explanation for someone's poor behavior, whether they're an outlaw, a germaphobe, or simply a man with a heart too broken to see the harm he's causing himself and those around him. And as life has it, he won't.

⇒XVI⇐

By 5 a.m., Jim had shat, showered, and shaved, in that order. By 5:15 he had a meal underway in his hotel room. Yup. Jim's back at the Fancy Hotel. Jim found his muse. It had been sitting by the room's oven the whole time. It leaked into the drawer that the whisk was sleeping in. The lights were dim, giving it a moody, Zenlike, misty experience. The room just got him. He hadn't asked for special treatment. This was orchestrated by fate. His brain had been working overtime to rationalize his presence in Cambodia since his exchange with Queen Pinmekalah the day before.

Jim had set aside his Nieke shoes along with the bottle of Pinmekalah's spice. He had something else burning in his mind; *someone* else was more like it. He thought deeply about Nora; running a fracking machine to mine his brain, he wondered what she might like and dislike in life.

Would she pass the olive theory? The lemon law? Would she put toilet paper on the right way? Reach for the imaginary check? Jim knew there had to be an emotional connection with the meal that could match the electricity he had felt between them nearly twenty-four hours before. And so it goes.

He prepped Bai Sach Chrouk with lemon zest and almonds that seemed to have coated themselves with ecstasy already. As a grounder and sweet connection, he made French toast with duck egg yolk that he'd purchased next to the stand where he got his Nieke's. He was sure Nora would be pleased with the twist of bee and tree nectar that Jim was feeling notorious for combining on this delicacy.

Meal ready.

Jim ready.

All that was missing at the marble dining table was a Cambodian spy.

≽XVII≼

There was a knock.

It was gentle but noticeable over the jazzy music playing from the kitchen area of the hotel room. Or perhaps Jim had his senses heightened, anticipating the moment of her knock. Would it be aggressive? Soft? Would she knock four times instead of the usual three? Would she knock to the beat of a song? The way a person knocks can send quite the signal to the one on the other side.

In this case? The knock was everything Jim had hoped it would be. Warm but curious. Apprehensive but friendly. Not quite song-like, but spiritual all the same.

Jim opened the door to see Nora.

"Did you always knock like that?" he asked as he leaned against the doorframe, a hint of a smile playing on his lips.

"Like what?"

"Gentle but noticeable. Almost as if you were asking permission."

"Maybe I was, but something tells me I didn't need to?"

"Funny, isn't it? Meeting someone for the first time and feeling like you already know them."

"You feel that too?" Her eyebrows raised, a mixture of curiosity and surprise in her voice, her inflection adding to the surprise expressed by her question.

"Yeah, it's like... I don't know, like there's something familiar about you."

"Maybe we've met in another life." She chuckled softly, but there was an adorable sincerity in her eyes.

The space between them was an invisible force, like two magnets uncertain whether they'll attract or push away from each other. The hands of fate were testing them out the closer they got to each other.

Nora broke the silence as both their brains and hearts processed the magnetic field of attraction between them.

"So, what do we do about it?"

"We could start with breakfast," Jim said as he gestured to the table he had almost completely set up.

"Breakfast sounds perfect."

Jim gestured for her to sit, their eyes never quite fully leaving each other.

Nora tilted her head slightly, a mischievous glint in her eye. A slight surprise that they were staying put rather than going out for a meal.

And so they began a bit of light banter. Peppering conversation back and forth between softball questions and small talk like their favorite food in Cambodia, all the way to what would constitute a "perfect" day, which inevitably resulted in the first mentions of any sort of sexual activity.

Above the table, Jim and Nora were in their own worlds, eating breakfast while conversation danced in the air.

But below? They were connected by the feet in their pajamas. They were like two trees that immediately rooted, not rotted. The mother duck had sacrificed her eggs for this moment in time, the French let others degrade their toast, and the honey and syrup performed a tango like the toes of the two who ate it up. In front of both of them, individual bottles of chocolate milk. The stuff held a soft spot in Jim's heart since his interaction with Queen Pinmekalah. In the background, a remixed, mellow version of Elvis was playing. Lo-fi Elvis. Kind of an oxymoron, really.

Jim curled the corner of his lip and asked in the exasperated breath of an Elvis impersonator, "Say, are ya, are ya enjoyin yourself, honey?" Nora giggled, covering her mouth so he couldn't see what two dozen dental demolitionists could do to his un-French toast.

Jim tried not to blink. It was so lonely in the world when his eyelids slammed shut. But there was bliss in being able to see Nora again when they retracted. He felt what a dog feels after its master leaves and returns. Time disappears. It returns. It disappears. It returns. It doesn't matter if it's a millisecond or a millennium; once they return, there's nothing but trusted love. Jim felt it.

Nora, too.

There's no need to entertain you with the entirety of their conversation. It was crisp and cute, like a vanilla wafer dipped in a size-one glass of two-percent chocolate milk. Unlike their toes, the conversation danced like spicy salsa, quick, short, and with few but fast syllables. Nora tossed back her hair as if she'd just finished spinning before reaching back to Jim with a question, which he grabbed hold of with his lips. The beat of their hearts led the melody. Table be damned when it came to the space between them. Jim ended up bent over it and Nora was on her tippy toes until both decided that the table was more of an impediment than a bridge between them.

Like a water bucket at a waterpark being filled with conversation, Jim and Nora were about to spill into the bedroom with screams of a different kind of pleasure as a wave of passion slid from sheet to pillow to comforter to comfort her on her back on the floor on clouds nine, ten, and eleven.

Jim's hands worked like a poor pocket thief losing a game of Operation as Nora felt him touching each and every sensitive part of her body. Salsa turned to smooth jazz turned to upbeat jazz turned to a static electric tune of ecstasy as Jim's stature overworked Nora's sound system. Electricity. Eeeee-lectricity. A current of orgasms flowing through each other, neither grounded in reality. Reality was a distant future. A lie of the past. An unnecessary present. Eyes wide open.

Jim played DJ with his tongue on the small disks of her breasts until Nora's lips found their way down his briefs, and then it was anything but brief. Banana split for one.

Their bodies, lips, and tongues played tag, ring-around-the-rosie, and hide-and-seek on the playground of sheets and blankets until both were exhausted. Satisfied. Winners.

"Better than a lemon parfait," Jim breathed out.

"What?"

"Nothing. You're incredible."

"Same same."

⇒ XVIII ⇐

Jim wasn't himself as he lay with Nora's naked body beside him, with her almond scent and the remnants of playtime dripping down her legs and drying on the sheets and preparing to give the hotel's washing machines a run for their money. He was sharing secrets, unaware that secrets were what Nora was most attracted to in Jim. Not his eyebrows, his confidence, or his contact list. His secrets. Particularly the recent ones.

"I dream about people reliving their lives knowing what they learned the first time around, still able to apply that knowledge, but still, because they did things different-ly, their life went down a completely different path with different learnings, some of which are counter to the ones they learned before. There's just no perfecting life whether you can travel through time or not," Nora entertained him. "Siddhartha ate a sweet treat in his enlightened state with no trace of cravings, just simple enjoyment. That's how life is meant to be lived, whether one's in control of time or not."

"Hmph."

Jim looked in Nora's eyes, blinded by the light of his own gaze, for in hers there was deceit and deception mak-ing its way to the surface. Jim just saw waves of blue.

"Tell me about your restaurant."

"Well, it's a high-end, seafood around-the-world ethnic experience with an insect spin. I put a cultural twist on tra-ditional seafood ingredients and then an American twist on the unexpected ingredients, like colossal plankton on but-tered toast. Everyone is a chef at my restaurant; that's what I think differentiates us most. Food is made better when there's no status or ego in the kitchen. It's a level cooking field of passion, finesse, and experiments. That's what en-ables me to not have to be there twenty-four seven. We're not actually in the food-making business, we're in the idea business. Ideas about flavor and taste and socializing and connection. And people come in for our ideas expressed through the food on their plate. They dine not on ingredi-ents but thoughts, they taste not flavors but concepts, they scoop the remnants of innovation off their plates and into their mouths, and they then crave not more but different. Same same, as you say, but different."

It was clear Jim had described his restaurant a few hundred times already. It was almost scripted.

"And soon I'll have saved it from the hands of a neighboring seafood restaurant that is the yin to our yang. There's no coming back from where I'm going, but there's no competing with it, either. Plus, competition isn't the point for me. It's not business in this particular situation. It's personal."

Nora's heartbeat started to track back to where it was not but ten minutes ago. The idea of learning Jim's secret was more of a tease than what he did with his hands, although she grudgingly admitted to herself that it was not by much. She toyed with the idea of turning the room into her playground again, but she had to remember her mission. She *had* to, so she put her blue eyes back to work, staring into Jim's.

"Tell me more," she insisted, rubbing her hand across his narrow, barren land of a chest.

"This restaurant has never been about being the best in the industry, or the geography, or the field, or the kitchen. It's not about having or making more than another. It's why I founded the restaurant coalition of Brooklyn: to be there and support one another for the sake of better for better's sake. Some of the greatest people are in it. Gus. Frank. And others," Jim said, quickly abandoning the list on the tip of his tongue after realizing she had no clue who these friends were. "Competition turns good men and women into animals. Competition brings out the worst in people as they strive and struggle for status, when the reality is that the biggest battles are fought within one's head. And what so few realize is that we're all fighting the same battle. When you're working with seaweed from Greenland, tartar from Alaska, and miracle berries from Timbuktu, that moment of trying to make it all dance—it doesn't matter what Louise is doing down the road or Roy is chopping upstate. What's more is that sometimes you're not even competing with yourself. All competing does is add force to something that merely needs a melody of vulnerability and meaning. And the best way to find that in ourselves is to offer it to others. All ships rise with the tide, but tides are treacherous. Better to create a steady river of forward momentum that can be traveled together. You mentioned Siddartha. Ever wonder why he set up camp next to a river and not an ocean or in the land of ten thousand lakes?"

Nora didn't care about Jim's homage to competition, but she also couldn't help but appreciate it. She was learning more about him, like how she needed to be specific in her questions—she wanted to know more about his bet and plan to win it, not his philosophy on competition—but she was also learning how much of his heart he put into things; how, after everything she'd been told by the man who hired her, Jim might be well-intentioned after all. Hmph.

⇒XIX⇐

When Lemon was nineteen, he swallowed a golf ball to win the respect of a few trailer park boys who gave him shit for doing so well on the debate team arguing how wonderful the sport of golf is. Turns out that repeating yourself is a great way to win the argument that golf is a worthwhile sport to watch, regardless that Lemon didn't believe it was.

Lemon didn't care much. His big stature made it easy to swallow, and now when he eats anything and says, "This tastes like a golf ball," you have to believe him. He actually knows. And in case you're wondering, no, he didn't have to go to the doctor. He passed it on through like everything else he's eaten. His esophagus was coated with steel, his stomach a tamed volcano that could handle anything thrown in it without overreacting. His bowels are a guided slip n' slide and his anus a stout gate he and only he controlled through a series of mental pulleys.

Lemon never understood how people could describe food with words about ingredients and flavors and feelings and experiences they've never actually had. Good or bad. Five star or one star. Vomit to eat again or vomit period. "This tastes like garbage." "This tastes like floorboard glue." "This tastes like an apricot pit meets freshly squeezed soy sauce and moss grown on a grindstone in the garage of an 1850 house."

If you haven't tasted the elements you say you're tasting, your word was Tunisian mud to him. And yes, he's tasted mud from thirty-two different countries and Tunisian mud really is the worst, so he could say that.

Lemon's propensity for smelling and tasting everything over the years has won him more than the respect of some trailer trash. He's conquered bets and challenges that garnered him more than $40,000 and a few fancy watches, built up an immunity to a dozen different minor poisons—not that anyone has set out to purposefully poison him, but if they ever did...—sat on the supertaster council of some of the most profound food brands, consulted with ingredient scientists, and competed in a series, undefeated, mind you, of robotic taste tests. IBM's Watson has nothing on Lemon.

Naturally he has a ream of secrets of his own: insider knowledge that can help, harm or harrow the newest or eldest of restauranters. Lemon was there for Jim.

Jim never bet with, teased, or challenged Lemon. Nor did he idolize him. Jim saw Lemon Twist for who he was: a person, and a goddamn positive one at that. Jim didn't dictate what Lemon should do, nor did he follow in his footsteps. If you give Jim a Lemon, he's going to make a friendship that lasts. Equal parts give and take. A two-way street of brotherly bonding.

Lemon had treated Jim with the same respect ever since he first met him at Corn Wallace Theater during a food panel discussion on people's propensity for turning any original ingredient into something sweet. *Brains: Wired For Sugar*. The superest of super tasters were on the panel. They included Dr. William McGee, who made a condensed protein bar from acorn dust which his competitors stole and added sugar beet juice to, to outsell him in the store. "Same protein. Sweeter flavor." It's easy to dominate a market with a sweetened spun version of something else.

Also on the panel was Eddy Tenny Withiason, guru, follower of Bhaisaijyaguru, and herbalist. His mother ate nothing but plants during her pregnancy and he's carried out that habit through his plant-based, fiber-dense life of thirty-six years. He's known for creating the flavor graph, plant version, in which he categorizes edible plants by which flavor profile each best connects with—salty, umami, bitter, fat, sour, and, of course, sweet. You would think the bitter category would be the most filled one, but sweetness wins the quantity game there, too, even in the natural world.

Lastly was Lemon, who had tasted around, in and outside of this world. While all the panelists appealed to Jim, Lemon was of utmost interest, not because of the value he could give to Jim but the value that Jim could give to him. The value of selflessness when it was so clear everyone else wanted something from him: "Taste this." "What do you think of that?" "What's the next trend I need to capitalize on?"

In the middle of the panelists debating the cognitive sciences of sweetness, Jim raised his hand in the audience and asked a question; that to all but Jim and Lemon was a question directed at the panel but really was a rhetorical question that would make Lemon and Jim instant friends.

"What happens when everything is sweet, and we've found all degrees of sweetness? At some point, if the human pursues eternal sweetness in all that's edible, we'll become desensitized, just as we have to smells of bile, experiences of inhumanity, and traces of deceit and lies between good company. Isn't this pursuit a decision to follow down a path of self-assigned prophecy leading to a revolution? Sweetness is supposed to bring us temporary joy, leveraged as a piece of a larger puzzle, not the tool, tool bag, and the tool-of-a-person using them. When everything is sweet, isn't nothing?" *Herough. Herough. Herough.*

Jim sat back down, having blacked out his tirade on sweetness, half in seriousness and half in jest. It was not the wording he planned to share, but the wheels had been set in motion, sugar-induced and ready to go.

Lemon stood up from the theater seating in the front of a blank white screen and took a deep breath. A mixture of curry and lavender perfume swirled its way from the front row to his nose. He exhaled all the air in his lungs and swallowed, tasting rutabaga and wet cardboard.

Lemon believed that so much of taste was done with the breath, from carrying the aromatics to sensors that signified flavor to the brain, to how oxygen was more than a molecule, but a carrier of volatile aromatics. Meditators make the best tasters in his opinion. He would go through a forty-five minute regimented meditation before any of his tastings and when he taught others, he rarely shared words about tasting; it was "watch your breathing" or "you're not exhaling right" or "eating in a room with bad air is no way to dine."

Lemon took another deep breath, unaware of all the eyes on him, and walked out. The remaining panelists were baffled, but the moderator worked her magic to keep the session moving by calling on Eddy, who gave some ode to only having discovered twelve percent of all plant life and how it would be years until any human could be desensitized to sweetness.

While the audience bought this response, Jim wasn't appeased. If anything, Eddy had just confirmed that desensitization was inevitable.

After enduring more banter about sweetness, *sans* Lemon, and a little bit of talk about seafood and the degradable impact it had on sweetness, which only infuriated Jim more, Jim took the feet that brought him there and sent them back on the path they took from the conference hotel room.

"That was thoughtful."

"What?"

Jim was in his own head, still frustrated by the seafood comments. At the time, he had been beginning to plan Herough and the last thing he needed was degradation of his concept. Frustration leads to blindness, which is why Jim didn't see Lemon standing in the entryway of the hotel waiting for him.

"I said, that was thoughtful. You expressed concern about the path toward sweetness. I agree with you."

The surprise mitigated any starstruckness Jim might have otherwise felt.

"Thank you."

"My name's Lemon. Lemon. Lemon."

"Jim. Just once. *Herough Herough.*"

"A pleasure, Jim. Sorry for the repetition. It's a tic of mine. Anyway, it's quite rare that anything meaningful strikes a chord with a panelist these days. So much of it is memorized and positioned with yesterday's thoughts. Eddy is still working with data and a hypothesis that are both almost a decade old. Contrary to popular belief, there's not much that can be learned from the past, and even if there is, there's no problem in relearning it. The past puts more weight on us than it propels us forward. Forget the past but remember what it taught you. Forget the past but remember what it taught you."

Lemon could tell Jim wasn't sure what to say. He was processing. Jim did that a lot. Add it to the list of characteristics Lemon admired about him.

"I read about your restaurant concept. Seafood is a risky endeavor. Risky but respectful. It's interesting that as creatures originally of the sea, we wouldn't have fully explored that waterscape first. So many are distracted by the land, by what they can see. In all my years of tasting, there's not a problem that couldn't be solved with some element of the ocean."

"That's what I've been saying!"

"I know," Lemon smirked.

While most friendships start with a sucker punch to the face or some childish brawl or companionship over losing the same love, this one started with an affinity for the sea and a saltiness for sweetness.

$$\gg XX \ll$$

Jim and Nora had partially dressed and returned to the table to finish what was left of their breakfast.

Nora was in the middle of discussing the similarities between rap artists across nationalities. It was her turn to reveal information, though she was careful as to which information.

She said her cousin, a well-known rap artist in Eastern Thailand, actively listened to rap artists from different countries in different languages to get better in his own. To a normal ear or Earth walker, and despite so many words sounding similar across languages, it was incredibly difficult to rap in one language and use words of another. Consider the documented 3,454 slang terms of Khmer. They're translatable, sure, but not syllabically. Somehow her cousin had found a way to blend words across languages without interrupting the listener. The belief is that, the words, even if not understood, all still inspired themes and emotions that were relatable despite the language transistor. The words of her cousin's most popular hit "Choul Mouy" were his interpretation of Cap Kendricks & Edgar Wasser's "Medizin," in which he used words from a total of six different languages and asserted that if everyone was drunk, he might not want to be sober at all.

Thus, Jim learned that it was all the rap songs Nora listened to from various nationalistic artists that enabled her to fluently speak four different languages, though, Jim noticed, she always had a soft syllabic sway to her voice, no matter what language she proved to Jim she could speak; it was like a smile was always present, no matter what word she said in what language with what inflection rhymed with what word with what intention. Her lips didn't even need to curl, though Jim wished they would so he could see the petite wrinkle on each side of her cheeks again.

"Sweet cheeks," Jim exhaled softly and unintentionally.

"*Was?*" she answered in German. Translation, if you don't know, "What?"

"Nothing. Sorry. Just getting lost in something."

"*Was?*" she responded again, but this time more inquisitive and flirty, as if she already knew the answer.

"Nothing. Carry on. I want to hear you rap one more time," Jim said, not giving her the satisfaction, but also not taking his eyes off her smile. Everyone loves a little tease.

Annoyingly, Jim's phone began to ring in the middle of Nora's performance of a Beastie Boys and Frank Sinatra remix; it was so wrong that it was right, and with someone as beautiful as Nora dialecting it, it was like a waterfall of letters and syllables with the scenery more beautiful than the water that falls from it. As for the ringing phone, its beat wasn't steady enough to rap to. It was Lemon.

"Are you doing what I think you're doing, Jim?"

Nora watched Jim's face turn to fierce determination. She tried to lean closer to hear.

"It's underway, Lem."

Lemon sighed so heavily that even Nora heard him from across that monkey gym of a table.

"You don't have to do this, Jim. You can do this on your own. You've got the attitude. The smarts. The resources."

Jim stopped him. "There's no stopping a con man by standing still and just doing what we've been doing, Lemon. You know that'll be our demise. Like I said, it's underway. I've already got the spice and I'll be heading to Budapest next. I'll be back in time for the conference."

Jim held the phone in front of him for a few seconds before hanging up; it was silent acceptance from Lemon, but Jim was questioning whether he'd say goodbye to his friend, considering if he was right and should turn back, but who would Jim be kidding? He'd already met with Queen capital letter P. Like he said, *It's underway*. Jim tapped his phone and the call ended.

Back 5,638 miles away from Jim, Lemon didn't wait for Jim to hang up. He had stuffed his phone in his pocket, still connected and now mixed with lemon drops that he'd pull out ironically in front of guests to entertain them after being introduced, along with the passport that he'd be making use of that evening (in Hungarian time) to find Jim hungry in Hungary.

"What was that?" asked Nora.

Jim wasn't about to say, but he wasn't about to let this Cambodian gem out of his hands either by coming off dismissive, secretive, or obtuse. He hadn't felt this good with anyone in quite some time. Nora was sweet. If sugarcane were a person, it would be her. He clearly had a way to go before he was desensitized to sweets.

"I leave for Hungary this afternoon... it's a work thing."

"I'll come with you!"

Jim mentally hesitated, but Nora needn't be a mind reader to tell.

"Úgy szép az élet, ha zajlik," she said. "Hungarian for 'Life is beautiful if it's happening.'"

That sounds like something Lemon would say three times in a row.

Jim knew where he needed to go and what he needed to do, but he also knew that he couldn't speak the language. If there were ever a time to accept a hand, that time was now. And how lucky for it to be Nora's smooth, caramel-swirl-colored hand and the delicate power it held, having had a delightful taste of what she could do with it already.

⮞XXI⮜

Of all the airports Jim had been in, he couldn't stand any of what got sold there. It was a fucked-up eco-system of tchotchkes, candy, shirts that are purchased in the wrong size, and items overpriced because they were deemed as essential as water in the existential desert of the airport. Of course, the water was sold right next to a drinking fountain from which one could fill a bottle, of which bottles were sold right next to that, and unnecessary backpacks with water bladders were sold right next to that. Even in the Cambodian airport, after the bribing and security guards and the trafficking of so many illegal goods, there were shops. Shops with musty perfume, shops with delectable tequila, decent rum, and despicable whiskey. It's not really an airport. It's a mall with airplanes entering and exiting. And don't even get Jim started on the lack of bathrooms. You know that thing people need to use but you never see needing them to use in movies?

Speaking of which...

"I need to use the bathroom," Nora said as she pushed herself up from lying on the floor of Gate C4 as they waited for boarding time.

In the bathroom, she did more than relieve herself. She also sent a text out as quickly as the toilet flushed. *We're on our way.* In the mirror, Nora saw a war happening on her own face. One side held firm with stoic motivation and tight skin and the other showed empathetic eyes and quiveringly loose lips. Dear Lord, a white hair had already shown atop her head, drooping down her forehead like a foreboding cross. Before the bathroom text, she could have left Jim to venture on his own and see it through himself without confrontation. But that was one flush and hand-wash ago. She grimly pulled out the chastising white hair. She had a mission to finish.

Back in the waiting area of C4, Jim was trying to comprehend why his life felt like a movie, wondering about the rap artist scene of Budapest, but over all of that was the far heavier thought of what he'd soon have to sacrifice.

Jim looked at the hallway waiting for Nora. He needed to taste her lips again. A few times, actually.

⇒ XXII ⇐

The flight wasn't the longest Jim had taken. Nora either. But it did take almost a full day.

Typically the longer flights are more comfortable, but despite all the technological advances in the world, the seats were still cramped and the TVs on the headrests did nothing but show the map that seemed to be delayed and never provided an accurate time of arrival. Apparently the airline had since given up on providing any updated tangible materials to read. Half the seats were even missing the safety belt instruction sheet. It was in some purgatory between olden times and new-age tech, the messy middle, the result of a lack of care; such is the world, really. Yet, somehow, they had plenty of earbuds to sell, for people to plug into the non-functional TVs. There's not many in the world that are as out of touch with it as those who fly all over it.

None of this bothered Jim. He had Nora to talk to. Questions to ask. Anything to take his mind off what was soon to ensue once they landed. He looked Nora over as she sat beside him. He noticed the tattoos on the back of her left hand, in the crevice between the pointer finger and the thumb. He saw her bottom lip was tighter than normal. He could see a scar on her shoulder. She had freckles on her face that spilled down her neck and down to the scar. All these little details Jim hadn't noticed before, back in the hotel. Lust was to blame for the lack of observation. She was also fidgeting her leg. Was she always a fidgeter? Jim could hear the seashell ankle bracelet she wore. The bracelet with charms, too. He wondered where they came from. Which came first. Was there any significance to the charms? Perhaps he could start there. Yeah. That was a good ice breaker. He wasn't sure why but Nora looked like she could use it. She was stressing outside as much as Jim was stressing inside.

Before he could open his mouth, Jim looked back up her body to realize Nora was dozing off, perhaps fighting a slight nightmare given the trembling, or at least trying to sleep. Eyes closed. Head now angled away from Jim. Jim chalked it up to an intense dislike of flying. (Although, dear reader, it is everything but that.) He'd given her the window seat. The comfiest of sleeping positions available on a flight.

Now looking past Sleeping Beauty, Jim could see clouds. How meaningless they appeared up close, yet how powerful they could appear from afar. Jim decided to take this time to prepare his mind, Six Sigma–style. Time to drop whatever might hold him back or slow him down. He was going to have to be ready. Clouds, be they big, small, in front of him, gray, white, or behind. Clouds be damned.

Jim reminisced about a time when he was foraging the land of a friend's thirty-acre lot for swamp mushrooms somewhere between New York and Pennsylvania. It was a mere few weeks after opening Herough. It had been the first time Jim felt like he could actually leave the four walls of his restaurant. How vile his friend thought mushrooms were at the time. The kind of plant that says, *Hey world, throw dung on me and watch me grow,* but Jim was doing what Jim always did, what Lemon always reminded him about; Jim tried whatever he could get his hands on. Careless at the time of what might be poisonous, he would lick, taste, and chew everything he found; no need to swallow it, after all, even though that's what Lemon did (remember, reader, Lemon's stomach was like a gestational volcano... Lemon could eat a Pacific poisonous newt and still be okay); merely licking and chewing is how Lemon rationalized that Jim didn't get sick or die. Jim knew that wasn't entirely true, but also knew it was a risk worth taking to hone his acumen with food and flavor.

Some mushrooms he licked that afternoon numbed his tongue, some moss on other mushrooms stuck to his teeth like glue. There was no shortage of mushrooms to try, but the real kicker for him was the three-mile river that flowed through the center of the land. It was as if the mushroom fields were merely a distraction, a wall of safety for what lay between the two fields of them. It was on that river, sandwiched between mushrooms of all sorts, that Jim found the greatest delicacies of crawfish and seaweed and snails, juices and jams and other things to squeeze, shape, and grill. And the insects—it was a breeding ground where he could experiment with the flavors of insects at all stages of life, from larvae to adults ready to lay larvae. Jim had quite the pair of ears on him, too, not that they were cauliflowerlike or abnormally large, but he had ears for insects. The chirps and cricks and tat tat tats. Nature to him was nurture to his heart and, more importantly, to his stomach. Nothing quite like the sound of a roly-poly or a pill bug, depending on where you're from, rolling itself up right before being sautéed. It tastes like shrimp, something we know Jim also loves. When Jim thought about the insects, he thought how much they love trees and how much trees must hate them, for they move and move and take and take. Trees, of course, take sunlight, energy, other plants' roots, nutrients *and* give oxygen, aura, shelter, and so on. But trees, they don't move. They stand still. They are masters of the vertical plank, which stops time. They're the only thing in life that grows standing still.

The thought of it all made Jim as drowsy as the last mushroom he licked on his way out of his friend's field, baskets full of all the findings he'd bring back to Herough. *Sans*—funnily enough—any mushrooms.

Jim was manspreading in his seat to get comfortable, his leg nustling the knee of Nora like a blanket. It was time for Jim to fish the alphabet and catch some zzzs just like Nora clearly was doing.

Right when Jim woke and started working on the mental Rubik's Cube of time—again, the estimated arrival time on the screen in front of him couldn't be trusted—the pilot must have pressed a button to release the wheels of the plane from their own slumber in preparation for arrival in Budapest. Before they touched the ground, Jim could smell the stench of the country. And from the look on Nora's face, she could, too. The smell was like a nightclub that hadn't been cleaned in years or what would happen if you stockpiled gym towels for a year without washing them. It smelled like an elementary school playground on field day in the middle of summer. Why they've never made scented wood chips for these playgrounds, we'll never know. Someone tell P&G that they're basically leaving money on the table.

As they waited to be let off the plane, Jim was racking the depths of his memory for a map, a mental map of where he needed to go and what he needed to do. He sifted through his memory; the books he's read, the songs he's heard, the whispers in the industry, anything he's heard about the Shaman Denny, a Vedic astrologer and qigong instructor with an intuitive relationship consultancy. With all the stories Jim has heard about him, he always thought of him as a hippie nomad, but that was when Jim was filled with doubt and zero need for Denny's insights. So here we are. Queen Pinmekalah had confirmed it. Validated it. She damn near ordered it. Jim's shoes were made for walking.

Jim, now that he holds the one artifact given to him by Pinmekalah-lah-lah-lah, seeks the one person who can guide him further on his journey to turn this bottle of chocolate milk-sand into something culinarily viable.

Despite having slept the entire flight, Nora didn't seem altogether refreshed; to Jim, though, she still projected warmth, gracing his peripheral vision with optimism and passion for accompanying him on this journey.

But here's the reality, dear reader. She didn't sleep an ounce. In her line of work, sleep doesn't come easy, and despite there being less than an inch between them on the flight, and zero inches at the knee, she had to maintain her emotional distance.

Jim, on the other hand, was out colder than the other side of the pillow. He caught more zzzs than his fishnet of dreams could contain. He slept deeply enough for both of them. The weight of what-ifs has that impact on people.

Alas. Both were now awake and following normal disembarking procedures for the plane, and embarking procedures for their journey.

They grabbed their bags from under the seats in front of them, proceeded through the airport, yet another shopping mall of sorts, albeit this time smaller and with more interesting trinkets like bathtub keychains shaped like penises, neon light necklaces, and, yes, unicum, unicum, unicum. The one drink you can't say no to when offered. Such is tradition. Albeit one that Jim had not yet imbibed, though he planned to make a detour of sorts at some point to do so. For now, he sought out a map of Budapest, something, anything, to at least get a directional decision on where to go to find Shaman D.

Though Nora was patient with Jim, Jim privately worried about her willingness to remain with him, especially when not even he knew what was in his future or where his future was.

"We should visit one of the fountains while we're here," Nora mentioned.

The fountain! Of course. Shaman D rests his As, Bs, and Cs by the Escapades. He could hear rhyming verse from the book in his head. Maybe having Nora with him was good fortune after all. How coincidental that she triggered the memory bank to deposit the one slip he needed to finalize his mental map, his clipped compass, his directional awareness.

But coincidences, as Jim would soon learn, are never coincidences. They're intentions that surprise or agendas that reveal themselves without an author's name scripted on them. They're usually not predestined experiences, but actively destined, preordained, masterfully manipulated ones.

In truth, Nora could tell he was struggling; after all, they had circled the innards of the airport a number of times, oddly stopping in front of the high-stacked rack of off-brand, watered-down map and magazine memorabilia meant to stimulate the economy with tourists leaving the country but wanting to remember the highlights of their stay. Given that there were so few of them, it was critical the country did whatever it could to get them to leave on a high note, for that's the single greatest indicator of them making a return visit.

Though Nora knew of the fountain and the shaman who resided there, we've now reached the extent of her knowledge. The texts on her phone that she read while Jim was asleep on the plane said two words: *Shaman* and *Escapades*.

In fact, if it hadn't been for having walked around the same magazine rack a dozen times in the airport, she might not have connected the dot of Escapades to the *Fountain of Escapades* that adorned nearly every tourist-targeting magazine on the racks.

A tourist attraction? Intriguing.

⇒XXIII⇐

It's a manual process to test the size of socks, no doubt. Literally three people in the mill will take the sock and stretch it out on a board to get a measurement, and if at least one of them hits the mark of the size they're looking for, then the batch is good. At the same time, there are endless variables at play regarding the stretchiness—and thus the fit—of a sock. The temperature, obviously. The transportation method: Is it vacuum-sealed? Or exposed to oxygen? How long has it been traveling? Is it piled on with other items and thus squished? Endless variables all affect sock size. At that rate, it's almost worth removing the three men from sock-stretching duty because there are too many other variables that assist in a stretch. But what's a process if not befuddled by a little human involvement? If the error is already going to be there, might as well have a human play a role in making it larger. This was a lesson for Jim, though not about producing socks. It was a lesson in process and automation. Either go all in on automation and remove any human intervention, or stick entirely with human intervention and be okay with the size and growth of a company that uses gut and brain and heart over wire, keyboard, and Wi-Fi connection. Could he automate everything in his restaurant? Sure he could, but this is Jim. He wouldn't, and you can thank his socks for that.

Jim and Nora had to have passed sixteen sock shops already walking through town. The first few were interesting, to watch the process and reflect, but now it was just a sad sight. What's Hungary's deal with socks? No matter. Each shop they passed by reminded Jim of what he had built and what he stood to lose to Phil.

"The fountain is that way, not far from here." Nora pointed to a billboard on the side of a building. Thank heavens she could read Hungarian.

"We need to do something else first... and last," Jim said with a wisp of trepidation. Or was it nervousness? Disappointment? Something was off and Nora picked up on it.

"What?"

"Eat, of course!" Jim proclaimed, trying to put a pep in the steps his words took. Known to Jim and Lemon but unbeknownst to Nora or you, the reader, Jim would shortly trade his taste buds for the magic to be imbued into the chocolate milk container he's hauled all this way with him from Cambodia.

Nora was taken aback; it was a shock to stall all the anticipation that had been built up inside her to discover what it was Jim was chasing, but suddenly her belly rumbled and gurgled, and she had the sensation that it was eating itself. In feigning sleep on the plane, she'd mistakenly passed up the free bags of animal crackers. Damn, could she go for some animal crackers now. They reminded her of a rap her cousin made when they were kids; he rapped all the zoo animals' names but in a way that mispronounced each of them. "In the back, there's the giraffe ('grrr-af'), and behind the post is the rhinoceros ('rin-no-iss-or-iss'), over there you'll find the calf ('salf') and over here you'll find the fish ('phish'), all of life is allopoiesis." Oh, her cousin. The thought invited a smile to her face. Those cheeks Jim had fallen in love with were back.

"I've read about a place near the river, but it might take us a bit to find it. It apparently doesn't have a sign or any advertising or lights. It will look like any number of these homes, but inside is an entire tree house, literally a tree, with nooks and crannies and cute hideouts that you have to access by climbing a ladder. They make remarkable Darjeeling tea and waffle cookies, and they serve only one main dish: duck. But not just any kind of duck; it's a three-way cooked duck with a secret drizzle that embodies each of the decoctions of cooking."

Nora had Jim at "they make remarkable." What a fantastic expression. To make something and then to make something worth talking about. Truly anything could have followed the expression and Jim would have been in. Thankfully it was a restaurant that followed, and now so would he, but not before she lit a little candle of lust in the moment by walking up to Jim and kissing him on the lips, unprompted, unadulterated, unrestrained. The kind of kiss that people dream of getting. This kiss was a seal that would prevent her from spilling her secret and from Jim drawing it out.

"Dessert first, huh?" Jim said with a crisp smile, glistening with the sun reflecting on the wetness on his upper lip left by Nora.

Now *that* is what he'd call remarkable. Ducks flying backward be damned.

⇒ XXIV ⇐

I love a life of the interesting. Interesting experiences, interesting flavors, interesting restaurants. And especially interesting stories. Stories that entail a clash of romance lost, debts owed, and romance renewed, found on the path of paying off that debt while filled with endless anguish and uncertainty, but somehow also an unlimited source of grit, gumption, and gumbo.

Stories like Nora's.

Shall we learn more about our damned damsel, our sleek-skinned spy, the apple of JimBo's eye?

Nora's mother was Thai and her father American. Her mother posted a note throughout their village in Thailand that read "For sale: baby clothes. Never worn."

Miscarriages and premature deaths were the norm in her village, but the reality was that Nora was born ten pounds and seven ounces, an absurd weight for an infant of Thai descent. She was so large that none of the baby clothes her mother had acquired fit. And just as Nora didn't fit into the clothes her mother had laid out, Nora's father didn't fit into the culture her mother had laid out for them, and he was off. When Nora was old enough to be told about her father leaving her and her mother alone, she was outraged; she, like her mother, posted a note throughout their village in Thailand except this one read "For sale: man's life. Never loved." It didn't take long for cultists of Thailand to respond. There was no harm in responding to inquiries like these, even if they were false. The various tribes were too deep into the Royal Thai Police's pocketbooks. Right next to the belief of inner country peace, Royal Executive Officer Batuk Cho-Cha believed in population control, and if anyone was motivated enough to put out a hit on someone—and pay for it—then that someone had it coming. "Let them wean themselves out. We'll gladly help," he would say. Of course, it was a simple strategy to keep his wallet and Bahn accounts full.

It just so happened that Batuk was traveling through Nora's village on a competitive tour of billiards throughout Thailand—*there's nothing as precise and peaceful as billiards,* he thought—when the notice was posted, and he did what the post meant him to do: He noticed.

Everything was a signal to Batuk. He would find meaning in the meaningless, which was disruptive, but still more disruptive was his use of signals. Although Thailand is a country that is exposed to very few tornadoes, Batuk had tornado sirens installed throughout the country. This was not so they would be there if ever the people needed a warning—there is nowhere to hide anyway, without basements or safely built structures—but so he could have the sirens tested each month. And month after month the entire country would endure a shrill signal of safety, as well as a reminder of Batuk's strong reign. *The one who is on everyone's mind the most has all the power*, Batuk journaled.

Aside from billiards, performative signaling, and turning face when people requested a hit man or woman, Batuk liked to lead by example and, as such, from time to time, typically on a day preceding a half-crescent moon, he would participate in a hunt. It was training for him, really, something that the police couldn't replicate no matter the elaborate setup of practice courses, books, or virtual trials. This was raw, animalistic practice. The good stuff.

With the day being one that preceded a half-crescent moon and the fact that Batuk was on a winning streak and riding a massive stallion of pride from it—though I dare say any opponent that actually could beat Batuk would allow him to win anyway for fear of retribution that was never in a form of a rematch. It has been thirty-four matches since someone made the mistake of accidentally winning, and Batuk was ready for a real challenge. He set out his troops to find Nora, the one who posted the notice, the one who sought out the man who didn't love. "How dare one not love?" Batuk said. "Life has no shortage of love; it's the one thing that retains peace and unity." Honest and heartfelt words coming from a man who was about to assassinate another. (What a beautiful word, *assassinate*. Two asses in one word paired with "innate," something so strong and driven and respectable, for if anything is innate, it is the concept of competition with oneself, which is all that killing another is.)

In the middle of Batuk's rumination, his police deputy returned with Nora, *sans* mother, for obvious reasons.

Nora was eleven at the time; old enough to be upset about her father leaving, but not yet old enough to

understand her actions following the revelation. She merely posted the notice out of anger and resentment at her
father.

Batuk was surprised to find an eleven-year-old girl in
front of him.

"Are you the one who posted the notice?" Batuk asked
with certainty that she couldn't be and already thinking of
the punishments for the troops who mistakenly brought
her to him.

Nora was too startled to respond, but Batuk's deputy
nodded his head to answer for Nora.

"And what is it you have to give in exchange?"

Nora's thoughts raced in dizzying loops, chasing their
own tails in her mind. Ring-around-the-amygdala. Was this
meant to happen? Did she actually want it to? Could Batuk do it? (She'd only ever heard of Batuk a couple of times
in her life, but never in a positive light. The question she
should have been thinking is *would* he do it? She knew he
could.) Did she have any right to put a call like this out? The
only question she could answer was the one of what she
has to offer in exchange.

"Nothing, Mr. Batuk. Nothing."

Rather than taken aback, Batuk was intrigued. Never
had he ever participated in or heard of a hit being posted without any exchange to be made, let alone by an
eleven-year-old.

"Well, you can color me intrigued by your notice. I will
do it, but not in exchange for nothing. You are young, able,
and clearly have an internal compass that aligns with the
way our country can retain peace. Tell me about this man
who did not love."

In most, a moment like this, of strickenness and star-
tlement, a moment that one couldn't imagine being in
when they woke up in the morning, silence would fall on
them. But for Nora, the waterwheel's first bucket was filled
with liquid thoughts and so it began to turn, powering

Nora's vocal cords to share all that she knew about her father, which wasn't too much, but Batuk found even more pleasure in the comparative lack of information; a chase, a hunt would ensue. A righteous one. But on one condition.

"Thank you. I will find him and end his misguided life."

Of course, when Batuk said "I," he didn't really mean himself. He looked at his deputy and nodded in the direction of the door, now with his assignment to fly to the United States and take the life of a man that should have been taken eleven years prior when he made the wrong choice.

Now, we won't find out if the deputy succeeded because he never returned. Perhaps he's still searching for Nora's dad. Perhaps he found America to be a better country to reside in. Perhaps he, himself, found love, say, at an airport layover in Belgium and decided to stay there.

The success or the failure of the mission, the return or not of his deputy, was of little interest to Batuk. The deputy wasn't the first to be labeled a deserter, but this was one of the few that Batuk simply ignored. For all intents and purposes, Nora assumed she had what she wanted and Batuk had what he wanted even more. Nora's promise in exchange for the kill. A spy in the making, someone to become ten times the model of his deputy, a murderess maiden molded in the shadow of Batuk himself.

➹XXV➷

Nora never went back home or saw her mother again after her exchange with Batuk. With her servitude promised to Batuk, she was assigned to the special branch, the Wild Tiger Corp.

That evening, at eleven years old, she was branded with a Tiger tattoo on her ankle. From there she was trained under Batuk's most praised police chiefs—you know, the ones who stayed around—thrown into multiple cults to train and understand their ways, under the pseudonym Alora. Of course, over time she became Batuk's most prized possession, a signal of sorts to all throughout Southern Asia. She took up many other names while on Batuk's keen missions and traveled many more miles beyond Southern Asia than in it. She even crossed the forbidden pond to Tennessee, maybe where her father had settled down, but by the age of twenty when she visited, thoughts of her father had long since been erased from her mind; and, of course, a few visits to Timbuktu leave many with gaps in their memory.

To most, Nora was an ordinary person, but to Batuk she was extraordinary; possessing agility and empathy and risk tolerance and an insanely effective perception and analysis of her surroundings and the intentions of others.

He also used her for the more interesting missions, well beyond those that strictly aligned with violence and death sentences.

After taking on Nora and successfully wielding her as a secret weapon for years, Batuk, nearing the end of his tenure—don't worry, it's by choice, not by a caste system set in stone by some unknown ancestor—wished to find respite in things beyond billiards. He found buying manufacturing sites to be a lucrative and entertaining endeavor. With each purchase, he could learn about something unique while awake and make money while he slept. Over the years Nora's missions were often tied to removing obstacles, a smoothing process that would enable Batuk to easily and ethically—okay, that's questionable—acquire toilet manufacturers, 3D printer manufacturers, motorcycle manufacturers, aluminum can manufacturers. His latest (or should we say last?) endeavor was to purchase a food ingredient manufacturing segment.

The manufacturing companies Batuk acquired always improved tenfold. Not through some form of discipline, Six Sigma, military organization reform. No. They were improved with magic. Though Batuk was no fan of reading for pleasure, he often found himself reviewing ancient literature, chasing myths and legends and stories that to an ordinary person would be fairy tales.

Batuk sent scouts to find the crevice of ever-changing material, a meteoric creation at the crease of a tectonic plate that overflowed with a new material, neither plastic nor metal but nearly weightless and which he believed to be the strongest element to be found. It had incredible qualities such as holding warmth, never dropping below sixty-five degrees to the touch; nor did it make a sound when it was hit with something. It absorbed noise. Though Batuk used it for toilet seats, he may have sent some off to the Tiger Clan as a parting gift to wear before his retirement. The material is extracted only slowly from the crevice, so Batuk began with leveraging it for toilet seats, and though he had endless plans for more, particularly and selfishly, a pool stick next, the supply could only be obtained at a speed that limited him to toilet seats.

As for the aluminum, it was the recyclability of it that he truly led, not necessarily the manufacturing of it. Lava from an uncharted volcanic island in the Indian Ocean incinerates everything that's on the aluminum. It's certainly not new-age tech, except for the fact that it left zero emissions, waste, or energy to do so, as if the magical lava sucked the material into a black hole and deposited it in another universe. Suck it, global warming. You're welcome, ozone. Batuk was tipped off about the lava by the Hindu Paranas, Varuna, the god of the oceans and its vehicle the Makara, which is a crocodile for those not conversant in Hindu history. Batuk could give three shits about the environment, having destroyed far more than what his volcanic find has saved, but he became the poster child of innovation for sustainable manufacturing processes, which was convenient. And you know Batuk well enough now to understand that he liked the spotlight as long as it didn't reveal the shadow behind him.

And now Batuk would put the final nail into his treasure chest of manufacturing dominance after his purchase of the food ingredient manufacturer, Sessalt. Not that Sessalt was anything special. Sure, it was well-off and supplied a breadth of ingredients globally. It was an inspirational company, at the forefront of the complex challenge of world-class innovation and application of expertise in creating tasting solutions. It also happened to be a purveyor of all sorts of spices. None like the one Batuk would soon bring to the table, er, that is, none like the one *Nora* would soon bring to the table. It just so happened that Batuk had recently acquired a text on Cambodian history that led him to learn about the ancient history of Queen Pinmekalah and, by extension, the Hungarian Shaman. Knowing what was at stake for the spice he sought as well as his fascination with making this the largest magical convergence of his lifetime before he left the military police, there could be no mistakes made. So he had entrusted the mission to the one person whom he knew could get the job done.

≫XXVI≪

In Nora's multitude of roles, she made more connections than she made enemies. Well, enemies that remained in their natural habitats, anyway. She never knew what happened to those who returned to Batuk. Partly because Batuk didn't need her to. Partly because, deep down, she didn't want to know.

And don't misread *connections* as friends and fellows and felines. No. Not one could be described as a friend of Nora's. Acquaintances, maybe, but not friends. Most were simply in her debt or in Batuk's back pocket and understood how Nora would handle any situation that didn't result in them acceding to her wishes, requests, and demands.

With her network across thirty-four countries and two unclaimed islands within the thirty-third and thirty-fourth country, it didn't take long for Jim's name to be communicated to her, as well as flight details and timing details of his efforts.

Though she had a helpful direction in which to start, Batuk was clear on this one. "You're doing this solo."

Early on in her career, if one could call it that, she learned from Batuk how much less dangerous and more efficient a mission can be when others do the work. Whether she knew what would ensue or not, she treated everything as if it were a booby trap: Let others go first and see what happens. If nothing, then they could come back with what you want. If something, then they've revealed the path of least resistance through a process of elimination. The scientific method at its finest.

But this was the real world; they never came back, and that's how Nora learned how to get from point A to point B. It's easy once all the traps have been triggered. Curious that this time Batuk specifically requested that Nora remain close to Jim and assist and manipulate him, however; she needed for him to complete some ritual to create the spice. Alas. Now was not the time to question any direction. Listen and act. Do as she was trained. Her muscle memory would take it from there.

Now, at dinner, she felt as though the ritual was so near she could taste it, or was that the lemony duck Jim just placed in her mouth? She washed it down with Darjeeling tea, the camellia sinensis a favorite of hers, though this one was an oolong style, produced through a process including withering the plant under strong sun and oxidation before curling and twisting. Insight she learned from Jim. It reminded her of the Dongding from her native land, which her mother used to make when she was young. She hadn't had tea since then. She hadn't even thought of her youth since then. But that's the power of taste, isn't it? A mnemonic key to a memoric vault. Batuk was never a fan of tea himself. Batuk. She nearly forgot why she was here with Jim. Lost again in the flavors of the food swirling around her mouth, her stomach gleefully discontinuing its self-inflicted carnage to savor the gustatory experience Jim was sharing with her. And wait, was that Jim's foot touching hers again? Her emotions, disquietingly, were swirling like the remnants of the tea leaves in the cup in front of her.

This wasn't the first time she'd found herself a little lost in the moment, but in the past it had always happened without her recognition, and it had been much more short-lived. This time she not only recognized it but toyed with it like some proscribed fire, like a button a child was told not to press; she played with it under the cover of darkness, well-aware of the forbidden thrill it offered.

Jim had that effect on her.

Perhaps it was the knowledge that her servitude to Batuk was coming to an end. Like a senior in college, like a middle-aged man about to go on a diet, like a gambler realizing she had another hundred-dollar bill in her pocket the whole time, Nora was fumbling to stay focused. Could she be excited to leave the life she had lived for so long once Batuk retired?

Despite her knowledge of the light at the end of the tunnel, she hadn't even considered what she would do after. This life was all she had known. Any idea of normalcy had gone out the window after an eastern cultist chief did, too, early in her career. She thought back to that first mission and a smile blossomed on her face, one whose source Jim would not have guessed in five lifetimes.

On the other side of the table, the reality of the near future was weighing on Jim's shoulders like the boulders of Fontainebleau, despite the heart skip he felt at the smile that just appeared on Nora's face, sweet cheeks ever present with it.

Disappointingly, the food wasn't as remarkable as Jim hoped it would be. Well, that's only half-true. It was in fact remarkable, but those boulders on Jim's shoulders must have been putting pressure on all of Jim's innards. That is, all but those in his metatarsals, which were picking up the radio waves left from Nora sliding her foot across his, too. A response well received. Noted. Another data point of a dance while sitting down. Jim was fumbling to stay focused on his mission, too. Could he really live his life without a sense of taste? Despite his knowledge of the light at the end of the tunnel, he hadn't even considered what he would do after he put Phil in his place. This life was all he had known.

The tea was getting cold. The miniature bowls of *crème brûlée* were becoming empty. The time delaying the inevitable had been used up all too quickly, like a water gun given to a kid on a hot summer day.

As Jim and Nora walked out toward the fountain, their hands found each other just as their feet had minutes before.

They've come this far together, might as well go the rest of the distance. There was no *Baby, don't go* or a *I can't stay* dialogue here. No, sir. No, ma'am. This would get done and it would get done together.

⇒XXVII⇐

Shaman Denny had eyebrows so large they could serve as bridges from one land mass to another, from one chapter to another, from here to *farrrrrr* over there. Bushy, bold, and angled to align with his cockeyed eyes. It would be a disastrous journey by boat across his forehead considering the number of ridges and waves and wrinkles of skin. Sun-scorched wisdom buried within each one. He wore white sweatpants and a denim button-up with tribal patches handsewn across it. Off-white might be a better description of his sweatpants, which had clearly been through a couple of cycles of the life of a shaman. Redstone sand stains from meditating in the valleys of Orr, disoriented threads at a loss to where their homes were or where they should go next, with a discolored button clearly taken from, aha, yup, the topmost button of his button-up. Resourceful. Fashionable. The Denny way.

Shaman Denny was using a staff of sorts, hand-carved like a totem pole, to stir water from a fountain. Well, a well might be a more accurate description. There was no water spraying up, no change at the bottom of the water and no photogenic carvings in the marble around it. Though no water showers, there were showers of another element. You would think he was touching the wires of the car battery together in there with the number of sparks spilling over the edges of the well and up toward Denny's face. Better pray the sparks wouldn't ignite a forest fire in Denny's eyebrows. No firefighting crew would be able to put it out.

Jim paused his pace, let go of Nora's hand, and focused in on the man causing the magic to happen.

It wasn't the appearance that Jim gravitated to, or that anyone would gravitate to, with Shaman Denny; it was his energy. Like the sparks flying from the well, he glistened. It wasn't quite heat that radiated from him but a short, light but consistent network of translucent lightning, as if feeling what one sees when heat bounces from the ground and different air densities distort the light; he emitted waves of the stuff as if creating a personal bubble of tantalizing, electrifying, breathtaking (or perhaps breath-giving?) magic of a man. Needless to say, nobody was commenting on the shopworn state of his pants.

Jim and Nora, hypnotized by the glowing static, walked slowly beside Denny and the well; not knowing or caring whether they'd surprise or interrupt him, they walked right up to the well to look down inside. Like any good shaman doing shaman's work, Denny kept his focus and gaze on the dance he was doing with the magic. A shaman's work is only as great as the number of distractions he can ignore. Well, that's the math that goes with anyone's work, really. One plus none equals three.

In working with Batuk, Nora had never actually seen any of the magic materials used in his manufacturing, only the item that Batuk wished for to enable him to operate, but in front of her now she saw magic. A spark jumped out on her arm. It seemed to absorb directly into her skin and for a moment her arm felt invigorated, tingly, as if it had fallen asleep, but the best way she could describe it is that it was actually awake and well-rested. Magic.

Though Jim believed all the hoopla he had read about this journey, there had always been an inkling of doubt at the back of his mind. A faint whisper, ridiculing him for thinking that magic existed and he of all people could leverage its power. And now here he stood, inches away from it, so close that he could... taste it.

There was no understanding, recognition or concern of time at that moment. Nora and Jim took a step back now, satisfied with what they had watched in the well, and let Shaman Denny step and stir his way through the remainder of the dance, becoming the only two spectators of Earth's most ancient sport, flummoxed; the tingling sensation still present, but fading in Nora's arm.

The magic soon dissipated altogether, as if absorbed into the air that Nora, Jim, and Shaman Denny breathed.

"The water here was spoiled," said Shaman D, still peering into the well and shaking the remains of the magic liquid dripping from his staff. "There's a paper plant just north of here. And not the Mother Nature kind. Though from the fumes in the air and the chemicals they pour daily into the land, I'd bet my left leg that they make more than just paper. Each fortnight it becomes so tainted from run-off that it clogs all the pipes in the fountain's inner working, and it becomes undrinkable."

Aha, so it is a fountain after all. A drinking fountain.

"And every couple of months, someone shows up beside me seeking my use of magic, and every couple of months I disappoint them in my inability to make it last. You see, magic only remains so long as it's nurtured."

Shaman Denny finally made eye contact with Jim and Nora.

"Your efforts to get here were a waste. I've heard sob stories and crybaby long tales and I can only count"—Denny rested the staff against his shoulder and held up both hands, placing one back down—"yes, I can only count on one hand the number of wishes I have granted in the last three hundred years. You can turn back now if you'd like. Perhaps some fresh water from the well might perk you up a bit from the disappointment, and then you can be on your way."

Denny was neither ignorant nor malicious, simply matter-of-fact. Definiteness rang through his tone, but there was also a hint of exhaustion. Three hundred years? I'd be tired too!

Fewer than five wishes granted across all those years. The odds weren't looking good Jim.

"Will you at least let me try?"

And try Jim did. First he went on the emotional roller-coaster of persuasion by trying to appeal to Denny's heart. Jim shared his story of love-lost trials and tribulations of being a chef in New England and how much he's built at Herough and how it's all on the line. He shared his familial ties to the industry and the inspiration he could be to so many, near, like Gus, Frank, Lemon, and others and far, like a fella from Arizona that reached out to him for advice a day before the Phil shakedown.

Second, he tried the mental tugboat of persuasion by trying to appeal to Denny's brain. Why waste any more years giving away his gift to the world? After all, his intentions are pure. There is someone in Jim's life that is the paper plate in a fine-dining restaurant, egging others on to lower their expectations.

Then Jim tried establishing a rapport with Denny by sharing how he knows what it's like to have something to offer someone and the risk that they might abuse it. There's no industry that experiences that more than the food industry.

Finally, he tried the underrated undertow of persuasion by trying to appeal to Denny's stomach. Given how thin Denny appeared, this argument had to work. The quickest way to a man's heart is, ya know. He riffed recipes he would make for Denny before departing in exchange for his help.

Not a single argument prevailed. The one about the food did at least cause Denny to glance down at his stomach—performing magic was ironically an energy-*consuming* activity and he was in fact hungry—but that hunger didn't change his position in the matter.

"Pass," Denny said as he moved his staff from leaning on his left shoulder to his right.

Nora briefly considered laying the Shaman down to rest, taking the staff, and figuring it out herself. If there was one thing that's triggering to a person like Nora, it's not getting what she asks for. Alas. Batuk wouldn't be happy if she came home without the magic. Maybe the magic was in the staff? Maybe it wasn't? Then again, either way she would at least have something to show from her efforts, from her only failure at a mission for Batuk. How ironic to fail at your last one. Then again, in her line of work, any failure often meant it was your last mission, although for other reasons than Nora's present situation.

Denny turned and began walking away.

"Until next month, when another wanderer comes around."

Jim made one final last-ditch attempt, shouting: "Queen Pinmekalah sent me."

That put a pause in Denny's progress. He pivoted back toward Jim. The look on his face was crooked. Partially livid, likely with resentment, but equally excited by what might ensue. It had been decades since Pinmekalah sent anyone to him.

As proof, Jim held out the chocolate container of dust for Denny to see. He knew that Denny would recognize the innocuous plastic bottle for what it was, or could be, and he was correct.

"And the sacrifice. You're willing to make it?" Denny said inquisitively, almost as if giving Jim one last out.

Denny's face shaped itself into a constrained one, one that had written *don't you dare test, lie, or cheat me*. His tone went from matter-of-fact to dead serious, killing doubt and hesitation in its path to Jim.

Speaking of faces, Nora's lips now took a turn on Cautious Ave, and her eyes filled like a nervous pond. She hadn't known this part. Sacrifice? What did Denny mean? Did Jim know about this? What wrench would this throw into her plan? Nora was unhappy with her lack of knowledge in this mission, or as unhappy as she ever allowed herself to feel.

"Yes... I am." Jim spoke slowly. He needed the time with the word. His seal of fate, his statement of certainty, his self-consolation of his commitment. As you recall from Jim's first argument, so much depends on this. He has to do it.

In response, Denny pointed to a space in the land—something larger than a hill but not quite a mountain.

"Meet me up on Michelin's Mound at sundown. Bring that and nothing more." And Denny started walking away, only to pause once more and turn.

"Do drink some of that water. It's the greatest water you will ever taste." Denny had a smirk on his face. That's just wicked of a shaman to be so on the nose with Jim. Fact is, Jim would be without a sense of taste by nightfall. Even Nora picked up on the punch, the light dawning as she realized what Jim was planning to give up.

The sacrifice.

⮞XXVIII⮜

Judging by the position of the sun, and, you know, what his watch told him, Jim had about four hours before sundown. And yes, you're right in thinking that Jim is not only the type to wear a watch, but actually the type who uses it to tell time.

"What did he mean by a sacrifice?" asked Nora.

Nora. Oof.

Jim forgot she was there. Oops. Not that he didn't care, but his selfish séance and impending transaction took precedence over the present company. Sorry, Nora.

Being caught off-guard and not wanting to have Nora upset with him, he immediately spewed the truth. Hell, she'd already heard a summary of his life story; now for the second time, albeit a shortened version.

He spilled the beans, the burger, and indeed the whole watermelon of the situation. The sacrifice of his sense of taste, the competitive agreement he had with Phil, and the newest part of his story—the apology for dragging her into this mix.

Nora looked at the ground. Somber. Sober. Saddened. Jim could detect disappointment in the air. He was quite familiar with that. And it was certainly not what he wanted to taste as his last. It wasn't that Nora felt betrayed in particular, but it felt like she *should* feel that way; like someone had influence over her emotions; like... like, she cared.

Then, recovering from the tug-o-war happening in her heart and the mental journey of scenario-playing she was engaged in, she glanced back at Jim. She was in. With Jim. On board. Signed up. Enrolled. She didn't need to say it; her smile did that for her. Sweet cheeks revealing themselves with a newly polished shine of optimism.

"Only one question remains in my mind... what's with the bottle of chocolate milk... dust?" Nora asked, placing her gaze on the container.

"You know the magic Denny did on the water? There's nothing like the spice..." Jim paused to build anticipation and also to ponder if Nora would think he was insane. Well, she'd come this far with him (her tolerance for insanity must be high!) and saw the magic herself, so he might as well lay it out there, cliché and all. "...the Spice of Life."

Nora smirked, a perfect blend of giddy amusement and eye roll. No energy to refute anything or to quarrel with the situation. She looked around (in her head, not her world). Under any other circumstances she wouldn't have put it together, but these weren't any other circumstances, these were *these* circumstances; and now we have Nora becoming enlightened by her task and its impact on Batuk's conglomeration. *That's* why he purchased Sessalt.

Nora didn't doubt that even though there appeared to be only a small amount in the chocolate bottle, that sixty-four fluid ounces (not really fluid, but you know what I mean, the measurement of half a gallon) would be enough for him to test, analyze and adapt a way to manufacture the magic.

If he could do that, he could then dominate the food industry and beyond. In fact, with this single ingredient, he could become a powerhouse manipulating other industries, simply because ingredients like spices infiltrate all business, whether noticeable or not.

He'd own the restaurant and beverage and hospitality industries, for obvious reasons, but even unexpected industries like, say, the electrical industry, wherein engineers were beginning to design not just for the flow of electricity but in the flow of flavor; if, again, say, a child were to stick the plug end of a vacuum cord in their mouth or a husband would lick his hands to turn a hot light bulb after having it on and then lick his hands again after the bulb was removed to temper the heat on his fingers. Electrical flavors all around.

It's incredible to consider all the electrical items in every household and realize the fact that there are millions of scenarios in which people end up tasting the product. It's as if we never grow out of our infantile desire to put things in our mouth.

On top of that, more and more brands are investing in taste because *they* ran a study (and don't ask who *they* means, if you've never yet asked in your life despite being faced with so many news headlines citing them) and found out the numbers behind the power taste has in brand recall; something crazy marketing departments are having an era in. In the same way brands have worked the sense of smell into the purchasing experience, they're now tackling the Age of Taste.

Stealing the Spice of Life for Batuk would change more than their homeland; it would change everything far and wide, cities, states, across all geographies and types of land and water and air and fire. Batuk would reign and *what the hell*, Nora thought, he already has enough money to settle down lavishly.

And that's when a spark in Nora's mind took place. No magic this time, just the mischief which always follows spies, especially freckled ones.

"I believe you," she said to Jim. Her words were more than just a statement about the situation. True, they were an extension of her trust in Jim as a person. She believed he would do right with the Spice of Life in his hands. But behind that face of trust, that sweet-cheeked smile, she began scheming.

Before Jim could prod, question, or plunge the thoughts she held, she doubled down on her façade.

"I'm going with you tonight, but that means we have a few hours to swat like a fly. Are you thirsty?" She tilted her head toward the well.

At this point in time, Jim couldn't believe his luck. Not the manifestation of being at the perfect place at the perfect time for Shaman Denny, not that everything was going according to his plan and that Phil would soon lose his bet and his restaurant, but that it was going better because a divine woman, an exceptional partner, the engine, and the anchor to his boat of life was standing in front of him, on his side, a cheerleader, a friend, a confidant. Full steam ahead.

Jim cupped the water from the well in his hands, splashed his face, shook his hands at his side and took another scoop of water and drank from it. His eyes turned a deep earthy but bright brown, color flowed through his skin, his aches, his sores, and his scratches from his endeavor—and his life in general—disappeared. It felt like he was on cloud nine, which was too small a number to describe how he felt. All of his senses excelled, his brain became clear, whatever wax was left in his ears dissolved; even the dirt on his legs dissipated as the liquid pellets that fell from his face hit his ankles. He cupped his hands again and held them out for Nora to experience. She went through the same osmosis that Jim went through, her eyes turning a brighter blue, her freckles darkening, her blemishes, tiny scars, makeup all dissolved, disappeared, leading the way in an orchestra-sized vanishing trick. Her senses ignited, as well as her urges, too. Rather than his brown eyes, Nora stared at the hands in front of hers as if they were made of magic and what they were capable of—much of which Nora was familiar with from only days ago. Deep down, she knew the hands were holding back and that there was more to unleash and feel the passion of and moan about. If you could see Nora's aura, it would be bright orange, with sacral chakra knowledge waves sweeping and swaying around her skin, with an even brighter color radiating from between her legs, orange in hue but more deeply, like honey and nectar. You'd think it was Day-Glo down there.

Nora took Jim's now-empty hands and pulled him away from the well into a small respite of private foliage and pushed his hands down into her own private foliage.

His fingers, still dancing with the electric waves of the well water, burrowed their way through, deeper into the brush until they found their own well of lust sap and passion fruit; he weaved his fingers through the land's crevices like he was conducting Johann Sebastian Bach's Cello Suite No. 1 in G Major. Nora's body moved to the melody with the occasional jolt, likely ignited by the magic left on Jim's fingers from the well water. Whatever he was doing with his index finger, she never wanted him to stop, but all too soon Jim's symphony arrived at its crescendo, and Nora's body, too. Jim's hand followed its tracks back from its journey and into his mouth, deep down knowing that this would be the last time he would taste Nora's decadence. It was a good high note on which to end his tastebuds' career. No urchin of the sea, fast-food burger, or Darjeeling tea could hold a candle to this.

Satiated but not exhausted, Nora lowered herself onto her soft round knees to reciprocate the favor, pulling Jim's pants down to the same ground where she knelt. The cushioned ground, miraculously devoid of rocks and twigs, welcomed her knees as if making pockets designed specifically for them. The magic water that she drank from Jim's cupped hands had soothed her throat only a wind's breeze ago, but lingered in her cheeks and under her tongue, and still skipped across her palate. She placed some of the magic on her hand and started to stroke his own branch, blowing a raspberry on the tip of his shaft. It wasn't long before the magic that made her climax made Jim do the same. Mix magic with a woman who already knows what she's doing and no man stands a chance at lasting longer than a snowflake on a hot stove. His own nectar dripped in her mouth like white chocolate in a freshly baked cookie, gooey, but delectable from the magic of the well water.

They lay upon the grass, equally exhausted and refueled, equally expensed and invested in, equally grounded and uplifted. Whatever barriers they still had between each other, whatever concerns they had or worries about the other, they vanished the same as the magic from the well water and their hands.

They stayed there on the ground together, the ground hugging them as it had hugged Nora's knees only moments ago. They watched the sky transition from day to dusk. As the evening unfolded, the dominant azure of the sky softened, gradually fading into paler, more serene shades of blue. High above, wispy cirrus clouds caught the sinking sun's rays, transforming into brilliant hues of pink and orange that stretched across the horizon like strokes of an impressionist painter's brush. It looked like the well's magic had made its way into the sky, too.

As the sky above transformed, so did Nora and Jim's connection. They talked, ruminated on what-ifs, and this is when Nora revealed her own secret to Jim.

Yep. You read that right, dear reader. No further hiatus between knowing her secret and not.

Like a broken waterline, information spewed out. She divulged her mission to Jim and Batuk's intention to replicate the Spice of Life. She also revealed her own uncertainty about the future, what she would have done after returning with the Spice of Life, and now that she had decided against fulfilling her mission, how she entertained ideas of what she would do.

A lizard crossed the open area in front of them as silence took over after Nora spilled the beans, the greens, and everything on her whole damn plate. The lizard shone metallic green like crinkled tinfoil the hue of an evergreen with what remained of the night's light. Their knees were still touching and hands still holding, but there was an emotional gap between them; an air of uncertainty. Jim took his words with fork and knife and cut through the silence.

"Come back with me," he said. There was certainty in his voice. Jim was never one for shades of gray. It was black or white, this or that, all or nothing, there or here, on the bus or off the bus. When Jim made a decision, he stuck with it regardless of how visible a positive—or sometimes negative—outcome it would be. He saw it through until he made his next decision. Example A: He's lying in Budapest, for Christ's sake. Turning around wasn't in his nature. Even when he would drive through the streets of New York, he never made a U-turn, illegal or not. It was about what came next. Missed exit? He'd find another way. Jim didn't need to have a map, the directions, all the pieces of a puzzle laid out in front of him to move forward decisively.

Nora was the complete opposite, of course. Her life was built on a game plan, a book of rules and guidelines, structure and regimented missions and clear conclusions and constant evaluation and scenario planning. Life was a maze that she zigged, zagged, and paddy-wagged through. Hell, she wouldn't start *anything* until she knew her path and what success looked like. For any puzzle she worked on, she had the cover of the box in one hand. The life Jim was offering—no, requesting—of her was one that she'd never experienced before.

But you know what they say about opposites.

⇒XXIX⇐

The light above punched out its time clock and officially turned gray-blue, perfumed with a luminous murky cloudage. Dusk had fallen like a popped balloon from the sky, slow, steady, and ominous. Together, Nora and Jim stood up, leaving in their shadows traces of a plan to get what they both wanted—a life free from Batuk and Phil's pillaging wishes. They held hands, intertwining only two of Jim's fingers (index and middle) around two fingers of Nora's (ring and pinkie finger). Jim approached love the same as he did the meals in his restaurant—crafting a unique experience for any guest which leaves them feeling appreciated and memorable. Certainly Nora had never held hands with anyone like this before. Unbeknownst to Jim, Nora had never held hands with another in her life. It was invigorating; the magic of the well water was long since spent, but the magic of their future was fueling them now. As magic does.

Despite it being merely a mound, it wasn't a straight shot to Denny. Jim and Nora had to traverse brush, rubble, a few scorpions, and no shortage of avocets flying peculiarly above them along the trek. By the time they reached Denny, they could both go for some water, from the magic well or not.

At the top of Michelin's Mound, they found Denny sitting on a rock near an indent in the mound, almost cavelike, placing figurines, uniquely colored rocks, and old pieces of torn scripture around his staff. It was plain that he was readying himself for the magic he would shortly place upon the contents of the container. As instructed, Nora and Jim left their bags at the bottom of the hill, hidden between two rocks shaped like koi fish, and carried nothing other than the spice given to Jim by Queen Pinmekalah. They took a seat on the ground near a steady stream of water that they hadn't even noticed at first. Their eyes were all on Denny. Their thirst from the climb was forgotten. Now they had to do the thing that was their least favorite of all: wait.

There was silence from their mouths, but the nature around them, the mound, and the sky were alive. The river caroled, the rock drummed, the air whistled and waved the strands of grass just outside their nook atop the mound. Nora was already in an elevated mental state that came of having some definition to her future free from Batuk, but Jim was being weighed down with doubt and fear for the sense he was about to lose.

It was the sense that had gotten him into the business and to where he now sat today. Sacrificing it was his only choice if he wanted a future for his business and his life with Nora, who would be going home with him, with everything she currently carried with her in the bag at the bottom of the mound.

Jim was imagining a life without taste, trying to game-plan how he could continue to be the face of a restaurant without the ability to register flavor; he wondered if there was anyone he trusted enough to taste for him (Lemon was up there, but so it goes. Jim still trusted his own palate over Lemon's); he wondered if his own knowledge of ingredients, his tongue, and taste bud muscle memory would be enough to help him navigate the future, to teach others, to continue to lead in innovation.

Memory, after all, is an exceptionally powerful tool if used correctly. All too often memory is left, ironically, in the past, to fall dormant and unused. When you can dust the lock and pry its gates open, the alchemy of the basal ganglia, cerebellum, prefrontal cortex, and the pathways and neurons across each can trailblaze a path to one's desired future.

Even a sixteen-year-old has built a robust arsenal of memories that, if activated, can help him lead a luxurious life well into his seventies. Alas. Many are too focused on creating new memories—which aren't really "new" after all, they merely overwrite ones that already exist, or add a piece to one of the strands that are already there. So much focus on thinking outside of the box rather than using what's already in it.

Two ticks before Shaman Denny turned to address Jim, Jim came to a resolution about his future, a confidence in his ability to train and leverage all he had in his memory to date. He could do it without his taste buds. Fortunately for him, he already had a venue going for him, a repertoire of knowledge; he had momentum. He had something to live for, and now, with Nora, he had something bigger than Herough to develop.

"I'm ready," Shaman Denny said. And not a moment too soon, as Jim was a jiff away from remembering he'd no longer be able to taste Nora's lips again—the ones above or the ones below. Jim was prepared, broadcasting his focus and determination like he was a radio station atop this mound. A thousand miles away, Phil's ears started ringing. Fewer than five miles away, Lemon Fraser's did too.

"What is it you wish?" Shaman Denny inquired.

"I wish to hold the Spice of Life," Jim answered as he held out the chocolate milk bottle containing the powder, which, strangely enough, Jim hadn't even opened for risk of ruining whatever was inside.

"And you understand what you're sacrificing to hold that?" Shaman Denny asked, giving Jim his final opportunity to back out, return to the life he'd lived, forget that any of this ever happened.

"I'm ready," Jim said. Prepared, stoic as a satellite tower, even Nora sensed wave after wave of seriousness and commitment radiating from Jim. "It is what it is. It is what I wish."

Shaman Denny turned back to his staff, which now laid perfectly at the center of the objects. Shaman D began speaking in a tongue Jim had never heard before (and being in the food and beverage industry, there were few languages that Jim hadn't heard while at his restaurant). Nora, who was familiar with even more languages than

Jim, didn't know it either. Denny read each of the pieces of scripture around the staff, each scrap of language seamlessly flowing from one to the other. Jim could detect a rhythm, a song in the words, though he didn't understand any of them. Shaman Denny lifted the staff, replacing it with the chocolate milk bottle and then proceeded to tap the staff's end, which Jim now realized was sculpted like the roots of a tree, on the top of the bottle. Touching it only with the topmost point of the staff. In a series of electronic pulses and white flashes and gusty winds (the grass nearby holding on to the grains of soil as tightly as possible), in soothing vibrations like a middle mind state of gliding and turbulence, of a river of earthquakes, of the smell of roses and the touch of their thorns. Magic encircled the bottle, as if warming it, preparing it to metamorphosize.

Nora, even at her distance, tasted the electricity of the air, the energy circumnavigating the space.

Jim was in a hypnotized state.

Shaman Denny then moved the end of his staff, pivoting in place, to tap the point of Jim's head. It filled Jim up like a clown's balloon; though the feeling was invigorating, he knew what he would be losing. At the re-realization Jim felt a pull from within him; it tickled and agitated him as if he'd swallowed food down the wrong pipe. While Denny's eyes were closed, focused on managing the magic, Nora watched the energy from inside Jim flow out of his jaw-dropped mouth and into the staff. It wasn't quite like a life force leaving a body, rather a steady stream of essence. Nora watched and wondered when it would end, as if she'd been stopped at a train crossing.

Alas. There was a tail to the energy leaving Jim and into the staff.

Shaman Denny pivoted again and pointed the staff back at the milk container of spice, repeating the scripture again and again, until the last drop of magic from the staff's end dripped into the bottle.

Shaman Denny finally ended his recitation in the unique dialect and said straight to Jim, "Quickly. Cap it."

Jim remained in place, still in shock. Nora jumped in, grabbing the cap which was one of the handful of items encircling the container. Just as she began to place the cap on, she could see the magic begin to make a U-turn in the container, as if ready to escape, but Nora stopped it, sealing the magic within, as well as Jim's fate.

Shaman Denny, satisfied with the speed of Nora's capping the container, changed direction to speak directly to the still-entranced Jim.

"This is all you get, my friend. Use it wisely. And be sure to tell Queen P she better have chosen well this time."

Shaman Denny scooped up the parchments, tossed the knickknacks in a sack, grabbed his staff and set off on a new journey. Though he told himself to just carry on without a final word, he nonetheless turned back to Jim and added, "Also, your other senses will start to increase over the next number of days. Don't be surprised to hear things you hadn't before, smell things you hadn't before, feel things you hadn't before. One of the four who has received this gift went mad with the other sensations and killed himself with poison—he couldn't taste it."

Jim was breaking from his trance but was now left to wonder about the others that received the Spice of Life. Could Ambrosia be an example? Did Shaman Denny once have doves and bring the Greek gods the Spice of Life? In the bag Denny had just used to gather the items, also rested a notebook with answers to Jim's ponderment. Like any good shaman, Denny kept organized records, lest they be lost in the realm of his memory bank.

The first Spice of Life was in fact an exploration of magic, a happy accident. To win over the Greek gods, Shaman Denny concocted a string of magic to create the Spice of Life. While his first attempt satiated the gods, he knew there was room for improvement. Something stronger.

Something better. It was a spice, that's for sure, but not quite life.

Shortly after the failure in front of the gods, he figured he had to make a sacrifice. So Jim's hunch was accurate. Shaman Denny sacrificed his own palate for a spice he would never be able to taste. After being dismissed by the gods, he journeyed through the lands and tested the result of his magic on others—and in a few cases, people tried tracking him down to get their hands back on the spice. Fortunately for Denny and unfortunately for those trying to steal the spice from him, he had learned a thing or two about battling from the gods he'd spent years with while perfecting his magic.

The second Spice of Life Shaman Denny created went to a salmon fisherman he ran into while journeying through the upper peninsula. The fisherman cried and whined about how dull life was. Shaman Denny pitied him, performed his magic, and gave the fisherman what he needed to not only find peace in the wild of the sea but find everlasting pleasure, too. It's not a coincidence that salmon are now the world's most nutrient-dense food on the planet. He fed a female salmon the spice and set off a chain of evolution into the best-tasting seafood.

The third was to the mighty Queen Pinmekalah herself. He was training under her purview—yes, in the exact square that Jim set foot in only days before.

The fourth was a mistake, which is why Shaman Denny was so stingy about working his magic for Jim. Denny doesn't quite know what went wrong, exactly. Perhaps it was the person who made the sacrifice. Perhaps he stumbled while casting his spell. Perhaps the magic was only fit to bond to specific spices. He still wasn't sure. Whatever he did, it caused the recipient so much anxiety and stress over wielding such power—combined with the loss of the one sense that she treasured so much that she mixed all the spice she had with poison and ate it all. If she couldn't taste the spice, no one would, she figured. Selfishness at its extreme. After hearing this from Queen Pinmekalah, Shaman Denny and she decided to refrain from performing his magic going forward. There were plenty of other efforts to put his energy toward and he'd already found peace with what the spices he'd created had given to and taken from the world.

That was, until Jim showed up.

Now, Jim was the fifth, with his stamp of approval from Queen Pinmekalah herself.

Jim licked his teeth for some flavor of familiarity. He moved his tongue around in his mouth and swallowed, trying to pick up on any remnants of the *crème brûlée* from the restaurant before. Nora's lips. The dirt in the air. Nothing. He licked his finger. Nothing. No flavor. No recognition. No connections being made in the brain. No memories resurfacing from the ignition switch of a flavor. No mental tasting notes. No more tasting Nora's lips. Jim stood there in distaste of himself and his choice. Well, that's probably not the expression to use right now. Jim stood there in *revulsion* of the exchange he'd just made. A fierce battle of regret and excitement ensued between his two ears. A fight for the way he would walk out of this. His stronger friend, determination, won the battle, but only by a hair. Hopes up high. Head down low. It would be the only way to go.

Jim sacrificed his taste buds for the Spice of Life. To be the one who could give it but never the one to taste it—or anything else again. The volume was not large, merely a half-gallon, but if used wisely and in small quantities, the Spice of Life could last the rest of his life. It would win him the competition. It would win him more loyal customers than ever before. It would win him Nora's endless appreciation of anything and everything he made—even when he experimented. Though, the truth is that her love for him already would make her stomach blind to imperfections. It would take any failure in the kitchen and turn it into a

Michelin star meal. It's the kind of safety net people fantasize about having when they take a leap of faith.

This was going to take some getting used to. The loss of taste, yes, but also the bottle of power.

Jim turned to Nora. A bottle of the Spice of Life in one hand and a wish to have her hand in his other. It was time to go home, win the Fork at the convention, and begin their lives together, *sans* taste, but not *sans* spice.

However, unbeknownst to them or even Shaman Denny at the time, another man was on the mound near them, only a handful of yards away from the action, watching and waiting for his opportunity.

The magic she witnessed, the way her heart was beating for Jim, the playful thinking about the promise of her future made Nora blind to things she wouldn't have normally missed. Blind to her surroundings. If only Jim had taken a sniff of the air, he'd have detected something sour.

⇒XXX⇐

Amidst all this fantasy, Jim and Nora forgot they still lived in reality. As in, they needed to make the trek back into town, take a tram to the airport, spend another eleven-hour flight going to NYC—and the whole figuring out what to do if Batuk sends anyone after her, that's still on the docket, too. But that was a lower priority than getting back home and to the conference. No other stars would align if Jim didn't make it back with the spice. He needed to ensure nothing would go wrong before then.

Of course, everything would go wrong. That's what happens when you don't want it to. And it definitely happens when you *really* don't want it to.

A quick tangent, if you'd be so tolerant, dear reader. Jim notoriously wrote two essays of his own in high school on the harm, waste, and negative impact trams have on the world. He riffed on the despicable speed of movement; the fact that cars are more likely to kill you when you get off the tram than peanut allergies kill people; the fact that no one has fallen in love on a tram, despite the incessant number of times that it must make an emergency stop. People repeatedly fall forward on one another, but no one has fallen in love with the person they fell into? *Blasphemy*, Jim thought. He complained about the poor design of having nothing to hold that's positioned at the right height. He wrote about the awkward length of the step on or off the tram, musty moist seats reminiscent of old diner booths that have been falling apart, and such an odd humidity regardless of the temperature outside, making a cauldron of stink with windows that can only be lowered by an inch and no more. If all of that wasn't enough, the second essay included a section titled, "Trams For Dummies," and included a bulleted list of a few dozen ways that something can be stolen from you while on a tram. Did you know that sixty-five percent of all thefts in cities with trams, like Hungary, for example, happen while on a tram? Literally on it, not at the station, not in the cab to the tram, not at the sketchy drug store on the other side of the street or in the public bath. Nope. On the tram. His high school English teacher couldn't help giving him at least an A on the assignment. And it's certainly safe for us to assume she hasn't ridden a tram since.

The trek back into the nearest town was the easy part. One foot in front of the other. One hand on the chocolate milk bottle, one hand in the sweaty palm of Nora's. In the fourth hand of the duo there was a bag of snacks they picked up right at the edge of town at the sketchy drug store. Wrapped orange brandy muffin with walnuts. Bircher muesli. A can of acai seasonal fruit juice and beef jerky. (It reminded Nora of the protein-dense care baskets Batuk would give her each time she returned. Now she was giving herself her own care basket, er, bag, rather.) Nora was starving. Jim, not so much. Hard to have an appetite, a craving, an urge to consume, when there's no gratification to it. He was afraid to face that reality so soon, not being able to taste his own saliva, the sweaty salt of the air. Not tasting the leftover lip gloss from Nora's lips was already a lot for him to handle. He'd put off eating if he could for now.

Alas. Malnourishment is not a smart move for someone carrying something so precious they wish to keep safe. The lack of nutrients, vitamins, and all-purpose energy leads to lethargy, hallucination, and headaches. Nora could see the weakness on Jim's skin and encouraged him to have a bite of her jerky, but Jim's a stubborn and emotional one. Jerky. He put the words together in his head that would describe it, but he couldn't imagine the flavor of the words. Just a big stupid iron gate in his head preventing the flow. He whispered the words, "teriyaki," "umami," "ketchup," "habanero"—bringing each syllable to his lips, but tasted nothing as he thought of them.

They reached the tram, purchased their tickets from the standalone ticket terminal machine. Nora polished off her goods, not even giving Jim a second chance at some nourishment. Jim was thankful, but he was also starting to hallucinate. He was more tired than a cheetah at mile fourteen. That same cheetah would have stopped to look at the sunrise that was now in front of Jim and Nora anyway. There was a blue gray crust that cracked and gave way to purple and orange waves; no dance electronica nightclub jamboree could compare to the light show that was in front of them. There was, however, a tram, which rolled up and blocked their view of nature's performance. Under normal circumstances, the intrusion would have made Jim recall his essay, and might even spur the desire to somehow return to it or rewrite it, adding this particular nuance of an experience. But Jim was distracted. He bit his tongue—frustrated that he could still feel the pain of a bite but not the flavor, nothing metallic, no hint of penny, no *soupçon* of salt from the bit of blood that pushed its way out from the tiny hole his tooth pierced during the bite. Distracted and aggrieved, Jim boarded the tram with Nora. Immediately Jim wondered why the magic couldn't have taken any other sense away instead.

The tram smelled like a balled-up tank-top that had been used to stop a toilet from overflowing, and had failed to do so. It reeked of boiled clams soaked in goat shit and ammonia. In all his years of working in a kitchen and experiencing some of the worst combinations of aromas, Jim never experienced a smell like the one he smelled on the tram. Perhaps it *was* time to revisit his essay on his hatred of trams.

Nora didn't seem to be phased.

"How are you breathing?" he asked.

"What?"

"How are you breathing in this air?" he repeated.

"It's not so bad," she shrugged.

And then Jim remembered Shaman Denny's warning about his other senses becoming more acute. Dear God. Jim wished he would have bought an air freshener while at the drugstore, so he could hold it up to his nose. Or maybe two, so he could dangle one on each of his ears like earrings. He longed for the next batch of flowers he could smell or when his nose would be between the legs of Nora again. Anything to counter this worst smell of his life. And to think he originally thought the normal smell of Hungary was bad. It was ten times worse inside the tram, and twenty times worse with his heightened senses.

Nora entered the tram and a food coma, not from overconsumption but from simply not having eaten in what felt like forever. The bag that previously held her various snacks now held the Spice of Life. Not only did they both need their hands to hold themselves upright while on the tram but Jim also believed he could keep a closer eye on it. Of course, his eyes were beginning to cross. He was hallucinating about the railings turning to liquid the way the chill of the metal combated the heated sweat of his hands. He hallucinated about which way the wind was being sucked through the window slits. He could see the damn hydrogen particles, pouring out and over. Jim rubbed his eyes, let go of the handles hanging from the ceiling of the tram and fell forward. Nora caught him but dropped the bag in doing so. She got him situated as much as she could as quickly as she could. Not that Jim was all that heavy, so much as Nora was simply petite despite being a strong kind of petite, and remember her food coma. Her whole body would have liked to have kept rolling onto a couch somewhere. The rail beneath was grinding and shaking Jim's insides. Shaman Denny wasn't kidding about the senses quickly making up for their lost friend, but need they do so in such a mind-crushing way? Nora grabbed the bag with one hand while keeping the other on Jim, trying to offer him some center of gravity as they stood back up.

Being so fatigued from overstimulation, Jim even thought he heard Lemon's accent when a wide gentleman rushed off the tram in the back, tripping on his way out (again, the danger of the tram is all too real), and grumbled, "Fuckin' trams."

When they arrived at the airport and the tram was finally in the rearview of their lives, Jim was still feeling like he had overdosed and was going through withdrawal at the same time.

He held one arm around Nora, who was feeling more reenergized now that her body had consumed the food rather than her muscle, though she looked forward to the next time she might lay in a bed to rest her eyes.

They boarded their flight without any claims, without any airport security, without any body scans. Nora merely nodded to the TSA agent standing beside the clerk and showed the tattoo on her ankle. He asked where they were heading and escorted them onto the plane. She was going to miss this sort of power in the States. Jim didn't pay much attention or notice the speed at which they went through the airport. He kept clapping his hands over his ears at the droning sound of all that happens at an airport, hitting him like he was standing in front of a speaker at a death metal concert. It was as if his brain was a blender and someone was throwing silverware in it to see if the blender could blend metal. It could. And it kept blending, moving from "pulverize" to "puree."

At 38,000 feet in the air (according to the back of the headrest in front of them), Jim was officially passed out, snoring—loudly. Could the sounds he was making be made any louder? Nora hoped this wasn't what she was in for in the future. She wasn't suffering from Jim's sensory overload but she did have a fairly acute sense of hearing when focused, having needed it in her line of work.

Nora didn't fancy movies much. She saw maybe one or two with her mom when she was a kid and then walked in on Batuk enjoying a few himself. She wasn't sure if it was just poor scenes and movies she was exposed to or if she simply didn't have the time to waste on something so mindless. She turned off the screen on the headset in front of her. She didn't even want to watch a pixelated airplane hover above a pool of more broken pixels, guesstimating the speed, elevation, and time of arrival. How pointless it is to give an estimate of facts (oxymoronic in itself) that mean nothing and that one has no control over. Airports act like flying is some nationally televised sport, rambling on and on about statistics and figures that are absolutely meaningless. Aside from the speed, elevation, and time, they also fed you screens consisting of numbers of models of airplanes, what year the combustible engine was invented, the longest distance a paper airplane ever flew, the name of the pilot and his grandmother, and what he had for breakfast each morning at the pilot academy. And so on.

Sitting there, Nora dropped her eyes between her legs where the bag rested. Curiosity was destined to kill the cat. Up to now, she hadn't even wondered what the Spice of Life would taste like, but now, up in the air, with Jim asleep, her future feeling uncertain, the world seemed to have stopped even though she could see the clouds moving past them from the other row's window.

The flight was severing her past from her future. She had someone by her whom she trusted. That was a new feeling. And she was more excited than a butterfly being let out of a jar. Just a taste wouldn't hurt. Jim wouldn't know. Her brain kept whispering all the reasons to do it. So she did. She needn't check if Jim was still asleep, the snoring checked that cautionary box. She lifted up the bag, opened it, stuck her hand in and searched beneath the empty bags of snacks she had left in it. Then she put two hands searching. If she'd had a third hand, she would have stuck that in to assist with the search. Then she dumped the contents out on her lap. Outwardly she was scared into silence, but on the inside, she was screaming loud enough that Jim could hear it. The snoring stopped.

Believe it or not, there are more times in life than there aren't that there's simply no turning back. Take for example, being on a roller-coaster as it gets to the top of its first hill. Or the first time you say "I love you"—and *finally* hear it in return. Or when you're already on a flight heading 4,352 miles away from where you want to be, flying at a speed of 880 km/h, at an average elevation of 38,000 feet with a bag you thought contained a bottle of the Spice of Life but didn't. Quite literally, there was no turning back.

≽XXXI≼

"Fuckin' trams," Lemon blurted out, hanging onto the bottle of what appeared to be chocolate powder inside with both hands so as not to spill its contents.

His toes were going to hurt that night, having just smashed themselves against the pavement of the curb, the bell from his feet rose all the way to his brain and DING—instant winner of pain. Of course, Lemon wouldn't have time to feel the pain beyond this moment or collect a prize for it. He couldn't. He had thirty-two separate meetings across eight different countries (Austria, Italy, Spain, Gabon, South Africa, Chile, Jamaica, and United States of America, for those wondering), all of which needed to take place within the next seventy-two hours—accounting for time changes. The location for a meetup was always planned near an airport or fast mode of transportation, so it could be a quick arrive-and-leave, come-and-go, give-and-take situation. The name and location and time was planned out in the small square notebook kept in Lemon's back right pocket. He began running—well, some odd form of running, not quite a limp, but serious avoidance of putting pressure on the big toe of his left foot. He looked like a penguin preparing for a triple jump on a medieval boat in rough seas. Picturing it? Good.

While Jim and Nora made their way on their plane back to LaGuardia, Lemon made his way from the blasted tram to the much more honorable train, destined for Austria. It had been a while since Lemon was this nervous. His nerves trembled harder than the train's wheels on the tracks below, or the gravel underneath them, or the tectonic plates underneath them, or the molten lava of Earth's core underneath them. For the first time in his life, Lemon had put his industry insider status—himself—in front of others, even his friend. It was all a bit jarring, but it's also show business.

Deep down, Lemon had known it would happen eventually; he had merely been waiting for the time to be right, the opportunity to rise like a spring flower, the chance of a lifetime. Everyone in life eventually finds a five-dollar bill on the ground. For years he had done the dirty work for others, put others ahead of himself, lived a life of positivity because he was elated to see others succeed. And to a degree, his latest motif accomplished that, too, though he would burn a few bridges to get there. Sure, it was generous for those in the industry to pick up his tab from time to time for all his help, but no one ever asked what *he* wanted, nobody ever put his wants or wishes ahead of their own. It was always "Lemon, I need this," "Lemon, do you know that..." "Lemon, what have you heard about her?" and so on. It was take, take, take. And a fair "thank you" simply wasn't enough.

This plan of Lemon's wasn't difficult to construct, and to this point, it was a whole lot easier than he thought it would be.

Being the king of knowledge in the industry, of course he had heard rumblings about the Spice of Life, and of course he paid attention to international conglomerates and those seeking to enter into the industry. He knew of Sessalt. That's the mark of an insider that no one tells or trains you for: that you need to be an insider of your industry and an insider of all others who might want to enter yours. A country border was no excuse to limit your knowledge of those outside it. Nor language. Nor ethics. He'd had an idea what Batuk was dreaming of even before he'd assigned Nora her task.

It's not that Lemon was wholeheartedly devious. He knew that if the Spice of Life were real, he could spread its virtue far and wide in a way that he could: 1. profit; 2. benefit his many connections; 3. prevent anyone (namely,

Batuk) from trying to reproduce the magic spice. (I told you he had good intentions!)

Lemon also knew he had to move quickly with giving out the spice. He'd seen enough movies as a kid to know what happens when someone has what others want. The faster he got rid of the spice, the safer he would be from anyone trying to track him down again to get more of it. Give it away. Make money. Move on. That was his three-step plan. Although it required far more steps than that, according to his fitness tracker.

And so, Lemon arrived in Austria and gave a few dashes to Tobias (pronounced Toe-bias). Tobias headed up a bakery that his parents had handed down to him and his great grandparents to them. He intended to bake it in only the pastries that he would bring to competitions to ensure he would win. A smart man knows how to make a little go a long way. He baked for the award system, not the public. Can't win the lottery if you don't play, he figured.

A few dashes went to Alessandro, a widow in Italy, who, contrary to your stereotypical thinking, decided to use it not in pizza, but in her curry dishes to please the parents of her deceased husband.

A few dashes went to Francisco Maria Lucia Martinez and his four brothers who ran a coffee bean farm just outside Athens. They were in serious debt and needed a quick fix for their troubles. Their answer? Go deeper into debt by paying Lemon so they could eventually climb out by using the spice in their coffee blends.

Lemon then hopped over the Mediterranean to give a few dashes to Seke in Gabon, Imka in South Africa, Koralina in Chile, Devon in Jamaica, and, last but not least, Phil, in America.

If you tracked Lemon's travels, it damn near made a smile across the globe.

Lemon did his research, hit up his Rolodex of contacts, examined thoroughly the ripple effects of what giving the spice to each of these people would mean to the industry at large.

This was trickier than time travel, more difficult than deciding on life insurance, and required more mental foreplay than a first date with a gal you met on a Christian dating website when you don't practice religion at all.

Oh, how much of a mess it would be if things didn't go right.

Lemon could have broken his foot stepping off a tram for Christ's sake and not been able to make his meetings. Not to mention the *years* of trust-building and information-observing that would all be lost if he were to make a bad choice. He thought it would be like the time when he was young (before he put on the pounds) and was bicycling too fast and his foot slipped off the pedal. The pedal, of course, continued to circle, boomeranging back to smash Lemon's fibula and crack it. The brakes, of course, were activated by the stoppage of the pedal rather than a handle on the handlebar and so the brakes were squeezed as hard as the plastic pedal squeezed into Lemon's leg—flipping Lemon over and cracking three more bones (arm, wrist, and rib) while giving him a sheet-sized scar along the side of the leg that's so large it can only pass off as a birthmark; no one would believe he picked a scab off a tennis court-size portion of his leg. Failing would be a lot like that, only the scar would be much larger and he would lose the friends who he was riding life with, maybe a leg too, none but your outside author knows.

Hours before the convention, Lemon, black-eyed, fueled only by a miniscule airplane pouch of peanuts and a bag of Doritos he'd pinched off a cab driver in Jamaica, arrived back in New York City to deliver the last few dashes of spice and see the last landfill-sized deposit into his bank account. This man was running on pure adrenaline, the carrot of a lush and early retirement dangling in front of him. One more exchange and then he would be off to some lonely island, expertly curated for celebrities to use. A hurricane-resistant hut on a distant but tropically luxurious piece of land somewhere in the middle of the land trek of a smile he just made. Those were steps he wouldn't mind retracing. He could do it at his own pace. The carrot was his. The satin sheets, endless drinks, and beach views were his.

That's what he would have said he wanted, had anyone asked him in all these years.

In another life, Lemon would have been a celebrity himself, paparazzi and all. Of course, there are people in this world who wonder about being something in another life and also wonder about being something in *this* life. Lemon was the latter and understood the ladder to the top was acquainted with how high the bank account got. And if you looked at Lemon's now, you would think he'd struck the lottery.

You can buy anything with enough money. Just like sex, everyone has their number. And Lemon had his for each of the spoonfuls of spice. Enough to equate to, well, living life out on a luxurious island. An orgasm from life. A selfish legacy, but a legacy nonetheless.

Lemon met Phil where only the dirtiest of deals are done, a Dairy Queen parking lot right behind the convention center.

Lemon's chocolate milk bottle was now empty, not even a hint of an aroma of what it had previously held or the smell of the plastic now that the heat could shine its way through the entirety of the bottle's surface. The smirk on Phil's face extended long down and past the other end of I-90. The smirk on Lemon's was broken, half-flipped like a DQ blizzard. Half was lifted with the ballooning of his bank balance and half turned down by the turmoil he was costing his friend. His former friend, he guessed.

"You're a wise one, Lemon," Phil managed to squeeze out of his smirk like all-natural squeezed lemonade, all bitter, no sweetness. "And you swear this will do what you say it will? It'll win me the competition?"

Lemon had a frog in his throat and he sorta croaked out his answer. "Yessum, and then some."

The frog had been stuck in his throat since he took flight to find Jim and track down the Spice of Life. He read a proverb when he was little about swallowing a frog at the start of your day. It means to do the hardest thing you need to do first and then everything else becomes easier. Weirdly, the proverb never said anything about what to do when it gets stuck in your throat. Guess Lemon was figuring that one out.

"Yessum, and then some," Lemon said again.

With the transaction made, Lemon wanted to still give Phil a scare, if anything, as a final act of friendship for Jim. "But I'll warn you that JimBo's a clever guy. He's like a bouncy ball. The harder he hits the ground, the harder he bounces back up," Lemon warned. And to put a little extra nail in the coffin of fear that he was trying to bury Phil alive in, "And that spice might win you the bet, but I know Jim has some tricks up his sleeve, too."

Phil's smirk lost some mileage. "What do you mean, tricks, Lemon? There are no tricks. He'll be finished. A gentleman's bet."

There was a twinkle in Lemon's eye, a little sour patch. A dash of pain for stealing from his friend, but a tinge of good and honest belief within him, too, that this would merely be a battle lost, not a war. He could not let himself believe otherwise and still think well of himself. So he didn't.

Lemon pivoted on his heels with a little "uh huh." It damn near sounded like Jim's laugh with a puff of air at the end of it. *Herough-uh-huh.*

Lemon started walking off, that smirk finding its home on his face again and the frog cleared from his throat. He could hear Phil's hollers becoming drowned by the sounds of vehicle engines starting to line up in the Dairy Queen drive-through for an early morning treat.

Lemon was doing what few people ever risk doing in life. He was leaving his past behind.

He had one last plane to catch to Oahu and then a boat to ride to Seychelles where he would live out the rest of his days. It was time for Lemon to simplify his overly complicated life. Time to lose his red eyes. His weight. His burden of being *the* insider. Nothing but "Ing" activities for him on the island. Fishing, canoeing, swimming, eating, and buying things from Ingvar Kamprad Elmtaryd Agunnaryd (otherwise known as IKEA) to build while he smoked himself into a daze. He had chosen the island because it was shared with a very quiet but specific group of residents. Not gender-specific by any means, but mainly women whose husbands loved them so dearly that they took their own lives so their wives could collect the insurance money. It was a swift and remarkable trend that took place a number of years ago, before the insurance companies updated their policies to not pay out on suicides. If you looked at a timeline of number of suicides, you'd see a large three-year spike as man after man (and yes, some women, too) took their lives for their significant other. While some widows did right by the funds they acquired as a result, creating meaningful charities and giving back to their communities, others invested a token amount in some mental health organization and then took off for the island life on Seychelles—people who were ready to leave their old lives behind. It would be a great time, reader, to bid Lemon adieu; he has some margaritas to make and widows to woo. Lemonade, on the rocks. *Auf wiedersehen.*

⇒XXXII⇐

After Nora chokingly told Jim the situation of the bottle of spice being lost—damn, that frog is making its rounds in this novel—Jim became frantic in Terminal C and began screaming at the top of his lungs. Even retracing their steps, it would be too late for the convention. At first Jim was screaming about Nora and his soon-to-be-failed business. Then he started screaming. Just pure, primal hollering. He'd read something about scream therapy at one point and now seemed like as good a time as any to see if it worked, though to others at the airport, he could have chosen a better place to practice and Nora, on the other hand, being the one person accompanying Jim, wished he would have waited until they were more... remote, perhaps.

Alas. Here was Jim. His sound waves echoing off the terminal walls, drowning out the crying baby and her mother rushing to a cab, rippling roars louder than the barista's coffee machine at the intersection of Terminal B and the lobby, bellowing his anguish at a decibel level that made the jet engines outside sound like the soft hum of a piano key or the buzz of a bee. Finally, red-faced and out of breath, Jim fell to his knees and sobbed a good, just, and righteous sob.

They say a man should only cry a good cry three times in his life. The first is when his dog dies. That's one thing country songs have right. The second is when he messes up and needs to get his wife, fiancé, girlfriend, or partner back. There's no better sealant on the truth of a changed man than his own tears. More powerful than any words he can utter. The last is when a man's world gets as turned upside down as a burned omelet. This third cry isn't just about the one moment; it's about all the moments that have been held back. There's nothing to do but open the dam that has held back the lake of life's anguish.

Tears streamed down Jim's face with one salty tear taking a detour from his cheek to his lips and in the corner of his mouth. Tasteless to Jim. He sobbed harder as he wrestled with the pain of all his efforts and all his losses.

Nora considered trying to console him, but it wasn't in her nature. She was clueless as to how to even begin. The key to any good relationship is to treat the person how they want to be treated and let them know how you would want to be treated. Nora would want to be left to sob until the river ran dry. And so she let that happen for Jim despite every passenger, shop staff, pilot, and airport nomad staring both of them down.

A clueless janitor walked by and asked if they were done with their snacks, trying to offer some sort of help, or at least to gain a bit of the spotlight for the first time in his life. Jim had yanked the empty wrappers out of Nora's bag in disbelief of the spice not being within it. The trash encircled Jim like some sort of exorcism layout. A ritual of shame. A séance of disappointment. Nora quaked with uncertainty over how Jim would react to the janitor's intrusion.

Jim's face became a desert, devoid of water ducts. His eyes were closed, but he could hear everyone's heartbeats, feel their stares, smell the perspiration of concern from the flight attendants walking by, uncertain how to respond to the situation. This wasn't in their instruction manuals.

At this moment, at the nadir of his life, all of Jim's senses seemed to suddenly lock into gear, find their footing; they arrived home and were completely dialed in. A wave of control overtook Jim. For the first time since losing his sense of taste, he felt like he had a handle on his other senses. Instead of overwhelming him with a cacophony of sensation, they aligned like the stars of the Little Dipper, a row of baby ducks behind their mother, and a strip of cocaine—the first of the day.

He looked up at the janitor and quietly nodded his head, giving permission for him to clean the mess he had made.

Jim had another mess that needed to be cleaned.

⇒XXXIII⇐

Thirty thousand people would enter and exit the doors of the convention centers. This was the largest crowd the convention had ever seen. There were booths spread across the space like cattle. There were some piled with hunky-dory hometown baked-in-my-own-oven-at-home pastries and other stations that looked like a hospital laboratory, breaking and blending flavor particles at a molecular level. There were 4D edible burgers. 3D energy drink fountains. 2D edible origami. And no shortage of 1D men and women with the sole focus of trying everything they could get their now-greasy (thanks, 4D burger) hands on.

This year's convention appeared to welcome a whole sweep of other categories to present as well. Forks, sporks, spoons, knives, and other hand-crafted utensils. In this image-conscious world, what you eat the food with must be as picture-worthy as the food itself. Hand models for hire were at Booth 1317. French tips with French fries.

The massive ballroom had every food writer dancing, elated to be away from the here-and-gone reporting of local restaurants and not-so-breaking news of mistreatment and harassment in the industry. And the never-ending labor shortage, which is about the lack of skill more than an actual lack of labor. This was not just a reprieve, it was a damn fun circus of flavor, a tilt-a-whirl for their taste buds, a carousel of flavors that they could eat with their eyes. They even had squirt gun stations that allowed you to frost your own cupcakes at a distance, with a plush cherry awarded to the one who added the most frosting in twenty seconds. This was restaurateurs' chance to play consumer.

The convention started as it did every year, with the reciting of the national supertaster mantra: "Taste, taste, taste. Eat slow because haste makes flavor waste." They even had a live indie band ready to perform a few times throughout the conference. Naturally the pamphlets that were handed out during the event had recommendations for the food to eat with the music, a curated combination of senses for the optimal experience. It cost the vendors $15,000 to have their name paired with the music, but many gladly did it, not because the pairing was exceptionally special but because people talked about it, which was more valuable than $15,000 of cash that can't talk.

After the mantra, the place became a haven for gastronomic orgasms. Guests trying food that was advertised at each stand. Vendors sharing with each other food that wasn't advertised, pulling coolers out from under tables, sneakily grabbing the best of the best of their goods to share. It was commonplace for booths to have codewords to get access to the special menu items. At some you merely had to ask; others only gave it out if you wore a shirt with their brand on it. In preparation for this, believe it or not, a man showed up the year before wearing 198 shirts, well shy of the Guinness record of 260 but still damn impressive. What a brilliant buffer between him and the nuisance of other bodies touching, flesh to flesh, as they crowd in a line of their favorite stands. Everyone wondered if the T-shirt guy would make another appearance this year.

In the left corner, weighing in at 286 pounds, veteran linebacker, husband, and businessman, was a fella selling shirts with foodie quotes on them: "Another one bites the crust" "Weir-dough for lyfe," "Let the beet drop."

In the right corner, weighing in at 111 pounds and proud of it, butcher by day and tattoo artist by night, was Nancy Williams, who was tattooing guests of the conference for a good cause—to pay medical bills for kids who had gotten their teeth knocked out while playing golf. (It's surprising how many people can be in a group that you'd think would be so niche.) A good number of business owners were in line, ready to have their own logos inked on their skin, reasoning that if they did, perhaps they would start a trend and others would get tattoos of their logo as well.

That's the dream.

Perhaps "convention" is the wrong word for this theme park, this jumble of jubilee, this festoon of festivity—and its cacophony of characters. It was an introvert's worst nightmare and an extrovert's paradise.

For some, this would be the place to get their word out for the first time. Others were veterans of this convention. For Phil, it was a little of both.

We find him at the center of the food ring, schmoozing the judges of the Golden Fork, knowing full well he doesn't need to with the spice he has in his pocket. Phil didn't need anything else in his pockets. He even left his phone in his hotel room. He didn't like to be interrupted when he was involved in a business activity such as this, and there were plenty of photographers and journalists covering the conference; he didn't need for anyone to use his phone to take his picture. Phil only hoped that the picture included the face of Jim, too. The look of defeat is priceless in Phil's eyes.

"Annalise, how are the kids? What did your husband think of the basket I sent you two?" Phil said to one judge.

"Kluck. How are you doing, sir? How did that butcher that I recommended to you turn out?" Phil said to another.

Phil had even found a way to connect with the newest judge at the table. Someone did their research.

"Gratavius, how was your getaway from Yekaterin-burg? Looked like you were exploring Arizona, huh? Sonoran Dessert puts together some of the greatest pastes from frog's venom glands. Five dollars you put some on your avocado toast and had a trip, didn't you, you ol' dog, you," Phil said, but this time with a slight Russian accent, as if it would signal a relation of respect to Gratavius's origin and ensure he would grow quickly fond of Phil.

Above Phil, a working countdown sign hung that, up close, looked to be the size that you'd find on the scoreboard at Soldier Field. Though, this one somehow seemed to shine brighter still. If the ceiling lights were to go out in the convention center, the countdown clock would illuminate it just the same, albeit with an ominous red hue. The sign read 09:24. At this point in the convention, most bellies were beginning to bubble, taste buds were getting toasted, and egos were either stroked to the edge of pleasure or broken down like a nineties rock band van trying to make the run from Tallahassee to Tacoma.

At the five-minute mark, booths would stop serving, the countdown sign would shine brighter (with an additional red border around the numbers), seats would be filled at the east wing of the center (the best view of the judges and the closest to the exit), Phil would take his position at kitchen space #3, and the judges he was just wooing would take their seats at the head judge table. Unlike everyone else at the center, the judge's belly gauges were near "E." Not to say they were starving; they are food experts, for Christ's sake. Being starved would award an inherent bias toward the first chef's dish, so the judges were given a handful of tasteless biscuits so as not to sway the base flavor in their mouth, a slow carb biscuit that would make their metabolic system feel satisfied, though their stomachs still had enough room to hold a wedding party for the weekend or, you know, for the dishes of the next six meals prepared by the competing chefs.

Phil was making crayfish puff cakes with mustard seed vinaigrette and a spoonful of plankton. Simple to make, elegant to look at, and tastes incredible even before the spice is added. But what was so conniving about this was that it allowed Phil to beat Jim even further into the ground by not only winning the bet, but doing so with a seafood dish that *Jim* should be known for, albeit without the addition of insects.

Ah, that wicked, aphotic smile was back on Phil's face.

He glanced over at kitchen space #6, where Jim should be soon. Phil was surprised he wasn't there already. There's nothing more shameful than losing a competition except not showing up for it, forfeiting, conceding privately from a distance like a coward. Phil knew Jim was not that kind of man. Perhaps this was some scare tactic. Jim was trying to get Phil all worked up. Phil remembered how Lemon said Jim had something up his sleeve...

Nancy Williams was just wrapping up tattooing a well on Nora's right ankle. Nora figured her one tattoo from Batuk would remind her of her past and the new tattoo would signify the magic in her present and future. While it wasn't matching, per se, a clock's ticking of minutes ago Jim had gotten a well bucket and lever with a rope on his forearm. They both silently wondered what Shaman Denny would say if he ever saw them.

Jim had pulled off an emotional one-eighty since the airport. It was a combination of acceptance of his defeat, curiosity of what to do after, and, let's face it, excitement that Nora was still with him. It's not just that misery loves company, it also loves to have someone to pull them away from it. That's not to say Jim was enjoying being at the convention or excited by what was inevitably to come. No, dear reader. He was suffering, but holding it in like many do, taking the punches without expressing the pain of them on his face. Every time Jim looked at a booth and thought that would be interesting to try, he remembered that there wasn't a point if he couldn't taste it. All the secret codes he had memorized were worthless. Jim didn't even know if he could fake a reaction of enjoyment in taking a bite of Marko's Meatballs, so he passed by the booth without making eye contact, so not to disappoint his fellow colleague.

At this point, Jim's other senses were well dialed into their new normal and he was gaining a decent amount of control over them. For example, he could zero in on Nora's heartbeat and feel it move faster as he touched her hand.

He could hear a bride-to-be a few booths over talking to her fiancé about how badly she needed a churro. "Like, right *now*, honey."

Jim needn't use any superpowers to know her fiancé responded with a sigh and rolled eyes. His nose, however, was still a bit awry, almost free-spirited or like a melting pot, rather. All the aromas, good and bad, were registering in Jim's brain as a muffled dank cologne. It must have something to do with the sense of smell being joined at the hip with the sense of taste. Oh how rare it was for Jim to ever smell anything in life and not also taste it or, if he couldn't, imagine what it would taste like.

Though Jim and Nora were late to the start of the convention, they were early enough to jump into one of the breakout seminars before Jim needed to get to his kitchen station. That is, before the quick tattoo. That was Nora's idea.

The seminar was focused on the Slow Food Nation, and the speaker had intentionally gained 140 pounds off Italy's most garbage food only to show the dual impact slow food has on both our bodies and our environment. The movement preserves and promotes the traditional and regional cuisine and encourages farming plants, seeds, and livestock in a local ecosystem, focused on quality rather than quantity and—like our fat—speaks out against overproduction and food or energy waste. Patrice Carlyle covered it all, from politics, which was rarely talked-about at the convention, to how the same amount of water used to feed some cattle could be used to grow more plants that could feed far more people than the single bovine could, to actually eating as slowly as you can to both break down foods better, enjoy the food more, and fill up faster so as not to overeat. The alternative to the slow food movement in Patrice's eyes, the thing that would benefit the world just the same, was mass genocide. (Nora thought bleakly of how much she had already contributed to that. Not necessarily directly, but certainly indirectly with her line of work. She gaffed at the idea of slow food being as effective, but if that was past her and this was new to her, perhaps this was the other end of the spectrum she needed to source her energy from?)

"Did you know that the time it takes for your bag of lettuce—from which you undoubtedly have maybe a single serving before tossing the rest—is touched by no fewer than twenty-five hands, transported on four trucks, sways up to forty-eight degrees Fahrenheit and then twenty-five degrees Fahrenheit up to six times depending on the season..." and she went on.

Jim didn't quite buy everything she was trying to sell. She was throwing a lot of terms out that in this day and age have been filled with air. "Fair trade," "producers with pride," "ethical treatment."

"Did you know, slaughtering an entire family's cattle was seen as ethical in the native tribe of Hablaken in Sentinalyse Island?" Jim despised it when speakers assumed their worldviews were the same as others or, worse, that they should be even if they weren't. That being written, Jim still agreed with a few sentiments of Patrice's. Haste makes waste. You are what you eat. To wit, she tried adding a touch of humor to her speech by suggesting she had a sexy beast for breakfast that morning. No one in the audience or, quite frankly, your fine author, knew how to react to that other than to painfully chuckle and pray she didn't let the punchline bask for too long lest we would all shrivel and die, a nice slow-food joke death. Thankfully Patrice carried on quickly when she realized she didn't have a chance as a stand-up comedian.

The seminar ended with a before-and-after photo of Patrice, 300 pounds then and 130 pounds now. Beside each photo was an infographic of the waste and destruction caused to the Earth by the weight gain, and the positive impact she had on the globe with the weight loss. The skinnied-down version of life itself. Patrice Carlyle. Slow-food fed. The skim-milk version of a person. The end of her seminar produced a standing ovation with the photo. Seeing is believing, I suppose.

Jim stepped out of the seminar and looked up at the jumbotron of a countdown, which even a person on the brink of blindness could see. Jim briefly considered not competing at all, knowing how much of a disadvantage he had, given his loss of taste. Nora was the one that convinced him to carry on. Deep down, in the marrow of his bones, Jim knew it was logical to do so. Any food maker who made it into the competition could at least wear their participation ribbon with pride—which not many can do in life without getting laughed at. And maybe, if he trusted his hands and his memory and this adjusting nose of his, he could come out as the second-place winner, to whom the convention politely awarded a gray fork. (A silver fork was too close to a silver spoon, which no one wants to say they won. Insensitive, really.) Nora teased out the idea of opening a restaurant someplace else, a different concept. "I could be your taste buds," Nora said. "We can do it together." Nora was saying all the right words, but despite Jim's improved senses, it took a while for him to hear them.

Jim decided to make a fish soup called The Buddha Jumps Over the Wall. It includes abalone, Japanese flower mushroom, sea cucumber, dried scallops, and, because this was a special occasion, Jim planned to include a shark fin in it. This, of course, would include the seaweed extract he recently concocted in his apartment. And to one-up the dish, he planned to put chopsticks shaped like a pirate ship's plank across the bowl, layering it with lobster frittata. He called that part The Buddha's Hotel Stay. Jim appreciated the resonance of Buddhist cuisine at the same time it spoiled it. As any Buddhist knows, the Buddha insisted his followers not eat any meat... or fish. But the Buddha is flesh and bone the same as you or I and subject to their own quirks, vices, and hypocrisies. Jim's dish was the equivalent of a monk swiping right on a cell phone.

The jumbotron flashed with a two-minute warning along with a voice over the intercom to double down. "Two minutes to cook off!" In an absolutely glorious, harmonious synchronicity, every non-first-year attendee at the convention yelled, "thank youuuuu!" Jim couldn't resist joining in. It was muscle memory. This moment at every year's convention set the energy level of all those in attendance, primed them for the main event, signaled that though they were competitor, vendor, acquaintance, and enemy, they were one tribe, like a pack of hunters and gatherers bellowing out that the hunt-and-gather was a success, and it would soon be time to dine.

On Jim's way to kitchen station #6, he passed a new booth he didn't recognize. Prayery Farms. It was a chocolate milk booth, with no shortage of chocolate milk options, made by some righteous Christians in Bozeman, Montana. Aside from the mint chocolate milk, skim chocolate milk, Turkish delight chocolate milk (which, counter to what the name suggests, is the most foul-tasting chocolate milk imaginable—it was merely there for the memory-creating moment of trying it and showing how wretched your face would turn after a sip), dark chocolate milk, white chocolate milk (which was a mind-bender because it poured like normal milk), and, last but not least, the sweet German chocolate milk. The banner behind the milk options showed the farm animals and their welfare situation. To the left was a list of labor efficiencies, most of which were gibberish to Jim. To the right was a list of awards as well as a minerals and vitamins chart that broke down the benefits of the silky brown substance. The belief this trust-in-God-not-the-farmers-almanac booth holder held, as did many at this convention, was that consumers were getting smarter and smarter every day. You could no longer appeal to the masses by merely listing carbohydrates, fats, and proteins.

No, sir. You needed to say it had 0.092 mg of niacin and 0.48 mg zinc and 5 ug of folate. The words that once scared people away now became the prominent factor in their decision to purchase a product or not. Even four-year-olds were asking their parents how much alpha-tocopherol was in their unspillable sippy cup with a bendy twisty straw. Beneath the banner was a pirate's plank of bottles that had been emptied, perhaps into the salty seas, but empty nonetheless. Jim imagined that the one bottle not on display here, the one he treasured most, was emptied by now.

Nora would have consoled him in that moment had she been by his side to witness the irony, but she was off to find a proper seat for the show. This was a first for her. Previously, at any sort of entertainment-like event in her life, she would typically be up in the rafters, prowling in the back alley, or dressed as a concierge, a clerk, or perhaps even a noble cowboy. (Definitely ask her about *that* story. It's a doozie.)

Jim took a deep breath, a gallant one, a sigh of a one-man army. In his partially processing mind he recited a phrase Lemon taught him early on: TMNW.

No, fine reader, it's not short for Teenage Mutant Ninja Weasels. That's preposterous. It stands for "this might not work." Lemon, with a single inspiring breath, had gone on one of his motivational spiels about how there was no certainty in *anything* working, but what mattered was that the impresario chef did his art anyway and gifted it to the world knowing full well it might not work, but whether it was working or not working (sorta like Jim's taste buds) wasn't the point of a remarkable person. Jim replayed the speech as if he had DVRed it in his head. It replayed a third time in his mind as he got to kitchen station #6.

At kitchen station #1 was the Fork winner from last year.

The man at #2 looked to be a macho Italian or Hispanic.

It was hard to tell his ethnicity behind the *lucha libre* mask he wore. The thinking of the man was that no one will think you're great, even if you're great, unless you're also noticeable. Soccer players with pink hair. Bowlers with a metal leg. Dog walkers with big gauges in their ears. (The walker, not the dogs... though there's an idea.) That was the one, two punch of this *luchador*.

At station #3 was the malicious, malevolent, villainous capital P, Phil.

Station #4 was Calypso Sherain, a smolderingly hot woman who only got the spot because of some relationship to the organizers. So goes the game of life.

Station #5 was Wiley Dae, a firefighter known for his Korean bulgogi, which literally means "fire meat." He was a master of marinade and slick with slicing pork, great at grilling, a beast with barbeque, and a gangster on the stovetop grill. He was a newbie to the competition, but his reputation brought in a whole coleslaw dollop of fans. Jim didn't know much about Wiley, but the air of confidence that surrounded him made Jim wonder if *he* was the one to worry about instead of Phil.

Last, but certainly not least, as the saying goes, was station #6 at which Jim stood, a rally of endorphins gathering in his brain. *Focus*, he thought. *Focus on what you do best.* He corralled the endorphins, but he also couldn't help but glance over his shoulder and see no shortage of enoki mushrooms at Wiley's station behind him. Damn, those were going to taste good.

A shadow cast over Jim's station and he turned to find Phil standing in front of him.

"I didn't think you were going to show. That would have been a smart move, actually. Anyway, hopefully you let your team know that today would be the last day they are working because your restaurant will be closed indefinitely tomorrow."

Phil wasn't wrong. A polygraph could see the straight

truth he spoke. Somehow, Jim knew it, too. But after all that he had been through, Jim could do the only thing Jim could do... keep going.

Resolve ironed out the wrinkles in his cheeks and purged his eyebrows of their menace and disdain for this burly man. *Focus.* And so he did.

"I've trained for this, Phil. Far longer than you. You might know the recent vacations of the judges, their kids' names, or what NHL team they're season ticket holders for, but you don't see into their taste buds and how it's taste that influences memory recollection, not the other way around."

Though the spaces were already set up the way that each chef had asked, Jim turned his shoulder to move some items around in preparation of the competition's start and to serve Phil a block of cold shoulder.

With a wide "hmph," Phil returned to his station. *This guy doesn't know what's coming,* he thought savagely.

Before the big red clock turned to zero, only to be reset to another hour's countdown for the chefs, and the cooking competition would begin, Jim scanned the audience. He found Nora without any effort; he could still smell the jitterbug perfume she sprayed on her from the "try me" bottle from one of the booths, edible and great-tasting colognes and perfumes for the inevitable instances that your mouth is open when you spray yourself fresh. Jim was beginning to appreciate his other senses, though his tongue still tossed and turned in his mouth, unable to fall asleep, despite Jim willing it to. He continued scanning the crowd and paused at a vacant seat, J8. That was odd. Lemon always sat at J8. A superstitious man, Lemon always sat in row J for Jim and 8. Well, what's a cleverer number for a food convention than 8? But the seat was nearly empty except for the bit of cavalier scarf that dangled onto the armrest from the foxy lady sitting in J9. Jim had to brush aside his concern about Lemon. *Maybe he's just late.*

In true WrestleMania fashion, spurring the energy of all contests—especially the *luchador* at station #2—there was the sound of a bell being whacked with a mallet three times. Ding, ding, ding.

Our chefs were off. This wasn't the *Great British Baking Show*. As mentioned, the kitchens were prepped, the menus submitted by the chefs weeks ago with excruciating detail of everything they would need to create their dishes and anything they thought they might need to use as a game-time decision addition. Naturally, chefs could bring anything in the day of, too.

Each of the chefs moved as smoothly as if they'd done it a million times before, dreamed of it, spent 128 hours on a virtual training program living the situation. Of course, there were some last-minute tweaks being made. That's art, isn't it? Science is calculated, hypothesized, attempted. Art is spontaneous, risky, a leap. Wiley decided to bring some homemade sourdough to use as a holster for his meaty weapons of choice. It was a last-minute bread breakthrough he'd made at his mother's when he was visiting before the competition. The trick? Rosemary.

The Fork winner from last year topped her dish with an edible Golden Fork, an exact replica of the crown she wore as she cooked. Someone forgot to leave their ego at the door.

Rather than talk to one another, the chefs merely talked to themselves. Unlike those baking shows you see on TV, no MC was interrupting them, getting up in their faces, spiking them with dialogue or poorly written jokes. This was a sport, and true of a sport, the audience acted as spectators. And true of spectators, they weren't one hundred percent focused on watching these artistic scientists at work unless the chef gave them reason to be. The audience wasn't quiet, of course. They were placing bets and high-fiving those sitting next to them when Wiley created a flame that rose to the heavens above, making the jumbotron's red glow even redder. This matchstick of a man wasn't just making food, he was playing his sport with the intention to fuel the audience. Their meters rose, as did the volume. On the Richter scale it was a 3. The volume rose as high as the flames in the convention center. The other chefs started to perspire. Not because of the heat of the flames but because of the heat of the competition. Then each artist started to put on a show, entertain, and actually perform for the audience to compete with Wiley.

Fortunately, the convention center was built to withstand anything with a Richter scale rating of 8 or lower. The foundation of the building would make Le Corbusier jump out of his shoes. Cinder block on cinder block as the core and no shortage of green space surrounding and rising to the rooftop of the center. It was as if Mother Earth was holding it down and in place. Through nature, the contestants and attendees were connected to the sacred.

Jim just did as Jim does. Working with a bit of an emotional limp, he didn't try anything new or unique, undocumented in his plan. He followed suit. It smelled right. It looked right. It felt like he was going through the motions right. This would be an incredible dish even if he was missing his secret ingredient that would have guaranteed a win. That's all he needed in this competition. A win. A win to save his work and his reputation and a future for Herough. At least a future he would be a part of.

Jim overheard some audience members talking to one another. He could hear the bets against him, deflating his soul; and then he heard bets for him, inflating his soul back up. Being a blow-up tube must be exhausting. Those betting against him could see the exhaust fuming out of Jim's pores. A leak in his tube, and this time, not a play on a vegetable.

Nearing the end of the cooking time, all the chefs began barking and bragging to one another. Wiley told Maria at station #1 to stick a fork in it, throwing the fork of a phrase back at her. Lucho Libre shouted something incomprehensible almost to himself. Naturally, Phil joined in on the fun with more maniacal egoism than anyone before him. It was his raw confidence in winning despite the showmanship antics of competition like Wiley.

Trudging through, Jim worked to put his final details on his plates as the jumbotron of a clock flicked down to a mere minute and ten seconds remaining. The Golden Fork winner of last year submitted her plates first—"if you're not forkst, you're last," she said with a wry giggle, as spicy as a nine-year aged rye whiskey.

Phil readied his dishes to be brought to the judges, but before waving the plates' chauffeur, he hollered over to Jim. "Hey, JimBo. Let's imagine I gave you an out right now, this would be your last chance to take it. Of course, I'm not going to give you that opportunity. With this bit of spice, your fate is absolutely, unequivocally sealed," Phil shouted. "Remind me to thank Lemon again for this spice if you ever see him. It tastes like magic."

Jim looked over and saw Phil dust his plates with the last bit of spice that oddly came from a plastic container. What appeared to be a chocolate milk bottle, to be exact. *It couldn't be*, Jim thought, but his improved eyesight wouldn't deceive him. The crane of his mandible broke, and his jaw fell to the floor like a broken paper airplane; a besieged castle gate; like a magician's curtain dropping too soon and revealing the secret. Anger swelled and he was ready to erupt like a child's science fair volcano. He managed to squeeze a few syllables out of the craters in his diaphragm.

"Lemon gave that to you? From where?"

"Oh, so *now* you'll talk?" Phil mumbled something about Budapest. "And it cost a pretty penny, too, from me and apparently others, since this was the last of what he had. But boy, I took a finger swab of it an hour ago and my taste buds are still elated. Damn near lost my finger to myself!"

Jim's jaw was still hanging out on the floor, no interest in getting up. It found a couch in the crease of the concrete. It might as well get comfy; it would be staying for a while.

Phil could tell he had the edge and that he'd found a soft spot in Jim's gut. Phil couldn't resist poking it more. It was a big red button and Phil was a child.

"From the looks of it, two things have to be true. One, you know what this is and two, you don't have any. Poor Jim. Not even Lemon's looking out for you," Phil explained like his words were salt on an open wound.

Phil's eyebrows hit the ceiling and bounced back down as he tossed the empty bottle in the recycling bin and signaled his escort service over to deliver his dishes to the judges. As they took them away, he sucked his finger again, making a "muah" sound and ejecting his fingers away from his mouth. Equal parts celebration, equal parts eff you to Jim. A signature gesture of delight and deliciousness and completion and fulfillment in Western culture, but really, he was also attempting to get whatever spice might have been left under his fingernail from that swab. It truly did taste like magic.

☙XXXIV❧

The first reaction of any spectator of a fire isn't "there's a fire" or "hope no one is inside" or "better call Wiley." Nope. The first reaction is always "Damn, I can feel the heat from here."

For some reason, our sense of touch is the first to reach our brain. Not the sight of the kaleidoscope of flames, not the sound of a life of passion cracking and evaporating, not the taste of charred dreams and two-by-fours. The ferocity of the inferno paves its way onto the skin, sizzling through the soul on the inside just as the hair on the outside disappears.

There was no shortage of spectators watching the restaurant, Herough, burn in flames. Some spectators were soaked in whiskey. Some who worked third shift had been roused by the sensation. No fire controllers were there yet, and the building was nearly a third gone, rapidly turned to ash by the power within. Every spectator was now wearing a perfume of burned seafood. That's one that doesn't come off in the shower and why seafood restaurants are one of the toughest to make succeed—just one burned dorado, one oversautéed trevally, one crisped wahoo and the stench sticks around like some superpowered aromatic flea. This may be something you have not experienced, dear reader, as many a seafood restaurant will close for the day to air out their dirty laundry if they burn something to the nth degree. The missed revenue of the day isn't nearly as bad as what they'd lose if folks like you and I visited and had our experience ruined by the scent. Hell, these spectators in front of Herough right now? They won't act as spectator at another fire in their life because of what their wives and husbands will say about their stench when they get home.

By the time the flame wranglers showed up to douse Jim's restaurant with fire retardant, it was nearly gone. It was a token gesture. They merely followed protocol so their chief wouldn't chew their asses for not doing it. Other times they sprayed on in the event they might save a prized possession or some remnants of writing, but this restaurant would soon become a memory hole. The white paste spurted out like a freshly opened and squeezed bottle of toothpaste, forceful but heavy, smothering the remaining flames with a grizzly bear hug, putting them into permanent hibernation.

"Turn her off," hollered one of the firefighters at the head of the hose. "It's good enough," he bellowed over the hisses and smacks of the embers on the ground. As in, *it's good, now, enough.* The chief showed up just as the hose was wrapped, tucked away to slumber until another fire undoubtedly arose—hopefully one it could do a better job at than this one, and one that didn't result in the kind of stench they all stood in.

The spectators became players in the game as the chief interviewed them, attempting to understand the reason behind the fire that had consumed Herough.

One spectator said she was on her routine walk with her muppet of a dog, who was being incessantly pesky about the route to take, bringing her down this particular block. Her usual pet food included ground salmon; naturally she was drawn to the smell of cooked seafood. After a few more minutes listening to the love/hate relationship with her dog, its "digestive habits" and "incurable tendencies," the chief moved on. "One out of ten," he muttered to himself.

Only one out of ten spectators ever have a worthy contribution, and even when they do it's usually just the tip of an iceberg, a hair of a lettuce, a tombstone of a deceased.

The trouble is that one spectator can waste so much of your time that others with something actually useful to say may end up leaving when the fire hydrant's tubes get tied and the show is over.

This was one of those times.

The chief switched from listening to the woman's canine conundrum, to listening to a nearby shop owner chewing the chief out for not arriving sooner to put out the fire and prevent the smoke from swooping and swaying, praying and prancing along the street—ignorant of "no smoking" signs posted outside the buildings and forcing the shopkeepers' customers to take a rain check on their "necessities" or even stop at another shop for the same goods farther down the road.

"It only takes one time! One time when a customer goes somewhere else that they find something better and form a new habit. This great bowl of smoke that you failed to prevent might cost me thousands in revenue and dozens of repeat customers."

The chief wished the fighters hadn't put the hose away; this man could use a dousing.

All the while the chief was being paid city tax money to provide inauthentic therapy sessions, the one spectator who could have contributed to a report worth reading scurried away, leaving a trail of regret, partially for the bet he'd made with a man who'd now left his bank account $3,000 lighter, and partially for the bet he'd made with a man who said he would set fire to a restaurant. This character thought the man was senile, joking about setting a restaurant on fire. That would be ridiculous. Alas. They shook hands, a gentleman's honor system, and the man proceeded to jigger with some valves on the side of Herough's building, slip inside with a key to the back door and when he returned, angry flames already trailed behind him, chasing him, only to have the door shut in their face, enraging them more. The man hastily requested the check be written by the bystanding better and the man obliged. He was stunned. He had no words to express. None to argue. His brain was still processing the bet and the fire. It all happened so fast. "Better take off before the police arrive," the pyro said to the man as he bolted away with the check in hand.

Had the bet-maker hung around with the other spectators and patiently waited his turn to be interrogated by the chief, he would have been brought into the station for further questioning and then to a courtroom for additional requestioning while a stenographer took notes, which while somewhat unreliable, is found to be more reliably binding than a statement of "I solemnly swear." The court conversation, had it occurred, would have gone thusly:

Chief: You understand that everything you say is going to be taken down by the stenographer.

Character: Uhm. Sure.

Chief: Please respond with definitive answers. Yes or no.

Character: Yes.

Chief: Your name? Age? Address?

Character: Kyle McLehren. Twenty-seven. 13 Rost Street, Apartment 37.

Chief: Occupation?

Kyle: I was recently promoted to manager of the Diagonaly Bowling Garage.

Chief: And at 4:30 p.m., whilst the world's most renowned culinary convention was taking place, you were...?

Kyle: I was on my way to work. I had the night shift. I just stopped in my go-to street shop to grab dinner and a snack to-go.

Chief: Did you, at approximately 4:35, set fire to Herough?

Kyle: No! I swear! It wasn't me.

Chief: So you know who it was?

Kyle: Yes. Well, no. Well, it was sort of me, but I didn't do it.

Chief: If there is a time to talk, son, it's now.

Kyle: There was a man with two duffel bags that approached me and asked if I was feeling lucky today. He unzipped one of the bags and it was money. A lot of money. "I'm a betting man," he said. "And I bet you $3,000 that I'm crazy enough to set fire to a restaurant."

Chief: Can you describe the man?

Kyle: He was large. Like, fridge large. He was well-dressed, though obviously perspiring and now that I think about it a little out of breath.

Chief: Carry on.

Kyle: Well, I was ahead of schedule to get to work and figured I'd entertain this guy, thinking he was on crack or something. I thought the worst-case scenario, maybe he gives me $3,000 out of that duffel bag of his. I really needed it too. My car needs a...

Chief: The guy. Can you tell us more about the guy?

Kyle: I. Uh. Well, I went ahead and bet him $3,000 that he wouldn't set fire to a restaurant. I was just playing his game. Honest. I didn't even know we were standing by a restaurant. I don't pay attention to much. I just walk my path every day, stop at the same convenience store if there's time before my shift, and keep my eyes down in front of me.

Chief: You're telling me that a stocky fella randomly came up to you with a duffel bag of cash and got you to bet him $3,000 that he *wouldn't* set a restaurant on fire?

Kyle: Well. Uhm. When you put it that way... Yeah? I guess I did. We shook hands on it.

Chief: And you had no knowledge of Herough being the target of his arson?

Kyle: No. Not a clue. Honest.

Chief: You can leave the honesty to the stenographer, kid. What happened next?

Kyle: Well, we walked to the back of this restaurant, Herough, he set his duffel bags down and he unlocked the back door, went inside and just a few minutes later he quickly walked out, slamming the door behind him and trapping the fire that was following him within.

Chief: And you just stood watching?

Kyle: Well. I. I didn't think he was going to do it. I thought he was just playing with me. He had a key, so I figured maybe it was his own place.

Chief: Witnesses already confirmed that it wasn't Jim Herough Bois, nor any of his staff when all provided aliases for themselves. Bois was at the convention the whole time.

Kyle: Well. I didn't know that.

Chief: Continue with your story, son. Every detail matters.

Kyle: Am I going to get in trouble for making the bet? I didn't do anything.

Chief: Now isn't the time to discuss if the ideator is subject to the punishment of the crime of the executor of the ideas, Kyle. Now what happened when he came out?

Kyle: Well. I. Uhm. I didn't have a duffel bag of cash like he did. Just my checkbook and so I wrote him a check for $3,000. I guess I hoped the punch line of his joke was that he wouldn't take it, seeing that he had a duffel bag full of cash anyway, and then I could still withhold my honor for fulfilling my end of the bet.

Chief: And to whom did you write the check?

Kyle: Oh! He said "Main Squeeze".

Chief: That was his name? Main Squeeze?

Kyle: Well. I. Uhm. I don't know. It's just what he had me write on the check.

Chief: And then what?

Kyle: Well, sir. Well. He took the check. And suggested I get on with my day as the flames were making their way through the crease of the door. That I should get out of there before the police came.

Chief: Then he left? That was it?

Kyle: Well. Uhm. I think he muttered something to himself as he was walking away. I could barely make it out with the fire crackling inside the restaurant.

Chief: Get on with it, boy.

Kyle: He said something like, "I'm on my way, Seychelles." I don't know who Seychelles is. I swear.

Chief: It's an island of widowers and retirees, my boy. It'll cost too much to track him down. And the government there isn't like the government here. He's the one.

Kyle: So, what now?

Chief: With this on record and the rest of the bystanders interviewed, this case will remain open, but it's as good as a case closed. Damn. Seychelles. Unless he leaves there... That's not information you need to know, however. Was there anything else you would like to add?

Kyle: No. I. Uhm. Well, yes. I don't know if it matters or helps, but he was smiling when he came back out of the restaurant. He said, "There's nothing like the smell of a good deed to make up for bad ones, is there?" I didn't really know what he was talking about. I just nodded and he was off.

Chief: Curious.

Kyle: Yea. Curious.

Kyle didn't hang around like a hummingbird who found a dish of sugar water. He flew off just as the Mr. Now-Retired-Fraser instructed him to. Like a child trying to come up with an excuse for late homework, Kyle got to scheming up a story to tell his girlfriend as to why it would be a bit longer before he could afford a car repair. Of course, she wouldn't bite the words in the air he breathed. His lies would fall like hammers on a sword, sharpening the end of their relationship. Tough to commute an hour and a half for love with a broken transmission. But I digress, dear reader, for this isn't an epic about a man named Kyle and the struggles of dating in your twenties.

Fraser never cashed the check anyhow; he framed it instead. Still hangs in a bar in Seychelles, if you ever find yourself there.

⮞XXXV⮜

Today was Batuk's birthday. The day he celebrates the fact that the celestial gods tubed an egg down to Earth, bituminous and evil. It was their way of keeping humankind on its tippy toes. Batuk had been raised by a village outlaw. Despite how much he consumed as a child, he grew as slow as *chicha* is made. Life chewed and chewed and chewed.

By the age of fourteen, he was fascinated with trinkets and death, curious what happened after the chewing stopped. He wrote a requiem for his outlaw caretaker, who was far from old, but he wanted it for good measure; he knew her tape would be run shorter than her aesthetics indicated.

His fascination around death grew and it was all he could talk about, that is, if it weren't for trinkets to distract him.

"You don't need oxygen," he told the other boys in school. "You can die just fine without it."

And then he'd take their doodads, bombkis, push pops, and belly pins and proceed to tinker and tanker them into something better—sometimes more precious and oftentimes more lethal.

Batuk would hoard and then organize his collections based on how likely they might cause someone's death. Batuk's the reason all manufactured products will say *choking hazard* this, *do not swallow* that, keep away from your jealous sibling and jealous ex for that matter.

Batuk was fascinated with his birthday. It was the one day a year that he chastised the grim reaper himself, blowing candles that stood like middle fingers to fate. In death we are all the same, and Batuk liked being different.

On his sixteenth birthday, he read the requiem he wrote for his outlaw of a caretaker and set off to join a nearby tribe. He traded trinkets for a higher rank in the cult and they quickly learned Batuk was a portent of death—smelled and sounded like it too, his words sticky like black tar, his scent like the fart of a rain cloud, and they sure had good use of that kind of scary, that kind of grimace of life, that kind of talent.

Batuk, being the crackerjack he was, stole back his trinkets the first night, but along with them, he clinched an object not of his own. A book. The cover was smeared with candle wax that smelled of Gotu Kola leaves, the binding made from porcupine thistles.

The book was entitled *Ashton Grimoire* and had a black lady slipper pressed into the leather on the back of it with a time turner, what appeared to be sperm swimming, and some Khmer scripture.

After some sly conversations with various cult members, he was informed about a brahman who the cult had robbed a few years back. It was like Batuk was a spy at sixteen. While people on the other side of the world were driving for the first time and trying to get laid in a parking lot in the back of their Pontiac, Batuk was busy with espionage on a whole other level.

It didn't take Batuk long to find the brahman; no one in the cult questioned where he went at night, anyway. Funny to imagine a recruit that no one questioned or spit slurs at, but that's Batuk, after all. Even back then he carried the air of a leader.

After finding the brahman's tribe, Batuk learned that the brahman had been exiled by the group for his inability to thwart thieves. Little did they know. Singular. Thief. Name starts with the second letter of the alphabet. So it goes.

Batuk found the brahman the next night. The weakest of hearts fail to flee far from home. Batuk traded his trinkets yet again, this time to the banished brahman in exchange for lessons in the language of the book. The brahman earned his right to return, and Batuk learned the secrets the pages of the book held.

By his twentieth birthday, Batuk had sought out more spellbound texts, and, discarding any language about spells or sorcery he could do himself, he sought after the objects that others had already sacrificed their lives for. He quickly picked up on the fact that any magic acquired required a more monumental sacrifice, and he wasn't keen on sacrificing anything himself. Batuk knew better than to do the dirty work himself when others had already done it or would do it for him with the right information, direction and, you know, pressure.

Today, on Batuk's sixty-fifth birthday, he ruminated on his insidious plans. Reflected on his perilous expeditions (perilous to others, mind you... not him). There was something in the air around him. Poison gas? Broken auras? Light refracting off the evil thick skin of his body?

There was a triple knock on his door, which, disturbing Batuk on one of his favorite days, was as dangerous to do as dog paddling across the Nile. It was one of his messengers, a fact made obvious to Batuk by the triple knock that was reserved for him specifically. When you reach the notoriety that Batuk has, everything is done by a code.

This was someone who actually would dog paddle across the Nile if that was what it took to carry a message for Batuk. Partly because of his allegiance, but more so because Batuk wouldn't lend him a hand back out of the Nile if he didn't deliver the message. The young man pushed the door open. Batuk wasn't one for opening doors himself. Metaphorical, magical, mythical ones, sure. But not physical ones. That's a layman's work.

The man who stood at the door was wearing torn khaki shorts. His knees were hairless from years spent using them in his line of work. You'd be amazed at how much crawling a messenger does. The world believes they run, run, run, when in reality they crawl more than anything. At least, the ones with the most important messages do.

"Sir, your eyes in America report things are going as planned."

You'd feel like today was the young man's birthday by the tone of his voice. Though it's not often he had to bring unwelcome messages to Batuk, he'd done it enough to discard the bliss a thousand positive messages could carry.

Batuk's voice remained strident, but the young man noticed the edges of his lips crack upward.

"Do you know why I work hard?" Batuk asked.

The young man knew well enough it was a rhetorical question.

He'd made the mistake of answering one of those with Batuk in his early days as a messenger. ("Early days" as in fifteen months ago.) It's a mistake one only makes once. Tongues don't display scars, but the sensory receptors in them have the greatest of memories.

Oof.

"I work hard to work smart because when you work smart long enough, you learn how to work fast. When you work fast, you can do more. And when you do more, you have more opportunities to work hard to work smart. That's why I've been able to achieve so much in sixty-five years. Be sure all who work beneath me know that."

The messenger nodded, departed, and in front of the closed door behind him, gave a gargantuan sigh. Batuk wasn't joking about his order to inform his entire army of servants.

He'd better get crawling.

⇒XXXVI⇐

The judges had their work cut out for them; they were faced with some of the most dainty delicacies of their already-delicious days.

One plate tasted like imagination; another brought them back through five lifetimes of reincarnation to experience the berries of history books. Another took their taste buds through a tortellini tango tantrum for two. And Wiley's bulgogi even made one judge say that she would never want to eat any other meat again, not even her husband's sausage (to the angry eyebrows of her husband in the audience—"there's nothing like a little tension to improve the TV ratings," she would argue to her husband later).

However, after trying Jim's insect-inspired dish, the dictyopterenes had her craving her husband's meat after all. Believe it or not, nearly a decade ago they started requiring all judges of the competition to masturbate no sooner than an hour before judging. This prevented the obvious bias of what they might have wanted to eat with their eyes, as well as any biases which might arise from food products that excrete pheromones.

There were, however, a few seaweed-derived pills that could refuel the tank of lust faster than an unfettered cosmic explosion filling the blackest of holes. For Jim's plate, he manifested the essence of Aphrodite, with Jackson Pollock's orgasms of orange, surrounded with Hooker Lips soaked in the waters of Banpo Bridge water and papaya juice. The plate was a masturbatory melody of tree and sea, a fine emergence of art.

Before Phil's interruption earlier, Jim had scooted through the cooking stations and fed Nora a spoonful for good measure; he might not be able to enjoy its effects, but he could enjoy the results of its effects on the finely cured flesh of Nora. Her smile split his heart in two, finely sizzled, and sealed back together. He may no longer be able to taste, but he could still feel. Thank Krishna for that.

There were sparkling stars in Jim's eyes, a refraction of hope coinciding with the lights from above. For a second he thought he tasted excitement as he saw the faces of the judges experience the dish he'd constructed with all he had in his heart and head, for their hearts and heads (and heads).

The air was soft in the convention, as if every audience member was holding their breath, conserving what remained in their tanks, living in the surreal space of deprived oxygen, uncertainty and relief that their cooking's the cooking that's being judged. Jim was clinging onto hope tighter than a cowboy running from the law. Maybe Phil's spice would fall flat, maybe the magic didn't work; how would Jim know? He'd never even tasted the spice.

It's incredible how many possibilities hope managed to place in Jim's mind. It scrolled through them like a slot machine; he was sitting on a prayer, standing on a dream, living on a lottery ticket that he'd strike big.

Alas. Dear reader, I must disappoint.

Phil's food hadn't even touched the tongues of the judges before Jim knew his fate was sealed. The mere radiation of magic revitalized the lips of the judges, mesmerized their eyes, made the hairs in their nose dance. The magic performed plastic surgery, Lasik, and a massage of the lips. Jim could sense it all. And the moment their mouths enveloped the forkful of Phil's food, it was like their mouth became the container in which the spice was gifted its luxury by Shaman Denny; it was as if he was performing magic right in their mouths. Taste buds titillated. What started off as a close-quarter combat of cooking now became a Ferrari driving down I-95 passing up roadkill. All the other competitors coughed from its fumes. Jim wanted to curl up and die. Compared to this, his dish was as good as carrion.

Have you ever wondered why movies never show what happens to the losers of a competition or a race or a bet? It's because it doesn't make for a good show. Misery may love company, but company sure doesn't love people watching their misery like a spectator sport.

The scenes would show a deflated dud of a walking radio, a catatonic coconut with legs. It would show a knight in dulled armor attempting to console himself. It would show the protagonist wading through their day, just as lame as an ocean wave far out at sea, meaningless so far from shore.

And Jim sure waded.

Waded through the sea of audience members fishing for Phil's autograph, the crowned king, the conqueror of the Golden Fork. Jim waded through the lie of what he thought was a remarkable dish. He even waded past Nora, leaving her behind in the crowd like she was leftovers. Disappointing us further. Just so you know, reader, Nora would have chased him had she seen Jim leave, but even her professionally observant eyes saw nothing with the storm of people raging out of their seats to the chefs' table for Phil. The room was like a football championship where the crowd storms the field. A rodeo. She had to play I, Spy. Jim was Waldo.

Waldo's wading took to waddling with disappointment. He was like a penguin riding a tandem bike. He found himself finally out of the waves of people and now stood outside, taking a breath of air and feeling undeserving of even that. He smelled a bit of cinnamon in the air. Nora.

Nora found a spot near Jim, silently, letting him feel the wake of emotion. A trail of umbrage boiling over his kettle, the last of the lemon being squeezed from his heart. Life had stomped him. Not like a bug, one step and done, but like a Beanie Baby on fire, repeatedly to douse the flame. You could say Nora was in just about as much shock. She'd accomplished a lot in her life. Unfeasible feats. But even her mastermind of a brain couldn't piece together how that bottle of spice had made its way from being "lost" a thousand miles away to "found," now empty, here and only moments ago. She'd thought Jim had this in the bag. She really did.

Jim hailed a cab and, bringing both his manners and the rest of his sorrow, let Nora in first. "Herough" was the only word he uttered on the car ride, to the cabbie. Jim watched the cityscape scrape by. They passed no shortage of city graffiti. As you know, Jim is a fan of street art, but the truth is that actual graffiti is a language Jim never learned to read. Like any art, it was an insider language. But graffiti isn't something you need to know how to read to know how to feel about it. The graffiti he saw resonated with his heart, ache, fading, and oppression. The noise of the city acerbated his eardrums. Jim's nose twitched at the halitosis of the cabbie. Nora could see Jim's distress hanging heavily in the air; she sought to slice it like a knife through an overripe avocado skin. From the moment Jim lost, she began searching her mental wardrobe for something she could slip on that might help her assuage some life into Jim. Nora had to reach deep into the wardrobe for the garment of empathy, which she had never worn. Aha! There it was in the deepest recess of her noggin. She put it on hastily (not quite doing the buttons up correctly) and set off to see what Jim thought of her now.

"Jim... You have to cheer up."

Oh, how threadbare that robe of empathy was. One should know the last thing you say to a sulking man is that of an order like a doctor's note. Nora tried to readjust her habiliment.

"You still have so much going for you. You made a wonderful dish; I'm sure their lips are still bellowing like a bull for more. And you have your other senses."

And in another volley to entice Jim back into the sky of positivity...

"And you have me."

Oh, sweet Nora. She had some learning to do when it came to empathy. The second worst thing you say to a downtrodden human are words that are meant to distract them from the harrowing reality they're looking into the eyes of.

Jim's blinders were on, honey.

Jim turned further away, nearly looking out the back window, icicles forming on his shoulder that even a yeti would struggle to climb.

Nora tilted the hat on her noodle; in the pocket of her mental robe she found a note her mother had left. Nora was overtaken with emotion, understanding, and forbearing. A soft-shell taco warmed her heart. The note expressed how her mother felt when her only daughter left. Through a little divination ritual, she'd left a mental note for Nora to find when she needed it most. It brought a tear to Nora's eyes, a light ripple of salty water caressing the beach of her eye lid.

Now. This. This looked good on her; emotive, exotic, like a mating call, but still she searched for one more utility to garner. A good pair of gloves to embrace those stalagmites hanging from Jim's ethos. She found them in her back pocket, put them on and readied herself to jump the plane into a pool of liquid understanding.

"Jim, I can feel how awful you feel. I'll never be able to understand what you're going through, but I feel it. I feel your bones ache and your brain working overtime to understand it yourself. I see you, and I want you to know I'm here for you. Here through the prickly thick of it, and I know there's nothing I can say to make things better and that you've gotta work through this maze of a situation in your mind yourself. I trust that you will; with all of my soul, I know that you will. Jim. Will you look at me? Jim... I'm still proud of you."

A pool of metaphorical water was seeping into the seats of the cab. The cold shoulder was melting. Jim angled back to face Nora. He didn't quite give her a smile, but she at least broke the seal of his somberness. His lips were set on the playing field of his face as his eyes rose to the height of Nora's.

"I appreciate you," Jim sang. Nora beamed love in return. She had it in her all along. They'd strategize a way to move forward, together. The baggage we all carry is only a burden until we decide to unzip it and use what's inside.

"You said vu vanted Herough, vight?" the cabbie asked with French hanging onto each word for dear life, somehow mixed with a tinge of surprise and a touch of concern.

"Yeah," Jim argued, bravely, through the moment and tension built in the back of the cab and between him and Nora.

"You might weesh to have a look. I don't think you weel be dining zere today."

Even before turning to look in front of them, Jim saw flashes of red, white, and blue reflecting in the eyes of Nora, and it wasn't another flag flying at half-mast.

Beyond the police and lights was something far brighter, a vortex of moonshine, what one sees when they look down Satan's throat. They could hear the sound of Satan going "ahhh" as the flames swelled the final remnants of the building. The alarm sounds Jim had heard through the cracked window were not just his head pounding. It was the ongoing buzz of a firetruck.

Jim's breath slowed to the pace of the saddest song you've ever heard. His soul flooded with melancholy. Depression tapped him on the shoulders and laid itself from one, across the neck and over the other, holding him like a blanket of death. Jim looked up and actually thought he saw a scythe in the clouds. He ached from his losses. His taste. Gone. The competition victories. Gone. And now his restaurant? Dust. Smoldering like Satan's shit. Gone. Gone. Gone.

Stuck in the backup on the street, the cabbie turned on the radio, flipped a few dials on the dashboard and found a news station covering the incident. They were interviewing the chief.

"Our crew acted as fast as possible," said the chief. "We tried to save what we could," he said. "We're working to figure out the culprit who set the fire and appreciate any tips those listening might have," he said.

Everything was ripped from a script he studied. In fact, he carried the script with him everywhere he went, along with a porcelain cross gifted by his grandmother, and a condom, of course. Damsels in distress, you know.

Not five minutes before the interview he'd pulled out his pocket-sized, black leather notebook and thumbed through its pages, passing dog ear after dog ear in an attempt to find the "restaurant on fire" header. In a dog's bark of time, he rememorized his lines and set out with a stern stance of confidence, an erected statue of class, a veil of calm as the media surrounded him like blood-sucking moths to a light full of juicy stories.

"Ah, such a tairrible zing to happen," the cabbie shared absentmindedly to his passengers, lowering the volume of the radio.

And a moment, a split hair of a second, an atom's tick before the tock of Jim breaking down like a rockslide of life's excrement, a minutia of a minute before Jim would decide his life was a drain pour, the cabbie shared one more thought to the air, and that thought surfed the waves of the musk, smoke, and halitosis into Jim's nasal passages and up to his brain.

"I bet he set it on fire for ze insurance money," serenaded the cabbie. "*Après la pluie, le beau temps*. After de rain, there's good wezzer."

Jim wasn't one for umbrellas, as we know, and a good thing, too. Had he been using an umbrella, he wouldn't have been able to feel the stickiness of the words, sense the acidity, and experience the citrus in each drop. If life gives you lemons, make it rain lemon juice.

⇒XXXVII⇐

The following is a letter imaginatively crafted by Lemon Fraser for Jim to find one day. In his mind, he'd somehow hire someone to hide it under a loose brick in the back of Herough in hopes Jim might find it. Alas. It's strictly imaginary. Purely made up. A lemon drop of illusion. Maybe.

Hey there Jimbean,

Not sure where to start here, but I guess apologies are in order. I hope by the time you're reading this that you've realized my good intentions. I'm sorry you had to go through a perilous experience.

Anyway, I hope the fire brought a ship in close enough for you to swim and meet it. I hope that the lady you were with on the dreaded tram is still with you and you didn't take the loss of the spice out on her. Fate worked its magic that day, and I needed to get out of the industry, out of the business, out of the Rolodex of all those who worked to use me for inside knowledge. Yes, even you, good buddy.

It's wonderful here; no six million ads racing through your receptacles daily, no bombardment of pompous phrases, no shackles of consumerism here. Pure lagom— everything in moderation.

I had best be getting back to my morning marg here. I hope you understand why I had to do what I had to do.

From your best man, beloved confidant, and propitious pyro.

p.s. Live your life in immersion.

⇒XXXVIII⇐

Jim didn't reveal his identity to the cabbie. He didn't face the onslaught of media wanting to speak to him. He definitely didn't return to the convention, where the news of his fire spread like the news of who kissed who in second grade. There was a goddess to see again, an insider more inside than Lemon, a queen he needed to revisit whom Jim knew would have something to say or so help me God.

"Cabbie. There's been a change of plans. Please take us to LaGuardia Airport," said Jim. His voice was ribbed with resolve, like two skeleton bones knocking heads, like an elephant's fart—there's no holding back once the motion has started. The resolve was caked with mustard, squeezed with icing. It had something hidden inside it. Curiosity sparked. Nora tried to find out what.

"Jim, what are we doing?" Nora asked hesitantly. Having years of practice and study of nonverbal displays, she knew that Jim's demeanor didn't quite match what she expected him to be showing at the sight of his burning restaurant. A bit of charred grouper whisked its way through the cab's air conditioning vent and the smell, perceived by passersby as an overloaded circuit mixed with boiled Band-Aids, should normally be making Jim wince with his fully steamed nasal factories. However, it seemed to only fill Jim up with drive rather than sorrow, confidence rather than uncertainty, jasmine tea rather than timidity. The cabbie was stepping on the gas, but it was Jim who had the wheel.

"It's time to retrace our steps and undo what has been done," Jim clarified. Each syllable was steeped in a pot of grit and gumption.

As one does in any scenario that impacts them, Nora thought about herself. She could tell Jim didn't care whether she joined him or not. She didn't let the arrow from Jim's quiver of a mouth pierce her heart, though. She was just aloof with gratitude that Jim wasn't suffocating from sorrow. In fact, this energy, this dignified aura, this translucent bear coat he wore, as if he'd just won her old tribe's hunting games—it sprinkled her garden moist and almond trees started to grow. She wished he would pluck them with his tongue.

The cabbie, pegging his two passengers as crazies—as there's no undoing what has been done in life, he reasoned—rather than culprits in the case of the fire that was fading in their rearview, stuffed his Bluetooth speaker in his ear further than a cotton swab until it was good and tight, tapped the button on it and with the sound of a Snapple bottle top, he was transported to a conversation miles away from the one taking place in his back seat. That was the one wherein Jim filled Nora in on his plans. The map to the future she was longing to hold. A familiar destination.

But like any good plan, it certainly wouldn't go according to itself.

Batuk wouldn't let it.

Jim knew in his heart of hearts, his hope of hopes, his inkling of tinklings that Queen Pinmekalah would still be right where he left her.

So after many intolerable airmile hours Jim once again found himself in the string of markets, with an overwhelming fish smell that reminded him of Herough and made a little sadness bubble up to the surface before it popped like a cork and set off to burden someone else.

There's nothing like reaching into your bag of willpower to keep the mind on course. This time, though, it felt familiar, and familiarity gives anyone an edge over whatever unfamiliar might try to wiggle its way into the scene. Not only did the sensory experience feel familiar (*sans* taste, of course), but he had in one hand his sack of willpower and in the other, Nora. It was in this space of familiarity that Nora finally felt like he wanted her there. If an anchor is what he needed her to be, she would be it. If the other half of the avocado of life is what he needed her to be, she would be that. And if a lover is what he needed her to be, she would be that. By God she would be that.

The unfamiliar in this familiar situation was the haze in the air, enough that it only let the sun illuminate a fair few feet of distance. It wasn't impure smog. It wasn't pure dust. It was a cloud of uncertainty. No problem for Jim; he let the familiar lay the tracks for his feet. He let the familiar sniff out the goat meat stand. He let the familiar follow the hanging lights that zigged, zagged, clinged, and clanged from one corner of a stand's tapestry to another. He let the familiar take him right to the spot where *she* sat. For a moment his feet wondered if they might even find the familiar shoes he left behind, and then they hoped the highest of hopes that they needn't leave another behind with this exchange. Laces crossed.

Upon arriving at the familiar, however, there was something lacking. Queen Pinmekalah was nowhere to be seen through the fog. It's not that she had picked up and left everything. Right?

There was something happening in Jim's head tank. A lower man would have defaulted to the worst-case scenario. *She left for good. She died. She'll never come back for me. She knew I was coming, and I was the last person she would want to help.* All thoughts were categorized in the default section of his brain's filing cabinet, but this time he kept that drawer (and it was a hefty one) closed. Behind it, he opened an envelope that read PATIENCE. And so he sat and encouraged Nora to do the same. For good measure, Jim took his shoes off and asked Nora to as well. He slid them both under the empty table in front of them.

Pinmekalah was close. Jim could sense it. And, here, his almighty senses hit it on the nose. You could measure the distance Pinmekalah stood from her shop: sixteen alligators; .000354 parsecs; 183 mangoes in a curved line, like a tilting staff. That staff that had soiled her in certainty that Jim would return, but let in a bit of apprehension if she would make it that long. So she hid and watched her stand from a distance. Though her ears may be growing weak, she could always hear the rumbles of rumors, though it strained her as much as skinning an alligator back with a dildo. The air carried consonants, vowels, and diphthongs in its currents. The Scrabble puzzle of dialect was deciphered in the Office of Deciphering. That lies just next to the amygdala. The code read:

Batuk knows of Nora's intentions. He's sending Croy.

Sealed with the wax of warning. Stamped with the ring of peach rings. And sent in haste. Pinmekalah wasn't one for getting into emotions over the years. Her immortality stems from her disciplined avoidance of them, like a mouse avoids a cat. And at the faintest meow of fate, she hid. But this time the squeal of destiny loomed like the smell of manure spread on a midwestern field, and it sang like fairies in a crop circle (crap circle?) before leaving their artwork without a trace. Pinmekalah actually felt something for Jim. She saw what the bottom of his shoes told. She'd heard through the grapevine about his success in acquiring the spice from Shaman Denny. She sensed his determination beating the drum, echoing like a swallow in a coal mine. Did she detect a trace of love, too? She thought she might have, though today was a more fragrant day than normal. The Jasmine traders were coming through. It was the one day a quarter that the stench of fish, other dead animals, and grease—oh God, so much grease—didn't just get pushed to the back seat, but to the trunk, entirely.

Three stories up, in a partially vacant, partially remodeled apartment complex which sat above a fish pedicure place, Pinmekalah wondered if there was a phylum Chordata in the world that would do the same to the soles of shoes as they do to the soles of human feet. Might they one day ruin her art of understanding a person by the bottoms of their shoes by exfoliating the rubber, stimulating the plastic flow and air circulation, removing the bacteria and foot odor? Might she nevermore smell what one has stepped in? She hoped that fish would forever fancy the phalanges of man and not the tarot pack of shoes the world has manifested. Rather than woe herself with the concerns of the distant future, the jasmine smell kept her tied to the chair of the present, loose enough for her to wiggle her nose but tight enough to not lose her focus on scouting for Jim.

When she spotted him, she experienced an involuntary contraction of her diaphragm, a hiccup that took her up out of the Le Corbusier-inspired seat beneath her. From there she began a series of signals that would maintain her safety and eventually lead to her connecting with Jim.

First, the curtain was pulled three inches wider, a match was lit and a half block away another match was lit, which signaled to the boy playing soccer in the street. Pinmekalah had wisely placed him there so that the net would be in the same line of sight as the window. Once the boy kicked the ball, hitting the post and hoping that his teammate would go get this one—he was tired of chasing the ball when not actually playing, it was the main drive for him to practice enough to be trusted with Pinmekalah's task—his eye saw what he was told would at some point glow this weekend. The boy ran opposite of the soccer ball and under a flowerpot, grabbing a dirty two-inch piece of paper that now smelled like the soil it had lain under.

Making a Cruyff turn, he went onward to Pinmekalah's stand and sought out the couple that had been described to him. A man with a beard the color of a #2 pencil that stretched its legs from a chiseled chin. He would be flushed. His determination would show in his straight back and wide shoulders, assertive but disciplined. With him, likely hand in hand, would be a five-foot-four-inch woman made of smokey quartz and carrying with her only a sturdy cloth tote with leather at its handles and bottom. The square neckline shirt she'd undoubtedly be wearing would show the few freckles that had found a home on her face and a family on her neck.

Though the description Pinmekalah gave the boy was thorough, it was still a complicated task to ask of the constantly wavering mind of an adolescent. Fortunately for the boy he needed only to connect two dots. The dot of the description that was given to him and the dot on which the couple stood, which happened to be a stand void of its merchant—and who would go about that for more than a few seconds, let alone someone sit in front of it?

The boy continued, step by step, fulfilling the Queen's request.

He bumped into the couple, a little more aggressively than he had wanted to. Alas. The excitement got to him. Catching his footing, he asked the gentleman if he might want to smell what he stepped in? And without waiting for the inevitable annoyed and curiously disgusted "no," he held his shoe up and put the note at the bottom of it.

"For you."

Had the boy not peeked at the note prior to placing it under the plant pot as told, we might otherwise not know what it read. Alas. A boy can always be trusted to read what one is told not to. On the note was a map and one line of text: "Meet me ASAP."

A.S.A.P. After Satan Alienates People? After Satan Arrives Peacefully? As Soon As Possible, when the moon is half-crescent? As Pinmekalah saw Jim and Nora read the note, Jim chuckled at the unique ways one might guess at an acronym like some mix-and-match wheel of fortune. After seeing a smirk of the wise, a smirk that wore its own beard, long and gray, a smirk than had read an encyclopedia two times through in its entirety, Pinmekalah climbed down the stairs, snuck out the tail of the fish feet therapy shop, and began her trek into the wild under the radar, a few clouds, and a god that might or might not be willing. Only in the wild did she feel safe to discuss what needed discussing.

The boy surprised Nora, although unto others, he merely looked like any other boy wanting to barter with a tourist over something they picked that another tourist had dropped at some point or another. Some of the richest Cambodians got their earnings by trading up items with tourists.

How easily convinced others are, especially Americans, that they can benefit another by taking and giving something else of equal or minutely more value. That tingle was a Patronus to doubt, a hydrant and hose to fear of failure, a perfume to the Brussels sprout smell of apprehension.

Jim heard an inner voice chanting of trust, and Jim acted on the sentiment.

Enlightened by Jim's own elated reaction, the boy also slid a red fabric bracelet upon Jim's wrist. One could have supposed that it was made of threads people had pulled out of clothing in frustration because it decreased their perceived aesthetic of the day, but to the boy, to Nora's cultural roots, the bracelet symbolized two statements.

First, as the boy put the bracelet on Jim's left hand, it would display to everyone in the world who might see it that the guy has transcended into the skies of love. Both taken and given.

Second, as the bracelet was red, it would ward off death and the *fin* which he, the ender of lives, the transporter to After, the slot machine of purgatory, wielded and, as such, the armorist of the armband would be safe in immortality's ring of red.

Nora was turning red, too; not as deep as the bracelet, but still rubicund like a strawberry balloon, about to pop like a pimple of embarrassment when the significance of the bracelet on Jim's left hand set in.

Not the immortality piece—that was part of a children's tale. But the love part, that was as real as her heartbeat.

Then she saw the glow that emanated from the arm, shoulder, neck, chest, and body of the wearer. Nora felt like someone had turned on a garden hose in her pants, sat upon dewy grass or spilled a martini, one part vermouth that's dryer than a cottonmouth and six parts gin harvested and distilled in Santa's workshop. She thought she might garnish it with a pair of olives and skewer. Stirred, not squeezed. Drink up, buttercup.

Jim asked the boy if he could help him navigate the directions. The boy shrugged and pointed to another shop with a leather canopy and even more bonded leather underneath. It was a pop-up bookstore; one might even call it a map store. Maps that make them mental masters of a sport. Maps that are designed for those seeking self-help. Maps about graffiti, salsa (the dance and the dish). Maps about immortality, Buddhism, and sun-worship dance.

Jim thanked the boy and pivoted his posture like a board game piece and life's grip moved him into the shop, wherein he asked for help reading the map he had in his hands.

The boy, having succeeded in the occupational checklist provided by Pinmekalah, returned to his soccer game with a smile as he contemplated what candy he'd buy with the money Queen P had promised him.

The merchant took hold of the map and observed it, as though he hadn't seen it before. But he had. He drew it in point of fact. His initials were right there on the backside corner. B.S.

Barry Salzor.

Poor initials for a map maker and author whose business is making maps and stories that people are meant to trust. Like many innovators, he made most of his business selling maps made by others, too. His personality might better fit that of a puzzle store. He continued acting like he was investigating the map, while actually wondering whether anyone had come up with a way to eat biscotti without crumbs air-striking one's entire lap, each almond piece exploding like an atomic bomb, each breadcrust like a Tomahawk, a chocolate chunk like a bundle of C4. He needed to make it appear like he had no knowledge of the map, lest someone come looking for what other treasures he knew the directions to, or worse, any one of Batuk's spies.

While his mind thought of the Italian delicacy, his tongue started to speak about something else. He gave Jim and Nora directions as if he'd practiced what to say, which he had, per Pinmekalah's request to ascertain accuracy of information. She gave him a snarl you couldn't shake a snake at when he shouted, "But I'm a map writer by trade!" But to Pinmekalah, even the most expertly trained person still needed reminders of even the most basic, expected, and assumed tasks. *Yes, map writer. That is why I give you the most reminders,* she thought, but instead she released that snarl.

The instructions the map maker, the bookseller, the— for lack of better term—biscotti nut case of a man were relatively brief.

Jim followed along just fine. Nora was bored. There was already an air of familiarity for her here. A game of search and, perhaps, destroy? You know what they say about old habits...

Jim and Nora followed the map-maker's instructions, both their subconsciouses being bold and thinking, *well this is a simple, straightforward, and short path.*

But as they would find out—just around the sandstone bend here—about this map and every map ever is that a map might show one thing, and reality another.

Their hike was a short one, but it was in a traffic jam of roots resisting downward growth, making U-turns, veering down a no-left-turn lane, and pitcher plants pouring their petals across the path like a baker's flour on bread dough.

It took twelve minutes to go two steps, hacking through the weeds with the machete the book merchant gave them. (The merchant rationalized selling weapons, but only ones with inscriptions on them. The shortest books written on metal. This particular machete had *afai e te le taumafai, ua e toilalo* etched on it, which the bookkeeper said was something like "if you don't try, you fail" in Samoan. It had been found in the sea by a treasure diver. And while the merchant did really want to share the story of how he acquired it, he stuck to what Pinmekalah had requested of him and tucked his tongue into bed without a bedtime story for his guests.)

On the path, a hippie rock decided to hitchhike its way (*sans* approval) in Nora's shoe. The itching pain of it reminded her of the amount of trailblazing she had had to do in her days. She huffed a bit at the thought of them already being in her past.

No longer her present, her MO, her life.

She fiercely shrugged the memories away on the tail of the huff and threw the hitcher with it before it ever reached its destination, freeloading between her toes.

Aside from the buzzing of the flies, there was another hum in the air, high up in the air. A single-engine, two-person needle-nose of a plane, a sliver in the sky. Jim in his hyperfocused state didn't notice it; he was too frustrated with the flies which were continuously landing on his skin. It felt like he was riding a bike shirtless in a hailstorm. Jim appreciated the incredible scent and hearing he had now. The heightened sense of touch, though, was something he was still getting used to. The map paper felt like sandpaper in his hands. His pant belt felt like a snake working to compress him into lunch. And those flies bombing his body from above! It was like a mosquito bite if the mosquito had a drill bit for a nose.

Again, Nora was reminded of missions she had performed in which she'd ridden in a plane such as the one she could hear and see in mere patches between the leaves of mango trees. Planes like that were great at three things.

Getting somewhere quick.

Getting somewhere small or otherwise uncharted.

And getting one's stomach muscles tested to see if they could contain all that the stomach had consumed recently.

Admittedly Nora had a great track record, but not a perfect one. Like her stomach had on a couple of trips, the path they were on performed a pirouette and finally spit them out upon a stretch of barren land, except for a few large kettles being dripped full of rice wine.

The kettles were surrounded by what was evidently a homemade confetti of pepper, cardamom, coriander grains, garlic, galangal, ginger, and star-anise—either that or an experiment to add a flavor to an otherwise flavorless alcohol. Though it looked like a mini distillery, the process is much more akin to the brewing of beer, converting starches into sugars and sugars into alcohol. Except that if one were to stick one's tongue under these drip, drip, drippings one would get to experience the shock of 20% ABV liquid pounding the palate like tennis-ball sized hail on a car roof made of styrofoam.

The brew master herself stood by the end of one of the pipes that gave way to the open air before skydiving its way into the basin of the pot, wherein Pinmekalah would add a combination of spices to flavor. She held a cap, upside down, to catch the wine drippings. Two caps were already filled and set on a beaten-down brown box which rested its weary boards on the hard soil, inches away from three much softer bases: floor pillows. (Or should that be ground pillows?) With the other hand, Queen Pinmekalah waved at the two visitors to her sake-soaked dojo, directing them to take a seat and make the box envious. The queen had a different energy about her at this meeting. On the face of it, it almost felt like she cared, which is an interesting evaluation for one to make given people are conditioned to either not notice when someone cares or to not appreciate it when they do.

It must have been the increased senses of Jim's that picked the fact up off the ground where it kept the box company, because Nora wasn't smelling what Pinmekalah was stepping in. It was Nora's natural guardedness and focus on threat assessment (boy, is it hard to rid a dog of old tricks) that prevented her from immediately sensing Pinmekalah's good intentions. (It's worth noting: Being able to perceive a lack of bad intentions is not the same thing as being able to perceive good ones.)

Nora was still wired to the default setting of people acting in such a way as to benefit themselves. She sent part of her head off to reset the wiring while the remainder focused on telling the rest of her body to do as Pinmekalah gestured, though with a drip, drip, drip of trepidation.

When the third cap was filled so the top of it looked as flat as people in the Middle Ages thought of Earth, she removed it from the drip, drip, drippings, brought it over to the sullen box and took a seat upon the third pillow.

Queen P gestured for them to drink the sake, as she proceeded to do, but not before saying "Chul Mouy" three times (one for each person around the table), the Cambodian way to cheers.

Jim took a swig, now fully aware of his ailment and tried to focus instead on the tingle he felt on his tongue, devoid of flavor. Nora hesitated at first, but down the gullet the rice wine went.

"Beauty lies in the eyes of the rice-wine holder," Pinmekalah burped. It was a curious sight to see and sound to hear. The elegant and constrained queen had become as loose as a yo-yo. She sat on the pillow lazily like the eighty-third busker on State Street, belched a couple more times (how long had she been here sipping the rice-wine before they got there?!), but somehow managed to radiate thoughtfulness from her pores. Jim could feel it. Jim felt everything but the turbulence the plane flying 5,000 feet above them was experiencing.

"You wouldn't believe me, but Oscar Wilde was a friend of mine back in the day."

Jim's steady enlightenment checked its watch and declared it time to take a rest. This made space in the vortex of time for the lizard brain to take command, trying to approach the present moment with hesitancy and deliberate concern (as all brain default settings do).

First up was this quirky, aged woman who looked like she'd been layered with cakes of clay. Jim's cerebrum dropped the "um" and quickly performed some grade-A mental math. If she were friends (with benefits?) with the wildest of Wildes? Well, that would make Miss Pinmekalah 119 years old or thereabouts. Certainly, that's impossible. The lizard brain was licking up all the doubt it could in the cone of Jim's head, all the worry and fear already dripped onto the ground floor of the cranium, enough to have made a puddle for Jim's consciousness to swim in. Waves of questioning why he was where he was, white capping with the thought of leaving for somewhere else, somewhere safe, somewhere familiar, somewhere that was anywhere but here.

But before the brain could send orders down to Jim's feet, Pinmekalah threw it off by feeding it more information, unrequested, mind you, about her more-than-acquaintance.

"Fingal O'Flahertie Wills was his middle name. You always know a friend from an enemy as one who you have told your middle name to. And you always know a best friend from a friend as one who remembers it. It was with him that I subscribed to the aestheticism movement, and it was he who introduced me to one of his secret lovers, an Irish shaman, turned friend, turned lover. (A lover being one who knows your middle name, remembers it *and* mentions it passionately during the throes of coitus.) Before Osc—he let me call him it, so I'll call him it now—*burrp*—and the Irishman—now that I'm trying to recall it, I never did get his middle name or his first for that matter, and to think I thought we were friends—*burrp*. Before Osc, I was merely a trader, barterer, keeper, purveyor of fine things, watches, wankers spec'd to King Midas'. But in meeting Osc, he taught me to look at food and ingredients like he looked at life, that being toward its beauty first rather than some moral, political, allegorical, doctrinal, theoretical, metaphorical, socio-economical, constitutional view.—*burrp*—"

Queen P, with the deft magic of skilled slight-of-hand, pulled three more caps full of rice wine from under the makeshift box table and prompted each to drink before she continued her story. This was no meeting for manners and she slammed hers back first.

Jim's jaw was on a tire swing, nearly sweeping the ground. His brain was trying to connect the dots and understand this woman. Alas. Pinmekalah's drunken words cast their net upon him and he didn't even try to wriggle, jiggle, or squiggle his way out. Even Nora shrugged her apprehension off her shoulders and let it fall to the ground, resting beside the tree holding the swing carrying Jim's jaw. Pinmekalah, at this point, was just revving her vocal engines, whacking the gong of her vocabularic chords, pinching the cheeks of her cerebrum. Or maybe that was just the rice wine talking.

"Life has to be lived intensely, and my findings show the best way to do that is through taste, though I had a pretty good argument with the Irish shaman about that. He said, 'Tis smell that be the blessing o' life. 'Tis the single sense that'll help recall ye memory the best, the sense that is the fastest for your brain to comprehend, the sense that led to the rise of the harshest dictators (they can smell ye fear, they can), and the most reputable peacekeepers—God didn't give Ghandi a big nose for no reason.'

"Ah, he went on and on about smell, so much so that he tried to give it credit for taste entirely. 'Ye can't taste well without it. Ye try to enjoy the flavors of barmbrack, the exploded raisins, fruits, and spices, the whiskey-soaked grain—ye try to enjoy that with your nose plugged, don't ya know.'

"Osc had to pull me away from shoving barmbrack up the Irish shaman's relaxed dining area. I know it's funny to

think of myself in that situation. You can withhold your—
burrp—expectations of me being a calm, cool, and collect-
ed woman. That was the only time I've ever gotten incensed
and I didn't shove anything anywhere, I merely left a plate
of barmbrack made with durian at his doorstep. That'll
show 'em.

"You see, the nose can be overloaded and shut down
one's entire nervous system, but taste? Oh, it has its thresh-
olds, but there's no harm done when taste exceeds them.
Bitterness? Ha. Anything more than 120 international bitterness units does nothing to us. We can't tell the difference between 120 and 420. And it's this core spectrum that
allows us to appreciate the vast differences in flavors of the
same. Consider chocolate for example. Oh, the range of
chocolate we can experience and we only appreciate the
range because of our limitations of flavor. There's beauty in
the constraints of chocolate and life is chocolate—*burrp*—"

There was no stopping Queen P. That is, of course, true
except for the moment in which she stood up and refilled
the caps with more rice wine while Jim and Nora processed.

At this point, both Nora and Jim were either in or they
were out. On the bus or off the bus. The two caps' worth
was already making Nora's aches dissipate and, as her
shoulders finally relaxed, her bra strap slipped down the
playground slide of her shoulder. Jim was grateful the magical transaction he'd made didn't take away the ability to
buzz, to tingle down his gullet, feeling like pop rocks on his
skin, fireworks in his blood, the quake of his spiritual tectonic plates sliding into the place they longed to be. Each
capful of wine they tipped back hit a little bit more than
the previous one. The caps made the beret of the Sahara
jealous of its dryness.

Pinmekalah sat back down and closed her eyes, but
continued to speak, though this time with a bit more astrin-
gency woven in her words.

"There's a reason the expression is 'so close you can

almost taste it' and there's a reason babies are born with the instinct to stick things in their mouth and not their nose. There's a reason the act of kissing traversed continent to continent and Eskimo kisses didn't last and why foreplay is better than one play."

That example resonated with Jim and Nora, certainly.

"That shaman was as sharp as a marble, he was, about the intricacies of taste. All that is to say, I must admit that he is the one you must visit if you wish to have your taste back."

Jim's neck nearly snapped in his return to reality, the tingles from the rice-wine just about completed their vanishing act from Jim's bloodstream.

"And..."

Now opening her eyes and lasering in on Nora's.

"Batuk knows. He knows you're heading to Kar Tresa's Crevice, he knows what you tried to do with the spice for yourself, he knows you've shaken your own magic eight ball to see your future."

Filled with paranoia and launched into immediate threat assessment mode by this news, Nora's neck swiveled so much that if it had been connected to a drill bit, she'd have found herself underground quicker than a crow caws at the sight of the moon playing peek-a-boo from behind a night cloud.

Jim didn't understand why the creases of Nora's skin under her eyes were valiantly trying to reform despite the soothing sensation of the rice wine, but he could feel the hair stand up on the back of her neck and her blood pressure rise.

The rice wine went to war with their bodies' fight-or-flight chemical concoctions, now brewing in earnest within them. A battle of two brutes. Throes of emotions.

Only one could win.

"Chul Mouy," Pinmekalah said three more times.

⇒XXXIX⇐

Pinmekalah and the Irish shaman, being both pals of Osc and, if truth be told, lovers (he, in secret and she as cover in an attempt to keep Oscar's homosexual affair a secret), they had been exposed to many a dialogue from Oscar.

As wise as Pinmekalah was, she couldn't grasp the idea that to shed oneself of an idea one must convince another of its truth.

Only then, in the throes of success, can one pivot; satisfied with the convincing and off in search of another big idea to shed.

While the Irishman would banter back and forth with Oscar, wildly shelling off idea after idea in between the tossing and tussling of flamboyish clothing, they would rest, enjoy a pipe at the sight of the ideas they would die to convince another of and the clothes on the floor. While one hand held a pipe, on the other hand Queen Pinmekalah had more questions than answers for Osc.

"What makes a big idea, big? Is it the status of the person who thinks it? Or the fascination a group may have about it? Does it depend on whether the journalists and media at large pick it up? Is it big when the critics write about it? Is it a big idea if you love it enough? Is it a big idea if it gets executed? What makes a big idea begs knowing what makes the world turn around, no? Or do we waste our time chasing and bantering about these big ideas as if they are fact, when we should be playing in the fiction of small ideas? Ideas that propel us forward, nonetheless, despite their miniature form...?

"...What about those ideas that don't need an army to execute? Maybe the world doesn't turn for every big idea, but rather leans ever so slightly with the small ideas, a subtle head tilt in agreement. And another and another. Until it's mad with motion and has made its salute to the multiverse and then, like an army junky, a child on a swing, a milking of a cow 'job's not done' 'one more time' 'is that all you got?'—momentum builds. And ever so slightly it turns, small idea after small idea. No need to wait for big ideas. Planets die standing still."

And Osc's response?

"There's a German sourdough guy who starts every one of his interviews by saying 'gluten tag.'"

Leave it to Osc to make one woman feel like one fourth of two pieces of catfish bait. She decreed that it would be easier to build an imaginary castle than chafe prose with the Grey Crow.

Alas. The Irishman soon took off, though it wasn't before he and Oscar had their exercise of homo-eroticism caught by the news media when a reporter climbed through a window to get a scoop on the rising fame of Oscar Wilde and quite a scoop he got. A snow cone drizzled with ecstasy, an ice cream flavored like a freshly pampered penny collection, a double-stacked gelato. Oscar, unphased, was reported by the journalist to have said "Es its Platz für drei"—there's room for three—once the reporter was inside. The article failed to mention, to wit, whether the journalist obliged or not. As is the case with any form of journalism, there's three sides to the story. The subject's, in this case Oscar; the author's, in this case the journalist's; and the truth.

Oscar ran off to who knows where. The Irish shaman headed to the Far East. Pinmekalah left London for Greece, affixed on learning why its culture had such a presence in Oscar's oeuvre, being that everything in life is beautiful and by comparison everything that is beautiful is good and when something is recognized as good, then one can truly say they are living. Time is a gift in Greece. It's why they call it the present. (Well, English visitors to Greece say that anyway. The pun doesn't work in Greek.)

In Greece she developed an affinity for the trades, the present of presents. She bought, sold, and bartered fruits, vegetables, and oils. Promoting herself, to even finer things. A dumb word, *things*, but the one that best describes the breadth and depth of her dabblings. She soon sought items in higher demand and lower supply, flavors that could be more controlled, in fact. She made homage to Cambodia, one of the largest exports of timber (there's nothing better than a steak smoked over a four-by-four), rice, fish (all varieties including those swimming, flying, and snorting salt), tobacco (both cured whole leaf and chopped leaves), and, of course, footwear. Though it wasn't just what got exported from Cambodia that provided a thrill of Asian sensations, it was all that made its way in and out of the country. Collectibles from Greece, crafts from America, and so on. Even more important than those handhelds were all the ingredients that passed through. Pinmekalah had a market already in her heart. It's said that her left ventricle echoed "same same, but different" when the aorta asked how much for a bit of blood. Wherever she walked, she walked on a magic carpet. Her mental space was simply a series of tents, poles, jerry-rigged infrastructures, banners, boxes, thickly threaded strings, clamps, and cooking equipment to sauté those great ideas of what to buy next, trade next, barter next, and, despite her good predisposition, steal next.

"The greatest artists steal," Oscar told her.

She bought his words and, had he asked her for twice the amount she paid, she would have taken out a loan for it quicker than she told the Irishman to put his pants back on whenever they heard a knock at the door.

It truly was happenstance that Queen P landed herself nearby the Irishman in Southeast Asia after her tenure in Greece. Coordinates pinning him somewhere between Ban Natouk-Louk and Ban Kang where he found with the Buddhists the enlightenment he never quite reached with Oscar. Well, that's not entirely true. He didn't necessarily find it in the concept so much as acquired it in his hand with his fingers like cigars, right down to the color. It was one of those sensations of knowing something is there even if one doesn't see it. It's the giddiness in a child's imagination on December's pagan holiday, the dog that knows a treat is in your hand, just not which, the feeling of knowing you'll get the job, but haven't received the offer letter yet. He did struggle with the fact that his new commitment forced him to unsubscribe from the weekly deliveries of *The Buzz*, published by none other than Bourdeaux Inc. It was his favorite digest, superior to *Cabernet Corp* and the *Merlot Daily*. But that's the slice of cake you've gotta serve yourself, but not eat when you seek to succumb to enlightenment quickly and in its entirety rather than the recklessly elongated way many others go about it. The Irishman detested the idea of waiting for his deathbed to reach enlightenment, so he absorbed from the handier of the two.

The Buddhist group he journeyed with happened to make one of the absolute rarest and finest of hot sauces.

The Buddhists had in their quaint library—if you can call it that, as it contained but one book—a mystical text presented long ago by the authors themselves, the Sun King and the Monkey King. The two gifted the book to a young Buddhist on the Mekong River, along with a map to find the caves that they now dwell in. The book's contents were scarce but scathing with a Scovillic script detailing a recipe for the Sun Monk Sauce. This sauce smelled of a swirl of Satan's sweat and fire lilies; merely taking the stopper off would fill the room with habanero and the gang who would play a tune nonstop, so filled with gusto that it had taste buds from miles away dancing like the floor was a layer of hot coals freshly delivered from the third circle of hell. Glutinous. Bituminous. Ready to explode upon contact. Its heat put ice water to shame, limeade to rest, and milk, well, not even chocolate milk could muffle the pops of the pepper's placenta, the piping of the capsaicin glands, the vibrating apex of its heat. But the flavor, by God, the flavor. If one could pay attention to the man behind the curtain of fire, one would find that their taste buds had been shocked back into life, once again playing bumper cars with one another, hungry hungry hippos with the liquid, and finding nirvana in the heated springs of the hot sauce.

When the Irishman heard that Pinmekalah had moved her bazaar headquarters just a spitting distance away (albeit a treacherous distance, a shortcut to death for many, a hop, skip, and trip for most), he passed word along about setting up a trade. Sauces and spices of his Buddhist colonies—if you could call them that, given they were composed of so few bodies. The trade included the infamous Sun Monk Sauce, for access to an array of vegetables that, unlike many of those the Buddhists grew themselves for their own nourishment, wouldn't otherwise spoil the flavor impact of their array of hot sauces (outside that of the Sun Monk's).

Pinmekalah agreed under the condition that he share the ingredients that he longed for as well as the list of what went into the Sun Monk sauce on that list. He obliged and wrote, "Mango Juice, Water, Onion, Wasabi, Thai Peppers, Garlic, Peanut Butter, More Garlic." Of course, he omitted a key ingredient from the list.

"Truer artists allow others to steal from them, but not their entirety, their soul. To be stolen from is not only a compliment, but one's way to make the world more beautiful. Certainly the one stealing needed it more than you. Certainly the one stealing it will find a way to make it their own. Certainly, well, if you're lucky, the one stealing it will make it better than you and in turn raise the bar for you, and so the world becomes more and more beautiful by the hand of stealing artists," Oscar told him.

He bought Oscar's words; had Oscar asked for thrice the amount he paid, he would have taken out a loan quicker than Oscar put on *his* pants at the sound of the knock at a door.

Through the back-and-forths, the Irishman and Pinmekalah came to learn even more about one another; not in the

sense of becoming friends. No. The Irishman saw Pinmekalah as a challenge, a reason for him to practice his Buddhist
ways of trust and release and meditation. She made him exercise his breathing more than any mantra in the temple.
He saw meditation as a muscle that if he focused on, within
the parameters of the temple as well as out, would help him
grasp enlightenment more quickly than the others who remained in the caves with their solo mantras.

And she? She sent along vials; little perfume bottles
filled with rice wine to tempt him back into the intoxicating
ways he had loved with Oscar. Rather than sign any letter
with his name, he always wrote the same reply. "Next time,
skip the rice." She thought she had him irritated.

Before the trades could commence in earnest, they
would have to create a trade path. Flying was not only too
costly, but anytime flights are involved, it's merely a path inviting tourists. Not to mention the way the mountains were
like a pair of jagged teeth made of chainsaws that sought to
cut down anything that came into a one hundred foot cord
length to them. They could only ship whatever could be
crammed into a little bottle, and the unreliable post could
take anywhere from weeks to "we lost it, try again."

Consequently in setting up their trade agreement,
they, and they alone, crafted a secret passage through the
wildness of green and greige, a combination of tunnel,
trail and wading through knee-high (to the Irishman) and
waist-high (to Pinmekalah) streams. It was laborious work,
drudgery—one of the few times Pinmekalah ever got her
hands truly dirty, and while the Irishman could work on
his half between meditations, his two meals (doused in four
meals worth of hot sauce each, naturally), head shaving (his
own and others in the group), and rest (bedtime was seven
p.m.), wherein he'd dream of wine and Oscar and doors being knocked, Pinmekalah had to work incognito and as her
schedule allowed.

Nonetheless, her network had steadily grown across countries, and she had become responsible for bartering, selling, and exchanging something more precious than physical cargo and something far cheaper to ship: information.

Information about ingredients, information about restaurants, information about gastric philanthropists, foodie influencers, entrepreneurs of cuisine. She realized that it was in her best interest to be a purveyor of information, because she could then use that to influence her sales of actual goods, seafood, for example.

Say a shipment of crayfish was coming into port and would go to waste if not sold within two days. She might send a word to the east coast of America that Galway was going to buy out all the crayfish, and just like that, she popped the cork of the buyers in Boston. By daylight she had too many eyes on her, too many searching for her, too many taking fifteen-hour flights to walk the market where she resided and do business face-to-face. So it was by the light of the moon, the ocean's source of energy, the wolf's twinkle of an eye, the pile of dandruff in the sky, the tinted mirror of the sun that Pinmekalah turned the trek to their halfway point into a salad.

She chopped trees like celery, sliced rocks like they were tomatoes, she carved and tossed all the radishes of the soil to the side, and, intuitively, she pocketed all the rice paddies along the way.

Three months of fracking by hand came and went like the fireflies of summer. The moon was tired of being an accomplice to Pinmekalah's necessities and her irises tired of working double time that of her hands. Little did Pinmekalah know that her half was the tougher half. The Irishman's took only a week, thanks to the already cavernous mountainside, his strong build despite his slender Buddhist ascetic, and that of soft rock, cushioned minerals, sulky sediment.

Pinmekalah, in no particular order, had been stung by a scorpion, had to behead fifteen snakes—allowing only one other to get away when a cloud helped the moon turn a blind eye—squashed thirty-six centipedes, rubbed fifteen gallons of premium calamine lotion on her mosquito bites, danced with a dozen monkeys, was scared into a solid piece of marble by the sound of a leopard's baritone "meow"— and not that cute, playful kind—formed, popped, and re-formed eleven blisters on her hands and six on her feet and one pesky rash on her calf that wouldn't go away no matter the ointment she used. No wonder she was a sucker for rice wine.

Over the span of time that she hustled to and fro while dredging her path, those who returned to visit her shop in person for a second, third or fourth time noticed a weariness eating at her skin.

She wrote about it to the Irishman, not exactly complaining per se, but communicating a hope that he might, perhaps, assist with her half. Instead, he sent her a kohlrabi hot sauce and instructed her to consume two ounces per day. She did so, albeit with an ABC extra stout in a glass with ice. Her skin started to smooth itself out and wrap around her cheek bones like a fitted sheet, her blisters ceased their boomeranging, the rash on her calf received its eviction notice and followed suit for fear of the ramifications.

"What is in this stuff?" she wrote.

Swollen, nearly spherical shape, kohlrabi in its entirety, stem, leaves and all, lemon, salt, apple cider vinegar, and both white and black kampot peppers that give it wine-like flavor and acidity.

Pinmekalah had dealt with her fair share of kampot pepper trades, being as rare as they are, but she had no clue how advantageous they could be to her health until now. Just as before, however, the Irishman omitted a key ingredient.

Reinvigorated with energy, Pinmekalah finished the thoroughfare in a matter of a fortnight after dipping into the hot sauce and beer but once a day at the end of it and feeling no fatigue the next morning when she put back on her hat of merchant, of trader of foodstuff and nonfood stuff alike. The range of her wares could take you from Sydney to Seattle and back a half dozen times; you could mix a bowl of alphabet soup and it would spell something she bartered, like a magician but with no magic required. If anyone requested it, she could pull it out of a hat within twenty-four hours—the Pinmekalah Promise.

Upon completion of their path, they decided they would meet on the last day of spring, full moon and all. Alas, the thickest of the weeds stretched their legs as far as they could that time of year, which required a bit of extra work to meet.

Overwhelmed by the amount of logistics that had been backlogged in her pursuit of the path, she worked tirelessly day and night. I truly do mean tirelessly, as she continued to season her pork and rice with the magic sauce he'd gifted to her. Pinmekalah was peculiar about the meals she ate, despite having access to every ingredient under the sun and the moon. She had an affinity for iced beer and rice wine and she stuck to a series of basics. Had you asked her, routine was the reason for her longevity, but we'll get more to that later.

When the day came for Pinmekalah to make the journey to the Irishman, she wished she had taken better care of her machete, because the long-neglected blade gave up and cracked in two after facing the stubborn vegetation. The plants were vigorously reclaiming the territory they'd once held. Though she managed to carry forward on the path she knew all too well at this point, she noted their recidivism for next time, dog-eared the reminder in the pocket of her brain. If anything, at least the regrowth would quickly cover up the trail and prevent vagabonds from following it or anyone else who inevitably would seek the hot sauces directly from the Buddhists.

The meeting went well, weller than either anticipated. It's a remarkable thing, the relationship that can be built between two people using only letterhead, pencil dust, and a roll of stamps.

It went so well, in fact, that Pinmekalah subsequently made frequent trips to meditate beside the Irishman. The meetings were lifted with conversation before and after meditation. In one weekend—a holiday from her trading which gave her the time to step away for longer than usual— she learned that there was actually magic in the hot sauce she had been consuming and that there was more where that came from. A handful of years passed this way: regular meditations, continuous trades, consistent hot sauce consumption, until one day a wandering shaman stumbled upon the path that Pinmekalah had recently given a trim. It was a shaman in training. Denny was his name. Big D, according to Pinmekalah (who had an immediate attraction to him, though that might have been the cannabis-infused hot sauce talking).

It was Denny who became the courier for the two over the years. He trained with the Irishman during the week and assisted Pinmekalah during the weekends, when the regulars, the tourists, and those who heard rumblings of the Sun Monk Sauce she sold only to those who asked for it in person, showed up. Not without displaying the soles of their boots, naturally.

Denny proved to be from another world with how quickly he picked up the hot sauce making, the marketing of goods, and the magic of it all. The Irishman even wondered if Denny had reached enlightenment before him. There was a little resentment there, but he graciously continued showing Denny all he knew of spice and life. Denny made up his own little hut on the west side of the mountains for quite some time until he decided to transport himself to areas that needed his magic; light touches of generosity he could make without ever being caught on to. He carried the magic with him to, say, a spoiled well, for example. By the time Denny realized that he needed to ditch the hut he'd called home for years, the Irishman felt he had reached as much enlightenment as he could with The Buddhists himself. So Denny made his way east, and the Irishman went west.

In a final letter to Pinmekalah, he shared, regrettably, that he would not be sending her any more Sun Monk Sauce, maintaining his half of the trade path, or writing her again; that he sought to find (later he'd learn it would be to create, or manipulate, rather, not just find) a new form of enlightenment, a new experience elsewhere in the world. He'd skate his path and ride the mountains like a half pipe to perform a one-eighty. The grasshopper had become the master, and the master was hanging up his figurative hat. The Irishman, in a quiply end to the note, shared with Pinmekalah that if she ever needed to find him for anything that she need only to follow her nose. What an ass.

As years went by and Pinmekalah carried on with her trade business—*sans* Sun Monk Sauce—she never did hear from the Irishman. But word travels faster than any tangible good does, and so she had heard rumors and epics about an ex-monk in the western hills. There were mentions of Kar Tresa's Crevice. A name familiar to her because it was a name on a map made by one map maker merchant with whom Queen P was friends with. One not far from the stand she sits at now.

ꙮ **XL** ꙮ

"Batuk, Lord, I bring both unfortunate and fortunate news. Does your excellence have a preference on which to hear first?"

"Croy, they don't stick the cherry on the bottom of the cake, now do they? On with the unfortunate news and we'll see if the cherry is sweet enough to discard it, like I'll do with you if you continue to disrupt my siestas. I am getting old, as one always does, but as you know, Croy, as life gets longer, my patience gets shorter."

Croy knew it well enough. Over the last twenty years of serving Batuk, Batuk had been increasingly quicker to chastise, faster to punish, swifter to discipline—not always with brute force, but carnal contention of his tongue, too. Croy knew, too, that to maintain his leader's respect for him, he couldn't quiver long and so he pressed on.

"Nora isn't coming back and the spice is gone."

It's a foolish leader that trusts a single person to execute his will without accountability, without any observation, without any contingencies in play. Batuk had never been that person until this instance with Nora. She had earned his trust. Batuk wisely assumed Nora would want to retire once she completed his request, too, and he would have let her, given all she had done for him and his empire. But this was a defiance of his will and sabotage of his soul, and it showed on Batuk's face.

While Croy avoided looking at it, for fear of the jawline cutting into his own soul, he pressed on, in hopes the good news might soften the scraggly daggers that the lines formed at the edges of Batuk's grimace.

"But she is on her way to Kar Tresa's Crevice. That's at the crease of Cambodia and Thailand, where the disciples of Vishnu reside. Lofty folk they are."

Croy should have stopped one sentence sooner. Batuk despised it when he was told information he already knew. His grimace grew, and Croy scrambled to recover.

"As my wise Lord already knows, of course. If you wish for her to not make it out of there..."

Croy raised his eyebrows to the sky. Long had he hoped for a chance to knock Nora down a step on the band's organizational totem pole.

While both devotees of Batuk, Nora had always been the first Batuk turned to. Trust was as green as gold to Croy and each request from Batuk that went to Nora rather than him was a kick to his ego and a notch on his mental wall of resentment. It was beginning to look like a prisoner's cell for a lifer. Today he would be released, or at least he hoped.

"Are you implying that I'd wish you to lower the population count of our best?"

Croy's tongue rolled up and choked his voice box long enough for Batuk to fill the void.

"The world's too busy anyway, too filled. The very amount of people is cutting into every industry I lead. A sliver here, a sliver there. And what happens as a result? Price increases. Taxes. Higher pay for poorer help. The mortality rate has been too low for far too long and the fertility rate, too high. To think that people continue to procreate when the entire world is shouting at them to stop. Shortages. Wars. I long for the days of simplicity, Croy. To answer your question plainly, yes. But I want her alive. Far too long I've left the most meaningful work to be done by others. Her life will be taken by my own hand. That'll be my real retirement gift."

Batuk could see the lust in Croy's eyes mixed with the disappointment of his lord's conditional request. In leaderlike fashion, Batuk relit the flame of cavalier's fire in his captain. His saw-tooth smirk bent upward as Croy now made eye contact.

"That's not to say she needs to be in good shape when she returns, though. Now off with you."

⇒XLI⇐

Pinmekalah had dished out more rice wine to combat the terror flooding Nora's body and the worry that began to unfold on Jim's brow in sensing the agitation Nora vainly attempted to resist.

There was a tidal wave of emotions that the rice wine simply couldn't keep up with.

Recognizing that the rice wine had met its match, Queen P shuffled through another trunk, pushing aside rice wine supplies, and pulled out a pen. She took the map that Jim had in his hand, spread it out on the ground in front of them and circled the name "Kar Tresa's Crevice." Though the pen tip touched the paper, no ink displayed on the page, though Jim, with his expanded senses, could see a hint of gloss, outlining the pen mark.

"This is where you need to go."

"Did you mean to circle the space?" asked Nora.

Pinmekalah took the paper and held it up to the sun, whose rays illuminated the invisible marks from behind.

"A map with a visible X marking the spot is a reckless request to have the map lost, found in the wrong hands, or fought for. Any X or O on a map, one assumes there is treasure or something of value worth pursuing. Be it true in this case, there's no need to take any risks. No hugs and kisses. This is luminescent ink, only visible when held up directly to the sun. You must hide the light to see the light. Such is life—*burrrp*"

Pinmekalah filled them in about the other shaman that might be able to help Jim and maybe even Nora. She admitted it had been years since she'd talked with him, but if there was anyone more powerful than Shaman Denny, it would be an Irishman that they could find near Kar Tresa's Crevice. Of course, she couldn't tell them directly where they could find the Irishman—she could only give them the same directions the Irishman had given her in the letter.

"The circle isn't exact anyway. Once you're there, you'll have to follow your nose."

This time, as she said it, a mental light bulb went off, a switch flicked in her head, a spark ignited a little epiphany.

She had thought the vague direction insensitively cryptic, but with Jim's advanced sense of smell, she was sure that they would find their way.

The only inkling of doubt she had was that the Irishman had never told her what odor to explore, what scent to search for, what perfume to pursue. Jim, of course, asked for clarification. So as not to not dissuade or disappoint the couple, she took a best guess of what they needed to sniff out.

"The Irishman has handled Sun Monk's Sauce so extensively over the years that it's practically soaked into his skin, maybe even his soul. I have a small, intricately carved bottle of this elusive elixir stashed away in a worn, wicker basket lined with faded velvet. *Burp.* That was a lot of words. This tiny treasure might just help you trace his path."

Now Pinmekalah looked right at Jim, a deep sobering connection digging into him with her eyes.

"If you succeed, be sure to put this sauce on a fish taco with a beer to chase it. In the words of someone wiser than me, 'Never underestimate how much assistance, how much satisfaction, how much comfort, how much soul and transcendence there might be in a well-made taco and a cold bottle of beer.'" I'd only add that it's missing a touch of hot sauce.

⇒XLII⇐

Nora and Jim were flown by a friend of Pinmekahal's to a strip south of Kar Tresa's Crevice—the closest place they could get, land, and pack before their incredibly short trip. They gazed up at the rock formation in the distance ahead. Its features were like a coffee filter, the bulges with roasted colorings making each boulder look like an emoji with cool glasses, like a repetitive lineup of Daft Punk front row fans, like salt crystals under a microscope.

"Are you ready for this?" Jim asked.

Nora snorted. "Am I?! Jim, I was bred for this, trained for this; this doesn't even look like it will be in the top five most difficult treks I've made. And in an area as desolate as this, at least there's no stealth needed, no clan trying to murder us, no community to trailblaze through."

Jim was a bit taken aback at the thought of what she'd done in her life.

Nora was, too. The memories were rich in her brain, their blood still had a pulse, and the exchanges, we'll call them, though in the past, were fueling her adrenaline now as she thought of them. It was a past version of herself and she knew it, but it seems they've found and nestled in a pocket of her present brain, nagging at the possibility that she may still be that same person.

Good ol' empathetic Jim, though, could see the tug-o-war happening, and took a shot at bringing her back to the moment.

"You know why they call right now the present?"

"Why?"

"Because it's a gift."

Nora smiled. That's all it took; a little cuteness, cheesiness, and heartfelt honesty from Jim to settle her nerves.

"You have a heart of gold, Jim."

Jim gave her a humble *herough herough* of a laugh as he grabbed her hand.

"Let's move forward. What's behind is behind."

The mountain sort of poured and fizzled down to where the couple stood, but its mouth gaped open for them. Nora and Jim thought they would mostly be climbing, but it turns out the mountains contained a labyrinth of caves. They figured the cave would take them to some hidden sanctuary, some carved-out dojo, and then they hit their thumb with the hammer of expectations rather than the nail on its head. The tunnel itself was dark and in the black they could both feel a steady decline, the way their weight placed itself more on their toes than their heels. The mountain seemed to know how to build momentum as well as the hypocrisy of the thought that the adage "it's all uphill from here," which can mean either ease or difficulty, steadiness or dizziness.

Though Jim couldn't see much (even heightened sensory muscles couldn't grant the gift of complete night vision, not the way the walls of the cave devoured every trace of light like a famished black hole, desperate to sustain itself after dragging all the stars within reach into its maw).

On the other hand, his nose, by God, his nose smelled really good diner coffee (an oxymoron, I know), the equilibrium of a roast and the croissant to go with it. He could smell the crust of the jagged protrusions of the walls, the crumbs of the naturally graveled floor. It was Earth's own bakery, and Jim was loving it so much so that it took Nora accidentally walking into him to realize he had simply stopped moving forward to appreciate the smell of the rubble, Earth's breakfast.

In the midst of the scents of earth and life, Jim followed the scent of the hot sauce, an enchanting bouquet that captivates the senses. The initial aroma was a sweet and tangy burst of ripe mango juice, blending harmoniously with the crisp, refreshing scent of mineralized water and the sharp, savory essence of onion. As Jim dove deeper, the pungent punch of wasabi tickled his nose, followed by the fiery, vibrant notes of Thai peppers. Layers of garlic added a robust, earthy depth, enriched by the subtle, nutty warmth of peanut butter. Amidst these vivid aromas, there was also a hint of something ethereal and magical, as if the essence of mystery itself was woven into the aroma in the air.

As they walked farther through the cave, the smell became watered-down and a light began to glow ahead. It was as if Earth's pastry case was growing stale. Certainly, the first cave they pursued couldn't be the right one to get them where they needed to go.

Alas, it was... and it wasn't.

For one, they were still at the bottom of the mountain. Though the view was rather different. In front of them stood a hut. Bamboo growing in the little acre of topsy-turvy land beside it. A stream pouring nearby with a tree branch hanging over it, leaves leaning into the water as if trying to take a sip; the water making its own tea from the leaning leaves. It was a mutual relationship. Nature in its most natural state.

A mere twenty paces away from the stream, and two paces from them, stood a bamboo hut. Not one to knock in the first place, Nora slid the door open to find the hut contained only a few items worth noting: recently used candles, a teapot over a presently extinguished fire, and a curtain that separated the hut into two spaces—one for living and one for meditating, made obvious by the Buddhist pillow beside the candles. Putting three and three together, they determined this was the hut once used by the Irishman and Shaman Denny on past trips. With a twinkle of Jim's nose, he could confirm the smell to be like that which he recalled smelling on the night he sacrificed his taste for the spice. Though there was a little more heat in the air, something Jim felt rather than smelled. Might it be the remnants of the Sun Monk Sauce?

Jim took the bottle of sauce out of the bag Nora had slung around her shoulder, decanted it, closed his eyes and took a deep breath. There were similarities and it became apparent that the smell wasn't just of Denny, but clearly of the Irishman, too. There was a distinctly Buddhist flair to the aroma.

"I've got a scent," Jim said, secretly even more impressed with his newfound animalistic capabilities. He scratched his ear.

Nora was intrigued by this new bode of confidence in Jim. She became turned on in a new way. She'd fallen for his spirit and softness upon their first meeting, but this hunter-like fixation and aura sent signals of dominance and determination she had only seen glimpses of in Jim before something had swiped them away. It was as if his confidence wore a suit jacket of its own now, and a rather sharp one at that.

Nora closed the door to the hut and before Jim could ask what she was doing, her lips were glued to his while her dragon tongue explored a different hut: Jim's mouth. Jim let it search while his hands explored Nora's body as if truly feeling it for the first time. Every crevice, every scar, and then his hands found the muscular hills of her stomach. With Nora's tongue slowing down, dragon tamed and tired, Jim pulled free and began to kiss her neck, making it impossible for her to maintain a steady breathing rate, let alone heart rate. His lips traversed her body on their way down to the hard-earned ridges and valleys of her abs as she removed her tank top and haphazardly removed Jim's shirt, knowing that any time she spent on taking it off was time he would stop kissing his way to her thighs.

Like the leaves and stream outside, both Jim and Nora nourished one another. They found a rhythm that matched a bamboo stalk thud-thud-thudding on the outside of the hut's exterior. The heat they made in the hut warmed the tea kettle until it sang in sync with Nora's bleats of ecstasy.

Jim, finally feeling satisfied with Nora's satisfaction, lifted her off his lap like a kettle from the burner. As they inefficiently picked up their clothes from around the hut like an arcade claw machine, they dressed once more, but included translucent hats of determination for a solution to each of their problems. Nora grabbed the Sun Monk Sauce, opened it again, and held it toward Jim's nose.

"Let's find them," Nora urged him.

≫XLIII≪

Within hours of the assignment from Batuk, Croy was on a plane that sounded like a dog fight, a garbage disposal stuffed with cinder blocks, a broken cuckoo clock—heck, a broken turkey gobble for that matter.

In short, it wasn't the lavish, luxurious, lofty air care he was used to flying with Batuk.

Alas. Any plane of a civilized size would be too large to land on either of the two runways available near-ish to the crevice. It didn't help Croy's nerves that the pilot was a spuddle of a man. Croy wanted to ask to see his pilot's license, but between knowing better and trying not to spew up his lunch of olives, crickets, duck eggs, rice, pickled onions, lamb chops, and a great deal of red wine, he lowered the garage door of his teeth and locked his lips in place.

The plane bobbed like blueberries in a beer. It was late evening, and the moon and sun just touched gloves to battle it out.

Within minutes, the moon rose victoriously, as the moon always does.

Croy wasn't one to find beauty in much aside from the few shades of green Batuk shared with him, but even he, the one whose eyes were primarily hued with greed, lightened a bit at the way the moonlight cascaded over the rock walls, valleys, moraceae, and cassava.

It was a part of the land he had never traveled, never seen photos of, and barely even heard stories about. As much of a leader Batuk was, he also wasn't a leader who would have given Croy some direction, a map, or at least a modicum of information.

Batuk trusted his tracking instincts.

In truth, even had Batuk given Croy some form of map, Croy probably wouldn't have used it. He was exceptional at sniffing out spies, finding the right pawns for Batuk to leverage, and apprehending his enemies. He was the kind of fella that plays the game to play the game, not necessarily to win quickly. Though, win he always did. To date he had captured three CEOs, four CFOs, two escapees, twelve conniving debt holders (five of whom paid off their debt with their lives) and has done the bidding of seeking out not thirty-four, not thirty-five, but thirty-six men who were named on "wanted dead" posters. (After all, it mattered to Batuk to keep close to his roots.) It was Croy who kept the irons stoked in the fire while Nora was on her lengthy adventures. It was Croy who wet his hands with life's sacred red wine.

A bit of air seeped into the plane by means of what appeared to be bullet holes and wafted through the cockpit, agitating the air like a child asking questions of her parent. "Are we there yet?" "Why is the pilot so hairy?" "When are we going to be there?" "Why does it smell like wet dog?" "Are we there yettttt?"

To answer the second-to-last question: the pilot. He smells like a four-week-old kiwi and has hair just like it; thin, young but fading, bristled white and brown—and everywhere. This was one attribute of the career Croy lived that he never understood. You couldn't do anything in life without interacting with a weirdo. A weird pilot. A weird traveler. A weird vendor. A weird craftsman. It's as if the world wouldn't move without the weird.

(Need I remind you of the weird portrait shop keeper, the weird contestants at the food convention, or the weird Louie-accented character we met briefly at the start of the novel? Yes, admittedly, even your beloved author must subject himself to a little humble pie, too. Weird.)

The weird pilot began descending the plane. The landing was as rough as the plane looked. Croy didn't believe in God or Shiva or any kind of deity, life was too short to put his mind on anything but himself, but as the odds of a successful landing by his calculations added up to roughly twenty percent, Croy did let a little prayer slip through his lips in case there was some deity with whom he hadn't burned his bridges.

Twenty percent odds were good enough in this situation and though it felt like the tires popped on landing and the bullet holes sucked the air out of the cabin rather than letting it in, they landed as safe as an armadillo rolled up like a steel Filthy Hooligan cigar.

After briefly inspecting the plane and giving it a nod of confirmation, convinced that it could still get itself back in the air once more for his departure (and God forbid that's the last time he sees it), Croy reluctantly handed the pilot a roll of bills and told him to wait on the dirt road like a caddie on a golf course. He had a birdie to kill.

The sun began its rise to redemption and popped the stars in the sky like zits. The day was finally breaking like bread at a dwarf's house and Croy was ready to play the first nine holes of the day.

On the western mountains, just south of Kar Tresa's Crevice, there were two different landing strips that hugged the jagged rock structures of the old hut, wherein our protagonists had recently performed the most historic and emotionally exhilarating of rituals.

Both strips were surrounded by a few small Buddhist communities. And calling them small may still be an exaggeration of their size.

Knowing that Nora had to have arrived on one of the two strips, it was a toss-up, like the weather, on whether Croy would be landing on the right one to start tracking.

He pawed at the ground lazily at first like it was some sort of scratch and sniff. Wallah! The odds continued to be in Croy's favor. Nora never concerned herself much with makeup or beautification methods, but she did have a liking for ambergris, the perfume ingredient made from the intestine of sperm whales. She hadn't worn any in several weeks, but it was such a habit of hers to wear it that you might say it was part of her now, in her skin and seeping out with her sweat. (Jim had come to associate the scent with his beloved since his nose settled into its new groove, too.) Croy didn't have Jim's nose, but he had to endure whiffs of the smell for years. He looked forward to never having to smell it again. All a matter of time.

Croy, in his zip-off jean shorts, sandstone shirt, and triangular Afghan knife (a *pesh-kabz* to be specific), a formidable weapon for close range combat, the kind of knife you'd expect Colonel Mustard to wield in the pantry of your grandpa's kitchen, he set off to track Nora. Croy didn't anticipate needing to use the knife. He knew his words could do far more damage to Nora (as they could do to anyone) than a formidable sickle. And, you know, reader, Batuk gave orders for her to be returned alive, and not even your beloved author would have Croy transgress the orders for fear of the words one would have to write. But, as a purveyor of economics, he knew it paid to be prepared, regardless.

A quarter of the way down Nora's scent trail, surprisingly heading west rather than north to the crevice, Croy flipped a rock that had been the roof over someone's head. A snake's head. An anaconda's head. A starving anaconda's head, specifically. Banters of black and brown with a child's crayon pattern of white leading from head to maraca. Croy let out a sound he hadn't since he was a little boy in Kilkenny, a boy who popped the cherry of a young fiddling gal within the village's 20,000 footprint on the world, a major celebration in an Irish village that size. This sound, however, was the kind of sound one makes after eating too much pterodactyl soup. The kind one makes that puts the screech of chalk on chalkboard in its place. The kind that has cops questioning where the street racing goons were performing burnouts for some ladies on the sidewalk corner *this time*. Was it to the left? No, north? West. West for sure. This was a girly scream that Croy, determined as ever, would rather let wither away in history, let it be overrun, and quickly, with other, newer and hopefully less embarrassing experiences.

It's funny to even imagine (and funnier still to write) about a sound like that coming from a man like Croy. Croy was no sugar or spice; he was everything not nice. His eyebrows were digging cemeteries at the center of his forehead. He had a matchstick tattoo on his forearm that was ready to set the world on fire. The Irish fiddlin' gal who had been Croy's first and only kiss said his lips tasted piquant with a twang of caraway seed soaked in whiskey. His spirit animal? A cut-throat shark that would die if he ever stopped moving forward. Croy lived his life in the fast lane, a scofflaw racing through the carpool lane without any passengers—he traveled solo, leaving nothing but a trail of broken hopes, cigarette butts, and a bit of blood (rarely his own). All that was to say, though the reaction of seeing the snake head was unorthodox for Croy, he quickly put his *pesh-kabz* to work and separated the snake's head from its body and kept doing as Croy did—he moved forward, following Nora's scent through some tunnels to a hut by a stream.

Alas. Croy found no inhabitants in the hut, but he did notice that Nora's scent swirled itself with perspiration and something else Croy couldn't put his finger on. Hmph. He decided to put his metaphoric tattoo to life and set it ablaze.

Once again he used his knife to cut a branch of a tree that hung over a spring just the same as he'd decapitated the snake head, but this time took the remnants and used it to agitate the coals beneath the teapot in the hut and closed the hut's rooftop hatch above the kettle to enclose the smoke and flame until it extended its legs across the entirety of the hut, catching the curtain, catching the pheromones, catching the pillow, catching everything.

The hut's flames roared like a preacher on a revival high, hurling a plume of smoke into the sky—a signal a good fifty times the size of a tea kettle's shriek, curling and twisting like a ghost with a grudge. Had Jim and Nora glanced south just then, they might've paused to wonder about the lone splinter of darkness clawing the heavens, a solitary exhale in an otherwise clean canvas. But they didn't. And Croy, inhaling the cocktail of charred wood and wilderness, turned his boots northward, toward the crevice where instinct whispered his prey would be waiting.

This should be easy, he thought.

Of course, when has anything that involves magic been easy?

⇒XLIV⇐

"**F**or fuck's sake, leave me alone!" Phil shouted at the knocks on the door. Hungover to hell and high water and back. There was a lingering taste of phlegm-soaked whiskey in the back of his throat and a touch of curacao that attempted to stimulate his dilapidated palate, but to no avail. Phil's ears were ringing like a death metal record played in reverse. He imagined someone playing an aggressive game of ping pong, each player at one ear. Player One just hit a let and a nerve tingled down to Phil's heel, pinching him all the way like an incompetent acupuncturist. Phil didn't quite care who was doing the knocking at the door.

Between you and me, dear reader, it's a reporter knocking, and Phil will be made aware of that in a moment.

After Phil was chosen as the winner of the convention's annual challenge and awarded the Golden Fork, he gave each of the judges a handshake and a wink. Then he did what any winner would do—he celebrated. Though the liquor of the alcoholic beverage providers at the conference was free (already making the goods taste good for that exact reason; you don't see anyone spitting out something free), it tasted a whole lot better as a winner (it's scientifically proven that winners who consume food or beverages after winning a competition tend to chew slower, enjoy the ingredients more, and actually have more taste bud receptors activated and processing than, say, the loser's. There's a reason why losers also tend to lose their appetites. Their body knows they won't enjoy it anyway.)

Anyway. Anyway. Anyway... the knocking persisted. "God damn it," Phil stated to himself as much as the person on the other side of the door. He heaved himself up off the couch, trying in equal parts to get his legs to support him and to recall what happened the night prior. Clearing his throat of mossy, citrus-infused phlegm and giving it a swallow, which he instantly regretted, the fog in his head started to clear, too, though the pinging and ponging inside remained.

With each step toward the door, a flash of memory returned between serves in his head. Whiskey. Dancing. More whiskey. A citrus *crème brûlée*. A tattooed fork inked by Nancy Williams (yes, reader, the one in the same who inked our protagonists hours prior). As Phil reached for the door, he looked down to discover the jet-black contour of a dining fork on his forearm. It had joined the previously inked batatas, sturgeon, and amaryllis. He nearly had the whole dining room table on his arm now. All that was missing was a highball glass. The thought of more whiskey made Phil pause opening the door to choke down some more of that phlegm that was crawling its way up his esophagus faster than a baby to its own bottle. There it goes. Right back down where it belongs. His stomach gurgled in disgruntlement. Phil opened the door.

"Phil! Phil! What do you think was the cause of the fire at Herough's?"

Then another person spoke.

"Phil! Where were you last night at 10:05 p.m.?"

Then one more.

"Phil! Phil! Chip here with the *Bugaloo Tribune*. Are you at all worried about a second attack, perhaps at your restaurant?"

The ping-pongers in Phil's head dropped their paddles. Phil slammed the door, trying to gather his thoughts. His hotel phone started to ring, and he answered. "Who is this?" Phil answered angrily and slightly gurgly... that phlegm was battling its way back up.

"I'm sorry, sir. Our staff tried to stop them. There are a few more outside, but we do have a vehicle waiting for you out the back."

Phil wasn't one to be caught off guard by some paparazzi. He'd had enough experiences in life that had desensitized him. However, it's hard for even the most-talented emotional-controllers to maintain their grips on a situation while hungover. Phil hung up the phone and scratched his fork. It was agitating him, the skin still a bit red and puffy. His head was agitating him. The whole situation was agitating him. He was flat out agitated. Need I write it again? You get it.

Phil was trying to make sense of what was happening. Being the referee in his head, he put an end to the ping pong tournament altogether after taking a solid swig of cold brew coffee he pulled from the hotel room fridge. The only pinging that remained was the persistent knocking on the door from one reporter or another. Phil figured he'd find answers in the one place anyone looks to find answers: his phone.

Of course, his phone was right where he had left it before he left his room to the convention the day prior. Right next to the microwave, in a *suahama-gata* bowl, with its naturally misshapen rim and assortment of hygge-inspired colors of earthen tan, diffused green, and bark brown; an infusion of a Japanese tea bowl and the Norwegian assortment of colors that sang of coziness and comfort. The phone looked happily situated. Phil was far from feeling the same.

Placing his thumb on the phone to unlock the screen, you'd think he was logging into the Associated Press breaking newsroom; texts from thirty-six different contacts, forty-eight phone calls (excluding the multiple attempts from the same number), eighteen voicemails, and six push notifications. The headline of the push notifications (of which Phil had set up for every restaurant he was seeking to take over until he did) gave the answer Phil was looking for.

"Seafood and insect-inspired restaurant Herough burned down"—Channel 28 news.

"Neighborhood rendered uninhabitable with stench of burnt Poseidon"—Neighborhood News, NY.

Phil's ears blocked out the incessant knocking and now hollering of the reporters outside his door. It took every ounce of energy to hold his hand still so he could read through the article's texts and voicemail-to-text summaries.

There are a few things in life that can sober a man up swiftly.

The first is laughing gas. The stuff they use at the dentist, holding a little mask over your face while you count backward from one hundred. As you breathe it in, you "ninety-nine" slowly "ninety-eight" go to "ninety-seven" sleep "ninety...." When you wake up, your hangover is cured. No urge to vomit. No stomach flips or rumbles. No headache. It's incredible what an hour's gas-induced unconsciousness can do to reset the body.

The second is when you've just woken up beside a woman with whom you want to have breakfast. No need for compatibility tests. When it comes to what the heart wants, your body works wonders to increase your chances. Goodbye hangover, hello charm.

The third is when your expectations get sucker-punched by reality. There was a part of Phil that initially thought the crowd and texts were talking about his win, but then he read words like "Might a restaurateur known for questionably shady tactics in dominating new markets be responsible?" or "One new seafood restaurant arrives, and another takes the heat. Is it really happenchance?"

Phil didn't need special glasses to read between the lines. The media were basically accusing him of setting fire to Herough. Phil laughed hard. Hard enough to finally clear that revolting phlegm, so your appreciative author no longer needs to write the word again. He laughed hard enough that the knocking stopped at the door as reporters pressed their ears up to it instead.

"Chowderheads," he said.

His laughter then took a dunk in a cup of more reality. Now Phil was pissed that he wasted his little bit of spice on the competition to remove Jim's restaurant, just to have it burn down anyway.

He could rebuild it, but it wouldn't truly be rebuilt. He couldn't rebuild the care and history that Jim had put into it. Phil couldn't just open it again and have all the previous regulars return with the knowledge that it's under new leadership... his leadership... the leadership of a person to whom the media is assigning blame for the fire, even if they weren't stating it directly. Phil was smart enough to consciously read between the lies, but the general public? Not so much. The media works in masterful ways with words and visuals; they can make you believe something in a way that convinces you that you came up with it yourself. Lord save us if the media ever learns to transfer the sense of taste through the TV, phone, or radio. Society would be done for. Everyone knows tasting is believing.

Phil's laughter turned from hysterical to maniacal quite rapidly. In every article Phil skimmed, he realized that not a single one quoted Jim.

"The [insert publication here] reached out to Jim Herough, but could not connect with him."

That was the line in every article.

Perhaps there was a way Phil could tell the media about Jim and his bet, then somehow convince them that Jim set the fire as a result of losing. The evidence stacks up. Jim lost his restaurant. Jim lost his competition. Jim left the convention early. Jim couldn't be reached. The one requirement to make the plan work was to find Jim before anyone else could. Phil couldn't be the one to do it, obviously, not with every reporter from the high rise of *Restquire* to the low-scum-filled *People* magazines following his every move. Phil cleared his phone of all the notifications, thumbed his way to his contacts, filtered down to names that started with "C," selected the third option, and hit "dial."

7,324 miles away a phone rang. The connection was weary, but a man answered. Phil could hear the crackling of fire in the background. Apparently, some people just want to listen to the world burn.

⋙XLV⋘

The Irishman was one who preached minimalism and held a fervent disdain for people's attachment to the digital world. In his mind, everyone he talked to in the "real world" was living a double life. The one they kinda sorta lived in brief physical moments, and the one they lived on their phone. He could barely tell people's skin color anymore since everyone seemed tinted blue. The impact of so much screentime, sadly. The Irishman prefers being called an Irishman and not a Buddhist because even the ones he had lived with had cell phones. Hypocrites.

As a minimalist, the Irishman didn't carry much; not physically, not mentally, not emotionally. He even wore flip flops without the annoying little thong piece that goes between the toes. It forced him to tread lightly through life, as one should do. Don't quite jump to total conclusions, reader; the Irishman is still as human as you or I, as we'll soon see.

Speaking of hypocrisy, the Irishman did carry one thing with him. It was massive. Heavy. It weighed down his emotional intelligence. It even aged him—a man that couldn't be aged. And that, my dear reader, was what he could do with a bit of the starlight that he, the Irishman, had only ever used in hot sauce. While he had originally taught Shaman Denny how to *blend* starlight, he could actually *bend* it to his will, too. In the world of enchantments and thaumaturgy, this was the difference between creating something and controlling it. The Irishman's ability made Midas' touch look like child's play. He put magic eight balls in the corner on a timeout to think about what they've been unable to accomplish, causing their little round windows to blandly say, *outlook not so good.*

"Come on, Grasshopper," Denny said, chuckling at how he thought the tables had turned.

Denny decided to bring up an old argument he and the Irishman would have in their Monk Sauce training days.

"You know that the nose needs the mouth as much as the mouth needs the nose, right? When someone tells you to follow your nose, there's a reason your mouth is always open. That air goes into your lungs, but taste goes to your circulatory system. Without taste, smell has nothing to dance with, no trail to follow—and with no trail to follow, no finish line to burst into ecstasy upon crossing."

Denny was just buying time; distracting the Irishman. Nothing distracts a man more than toying with his emotions. (One might say a woman does; but what in the world plays with a man's emotions more than a woman?)

So Denny teased him. He didn't need to let the Irishman know that he needed him for this final ritual. The Irishman would figure it out soon enough.

In the meantime, let's listen in on Denny bantering more with the Irishman. It's fun.

"But a splash of paint can be covered in weekday..."

"And I'll tell you, it swayed in the tree like a rocking chair…"

"Remember when you hollered at me to hold on to my socks, but I wasn't wearing any?"

The Irishman gave a grunted chuckle at the memories, but Denny couldn't hear it over his own chortles. The Irishman began wondering what he was doing with Denny again, anyway.

So life goes: Ask and you shall have your answer.

Denny stopped sniggering. He stopped altogether, actually. They were facing a dead end. A slab of mountain that stood in their way.

Unlike the Irishman, Denny carried a bag with him. Denny stuck his hand in the bag, and it went deeper than seemed possible from the outside. Eyes closed, Denny trusted his fingers to grasp what they needed.

"Aha. There you are."

Denny drew forth a tusk and handed it to the Irishman. The tusk seemed old, going by its porousness and white-speckled hue. Its small size made it clear that it was not from an elephant, walrus, or boar. In fact, it wasn't a tusk at all. Denny carved it himself from a prehistoric kauri tree that had lain buried under a peat swamp for more than 50,000 years. It shimmered with streaks of iridescence. It was so beautiful that it would make a female elephant believe that the size of one's tusk doesn't matter.

This moonfang had carvings on it—somewhere between calligraphy and Pollock art. The only thing they communicated was that some type of magic had been performed on the ivory at one point, like how a dent in a car communicates its past, but not its present or future. Denny continued to surprise the Irishman.

"But how?"

"Some secrets are meant to be kept," Denny responded with a wink. "Would you do the honor?"

As the Irishman looked up at the slab of wall in front of him, information started to percolate to the surface of his brain. The librarians in his head must have been working during this whole climb to find whatever memory vault contained the readings about where they were.

The slab in front of them was called the Chef's Slab. It was written in some book or another that behind it lay round rocks like cooking pans, and that at times the sunlight hit them at the optimal temperature for cooking. In the cracks that speared through the slab grew a variety of undiscovered herbs and spices—so new and electric they could restart a person's heart after cardiac arrest. Even larger plants grew on the outskirts of the crevice. Bulbous plants, reminiscent of gargantuan jackfruit but with a texture and protein framework that was even closer to red meat. In fact, somewhere between red meat and fish meat. Streams of saltwater flowing around the crevice like a neuron network provided the blend of minerals for the meatlike growth of vegetation. In short, the slab was a damn kitchen.

Standing in front of the Chef's Slab meant they were in the heart of Kar Tresa's Crevice, and the Irishman knew what to do.

In inspecting the slab further, he found what looked like a small crack in the slab from the ground up, shaped like a doorway. Not massive. Not perfectly rectangular. Not standard. Not unexpected.

The Irishman took the ivory crescent, placed the tip of it against the crack in the wall, and dragged it in a cutting fashion, steadily following the crack. As he did, the rock turned to dust, fell, and dissipated before touching the ground. Once the entire crack had been followed with the ivory, the remainder of the entryway poofed into nonexistence and the Irishman and Denny entered. The moment they crossed the chasm, the dust of the doorway the Irishman had just cut seemed to rise out of the ground to reform itself once again into rock. He returned the ivory horn to Denny and stared at him as if waiting for direction.

"And now we wait," said Denny.

The Irishman's face was puzzled, but the pieces were finding their proper places slowly but surely. The memories of this location were coming back to the Irishman. It had been hundreds of years since he was last here.

What did Denny know that he didn't? Thinking of the answer angered him, so he decided to let his eyes do some work and observe the aesthetic of the place to see how much had changed and how much had stayed the same. While most written documentation of the world never quite lines up with the reality, what the Irishman recalled of this place was spot on. The outside was a mere snack-shop compared to the inside. The outside was like a lazy Susan of ingredients. The inside, a whole damn pantry. A commissary kitchen. A cathedral of culinary chaos, where flavors clashed and harmonized like an orchestra of reckless virtuosos. It's as if the place had been untouched. A true rarity. Something the Irishman was welcoming to nourish his eyes with while they waited. His curiosity of why Denny brought him back here took a seat, while awe stepped up and took the stage.

≈XLVI≈

When you're completely alone in the middle of nowhere, it's not uncommon to hear a constant buzz. It's the buzz of the unfamiliar. It's your eardrum working to understand. But for Croy, the buzz was just coming from his phone. One of the perks of working with Batuk was that he made sure that one could be reached no matter where they were in the world.

"I'm busy," Croy answered.

Seconds passed and a smirky air dropped onto Croy's face.

"Funny you should ask," he said. "I'll make it happen."

You could say that Croy was an incentive-driven person. If there was a medal, he wanted it. Name on a list of top ten in the gym? He had to be number one. A wire-transfer of more funds than he knew what to do with? You bet. Even better in this situation was a wire-transfer of two funds for a single job well done. One from Batuk and one from Phil.

Keep your friends close. Your enemies closer. Those who actually pay you, closer still.

⇒XLVII⇐

Jim and Nora left a trail of ecstasy behind them. Shine a blacklight on the trail and it would have looked like a giant slug had strolled through.

While the high they felt was higher than the mountain they traversed, their feet were grounded back into reality—pebble in shoe and all.

Their trek was slowed from the exhaustion of all their merriment. The gravel seemed to reach out of the ground like some back-from-the-dead horror movie scene and grabbed their ankles. The path was telling them to stop. Their lungs, too. But they did the two things they knew best how to do: perspire and persevere. So it goes, one with the other.

Are we almost there?" Nora asked, looking up and seeing a protruding slab of mountain up ahead. The smell was getting stronger. "Almost," Jim responded. "Almost" being a little subjective here. It was another six hundred yards or so. But the energy of seeing the light at the end of their figurative tunnel traveled through their body, down their legs, into their heels. They kicked the rocks trying to drag them down.

As Nora was looking up with hope, Jim was looking down with a doubt. One of the pathway rocks must have found itself in the gumption gland of Jim's feet.

"You know you don't have to do this with me, right?"

Nora was getting a little tired of Jim's episodes.

"I don't *have* to do anything. It's not about what I've got to do, Jim. When are you going to realize that? It's about what I get to do!"

Jim took his eyes off the gravel monsters and looked up to lock in with Nora's gaze. They were four hundred yards from their destination now, but Jim took a five-mile detour into Nora's eyes as she continued.

"You don't think I've been aware of every decision I've made? The consequences I face for them? Even the wrongest wrongs. I made them. Sure, there are always variables like peer pressure or fear helping them along, but the decision was, is, and always will be, mine. Even when I'm told what to do. The doing is my decision."

Nora took a breath, less because of the physical strain and more in preparation for the relief she was finding in the words she was sharing. In truth, she's never had anyone to share with openly.

"When we were up in the plane together, I could have taken the spice and brought it back to Batuk. That's what I was supposed to do, but it's not what I got to do. Instead, I got to make the realization that the actions I take are a privilege; and from there, realize that there's no limit to the legacy I could leave and the control I could have back in my life if I were to change my attitude from what I *'have* to do' to what I *'get* to do.' I *get* to do this with you, Jim. Do you realize that you pushing me away would rob me of that joy, of that agency, of that solace in freedom? It doesn't matter that you're trying to be sweet if the result is no different than if Batuk himself were here threatening your life and forcing me to turn around. From here on out, I'll have no more of that forcefulness upon the decisions of my life. Not

from Batuk. Not from Pinmekalah. And, despite the feelings I've built for you, I won't have that forcefulness from
you, either."

Funny how people spend thousands of dollars to travel to some convention center to hear some motivational speaker in hopes that what they'll hear will help them
straighten out their lives, when in reality all it takes is chasing your dream, losing a bet, having your dream set on fire,
having the sense you care most about ripped away, and, to
top it all off, to get the love of your dreams taken away. Fortunately for Jim, she shared enough words to motivate him
before she was taken away.

Taken away, you wonder? About that...

In the time it took Nora to vocalize her life lesson, she and
Jim got closer to the Chef's Slab, but Croy caught up to them
before they reached it. The sludgy trail the two had left in
their wake didn't slow him down, although Croy had his
nose slightly scrunched from the scent of it all. If anything,
Croy covered more ground than even he could have imagined. The phone call from Phil put Croy into sixth gear.
He treated the mountain like the U-Bahn or a reverse luge
course or a slip-and-slide, extra slippery.

And Jim didn't notice a damn thing. Here's the thing
about senses; it doesn't matter how strong they are if you're
focused on something else. With Jim focused on Nora's
words and avoiding the gravel phalanges, he missed the
scent of evil (and Jim was even downwind of Croy!); he
missed hearing the careless crunches of rubber and rocky
road; he missed seeing the dust cloud of a devil doing a
Dartmouth Dip in the air trail of Croy. Often our senses fail
us because of focus.

Remember that thing about Croy liking to be number
one, the winner, the award-receiver? Would you be surprised, reader, if I also said he was a gloater, show-boater,

and rubber-inner? I didn't think so.

If Croy were to run a one hundred meter, he'd wait just before the finish line so you could almost catch up and he could cross it seconds before you.

If you were playing Texas Hold'em, he'd have a game in the bag and bluff to high heaven to get you all in.

When Batuk sent him on a hunting challenge in the wilderness of Wallonia, he had a clear shot at the heart of the beast Batuk wanted mounted in his emporium. Instead, he shot its bladder and watched him die a slow, painful death. He sat and basked in the sunlight and the sound of scraping for the afterlife.

This may seem stupid, but Croy would even milk a dried-out cow if you had bet him he couldn't. He'd find a way. Force a way. He'd make you pay, the cow pay, the farmer pay... all the way up and down the food chain.

All that is to say that in this moment, the opportunity to both capture Nora and kill Jim—it was too easy, too painless, too seamless, too fast. Shit. Jim was so damn focused on Nora that he wouldn't even have time to see his life pass before his eyes; something Croy enjoyed seeing in another more than any television show or gambling face of another that goes "all in" with him at the table. No. If there was anything Croy loved more than money, it was torture. T-o-r-t-u-r-e. Torture. And what would be more torturous for Jim than to have the love of his life (and the bane of Batuk's) taken from him?

Croy went full broom and swept Jim's legs from underneath him. Jim's face hit the ground first and those gravel gravediggers scratched at it. His brain hung in limbo of consciousness. The web in his head holding his brain in place was vibrating from the surprise earthquake, holding on for dear consciousness.

While a surprise leg sweep for Jim was something he never imagined avoiding, a surprise attack of any kind is something Nora was trained for.

Croy held a knife outright as if in a yoga pose waiting for Nora to make a move. *Namaste.*

Nora's feet traversed the ground as smoothly and simply as the wind itself, but no amount of focused wind can push its way through a wall of rock. And Croy was a wall of rock.

In one of the many villages Nora had needed to go through while on a mission, she overheard a mother chastising her son.

"But he deserved it!" the boy argued.

"You are a lover, not a fighter. But if you must fight, you are not to be the one to throw the first punch. That is not who you are."

Chances are likely the wisdom sunk into the memory glands of the boy, but they never did for Nora. Years of training habituated her to hit first.

While her punch landed, Croy used the opportunity to test his knife out on the shoulder of Nora's opposite throwing arm. Never bring a fist to a knife fight, I suppose.

Nora argued for a fair fight. She knew Croy, and realized it was worth a shot.

"Drop the knife and fight like a man, Croy. You're a cheater and a fraud, and you don't have the skill to compete with me."

Croy laughed, but the words seared into his ego, finding the soft spot and also a switch that turned his internal narcissism from a calm 98.6 up to a balmy 105 degrees. He threw the knife right in the ground in front of Jim's face, a centipede's distance away from his nose, making Jim's eyes cross further.

"So be it, Princess. I'll have you submitting faster than you can spell mercy."

The wind picked up and the few trees upon the mountain ruffled against each other; nature's "ding ding ding."

Nora wound up her good arm like a toy and released it at Croy. She hit 'em good, but was a few stomach hairs away from a direct hit on his diaphragm.

The reason to blame wasn't Croy's swiftness. When you're built like a boulder, you move like one, too. But on top of that Nora had to lean to nurse her wounded shoulder. Her brain hadn't caught up with the fact that everything she wanted her body to do would need to account for a few degrees difference.

Croy had placed his cut perfectly. Something he intended to brag about to Batuk. He knew he'd have the advantage against Nora. There's that. Plus all the knowledge Croy has of how she was trained, having seen a countless number of her strategies, tactics, and habits in practice.

Croy returned the punch to sender and the brute force of his muscle and the momentum he had acquired from being pushed back a couple of feet from Nora's punch meant his was packed even fuller. You'd think the punch was going on a month-long sabbatical with how much it carried. If it was a bowl, the smoker would be high as heaven off a single puff. The punch was definitely filled beyond fire code capacity.

That wind that Nora had danced with a bird's song ago? Well, that got sent back to where it came from (wherever wind comes from, I suppose) with the one hit from Croy.

Jim was watching the hit and Nora's stumble unfold, though at a forty-five-degree angle, given his head still lay parallel to the ground. He heard the wind leave her chest and slam the door behind it. He even heard the creak of a few bones just shy of their breaking point. As much as Jim's brain was yelling at his body, shouting orders to get up like a lieutenant, his body wouldn't listen. It still hadn't stopped trembling from the fall.

Dear reader, we're going to have to give Nora a break on this one. She's talented. She's fit. She knows how to fight. But anyone, even the best, has their bad days.

While Nora stumbled back, Croy kicked her legs from underneath her, too. His foot had crushed the bracelet she had on her ankle, cutting her skin at the same time as breaking its chain. You'd think Croy was a housemaid in another life, the way he could sweep.

"Ah, so that's how I looked," Jim's brain said to itself.

Nora's face was now parallel to Jim's and the ground's, too. The knife between them. Nora squeezed her lungs to get what tiny bit of air they had in them.

"Jim. The bracelet. The bracelet, Jim."

Now Jim's consciousness was putting back its disheveled home and with it, some bodily function and control. Every inch of Jim wanted to be a hero. To hit "return to sender" with Croy. The feeling of control was present for a fleeting moment before Jim's gut received the rippling impact of the tip of Croy's boot.

"Ah, so that's how the wind exited Nora's body," Jim's brain said to itself.

Moments later, Croy had Nora's hands bound behind her back. Her ankles were sporting a new bracelet of polypropylene. Her head and mouth wrapped with the salty and stained shirt, torn from Jim's semi-cataleptic body. Croy wanted her to taste her failure.

And with Nora tied up and immobile, he spat on Jim and told his borderline-unconscious body that he'd be back for him after he sorted things out with Nora, but not to worry, he'd make sure she was treated the best he's ever treated a prisoner.

With Nora over his shoulder, hardly struggling to carry her lean figure, Croy made the trek back down the mountain, out of Kar Tresa's Crevice.

He passed the hut he had set aflame. It was now mere ashes with the neck of the teapot slightly protruding from them like a phoenix beak.

Sometimes pushing, sometimes dragging Nora by her bonds, he made his way back to his plane and back in the air and back to Batuk. Praise and reward in front of Croy.

Back atop the mountain, a bit of blood and drool made a mini pool on the ground near Jim's mouth.

⇒XLVIII⇐

B ack in his hotel room, Phil's smile was so polished, he could shine his shoes with it. This wasn't Phil's first attendance at the Hangover Rodeo Show. He gargled mouthwash, chugged purified water from his fridge (specially requested: Nerve, a new formula of minerals that make your average electrolyte water taste like half-flushed toilet bowl water). He put on a fresh pair of slacks, shirt, cufflinks engraved like the head of a shark. He did, however, have to use a different hole in his belt to get it on. Then again, so does everyone the day after attending a food and beverage convention, or after a long night of sake bomb drinking.

All the while he worked on his presentation on the outside, he formulated the story he'd tell the press on the inside.

Years and years in the business, with no shortage of reporter relationships, and it still blew his mind how nosy, inconsiderate, and unstoppable journalists could be. He remained focused on thinking through the story despite the continuous knocks and calling of his name from those out the door. Over the last twenty minutes, he even heard a few new voices. Respond to one reporter, two show up in her place. Ignore one reporter, three show up in his place.

Good, Phil thought.

Phil opened the door and the barrage of questions came flying at him. If they were arrows, they would have blocked out all ceiling light in the hall. Phil, however, was the one with the power (or at least so he thought). He held a hand up and the points of the arrows carrying questions hung in the air. They fell to the floor and along with them, silence.

"Meet me at the convention center lobby and I'll answer all of your questions that I can," Phil said.

He knew better than to share words with reporters alone or to tell them he wouldn't respond to any inquiries. Doing so makes it too easy for them to spin what he says or bark up the "no answer is still an answer" tree of public gossip, and there's no public layperson to correct it in casual conversation with another or to simply hold the reporter accountable, too. It's hard to say something incorrect when you know you'll be called out on your bullshit, whether you're the question asker or the askee.

Phil squeezed his way through the hallway of reporters to the elevator. He paused at the hotel's entryway café, ordered, and enjoyed a quick cortado. Quick, but slow enough to signal to the reporters that he was in no hurry; he was in control of the situation; he had nothing to hide.

While the majority of reporters beamed off to the convention center lobby to get the best position, a few laggards hung back and watched. Veteran reporters. The ones that knew they can get as much of a story by using their eyes as they do their ears or mouths.

They could see the espresso taking effect, tightening the skin under Phil's eyes, forcing his foot to tap tap tap on the foot rail of the café bar. In all truth, Phil was actually trying to work out what had truly happened to Jim's restaurant. Fires don't happen by happenstance and Phil truly believed Jim had nothing to do with it. So what could have happened and who could have done it? Phil had his story set, but he was still curious about what the truth was.

Phil looked at his watch and figured he'd bought Croy enough time to tie up the loose end of his story. After all, he was called the Minute Man because of how quickly he could complete the challenges put upon him. And Croy seemed all too confident on the phone. Phil respected that.

Phil waddled his way to the convention center lobby with a bit of espresso swishing back and forth in his gut, his belly finding the extent of the stretch the additional belt hole gave him—perhaps Phil should have gone two holes longer. Oh, well.

The convention's PR team was already set up and fielding questions about their security and the attendance and the reactions of those in the audience when they had learned of Jim losing to Phil. In another corner of the lobby, the police were asking similar questions to the judges and other contestants. But as Phil walked in, all eyes went to him. He took a breath. He had his cool to keep. He had a story to tell. Most importantly, he had a crime to frame.

Phil walked forward to a small makeshift podium cobbled together from a white foldout table, a food crate, and a mic stand. There was no need for chairs. This wasn't a normal formal press conference planned weeks in advance; it was a press conference, and a hodgepodge one at that. Fat chance the reporters would have kept their bottoms in their chairs anyway.

"I'll answer your questions in a moment, but first let me share with you what I know that you may not."

Phil paused to build the anticipation.

He knew how to work a crowd.

Just as your writer is doing here and now.

Tempting you to know the words he'll say. The story he'll craft. The lie(?) he'll tell.

Deep breath.

"I've heard the news of Herough going up in flames, and I can anticipate the scrutiny around the fact that I've opened a similar restaurant concept right near it. I know my reputation is one of dominating markets, but I did not set fire to Herough."

Reporters were feverishly tapping away on their keyboards while the old laggards handwrote in their journals. A few cameras were recording the footage live. They'd slice and dice it like a Domino's pizza later on and sell it off to the other news stations that hadn't shown up yet.

"What you might not know is that Jim and I had become close frenemies. In fact, I gave him a tour of my establishment mere weeks ago. We talked about the industry and the neighborhood we were in. Before parting ways that evening, it was clear that Jim felt threatened by the impending success of my business and what it might take away from his own. The fear drove him to make a bet with me which I gladly accepted. We actually bet our restaurants on this competition. The loser was to forfeit their restaurant to the other. So I merely need to ask you all one question: Why in the world would I set flame to a restaurant about to be mine?"

Phil paused for impact.

"That's my question for you," Phil restated, placing his hands on his hips. Partially to set an impression. Partially to wiggle his hands under his belt so he could breathe better.

"Now what questions do you have for me?"

Most reporters were mulling over their questions. Most of them were based on the premise that Phil probably did set fire to it, so they were having to rethink their story on the fly.

One reporter, with his fly in particular still down, raised his hand.

"That's all well and good for you to defer the blame, but then who do you think did it?"

Phil smirked. Hook. Line. Sinker. God, these reporters are so predictable.

"I'm going to answer your question with another one of my own."

Phil paused again to tighten his smirk.

"Where's Jim?"

The reporters looked around the room, thinking, hoping, praying, Jim might reveal himself like a magic trick.

With no poof of smoke, the reporters started looking at each other to see whether any of them may have gotten the edge on another and had found or talked to Jim.

As Phil suspected.

None of them had seen Jim around. None of them had gotten ahold of him either. Hell, they couldn't even find his best friend, Lemon, for some form of alibi. Not being able to find Lemon was common (h,e was most likely off striking some deal or evaluating some new distributor or shaking some inspiring chef's hand halfway across the country [though in reality he was sipping a margarita half-way across the world]). However, not being able to find Jim was uncommon. After all, he'd lived and breathed his vision over the last hefty number of months. He attended neighborhood association meetings. He hunkered in his apartment trying new dishes. He was always at Herough or Gendrick's. Being unavailable was uncharacteristic to say the least.

While the reporters mulled it over and before they could ask more questions, Phil shared a few more words.

"Now I spent just a little time with Jim, and I'll admit I don't know him incredibly well. I have no clue how far he would go to achieve his business dreams... or to save them. From what I gathered from our brief encounter, he's a creative fellow, but also clearly a gambling one. And anyone who gambles is someone who enjoys the game of testing out their emotions."

"So you think Jim set the fire?" one reporter from the far back corner shouted. (And to think, the obnoxious ones are meant to stand in the front row.)

Phil was unphased by the heckling question.

"In my time, I've met many business owners, many chefs, many people in this industry. The only predictable thing about them is that they can be extremely unpredict-able when they're in an unfamiliar or unwelcoming envi-ronment, emotion, or... deal. I'm not saying Jim did it. I'm thinking the same as all of you in front of me. I'm evaluating what's the most likely situation. In the end, I'm choosing to see it as an opportunity to grow my space in the ashes of Jim's and I'll do my damnedest to go beyond the level of creativity and care that Jim did, regardless of the character he may or may not have become. And, I will, of course, continue to work with any and all authorities as necessary while tending to my own businesses."

With that, Phil walked toward the police, who had waved him over. He answered their few lackluster questions with ease, thinking to himself that any police responsible for questioning should be trained in journalism if they wished to gather any information of value from those they question. He then snuck through the hidden exit door near the bathrooms.

He actually did have other business to attend to. All the while checking his phone for a "C" of confirmation from a "C" of Croy. Phil checked his watch. It was a "C" of curious that he hadn't received it yet.

Hmph.

⇒XLIX⇐

Jim regained full consciousness in about the same time it took the sun to cook his dried spit and blood on the ground like scrambled eggs. In the balmy weather of East Asia? That's not too long. His fingers laid in the blend like cooked sausage links. Add a bit of sage to him and you'd have a Jim omelet.

Jim couldn't remember the last time he had taken a beating. He'd only been in a few fights in his life. One, drunk with Lemon, that ended as quickly as it started after realizing neither could focus enough to land a solid punch. One as a kid, participating in a neighbor's boxing match on the side of their house as an after-school activity. And one other situation with a kid who was pestering him so much that Jim beat him to the ground and then kept beating him, leaving a few scars where the skin opened like a portal above his eyebrow. In all of those fights, the worst Jim had gotten was a bloody lip. *This* was certainly a new experience for him. As an adult, too! He'd tenderized his fair share of meat in the kitchen, but never had his own body tenderized with such few kicks. Jim was as impressed as he was mad.

Exhausted and exhausting his last reservoir of energy to get up, despite the dehydration, despite the bruised ribs, despite the memory of a man hitting and binding up Nora slowly making its way through his brain, Jim got up and spit some blood out (unsure how fresh it actually was). Before his brain could work out what to do, think, or feel for that matter, his eyes had followed his spit of blood to a few strands of grass protruding from the ground, under the cover of a rock, which is why they weren't yet burnt and shriveled up. The green grass wasn't the interesting part, however; it was the bracelet poking its way through them that was interesting. Bracelet. The word rang significantly in Jim's head.

Jim extended his sautéed tentacles of fingers out and grabbed the bracelet. *Nora's.* He remembered the seashell bracelet and charms from the plane ride with her. He had only a glimpse of part of the bracelet back then. Now in his hand he could see every charm in all its detail. One charm was a Celtic cross, symbolic of the human desire to discover and experience the mystery of life. Another charm was of a scorpion. Another a flower that looked like the same she had tattooed on her back shoulder blade. But those were not the interesting ones. Those were all made of sterling silver. The unique one was the wood one. It was slightly larger than the others, but not so much as to be obtrusive to the wearer. The wood charm looked like a small talon or tusk of sorts; the point still sharp, but the wood was sturdy enough that it could easily hold up to any sort of beating it might get without snapping. In continued inspection, there were carvings on it, too. Swirls and stars.

Jim's heart sank like a boat with a cannonball-sized hole in the middle of it. The heart is fragile, after all. It was a glass boat, really. There's no extra escape boat attached to it. No life preserver. No tape that you can just slap over the hole. It kept sinking as he thought of what might be happening to Nora or who was cruel enough to ambush them.

His brain, now fully functioning, unleashed a hundred questions of what to do next. He stood there in analysis paralysis.

Should I leave?

Was that Batuk?

How the hell am I going to track her down?

How would I even get out of here?

Will I even make it? God, I'm thirsty.

How farther up this mountain did we need to go?

What's at the end of it? (From Jim's view, he could only see a tall slab ahead that looked unclimbable.)

Add *Are my ribs broken?* into that pool of questions for good measure.

Jim sure wished he had Lemon around to advise him. That's what Lemon did best.

But Lemon wasn't there.

Jim was alone. This time, not the kind of alone of being in his apartment alone. This was a *thousand miles away from anyone he knows* kind of alone. The alone of having lost someone... not to death (he prayed), but damn near close to it; from distance. The alone of uncertainty. The alone that was the opposite of fulfillment. He'd been robbed of his security. He was emotionally naked, physically bloody, and mentally afraid.

Jim closed his eyes. He could hear Lemon telling him to just "Breathe." That's what he always told him every time he'd get worked up about a recipe or a staffing issue or a city permitting issue or any issue.

It was an insider thing between Jim and Lemon. That was their safe word for letting the other know they were out of line.

"Breathe."

Jim took a breath. A big breath. With silence all around him. His head became calm. His heightened senses stretched to the ends of their capabilities. He could hear faint chatter. And that taste... there was something in the air. It almost smelled like... yes... exactly like what he had smelled from the well Denny had let him drink from.

Eyes still shut, Jim breathed again, this time exclusively through his nose rather than a body blend of nostril and throat. He turned in the direction of the scent. Breathed again and this time he could smell remnants of Denny, of spice, of magic.

He didn't need to decide what to do. Jim's nose did it for him.

And so he walked. Hiked, rather, given the incline and speed at which he moved. He put one foot in front of the other and kept breathing through his nose as the scent grew stronger. The bracelet Jim held tightly in his hand gave him all the energy he needed to continue. He'd see this through. For Nora.

A few seconds and a couple awkward steps on jagged rocks later, Jim was face to face with a wall of rock. The path ended. Even the smell he had followed up to the point had all but disappeared. Jim second guessed himself, wondering if he had missed a turn in the path.

No.

He was certain this was the direction to go in. He had to trust his senses.

Switching his sense of focus from his nose to his eyes, he looked around. Given it was him versus a slab of rock, it took all but two seconds for him to notice an arched shape crack in the slab.

With his empty hand, he pushed. He knocked to listen if it was hollow. He looked around to see if there were some sort of secret entrance kind of pulley system.

Nada.

Jim switched the bracelet from his right hand to left so he could try knocking on the slab again with his dominant hand, with greater gumption.

No success.

He let out a sigh of frustration. *This has to be it,* he told himself. After the sigh of frustration, he clenched his fists in it, only to feel a sting in his left hand.

Jim opened his hand. The wooden tusk charm had pierced his skin. This pissed him off even more. He hated how the world worked like this. One bad thing leads to another. Then you get frustrated. And then another bad thing happens. He stared at the tusk-like charm. In staring he noticed tiny engravings on it, one of which looked like an arch.

"Jim. The bracelet. The bracelet, Jim."

It was as if something took control over Jim's body. It was like instinct was Jim's sixth sense; it hopped in the driver's seat of his brain. He didn't consciously decide to take the tusk charm and use it to carve into the crack of the slab in front of him. He just did it. In a way, it felt as if the bracelet was doing it itself. Jim's brain battled between amazement and "duh, dumbass" as a reaction to the gold-like residue of dust falling from where the tusk carved.

His eyes were open wide, nearly stretched end to end with the arch. He considered stopping what he was doing in disbelief of its effect, but his hand wouldn't listen to his brain. It followed the crack and, in completing the arch, Jim looked in to see one unfamiliar face looking out just as quizzically as Jim looked in and one other, this time, familiar face, sneering at him.

"Well, look who decided to show up," Denny said, perched atop a rock carved like a stool.

There were about ten other stools in a curved line around a round table. Jim stood on his tippy toes. Nope. It was more like twenty-something stools, going all the way around a round table. Jim's eyes followed them all the way around, landing lastly on the stranger.

In realizing Jim was at a loss for words, Denny spoke first.

"Welcome to the world's most magical dining hall. I'll be the first to admit that I didn't think you'd make it here. I damn near bet the Irishman the rest of my secrets that you wouldn't."

Denny looked at the Irishman, raising his eyebrows.

"I've only ever come here alone, so despite his egging-me-on, it was refreshing to have some company along the trek. A spot of tea always helps, of course. And a little monk sauce to prevent the blood from pooling in our feet. Speaking of company..."

Denny leaned forward on the stool to look beyond Jim as if Nora were hiding behind him, waiting to bloom like a flower from behind or burst like a surprise party celebration.

"Where's that other half of yours? I have no doubt that you two have been attached at the arm since I met you at the well."

Jim looked down at the ground, took a breath, and regaled the adventures from start to finish. He told Denny and the Irishman of losing the spice, losing the contest, and losing Nora, the last of which happened mere minutes (or was it hours?) ago.

The Irishman appeared to be most interested in those parts referencing Pinmekalah while Shaman Denny remained stoic through the entirety of the tale.

"...and here I am. Hoping to figure out now how both to get my sense of taste back and Nora."

Denny, not missing a beat, winked at Jim.

"Well, today is your lucky day. Had you turned to chase with your heart rather than to chase your taste, you would never have made it to where you are now, in the company of two of the greatest manipulators of magic on the planet."

Denny looked at the Irishman. "What do you say, for love? For Pinmekalah? For the sake of putting those hands of yours into practice again, old man? I've got the blend, but I need you to bend it."

This Shaman Denny is a little bit of a hop and skip away from the Shaman Denny that he was at the well. He was still snarky, a test tube of attitude. Pointed, even, oddly for a shaman. But here he was... he was... hopeful?

If you were to ask him, hope may damned well be his secret to his own success, and the area where the Irishman struggled most. It's the only thing that one has control over when everything around them is chaos. It's the one thing to get one out of a bad mood. It's what enables a person to give ten percent after giving one hundred percent.

In this moment, the hope Denny had was the kind of hope Jim needed. He sucked it all in like a leech. Denny knew he would.

"Fortunately for us, we have everything we need around us to get your taste back, and quite possibly to get Nora back too," Denny said, spreading his arms out and looking around. "So long as we play our menus right."

Jim looked around the circumference of the space, beyond that of the table and stools, and saw no shortage of plants and living organisms—insects, in fact.

Jim knew a thing or two about plants and insects, but the fauna and flora around him were completely unfamiliar.

To the left were red flowers with a streak of blue on their petals and a protruding center of pollen that dripped yellow liquid into the ground.

To the right there was something that looked like an upside-down tree. Roots and rootlets where branches and leaves would be. Protruding from the ground were leaves, well and alive.

In another corner there were massive, weeping, bell-like melons that looked like a cross between mango and dragon fruit. Opposite the table, hidden behind the silhouette of the Irishman, were vegetables that looked like upside-down kohlrabi.

With Jim's heightened sense of sight, he could barely keep up counting the number of unique insects within sight—some that walked (some on four, some on forty legs), others that hovered and glistened gold from the sunlight bouncing off them, others that ate and drank what the garden had to offer, others that if you'd give them a decent squeeze, they'd be sure to excrete some form of paste. Somehow Jim just knew that the paste would be better than any man-made jam. Jim stood there in his dream pantry. He might not be able to taste any longer, but his tongue was still salivating as if it could.

The Irishman watched Jim experiencing his awe. A few moments later he finally broke his silence. The Irishman had connected the dots.

"Denny. Are ya sure 'bout this? For *him,* is it now?"

Denny's hope showed itself again while Jim was a little shocked at the immediate skepticism of the Irishman. Alas. It was clear there was some mixed chemistry between Denny and the Irishman. Jim didn't actually know who was the master and who the grasshopper at this point.

Denny didn't respond with words, he just nodded in agreement. And for once, it felt like he and the Irishman were aligned, on the same page; which is hard not to do when you are both sitting in the center of Kar Tresa's Crevice.

The Irishman and Shaman Denny looked up at Jim in unison.

"Are you ready, Jim?"

The thing about preparation is that it's hard to be prepared when one doesn't know what to prepare for. Jim hadn't the slightest clue what "ready" would even be. Nonetheless, he eased the firm grasp on Nora's bracelet to put it on his wrist for safekeeping, retying it where it had snapped. Jim had the feeling he'd need to use his hands for whatever Denny would instruct him to do. In putting on the bracelet, Jim felt some form of comfort army crawl its way into his veins. It was therapeutic to feel like he had a part of Nora with him. He knew she wouldn't be phased by a thing here.

"The bracelet, Jim."

The words hung in the air with the sound of insects chitting and chatting with their wings. Even some of the plants started to fluster a bit. It seemed as though the pantry was ready, too.

Jim took a breath and then nodded at Denny.

"Ready."

❧L❦

Batuk had a penthouse-like office, to be sure. But it was no lair. There were no secret trap doors, no torture chambers, no scream-proof rooms. "I'm not a monster," Batuk would tell people who first entered his office in awe of just how... normal it looked. Then he'd laugh. *Not on the outside, anyway,* he'd think to himself. The office was normal, at least for someone with more money than they know what to shake at. Sure, there was security. It was sixty-four floors up with a beautiful view to the east of the East Asian country of rice farms, paper mills, and land speckled with villages. To the west you'd see no shortage of warehouses and manufacturing plants, turning out thousands of branded products, each specifically stamped with Made In Cambodia. (Though they were truly made in Thailand. Batuk thought it close enough to not raise eyebrows but be different enough that if someone, an arsenic foe, perhaps, were to come searching his facilities, they'd have bit of an issue finding them. Batuk saw paranoia as a strength, not hindrance.)

At this point, Nora was easy enough for Croy to drag given her lack of resistance. Even someone trained as specially as Nora would suffer the same exhaustive behaviors from dehydration and a fair number of jabs, knicks, and knacks from the aggressive transportation Croy put her through to get to Batuk. Saying he was gentle would be a gross overstatement. To say he was even mindful would be grosser, still. Croy held her standing in the elevator ride up to Batuk's office. Nora did her best to conserve what energy she had by not resisting.

"You don't know how much joy this is going to bring me, Nora. Defying Batuk. Running off with the target. Losing the spice. Tssk, tssk. Once Batuk does what he wants with you, I want you to know my next task comes from someone who you should know, now that you have spent time with Jim."

Nora woozily swayed, her body wanting to crumble under the inertia of the elevator. She used a bit of energy to look up at Croy with curiosity.

"Does the name Phil ring a bell?" he smirked.

Admittedly, at first it didn't, but then her eyes widened. Croy must be referring to the Phil from the convention. But what did he have to do with anything?

"That Phil is an impressive fella. Someone who holds such a public-facing role in the world and who, if I'm being forward, couldn't break a cinder block even if given a hammer, could somehow get ahold of me as a contact awhile back. Alas. As you're aware: Money talks. This money, however, is hooting and hollering. Once I'm done here with Batuk, I'm off to find your friend Jim again. Taking care of him in front of you would be too easy. Plus, you would have moved on or let the rage fuel you. That would have made it more annoying that it already was to drag you down the mountain. It was far more enjoyable to watch Jim's disappointment in himself, incapable of saving you. I just hope the sun and the snakes don't get to him before I do. Knowing me as well as you do, you know how much pleasure I'll take in ending him."

Nora's body wanted to erupt like a volcano. She wiggled and squirmed and shouted. Though tied, she kicked off the ground hard enough to force slam Croy's face into the elevator doors. It might not have broken his nose, but it definitely bloodied it. A few drips fell to the elevator floor.

"You son of a bitch. I ought to just kill you now."

DING, DING!

The elevator doors opened and Croy threw Nora like a javelin from the elevator toward the doors of Batuk's office. Except Batuk's doors were already open. He had been watching Croy and Nora since they entered the building that is his Bangkok highrise.

"Croy. That's no way to treat our guest. Now go wash up your face. It looks like a bottle of ketchup pissed on it."

"Guest?" Croy responded blankly.

"Here's one of the biggest differences between you and me, Croy. I'm aware of and respect leverage, which one can only do if one is thinking ten steps ahead of others. You, however, are a cog in a machine and only focus on the orders given to you. Not the following circumstances or opportunities."

Croy had a look of puzzlement and then rage. He looked at Nora with a gaze as sharp as the knife in his pocket. In his head, his gaze sliced hers right off her shoulders.

"Let me spell it out for you, Croy."

Batuk took an agitated breath.

"First I'll compliment you on not fulfilling Phil's request. Not yet, anyway."

Croy was taken aback at Batuk knowing about the deal, but in truth, he shouldn't have been. Batuk knew everything Croy did, where he was, what he'd eaten, how badly he'd tortured someone, and so on. Batuk always had eyes on anything of interest. Always.

"It appears that Jim and I have more in common than you and me, in fact. Jim is unstoppable when it comes to desires. He draws on them like an unending fuel source. I've done some digging on the location you just left and have an inkling that Jim's about to come into possession of something just as powerful as the spice, if not more. Quiz time, Croy. If Jim has something I want and I have something he wants, what happens?"

Croy looked from Batuk back to Nora. His gaze much duller than before.

"That's right, Croy. And do you think having Jim see her bloodied and bruised will ease negotiations?"

Croy knew better than to not answer his question, so he shook his head.

Nora was enjoying this. For one, it felt like Batuk was taking a turn in his personality, being more diplomatic than normal. She chalked it up to old age. But second, she sure as hell enjoyed watching Croy look like a sad dog that just crapped on the floor, and its master just found it and was shoving its nose in it. If Croy had a tail, it would be between his legs.

"Exactly. Now if you don't mind," Batuk said sternly. "Please remove the bonds from Nora and go clean up your face."

Batuk then looked directly at Nora.

"And you, please do your best to refrain from laying a punch on him. It seems you've already managed a small nose fracture. That'll have to do for now. You two can hash things out further later on, once I'm done doing business.

I'd originally have put my money on you, but the ease of Croy's success and speed in bringing you here has me thinking I would have been better to bet on him at the start of all this."

Batuk must have had some sort of means of reading minds, because all Nora had been thinking about was sending her fist right back at Croy's stupid face. Alas. Nora released the tension she had built in her hands as Croy grumpily released her wrist restraints.

Knowing where she stood in this deal of Batuk's made her feel confident that she could agitate Croy further. She might not be able to use her fists, but she could now use words in a way Croy would understand without a doubt. The bit of freedom fueled the blood flow in Nora's body and she regained a bit of temporary strength. Croy still wasn't walking to the water basin in the corner of the room to wash his face, giving Nora the opportunity to put her words to use.

"That's right, you asshat. Listen to your master. And by the way, I think that dumb nose of yours is still bleeding. God, you're weak."

It took every ounce of Croy's willpower not to use his knife he already had out to free her wrists to now cut them entirely. Of course, the only emotion greater than his anger at Nora was his fear of what Batuk would do if he ruined his plans, and Nora knew this.

Admittedly, Batuk found it entertaining to see Croy struggle. The man had become entitled and egotistic over the years. Rightfully so, given his track record—and Batuk would continue using that to his advantage—but even Batuk found some delight in the novel experience of seeing Croy meet resistance.

Croy started to walk out of the office to wash up elsewhere, partly because he thought he was done with his work and partly because he thought that if he stayed, he'd most certainly defy Batuk's request to treat Nora like a guest.

"Not so quickly, Croy. You're still needed here. Clean up in the basin over there," Batuk said, pointing to the corner. It was as if Croy was getting a time out.

Once Croy's face was cleaned up, Batuk proceeded to share his plan with Nora and Croy. Well, *their* plan, really. He began by sharing a few more words about the magic that Jim was about to withhold so Nora and Croy understood the importance. Then he told Croy how to get ahold of Jim once he left the Crevice—and that if Croy wanted to stay on Phil's nice list, how he must do it before Jim made his way back to the States.

The plan was simple:

Find Jim;

Trade Nora for magic;

Tie up loose ends.

The loose end finale, of course, was that Nora and Croy would be able to settle the score they had against each other. As plans go, that would be that. Batuk waved Croy off and then directed Nora to a guest office that doubled as a bedroom for situations such as these.

"I don't need to tell you about your chances of escaping, or rather the lack of."

Nora had known Batuk a long time. He truly didn't. Nora was unphased. If anything, she appreciated the opportunity of a decent bed, decent food, and the time and space to think. That's what she needed to do. Think. Think of how she could save Jim. Think of how to finally cut ties with Batuk. Think of how she'd overcome Croy, since he'd already proved he'd win in a contest of strength.

In short, Nora had to think about how to survive. Fortunately this wasn't the first exercise of that survival muscle.

⋙LI⋘

Shaman Denny stood up, walked to a side of the slab wall and moved away the hanging vines to reveal a couple shelves of wooden bowls and wooden tools. These were not cave relics of a million years ago, though. They were wooden, sure, but they were clearly carved with grace. The muddlers had hieroglyphics on them. The spoons had stories. The whisks seemed to be made of a blend of wood and some sort of tantalic cotton. Denny waved the Irishman over to help grab the supplies and move them to the table. Once everything was laid out, Denny looked to Jim.

"Now, Jim. Make us something special to eat. No instructions. No reassurance. Just make us something."

Jim was taken a bit aback.

"How am I supposed to make something when I can't taste? I don't know what any of this tastes like," he enquired, already frustrated.

Denny looked at Jim like he should know the answer.

"Trust, of course. You know. That stuff made of instinct and thoughtfulness. That stuff blended from past experiences and the hopes of the future. You know. You don't need taste buds to trust your gut. Now you should start your work, because ours starts in..." Denny looked up to the sky that was turning dusk, "...about two hours, and the Irishman and I have a bit of preparation of our own to do."

Slightly dazed and confused, Jim stared at Denny.

Denny's response?

He pulled out a chocolate milk bottle.

"You... you have more spice?"

"You really think I'd just make enough for you? Ha! But don't get cocky about your dish just because I've got some spice here. There's still one more ingredient needed. One the Irishman over here can extract and bend to his will. One Pinmekalah doesn't even know was in the Sun Monk

Sauce. That ingredient, or its lack, is the reason I couldn't continue making it once the Irishman decided to go chase more enlightenment. Now. Like I said. Get to work."

Jim didn't immediately move for two reasons. One, still being in awe of the sneakery of Shaman Denny. Second, because any good chef in the world knows that the best recipes don't come from ingredients at their fingertips; they come from a pen and paper. Though, in Jim's case, a pencil rather than pen, which was in company with the other supplies Shaman Denny and the Irishman laid out on the table for him.

Jim took a seat on the stool that Shaman Denny had been sitting in while he and the Irishman walked over to some type of contraption Jim hadn't noticed, given how overgrown the plants were around it. The device looked like a telescope of sorts but also had a beaker system at its base. Shaman Denny stopped tinkering and bellowed at Jim.

"Well? What are you waiting for?!"

Jim averted his gaze and redirected it to the pencil in hand and paper on the table. He then looked around the pantry he was in. He smelled Darjeeling tea. He heard a thump thump thump of an insect that sounded like a rain dance. He saw a plant exchange drippings of a sugared water back and forth between its pods like Newton's cradle.

Jim combined his sensory intake with what he knew about balancing flavors, harmonizing mouth feels, blending aromatics, and accentuating his dishes with the unexpected. Ha. Unexpected. Given Jim couldn't identify anything in the pantry, the entire dish would be unexpected, at least by means of taste. Though Denny said he'd offer no reassurance, he sort of already had by showing that he had some of the Spice of Life. Jim figured even if he didn't nail the recipe, the spice would make up for anything it lacked. That was enough reassurance to put Jim into motion.

Jim started collecting ingredients that he noted on his paper (plant that looks like an onion, insect that looks like a centipede, the juice of that one plant drooping like a tilted cauldron, and so on) and checked them off, respectively. Even more respectfully, he thanked the plant and insects which he undoubtedly misnamed on the paper. Jim didn't always do this with the food he cooked with, but being where he was, he felt like he was on sacred ground, a temple of sorts. And being perfectly honest, Jim felt like the plants might come to life and kill him if he made a wrong move. They seemed to have personalities. Energy. Care. Some of which were eager to join the other recruits of Jim's recipe. Some a bit more timid or difficult to pull and persuade. Then as Jim picked the berries he had noted looked like gooseberries with a durian outside, checking off the last item on his list, he wondered how he'd actually *cook* the dish.

The Irishman was one step ahead of him and while he finicked with the contraption a bit more, he directed Denny to build a fire at the center of the table. It ceased to be a table, but rather a grill or stove top in addition to a workbench. Jim did just that. He got to work on the bench.

Denny returned to the Irishman spitting on a latch to get it unstuck.

"When are you going to fill me in on what this is meant to do?" asked Denny. "I have an inkling."

"An' why d'ya reckon folks be wishin' on the stars?"

Denny started to get red in the face. It's hard not to get frustrated when you're talking to someone who seems to speak only in riddles.

Continuing to tinker, finally getting the latch open, the Irishman answered his own question.

"Magic, that's why. Most'll tell ya it's only superstitious nonsense, a bit of a joke, or an excuse for how they managed t'get what they were after. Others'll call it the child's kind o' magic—hope, y'know—the start of believin' their wish might come true. But in all fairness to the life we're liv-in', the magic's real. This isn't some old telescope, now. It's a way o' catchin' a bit o' stardust. That's what goes into the Sun Monk's Sauce. That's what'll be in the food Jim makes. I can bend it here, but you'll have t'blend it like ya used to with the Sun Monk's Sauce." He paused to appreciate the face of Denny's reaction. His expression was studiously bland, but the Irishman saw beneath it. He'd never shared this process with Shaman Denny, and they were breaking new ground in their longstanding association. This was ca-maraderie at its finest.

"As for the actual plan?" The Irishman continued speaking though he stopped tinkering and looked at Jim working the stove like he'd been using it all his life.

"The plan itself, now, is we're gonna be creatin' a new flavor. A seventh one, so it is. A flavor that brings together the dish, the spice you've got there, an' the stardust. I've worked the stardust in with other bits before, sure, but nev-er alongside the Spice o' Life. Somehow, I've a feelin' you knew all this already, didn't ya?"

The Irishman glanced over to Shaman Denny to see a smirk on his face, and then returned his attention back to tinkering.

"You know, people forget there was once only one won-der of the world. That is, until more were added and more still could be added. There's no limit to the wonders of the world, so magnificent and majestic, why should there be a limit to equally abstract manifestations such as flavor?"

The Irishman appreciated the logic.

Shaman Denny took a sniff in the air. What was levitat-ing atop the grill and journeying its way to his nostrils was magnificent. He'd never smelled anything like it.

"Now then, if ye'd be so kind an' give that lever a good pull, tryin' t'level the whole thing out. I took it apart meself, y'see, so no one else'd be meddlin' with it. Never thought it'd be this tricky puttin' all the bits back where they belong.

Quick now, will ya? Time's slippin'. An' if ye haven't guessed, one doesn't just go n'grab stardust from the sky the way ye'd fetch a cup o' coffee on Main Street. We've t'time it just right with the shootin' stars, dancin' their own little salsa across the night. Once ye've brewed as much Sun Monk Sauce as meself, ye'll know well enough that dust from some stars works better than others. Ahh, there we are."

Jim wasn't paying attention; he was in the groove, his chopping and whisking and stirring and brisking a virtual dance of the kitchen cosmos. The Irishman looked up at Jim with just a hint of astonishment, like he was a sport spectator and Jim was in the final stretch of a race. The Irishman figured he had a few minutes to spare and didn't want to disrupt Jim from the flow he had found. And to think, Jim was doing this all without his ability to taste. Ha.

"Now's as good a time as any t'catch ya up t'speed on things, so it is," the Irishman said to Shaman Denny.

The Shaman D sat on the ground, but with a bit of lean forward, lusting for any crumbs of knowledge he might not already have. You'd think he was sitting on the edge of a thinking chair. Denny's eyes remained wide and his brain ready to absorb the information like the vegetables on Jim's table oven were absorbing the inscrutable nectars of the insects and flowers.

The Irishman took a different posture. Not of a master ready to teach his final lesson, but of someone who appeared exhausted by the weight he bore. Knowledge isn't just power; it's responsibility, and responsibility is heavy.

"The journeys we've taken, an' all we've uncovered on this land... sure, it's been nothin' short of incredible. We've brushed up against all sorts of enlightenment, but I've always felt the light of it all was a bit dim, y'know? Most everything we learned was tied to what's here—inside ourselves or under our feet. But what I've come t'see is this: The final ingredient, it comes from above. Not from some God, nor from a celestial bein', but straight from the universe itself.

Not somethin' ye can sketch in a book or paint in a drawin', but only what's out there—the sky an' its stars.

"I'll admit, I even gave in to swallowin' down the scholars' work. An' sure enough, like the wind itself, they've no clue where the stars truly begin, nor the means to test the strange bits inside 'em, or the auraric traces they leave behind. It took me time, an' no small bit o' help, to piece together this invention. Between you an' me, Batuk sparked some of the ideas for its parts. Mad, isn't it? What ye can learn from a soul without ever sittin' across from 'em."

"But for our sake, best not t'let Jim catch wind o' that. Still, it's insight I want you t'hold close. Observance, that's the key. Whether it's good or ill bein' done, watchin' tells ya more than meddlin' ever could. Interferin' only muddies the truth or slows the whole lot down."

The Irishman looked at the ground.

"The things I had t'witness to get here… the things Batuk an' the others have done… Jaysus, it's harrowin'. But I'm reminded, all the same, of what I've gotten out of it—the here an' now."

The Irishman tapped the telescope-like invention.

"This… this here's what we use t'trail the shootin' stars an' catch their dust in a container. An' it's true enough I can bend the magic of it all—though it's been a fair few years since I last did."

He paused a moment.

"It's both that simple, an' not that simple, y'see. Stars, they move fierce fast, so it took a fair bit o' practice trailin' 'em steady enough, long enough. The first dozen times I gave it a go, I came away with nothin'. But with time, an' a bit o' intention married to me attention, I caught a little… an' then I caught a lot.

"On the outside it looks simple enough, once ye've the steady hand for it. But on the inside—ah, that cost me. I walked a total of five-thousand, two-hundred an' three miles on me own two feet, near died in three caves—one o' them under the water—watched folk like Batuk commit acts I'd not wish on me worst enemy, an' gathered up crystals that were sacred treasures to half a dozen Buddhist groups. That's the short of it.

"Add to that the endless tinkerin', the consultin' with other shamans, scholars, nomads, even a handful o' spies... Jaysus, I could write a whole book on the matter."

Denny remained silent, feeling as though the Irishman wasn't finished. The Irishman took a deep breath. The kind that bloats the soul. The kind that precedes relief. The kind *Namaste* would breathe if it were a person. But also the kind a kid takes before blowing up a balloon on their own. The kind one takes before blowing the seeds off a dandelion. The kind one takes before blowing the candles on a birthday cake after making a wish.

"That's all t'say, I know rightly there's more out there in the world—more than this bit o' magic I've stumbled on. Same as I know there's more you yerself can do, an' more ye'll discover in time. An' that's why I've rigged this contraption t'crumble into dust after it's used the once more. Merely takin' it apart before only brought us back here again.

"But now, I'm content. Enlightened, if ye'd call it that— or maybe just plain satisfied with what I've given this world. After this, I'll be slippin' into another o' me spiritual hibernations—a reprieve, a bit of a rest. Sure, call it a vacation if ye like."

The Irishman reached into his pocket and pulled out an envelope.

"Now then, if ye wouldn't mind, pass this along t'Pinmekalah. Nothin' secret inside, I'll tell ya that much—just a few kind words for a friend who's well due 'em.

"An' as for yerself, I've no doubt ye'll see straight through whatever it is ye've gotten tangled up in with Jim an' Nora. I'll be eager t'hear the whispers in the wind o' what ye manage on yer own.

"Ye know now all I know. An' ye see it's not the information that gives life its meanin'—it's the doin' of it. Take Jim, now. Even he knows—subconsciously, mind ye—that makin' is better than eatin'. Have ye ever seen a soul put so much heart on display without sayin' a single word? Look."

Shaman Denny was chewing on all the words. They were pleasantly numbing. They tasted sweet enough that he wanted more but at the same time, bitter enough that he had had enough. It would take Denny a while to digest them. Anyway, he knew that right now his responsibility was to help how he could. He looked at Jim. The Irishman followed his gaze with a bit of a smirk at seeing Jim finish his art.

Jim had scraped the food he had made into a bowl and grabbed a bell-shaped plant and poured the liquid that sat inside it like a pool onto the table, extinguishing the fire he had used. He looked at the bowl. Stared at it, actually. Got lost in it, really. Emotionally. Spiritually.

The broth glistened perfectly. The vegetables were both long and straw-like, but there were also chunks of chewiness from the insects he'd tossed in, which gave it the perfect texture. He held the bowl up to his nose and took a deep breath. A soup of bliss, he thought. Jim just knew it would taste great. At that moment, he didn't want to give the bowl up. He had never poured his heart into a dish like he just had. He'd never felt *wu wei* like this. Giving this bowl up felt like he was giving a part of himself. It's ethereal to leverage every other sense but taste in the kitchen. He was restrained in one sense but relentless in others. He looked at Shaman Denny and the Irishman and asked the question a shark always asks after finishing a meal, a question only a person who wants to live life to the fullest asks, the question a soul asks before heading into the afterlife.

"What's next?"

The Irishman held out a hand to Shaman Denny, who handed him the bottle with the Spice of Life. He gently

tapped a sprinkle over the bowl, and Jim could smell it doing its magic. Then the Irishman held up another container, but rather than handing it to Jim like Jim thought he
would, the Irishman put it on the bottom of his contraption, leaned over and peered into the invention while he
felt for the switch on the side that would turn it on.

"Look t'the sky, the pair o' ye," the Irishman said as he
moved his hands around the contraption and turning dials
here, there, and over there and over here, while keeping
his eye peering through the looking glass.

"There you are," the Irishman said in unison with the
sswsht sound of the switch turning on.

In the sky, now blanketed black with what looked like
speckles of static, Jim and Shaman Denny watched stars
start to reveal themselves. Some disappeared as quickly as
they appeared. They looked back at the Irishman, followed
where he was pointing the telescope and saw what he saw:
a shooting star.

In the moment Shaman Denny merely saw a shooting
star, the same he had seen many nights looking up at the
sky in the desert with other Buddhists and nomads. Jim,
however, had heightened sight, and while it was not super-
natural, it was enough that he could see the tail of the star
turn into tiny particles that... it couldn't be, he thought.

They were falling down toward them.

Shaman Denny kept watching the shooting stars make
their way across the sky as Jim followed the dust from the
sky to nearly right in front of him and into the telescope.
Slowly but surely the container was filled with a layer of
stardust. Denny watched the star in the sky disappear into
the ether. The Irishman removed his eye from its place-
holder and grabbed the container while he turned to Jim.

"Grab the bowl, Jim."

Jim wordlessly did as directed.

The Irishman removed the lid of the bottle and poured
it over Jim's dish. To think, Jim had thought the broth

glistened before. The dish he had made began to transform. This wasn't your typical salt and pepper on top. This was pure celestial magic at play and to both Denny and Jim's surprise, the Irishman poured all of the star dust on the dish. Rather than taking the shape of a sand dune atop Jim's dish, it seemed to boil and liquify all the ingredients into a sauce. It intermingled like a marriage ritual.

Jim's sauce. Jim Herough's sauce.

"Herough Herough sauce," Jim said aloud.

Shaman Denny and The Irishman couldn't help but laugh at it. They were maxed with bliss. Overflowing with dopamine. The adrenaline rush they couldn't begin to describe (but if they had it might be something like: When you twist the throttle and feel a motorcycle surge forward, the world blurs into streaks of color and light. The wind grabs at your clothing and screams in your ears, a primal howl that drowns out rational thought. Your heart hammers in your chest, each beat syncing with the roar of the engine beneath you. Every nerve is electrified, alive with the razor-edge thrill that dances between control and chaos. The road beneath you twists and snakes, a ribbon that beckons you to chase it further into the unknown. Time warps and slows, and in that heartbeat of a moment, you're weightless—flying free with a grin that spreads wide under your helmet. The rush of adrenaline sets your senses alight, a potent cocktail of exhilaration, fear, and invincibility grips you tight and won't let go. For those fleeting seconds, you're not just riding a motorcycle; you're defying gravity and embracing pure, unfiltered speed). That was the spice, the celestial magic, Herough Herough's sauce: unfiltered life served in a bowl. Vroom. Vroom.

Of course Jim would make light of the situation with humor. Jim followed his naming ritual with actual *Herough Herough Herough* laughter. Shaman Denny and the Irishman, elated, couldn't help but join in. It was one of those rare situations when something so good happens that all you can do is smile and laugh in surprise and awe. One of those laughs that echo beyond the walls and across the land and up to the stars where the moon joined in. A rarity, indeed.

Their chuckles settled down into silence in sync with the powder turning the remainder of the dish into a liquid sauce, glistening, and turning a wavy green and red hue. Christmas in a cup.

The Irishman pulled a five-ounce bottle from his pocket and with the pour spout of the bowl, assisted Jim in moving the liquid contents from the bowl to the bottle. The contents of the bowl were reduced from the heat of the magical transformation, leaving just a bit more than five ounces in the bowl. A mathematical consequence of alchemy in that you get less from more, but more from less. The Irishman sealed the bottle. As he tightened it, both Jim and Denny were spooked at the sound of a series of loud cracks behind them. Thankfully the Irishman was holding the bottle lest it be dropped by Jim or Denny.

The telescope beside them cracked and crumbled. The ground where it stood was now covered with broken hieroglyphic wood, bits and pieces of crystals of varying color; even the looking glass was cracked in three parts. It didn't require a keen eye like Jim's to see that there was simply no recovering the equipment. It might as well degrade into the floor now. Its mission was complete and it was ready for the afterlife.

"Your device!" Jim yelled at the Irishman in panic.

""I know," says the Irishman, calm as you like. "There's a weightier matter at hand here, an' it's not about me nor that device. What ye've just done... what's in this bottle— it's a new flavour. Never tasted before, never made, never known, neither in the craftin' of it nor in the takin' of it. This is magic in a bottle, sure an' certain. It'll bring back your sense o'taste, set your body right again, an' with luck there'll be a bit left over for whatever else ye choose."

"Two words o' caution, though."

"The first is this: if ye hand it round to others, tryin' t'sell a dish, ye'll run it dry soon enough. Think o' Batuk, an' you'll remember what a body's willin' t'do—or sacrifice—for the thing they're after. Best advice I've for ye is savour it. Keep it close for the moments that truly matter. The simple ones. Like a bowl o'scrambled eggs with ketchup of a mornin', after a long night talkin' with someone ye hold dear. It'll be those small, ordinary moments ye'll lean on for the rest o'your days."

"The second is about Batuk."

"In my efforts to learn from him over the years, he knows what we've done here. He doesn't know how, but he knows the end result. He's tried a few times to capture me for my knowledge of the contraption that you just saw me destroy. It's no surprise that he's merely been waiting for me to put it to use again like I had so many times making the Sun Monk Sauce for Queen P. In thinking it through, chances are likely he intended for you to remain behind while he took the leverage he needed."

All of this news swirled and suffocated Jim. Being honest as he always was, Jim, in the time it took him to make the dish and watch the star dust get captured, had forgotten about everything else. The bet. His restaurant. Don't tell her, but even Nora. Now that devilish sting of reality sunk into his soul, but he held onto the calmness that the Irishman was showing in front of him.

The Irishman gave his warnings, but they weren't expressed with fear or doubt; they were given with the absence of sorrow or concern. *That*, to Jim, was the real gift in the moment.

Shaman Denny opened his mouth to speak—the calm of the Irishman didn't affect him quite the same as Jim—but the Irishman gave him a glance that could melt popsicles and Denny kept quiet.

Jim placed his hand out for the bottle from The Irish-man and thought deeply. His thoughts dug a hole, lay-ers deep enough that they reached the underbelly of the mountain they stood atop. The brain may not be a sense itself, but Jim was thinking as if it, too, was superpowered by the lack of taste.

Shaman Denny thought Jim would take a straight swig of the sauce now, get his sense of taste back, and figure out what to do about getting Nora back after. Hell. Even your dear writer thought that would be the logical path. So what if Batuk got the remnants of the sauce, if he got his taste back and exchanged the remnants for Nora?

But if we were to look at the situation with truthful eyes? The first is that the chances were slim to none that Batuk would simply let them carry on with their merry selves after getting the sauce.

The second, dear reader, is that Jim had a sensory ad-vantage. He could smell a lie. He could feel the tremble of fear. He could damn near hear thoughts before they left an-other's mouth. In most scenarios, other than, say, a tasting panel, this put Jim at an advantage. Anyway, Jim thought he'd gone this long without his sense of taste. What's a little while longer?

Jim placed the bottle of sauce in his pocket and looked back up at the Irishman.

"So, how does one find Batuk?"

≽ LII ≼

Most people, after learning they're being watched, try to research the watchers. The Sun Monk Sauce net-work carried back more than money and good will; it also gathered information about Batuk, which is why the Irish-man and Shaman Denny had been able to avoid capture all these years.

Nestled in the bustling heart of Bangkok, the head-quarters of the notorious entrepreneur stands as an imposing structure, a testament to his ambition and ruthlessness. This multi-story skyscraper pierces the skyline like a dagger, its darkened glass facade reflecting the vibrant yet chaotic energy of the city below.

Every floor was meticulously designed to cater to one of Batuk's myriad operations. The lower levels housed sprawling, high-tech laboratories for his nefarious experiments and innovations. Mid-level floors were dedicated to administrative functions. The upper floors were where Batuk's true power was evident: private quarters, opulent meeting rooms, luxurious executive negotiation suites. One master office had the most opulence and the best view. Of course, that was Batuk's. The building also had a few floors of hotel-like rooms that he offered to clients, customers, and employees in transition from one facility or product line to another. It even had a kitchen that took up an entire floor, a nod of accomplishment to the Sessalt acquisition.

For the last two days as Nora waited to be told what to do, she strolled and surveyed what she was permitted to after she had rested and recovered a bit from her wounds and wooziness. She was allowed to be in her room, naturally, but also had access to the kitchen, fitness center, entertainment room for some billiards, etc. Nora took in as much information about the space as possible. Though she had been to this building many times before, she had never been required to visit or monitor the floors that did not involve her business. She got a good idea of where the cameras were. She determined the typical rotation of the guards. And then she learned about as many of those staying in the other hotel rooms as possible—mainly from the billiard players. She even made time to practice some Krav Maga in the gym, visualizing Croy as her enemy the entire time, naturally.

She was in her home territory, in a way. But despite Nora's proclivity for getting herself both in and out of particularly dangerous situations, she struggled to see any form of convenient or semi-convenient way out without any help. It's also worth noting that her Tiger ankle tattoo no longer gave her any leverage. Despite Batuk's directive that Croy not cause Nora any harm, the angry assassin did have a couple of his men hold Nora down and burn the tattoo away. It was a form of exile from a unique, worldwide community. When you're Batuk, with properties across the globe, there's really no such thing as a traditional exile. Croy's searing transgression deprived Nora of a major asset, but the burn also gave Nora some of the solace she had been searching for. It was almost as if she was being given a fresh start. She'd have to make her own leverage. She might even run into others who have had their tattoos "removed." That is... if she ever escaped her cushy, but ironclad, custody.

One thing was pleasant about her stay in the skyscraper, though: Croy wasn't there.

Now reader, you might be thinking what your dear author is thinking: Why in the world would Croy leave Jim behind when Phil had hired Croy to put a tombstone in the ground?

Consider for a moment that a jaguar's success rate in catching its prey is a mere five percent. This isn't due to any lack of jaguaristic talent; rather, it's the joy and satisfaction of the chase itself. That "journey not the destination" mentality is the adrenaline soup Croy savors for breakfast, lunch, and dinner. And lest you think Croy is a nimwit, he had things carefully calculated in his plan to capture Nora and subsequently go back on the hunt for Jim.

His orders to intercept Jim at the Bangkok airport gave Croy a bit of time to handle some other business. After all, what Croy provided was a service. Primarily to Batuk, sure, but to plenty of others as well. Croy's email had a fair few new requests come in from the last few days. There were the typical "Husband did me wrong and I want him dead" requests and the all-too-common "I can't wait for my inheritance" demands. Croy always hit "delete" on those emails. They weren't fun enough for him. They were always followed up with "but I don't want him to feel pain" or "could you do it while they were sleeping?" Rarely would they pay well, too. No money. No honey. Croy did respond to one promising inquiry, however. A man whose brother was in line for the throne of some third-world country wanted to skip ahead in line, so to speak. The funny thing is that about a half-dozen emails later, there was an email from the heir asking whether Croy could eliminate the troublesome younger sibling. Ha. Say what you will about Croy, he's a man of his word; even though the heir offered more, Croy had already responded to the first message. A classic condition of first come, first killed. Right when Croy had almost cleared his inbox, a new message popped up.

From: Phil

To: Croy

Croy. Has something happened to you? Has he been taken care of? Get back to me.

Croy got agitated. He learned early in his career to not say something has been done when it hadn't, even though he was one hundred percent certain that he'd take care of Jim as soon as Batuk got his sauce.

(What his experience told him to write:)

To: Phil

From: Croy

I'm more irritated than you about him. I'll touch base in twenty-four hours with an update you'll be pleased with.

(What he actually wrote, in a fit of agitated impatience:)

To: Phil

From: Croy

The job is done. It took a bit longer for reasons I can't share, but it's the end of him. I made sure he suffered for the delay that was caused. Until next time.

The best,

—C

Croy set down his phone and ruminated on what he'd do to Jim *and* Nora. The only frustration he felt was which would be more entertaining to watch while he dispatched the other to the afterlife.

Jim and company had sort of forgotten about what a hard trek it had been up the mountain. They stopped at the hut that had been burnt to ash by Croy, and the Irishman extracted the tea kettle from the mound of charred wood.

"Pinmekalah sent me this long ago. She included a note with it about how she had tea to thank for helping her keep her nerves as she went through the trials and tribulations of growing her distribution network."

"We could probably all use a cup of tea right now, by that logic," Denny quipped, trying to lighten the mood.

It didn't.

The Irishman was wallowing in woe, feeling like he'd reached the end of his mission on Earth with nothing to look forward to.

Jim, in contrast, was metaphorically marching forth with both accuracy and fury. Just as Nora was searching Batuk's bastion for a way out of this mess, Jim was racking his brain on how he should approach Batuk, how he could make a trade, how he could get himself and Nora away to live their life out of this mess. A mess. That's all that this was. They just had some cleaning up to do. He almost believed it.

⇒LIII⇐

The Irishman, Shaman Denny, and Jim traveled together to the Bangkok airport. In case you were wondering, they got there by way of an alternative small private plane coordinated previously by the Irishman, as Jim and Nora's original guide had all but left them.

Both the Irishman and Denny felt a responsibility over Jim. Not exactly a paternal responsibility, but the sort a mentor feels for a mentee, or perhaps a tour guide for people who've bought their ticket and dutifully followed along.

They'd see him off from the airport with direction to Batuk's satellite headquarters in the States where the Irishman figured he would be—if not right away, then soon thereafter.

The airport is a funny place. Every person there has their own agenda. This is especially true in the Bangkok airport. There are few who work there that have not been paid off to look the other way or, sometimes, to get their own hands dirty. Airport? Business district? Black market? Chinatown? What's the difference?

Any guesses, smart reader, on who has had a great deal of dealings in the airport?

Ding ding ding. If you guessed Croy then you're a winner! Your prize waits for you under the seat of the corner post chair in gate A32 at the Bangkok international airport.

Since the Irishman, Shaman Denny, and Jim never had reason to conduct any form of business in the airport, they didn't know, despite their various degrees of enlightenment, that random police searches were just a front for more nefarious happenings.

Alas. Turns out they were "randomly" selected for a search and questioning even before Jim could purchase a plane ticket.

It was a safety protocol, the group was told.

Shaman Denny, who spoke the most Thai, informed Jim and the Irishman that they were being brought to a different room for a randomly assigned interrogation.

Great, Jim thought sourly. Every extra minute it took him reach Batuk was a minute that something terrible could be happening to Nora.

"Will this be quick?" Jim asked.

Denny asked the police in Thai.

"They said, 'time will tell,'" Denny reported.

"Well, that's not promising," Jim replied, his nose twitching at the scent of deceit.

The Irishman, though silent, couldn't agree more. What are the chances, he thought, that the three of them would get randomly selected? He shrugged off the hunch, answering his question rationally: It was rare that they traveled, so that's likely what set the trigger off in the event it wasn't truly random. He knew the three of them had nothing to hide, so he followed instructions.

Turn here. Walk through this gate. Turn again. Head down the escalator. Go through this unmarked door. Down another hall.

The three of them walked so far that it felt like they were traversing the mountain to Kar Tresa's Crevice again. In truth, before long it didn't even feel like they were in the airport anymore, but rather a bunker of sorts, both deep and long beyond the airport gates. Jim couldn't even hear the sounds of planes taking off or landing. Hmph.

After a few too many paces and increasing questions and doubts from the group—which were unanswered by the escort—the whole group arrived in front of a rotunda of sorts.

Not quite a room of its own, but not quite a full lobby, either.

The escort (not the fun kind) didn't speak another word. They simply turned around and left the rotunda through the door they came in. Jim, by now fully aware that this was no routine random search, was the first to notice that it was the *only* door in or out of the room. He heard a latch lock firmly into place when it closed. All three men were surveying the rotunda when the lights turned on and they saw Croy leaning against some dusty bookshelves on a wall.

He pushed off and then brushed the dust off his overcoat.

"I told you I'd be seeing you soon," Croy said, clearly directing his statement at Jim. "It's a bit of a bummer just how easy you've made all of this, though."

"An' what is it ye're wantin' with him, then?" said the Irishman, sternly, as if this were a simple inconvenience and the three would soon be back on their merry way.

"Two things, really. That little bottle, which Batuk wants, and then Jim's life. Thanks for asking."

Jim didn't need enhanced senses to know he was telling the truth.

The Irishman stood in front of Denny and Jim and continued to speak for them.

"We're already on our way t'Batuk. Yer services aren't needed no more. Now let us get back t'our own business—an' don't be even thinkin' o'takin' his life."

Croy laughed, sending maniacal echoes rippling through the rotunda. If the laughter were to leave marks on walls, it would have mapped out over twenty evil schemes. It was powered by pain, hellfire, and everything malicious.

"You can take your Irish accent and shove it up your ass. Do you even know who you're dealing with?"

Croy was about to continue but the Irishman stepped forward and confronted him. This was completely out of character for the Irishman, but after the ritual, his behavior had changed; he was more relatable, almost human, even. A touch lost, perhaps.

"I do. Yer nothin' but a no-good piece o'trash, the sort Batuk has t'keep on a short leash. We've our own lives t'live, an' I'll tell ya this—you..."

Before the Irishman could finish his sentence, Croy had taken his *pesh-kabz* and stabbed the Irishman through the stomach.

Slicing, in particular order, the stomach, a piece of the spleen, and the diaphragm, with the tip finishing its job by puncturing a pinch of his left lung. Blood flowed from the Irishman's mouth and from the hole the knife made. There were no words coming out of his mouth, no finished sentence, but a final half breath took a ride from inside the Irishman, up from his one unpunctured lung and journeyed down the slow and thinning waterfall of blood from his mouth. Croy held the Irishman up, though the body was lifeless and unable to hear, he whispered into one ear, "You won't say a word."

The Irishman's body fell to the ground with a thud that echoed just as Croy's laughter did.

"Damn, that feels good to have shut at least one of you up. A trifling addendum to my mission to bring you, Jim, to Batuk."

Jim and Shaman Denny were at a loss for words. The words had packed their bags and took off to Timbuktu. The words had dug their own graves and buried themselves alive. The words had tossed out their GPS and got lost on some neuron or another in the brain. The most they could muster was a gasp. Air that carried zero syllables.

Shaman Denny ran to the Irishman's body and held it up.

Shaman Denny was the first to speak up toward Croy while cradling the already coldening and stiffening Irishman's body.

"You'll pay for this," Denny said through gritted teeth. Denny didn't hear Croy's response, that he actually *gets paid* for this. The Irishman hadn't been mentioned by Batuk in particular as being necessary or not, but if he was with Jim and Shaman Denny, then there must be some merit to making him a permanent mute, an unwrapped mummy, a guy that's all but dead.

Jim's soul was as depressed as depressed could get in the moment. Jim heard the sadness in Shaman Denny's sobs. He could feel the absence of movement in the Irishman's body. He could already smell the start of a corpse's scent. He'd gone to two funerals in his life, but that was before he'd acquired his enhanced senses; he'd never actually smelled what death was like. His senses were overwhelmed. He joined Denny at the body of the Irishman, simply not believing what his eyes just witnessed. The smell up close wasn't just of death, it was of a life cut too short; a life nearly fulfilled; of a severed connection to another that was on the back nine of the golf course of life.

Jim had butchered chickens and ducks. He'd caught and filleted fish. He'd exterminated innumerable insects. But he'd never witnessed a murder of another person this close. Maybe a few close calls in traffic accidents, or there was that one chef that got glitzy with grease while grilling a steak and seared his own flesh in the process. But nothing like this.

It was almost overwhelming, but Jim's vehement focus anchored him. He quickly concluded that the best way to gain retribution for the Irishman was to move forward and actually retribute, not wallow.

"Bring us to Batuk," Jim said to Croy, pure anger and gumption in every syllable.

Croy, whose senses were not enhanced to superhuman levels and who saw nothing threatening in Jim's gumption, said, "With pleasure."

(Before the next chapter, I, your devoted author, need to explain something about Jim. Jim believed that drowning in sorrow over the death of someone you care about may feel like a profound expression of love and grief, but it can also be a disservice to their memory. At its core, this overwhelming sadness often stems from a deep-seated fear of our own mortality. This focus on our own pain and loss can become an act of selfishness, diverting attention from the joy and love that the departed brought into our lives. Instead of being consumed by grief, Jim believed we should honor their memory by celebrating their life and the positive impact they had. Embracing their legacy with gratitude and living fully in their honor allows us to find meaning and purpose, transforming our sorrow into a testament to their lasting influence on our lives. Any time between their death and this realization is merely wasted time. Jim can't stand wasting time. There's not really any to waste, so they say, anyway.

I thought it was important to say all this, dear reader, so you understand the spirit in which Jim was advancing on Batuk: filled with reverence for the life and incalculable gifts of the Irishman, blazing with anxiety and ironclad affection for Nora, and, quite frankly, royally pissed off.)

This page isn't meant to last. Burn it, bury it, or leave it in a public library.

⇒LIV⇐

Shaman Denny took some coaxing to begin with to get him moving from the rotunda to Croy's private helicopter. Croy pushed Denny up the stairs into the sleek vehicle, smirking at the sound of Denny's pain as his shins hit the step. This chopper was a far hop, skip, and architecturally advanced jump away from the little plane he had in the Crevice.

Prior to the door rising up and closing, Denny took a look back and swore to himself that he would retrieve the Irishman's body and lay it to rest in Kar Tresa's Crevice, where, to Denny, the Irishman had opened his heart the most he ever had.

The copter flight was short enough to Batuk's HQ, but though they had some down time (or would it be up time?), Shaman Denny didn't spit a word. He didn't even make eye contact with either Jim or Croy. He simply stared out of the window. If you had Jim's eyes, you would plainly see the battle on Denny's face between anger mixed with a lust for vengeance and heartfelt sorrow mixed with an attempt at not letting one's emotions best them. After all, Shaman Denny had faced no shortage of emotional and intellectual challenges over his training and life as a shaman, much of which was at the tutelage of the Irishman. He'd endured pain. He controlled his emotions when he fasted for ninety days straight. He's even tolerated the naivety of more than one amateur as he tried to train them. But nowhere in any literature or Buddhist teaching or Shamanistic study does one learn how to overcome the emotional rupture of losing someone close. They have tried, but no theory was serving Denny in that moment. The only thing Shaman Denny could think of as close to it is a broken heart, which was for him an abstraction since he'd never had a romantic partner. He had nothing to compare this to.

Jim, on the other hand, had felt such a thing, which may explain why he had a bit more composure. The searing flames of heartbreak temper a man.

Jim recalled that heartbreak while on the flight. Like Shaman Denny, Jim, too, was thinking of the time he felt as close to how he feels right now.

Thinking of his past always stirred up a complex dichotomy of anger, jealousy, regret, and, still, love. Jim thought about his last meaningful relationship, and the guy she was probably dancing with in Timbuktu. He spoke to the guy in his head.

"You'll never love her like I could love her. Never lead with as much selflessness as I could. Not care for her as deeply. Not motivate her and encourage her as much as I could. You'll never make love to her like I could. But what's even more important is that you'll never appreciate her as much as me. You won't be as inspired by her as me. You don't understand that loving her isn't what fulfills her most, it's her knowing that her love has a meaningful impact that makes her feel fulfilled. To be truly moved by her tenderness and by her tenacity. To let her love makes you the best person you could possibly be. No. You'll never love nor be loved by her the way I could." He paused in his speech to nobody as the reality of the death he'd just experienced washed over him again. "And you'll never understand the magnitude of what a gift life is, because you don't understand death."

Jim snapped himself out of his internal monologue, thanks to the turbulence they were experiencing on the helicopter.

Croy was awaiting his eye. He saw a pain in Jim similar to the one he so easily saw in Shaman Denny. Croy wished to expound upon it.

"Such a shame your friend had to die."

"He didn't."

"Well, obviously he did, given the fact he's dead. And soon you and Nora will be, too."

Croy looked at Shaman Denny.

"I'm just going to guess you will as well," Croy added. Denny remained still as a statue and tuned out of the conversation, still battling internally with his emotions, searching for peace in the endless blanket of white clouds out the window.

Now, in the light of the fancy copter, Jim had his first good look at Croy's face. One hundred percent brute, no doubt about it. Scars to show it. But the cut along his nose and a bit of dried blood inside it indicated that the injury was fresh.

Jim took a whack at the possibility that, maybe, just maybe, it was Nora's doing after he had been knocked out. Jim thought more about it and decided that of course it was. Nora wasn't someone who'd go down without a fight.

"Such a shame your nose had to be broken," Jim retorted.

Croy stood up and leaned over at Jim with his fist raised, a swallow's cry away from walloping him, from feeding him a fist sandwich, from giving *him* a nose job.

As you'd expect, Batuk's words restrained his fist, but the gesture told Jim that he had struck a nerve.

"Nora, huh? And to think I thought you were tough," Jim said with a classic Herough laugh, of the sort that we haven't heard since Kar Tresa's Crevice.

At this point, Jim knew that Croy really wanted to let his fist fly... but he didn't. Jim could sense the stress of restraint through Croy's body. He was fighting the urge with all his might.

Oh, this is going to be fun, Jim thought.

Putting three and three together, Jim concluded that Batuk had given Croy orders not to harm him. It was the only logical explanation for why he hadn't touched him yet.

Jim would test the theory by poking more at Croy's soft spots in a moment, but time was ticking and Jim had a burning question that he needed to ask now that he had Croy's full attention.

"I know what Batuk wants, but why not just take it and leave all of us alone?" Jim asked while placing his hands on the satchel of his that held the recently dubbed Herough Herough Sauce.

Croy was a bit more transparent than Jim anticipated, namely because this was the same question that *he* expressed to Batuk before leaving to capture Jim.

Croy explained that Batuk's response was "with time," and Croy imagined what that meant through the lens of what he hoped it meant.

"That means that once he gets what he wants, he'll either 1) Get more out of you that you didn't even know you had, or 2) he'll hand you both back to me to make it more of a game for me. Now that I say it out loud, that's probably it. Money is great, but he knows the real reward to me would be to give me a mouse to chase... or in this case, a couple of mice. Nora's good, no doubt about that. What will be interesting is if in the pursuit, she leaves your slow ass behind like she had to on the way up that mountain."

For the last handful of hours, Jim had been thinking of how he'd trade and escape from Batuk; that already felt impossible. Now he realized that even if he did, he and Nora had Croy to escape from, too. For a brief millisecond of time, Jim thought that maybe the Irishman had gotten off easy and he was the one that had actually drawn the short stick of this adventure.

Jim decided to do what Jim did best under stress: distract himself. His brain worked like that of an artist; the less it thought about what it needed to do, the easier it could solve any problems.

Some of the best dishes Jim created were when his mind was preoccupied with shower thoughts like how a splinter is the price of wood, or pondering which would be more embarrassing: a history of calculator input or search browser history?

As for now, Jim decided the best distraction would be to further insult Croy.

"What will be interesting is to see whether Nora kicks out a few teeth so you have a broken smile to go with that nose."

Croy was clenching the armrests of his seat. Jim could hear the plastic within them creak a bit from the pressure.

Shaman Denny, who had started listening in on the conversation when Croy shared the real (rather, lack of reason) behind letting them live, broke from his emotional paralysis and let out a small chuckle at Jim's last verbal dagger.

Small, but large enough for Croy to hear it.

"So help me God. If there's another word out of either of you in these last minutes before we land, I swear that I'll cut your tongues from your mouths. I don't care what consequences Batuk might deploy."

Jim sensed that Croy had been pushed past all reason and was speaking the truth, all of the truth, and nothing but the truth. He couldn't help but look at Shaman Denny and give him a friendly smirk. The vibe of "don't worry, be happy." The kind that says "I'm glad you're with me." The type that the one receiving it can only mirror in return.

Shaman Denny did just that.

Turns out peace was found inside the chopper, not out.

A few minutes after this exchange the copter began its descent. Once it landed, Croy escorted the two off his personal helicopter and directly into another one, branded with a Tiger logo on its side—the same as the one on Nora's ankle, although Jim didn't know it was no longer there—that flew them roughly fifteen kilometers to the rooftop landing pad

of Batuk's skyscraper. (Batuk only allowed his own chop-
pers to land on his building.)

Croy then guided them to the stairs. There were an awful lot of stairs, but Croy wasn't sure if the blood he had lost
on the elevator had been cleaned up and he wasn't going to
risk any final verbal insults from Jim.

Plus, Batuk had stairs installed from the entrance, to
a few particular floors, and to the roof, so whichever way
he and his guests chose to enter, they had a direct hike to
the conference room. It was another one of Batuk's power plays. Very little breaks a man down more than having
him realize his own lack of physique, stamina, or stating
it more plainly—fatness. When Batuk's guests arrived in
the conference room—this was a skyscraper, remember—
they were already half defeated and half at the mercy of
whomever would offer them an air-conditioned space with
an endless supply of cucumber water. Batuk loved to see
the looks on their faces after a deal had been struck when
they saw on the way out that there was in fact an elevator.
Batuk's chuckle of a goodbye always echoed up or down the
stairwell as his guests made their laborious exit while he
took the elevator with ease.

Croy knew his restraint was dangling by a thread and
he'd lose it moments before fulfilling Batuk's request. So
down the stairs they went.

And went.

And went.

And went.

And went.

Recently, Nora had been escorted up a few floors (though,
she was permitted the elevator—no surprise to Nora giv-
en Batuk's priority for cleanliness, you know, just beside

godliness; the blood that she had spilled from Croy's nose was cleaned up within hours) to a large conference room. It was the one that Batuk reserved for his most valued deals. Not that the room came with anything special; it was just where he conducted his first business-altering deal and each subsequent one that grew his empire.

Batuk was at the head of the rectangular table that stretched the length of the floor when Nora was brought inside. The floor was carpeted, but felt like walking on down pillows. Something in the room smelled sweet—not quite oven-baked cookies, but in that neighborhood. The view. By God the view. If you thought the view from Batuk's office was amazing—this beat it, *and* it wasn't even the highest floor of the tower.

Batuk gave the two gentlemen that had escorted her to the conference room a nod and they aggressively grabbed Nora's arms and restrained them behind her back. Batuk felt he needed to assert his authority lest Nora had any doubts.

"Just a formality, my dear Nora. As you know."

Nora forced her body to relax a bit, but left enough tension in her wrists to signal to the gentlemen that she was permitting them to restrain her, and that she could damage their faces just as she had Croy's if she wanted.

Batuk gave another nod and the guards left the room.

"You've never been in here before. In all of your time, the business you conducted was far, far away from where I conduct mine. You feel how comfortable the floors are? The view of paradise? That sweet smell? Turns out that baking cookies in a house you want to sell makes it sell more quickly and at a higher price. It's psychology, not snake oil. It gives me the edge of deals coordinated in here. Everything sends a signal to the people in it. Even you, whom I'd figured would be high alert, stressed, strained, high blood pressure, and such—even you are calmer here."

Batuk reached onto the table, grabbed a tablet, hit the screen a couple of times, and flipped it so Nora could see.

"See, your blood pressure is a nice one-twenty over eighty. Just a smidge higher than the average base. It implies that you're engaged, but relaxed."

Nora looked around for cameras or sensors. Surely it couldn't be the cuffs around her wrists that were sending the data. Nora knew well enough that this wasn't the room that Batuk did *that* kind of business in.

Batuk continued boasting.

"Everything sends a signal, and you of all people know how important signals are. Signals of desperation. Signals of loyalty. Signals of deceit. Even signals of love."

Batuk's words caused Nora to think about Jim.

Batuk left the tablet facing Nora as he started pacing back and forth at the head of the table, stopping before the window, canvasing the cityscape and the country just beyond it. The weather was prime for viewing distance today, no low clouds to block one's view. The weather. That was always the challenge of having a complete sensory advantage when conducting deals in the space. Batuk had considered a digital screen to simulate the view, but none of them felt authentic enough. The weather. It's the only thing that no matter the source you're reviewing, you have a fifty percent chance of being right. Either it'll rain or it won't. Either there will be clouds or there won't. Either the sun will shine, give you blisters on the back from the lack of sunblock, or it won't. Controlling the weather was on Batuk's list, no doubt, but a low priority. Maybe something he'd tackle in his next life. For Batuk, here and now, controlling people was far more practical and enjoyable.

"I'll tell it to you straight here, Nora. You are now a bargaining chip. You're only here to make things smoother with Jim. We both know he'll do anything for you. We also know that if you were out of the picture already, there's no way he would have agreed to come here. Not that he would have any say in it, anyway."

Batuk knew that a relaxed Nora was a Nora that would not try anything disastrous once Jim arrived. Batuk needed to keep her grounded in reality and not in love. Love makes you do crazy things.

"And between you and me, Croy has let his temper and lust for violence get the best of him on a few missions lately, so forcing him to restrain himself has actually given me some pleasure. Even a wildcard like Croy is merely a card in a hand of Texas Hold'em. Kudos to you on giving him a bloody nose. I couldn't have asked for a better test. You played the card I hoped you would."

Batuk let out a slight chuckle. It sounded like warm rubble in a blender set on a low grind setting.

Nora couldn't keep her face straight at the thought of having gotten one up on Croy. Her face snuck a smirk, small, but enough for Batuk to see.

Good, he thought. *Now she's at equilibrium.* Nora saw it herself on the tablet.

Batuk decided he'd spare a few more moments of this time to converse with Nora before he'd let the worry that was knocking at his mental door in, because he believed Croy should have arrived already. He knew he risked ruining the emotional control he had over Nora, but, truth be told, Batuk never *thought* of himself as a dad to Nora, although he sort of *felt* like one. He sat down at the table in hopes to not let on that he was stressed about something or that things weren't strictly on schedule. Batuk wasn't one to hold a poker face. He ended the lives of those who did.

"All that said about signals, I have to admit that I'm disappointed in you."

Similar to Batuk, Nora never *thought* of herself as a daughter to Batuk, but his words cut through her in a way that she *felt* like she was.

Batuk didn't need to look at the tablet to monitor the impact of his words. He could see it on Nora's face. Batuk felt an ounce of relief after saying the words to Nora. It felt good to let them go, so he leaned forward in his chair, eyes locked on with Nora's, and let a few more slither out.

"I've raised you and trained you, Nora. You were one of my best and I was so proud of the strong woman you had become. I just don't understand how you've fallen so far off your trajectory, a path that should have led you to rule others. Perhaps even others who have had less-than-wonderful upbringings. It pains me to even tell you what I had planned for you if you had successfully retrieved the spice. It was my final test for you and you... you failed."

Batuk, like Croy, but much less aggressively, was letting his emotions get the best of him. He took a breath and started to talk calmly again.

"That said, your failure and disloyalty over the spice has resulted in something far greater for me. Something I wasn't sure existed. Something that the spice was merely a component of. Something that's greater than the sum of its parts. In a way, I guess it had to be this way to get to where we are today and to get what will take my empire into its truest of glory days, even more filled with glory than if you had succeeded in your mission."

Batuk, now staring down at the table, was ruminating over the words that he had said more than he was evaluating their impact on Nora.

Nora didn't have a chance to express anything in return. Partly because she, like Batuk, was absorbing them. Rather than taking them to the brain, she was taking them to the heart. That path happens to take a bit longer. Also, partly because the doors had opened and Jim had fallen face first in front of them. Hey dere, ho dere, hi dare Jim.

Jim, though fatigued from the countless number of steps he had just taken, thought the moment before going through the doors was his last chance to give Croy a verbal left jab and a wordy right hook.

Rather than attacking with insults about his nose, Jim cut to the core and dished up a dessert of dialect about how soft and controlled Croy was because of Batuk. "Obedient to his master." "Merely a coward; a sheep in wolf's skin." Words like that.

Like a match to a firework, it was enough to set Croy off, which meant that Jim didn't walk into the room, but was thrown through the doors like a rag doll to land right in front of Batuk.

Batuk stood up in surprise that quickly turned to molten anger.

Batuk had a number of rules about his deal-based sanctuary.

One of which was the decency of a knock and, he, Batuk, opening the door for the guests. This made people feel like they were walking into a home, rather than a business deal. The airborne arrival of the newcomer was startling to Batuk, but not to Nora, who recognized the person as Jim from when he was still in the air. She rushed to him and, with her hands still tied, used her head to flip him over on his back to see his face.

"You're safe, Jim? Did you get what you were after?"

"Safe?" Croy asked, walking in the room after pushing Shaman Denny through to ensure he didn't take advantage of the disruption to make a run for it back up the stairs. "Far from it."

Jim opened his eyes and, cutting through the white of the ceiling lights, saw Nora.

Jim smiled and handed Nora her bracelet back in her tied hands as he hugged her. Nora had her answer in her hand now. With his other hand, Jim felt his bag to make sure the sauce hadn't broken open on his body to floor contact.

It hadn't.

Jim smiled larger.

Nora smiled in return.

Batuk tried to regain control of the room. He and Denny were the only two not smiling.

"Croy! What did we talk about?"

Croy apologized with a mumble, not quite meaning it, but knowing the consequences of not trying. Jim, with his peripheral vision, thought he looked like a sad dog, but didn't dare say it aloud now. Despite the situation he'd gotten himself in, he actually wanted to live. He knew he was in Batuk's world now, anyway, not Croy's.

"Nora, sit back down. Croy, *help* Jim up and into the seat over there."

Batuk leaned to the side to look behind Croy.

"And don't think I don't see you over there Denny. If you wouldn't mind, please get comfortable on the seat over here."

Denny resentfully followed the instructions.

Croy was the last to sit down in what he deemed as "his" seat, even though he'd only been in the room twice before as "leverage" during a deal.

Those in the room who moved had moved like they were pieces in a game of chess or kids in a classroom that the principal just walked into. Solemn. Resentful. As if there was energy to act out, but they contained it and followed the order of things.

Finally Batuk felt like the room was the way he wanted it. He was in control. *Mise en place.*

⇒LV⇐

Things were not working out as well as Phil had hoped since the public display of his framing the fire situation. The police had narrowed down the timing of when the fire began and confirmed with surveillance footage that the fire couldn't have been Jim's fault, because he was still at the conference when it started. Had Jim stormed off from the conference any sooner than he did after losing, the outcome would have been different.

Phil tried speculating that Jim must have paid someone to do it then; what else would explain his absence?

The media had a good run at that, too, but with the media and brands, there's a delicate threshold when it comes to bad PR.

At some point, enough turmoil about Jim would carry over into Jim's location, which would carry over to the new owner: Phil.

Phil knew better than to push things further and risk ruining his own business. Any PR is good awareness, but it's not always good PR.

Now Phil had to exercise his business acumen like he never had before. Should Phil:

A. Rebuild Herough under his ownership so that he could ride the cash flow of a good deed? Everyone loves a comeback story, right?

B. Build an entirely new business, crafting a new story and establishment, abandoning Herough to the dust of ancient history?

C. Let the space be and move on? After all, his competition was toast now (very very very very burnt toast, mind you).

Unfortunately for Phil, he didn't get to make the choice himself, let alone take input from you, dear reader.

The choice was instead made for him based on a couple of events.

The first is that he *finally* received a message from Croy. Not that Phil ever doubted Croy's capabilities. He knew that if, by some miracle, Jim had survived, then it would be in Phil's financial interest to rebuild Herough and return it to what people had come to know and love. That would pain him, certainly, but it would only need to be a temporary situation. Rebuild. Profit off of its restoration. And once people found other stories to sob over, he could change the business to what he wanted. Phil would look like the good guy. *That* would be good PR. Alas. Option A was out of the question since Croy confirmed there would be no return of Jim in anything more than an obituary, if that. Phil thought himself a bit stupid to even consider that Croy might not complete his task.

The second event was one of education. Now, Phil prided himself on the level of research he conducts into the markets he moves into. Since receiving the message, he started to execute option B: build a new business from the ashes of Herough. He had done deep research into the market, but not much about Herough's specific spot before placing his bet with Jim. To put it plainly: Phil never looked into who owns *the land* Herough was built on. In Phil's defense, he assumed Jim had owned the land and the building; he deduced that based on how invested Jim was in the space. No plans for Herough Two or Three or Four, the best Phil could tell. Since Phil's plan was never to take over the spot, merely push Jim out of it, he hadn't cared much about whether Jim owned the land or not. Hindsight is 20/20, of course.

While legally someone could make the argument that the location couldn't be Phil's and that, maybe, he and Jim never placed a bet since there was no paperwork or written agreement of the deal—it was verbal; a gentleman's handshake—without Jim's presence, there was no one to defend it, regardless.

Not to mention, who wants to own a pile of rubble and ash, anyway?

Add Phil's reputation onto the top of it all, and that meant even less interest in anyone going against one of the most successful restaurateurs on the East Coast.

Phil managed to wiggle around all of those "what if" situations, but there was one connection he couldn't crack to gain what he believed to be rightfully his: the landlord.

If you ever want to see what a defeated man looks like, take a successful person and put them face to face with someone they wronged during their childhood.

Phil didn't recognize the name when he acquired the landowner's contact info. He simply made the call, announced that Jim had handed over his business, it had burned in a fire likely at Jim's hands, directly or indirectly, and that Phil wished to rebuild.

The "rebuild" language had thrown the landlord off. Here's how that all went.

Landlord: "This is Trace."

Phil: "Hey, Trace. This is Phil, a restauranter. I know this might sound a bit unusual, but Jim, the owner of Herough, lost his restaurant to me in a bet and has since skipped town. While I wish I could say this was just a transfer of ownership type of thing, by now you've probably heard that the building has burned down, with some—off the record, between you and me I agree with the majority here—thinking that Jim had set it aflame before he bolted to spite me. I've moved on from being upset about it though, as it'll give me a new opportunity to build something from scratch. I'm just calling to connect on the paperwork to start up a new lease. I've already reviewed Jim's old lease and there are a couple of amendments I'd like to propose, nothing drastic, but just a thing or two that has been beneficial to have in place with previous restaurants of mine. Is there a place we could meet?"

Trace: "Wow. Wait. Herough burned down?"

Phil: "Shoot. Trace. I didn't mean to be the one to bear the news. I figured you would have already heard."

Trace: "Oh. Well, I don't reside in New York anymore. I live in the heart of Pennsylvania."

Between you and me, reader, Trace is being coy. Trace may be an introverted fella who does, in fact, reside alone away from the hub bub of a main city in the wines and vines of Pennsylvania, but he's lying about how much attention he pays to his property.

Trace doesn't just live within the vineyards. He owns them. He owns them because he's gotten talented at leasing land, buildings, vehicles—you name it. Of course Trace knew about the fire. Trace knew all about the politics of Phil entering the market where Herough had treated him so well the last few months. Trace also knew who Phil was. Phil wasn't just someone who wanted to take over the lease; Phil was once a pre-teen boy that pushed him around on the playground, punched him in the parking lot, and made fun of his pale skin, curly hair, belly rolls, and glasses in front of not just the girls in his gym class, but the entire school whenever he would see him. Phil was a bully. Trace was the one who had been bullied.

Phil: "Oh, well. Do you come here frequently? I'd love to put pen to paper as soon as possible."

Trace: "No. Jim always came to me."

He didn't.

Trace: "Can you come here? Here's my address…"

Phil was slightly frustrated, but it wasn't too far a distance to travel. He'd make a weekend out of it. He had time, anyway, while the contractors he had already hired without the landlord's permission cleaned up the space. He had the money. The means. The mission.

Maybe he'll have a glass of wine with Trace to celebrate. He had this in the bag

⇒ LVI ⇐

Pardon the brief interruption, dear reader. I thought you'd like to know that Lemon Fraser was still living the good life. Mai Tais. Beach. Ladies. He even bet a local bartender for which would shut down first: the bar or his liver. All to say, he was living a life of citrus, a well-rounded retirement, and no regrets. Not that he didn't believe in them, rather that the truth about the life Lemon lived was that he had the wherewithal to imagine the future of decisions he had yet to make and evaluated the unmade decisions based on how much he would regret if he did or didn't do something. Then it was simple: Do the thing that results in the least amount of regret. So, in truth, he had some, but they were negligible. They were probably enjoying the wave ride of liquid in his gut anyway.

Walk good, Lemon. Bottoms up. Penicillin will help.

⇒ LVII ⇐

Phil's physical bag was simple enough to pack. Phil couldn't recall a time he ever checked a bag on an airplane. He was the type who would just buy something if he needed it. He loved his luggage lugger carry-on that just about did every job one would need it to do on a trip. It came with a battery built in to wirelessly charge everything he had in it; the charge even reached in his pocket. He felt powerful carrying it around. He also liked the surprised looks on people's faces when they saw their phones start to charge while standing next to him, thinking something must be wrong with their tech. As you've learned, everything sends a signal, though some things are more obvious signals, such as the fact that the bag was embroidered with a saying that read "Cook or be cooked." Alas. It was a simple trip and Phil used the short airport and air flight time to select and amplify a restaurant concept he would put in Herough's place. He had a whole digital folder saved with ideas and now it was just running through another series of SWOT analysis of each and even more importantly to him, to ensure he didn't cannibalize any capital from his existing establishment neighboring the historic Herough.

Phil felt like he locked in on the idea right as the plane's wheels touched the ground. He hastened off the plane (which, given the shortness of the flight, didn't quite have a 1st class, which was where he usually sat). The driver he had hired was at passenger pick up waiting for him. Though Phil normally didn't care what vehicle he rode in, he thought he better play it safe and ride in something expensive, for lack of better words, so that Trace would gain confidence in Phil's capabilities to profit. There are those signals again, remember?

And so they drove a fair distance away from the airport and nearest city. Soon they reached the start of some vineyards. Then they kept driving through them. And kept driving through more. And kept driving through even more.

"Are these all part of one property?" Phil asked the driver, assuming the answer to be no.

"Sure are. Benson Vineyards. You must not be from Pennsylvania, huh?"

The look on Phil's face he saw in the rearview mirror answered his question.

"It's the largest vineyard in Pennsylvania and one of the largest producers of wine in the Eastern half of the U.S., though here's the catch: They don't send it anywhere outside of Pennsylvania."

"Ah," Phil responded. That explains why he wasn't privy to it. Phil didn't like to pay attention to anything that didn't actually involve him or that he couldn't control. The shooting in Wyoming? Whatever. The unique but incredibly simple and stupid sculpture that the center of debate between artists in North Dakota and the taxpayers whose money had paid for the sculpture? Why would Phil put any brain power to the topic? It didn't impact him in the slightest. He also applied this thinking (or, I suppose, the lack of it) to international royalty, classical music, presidential elections, hate crimes (specifically any *not* near his restaurants), and the ever-rotating top trend that was "sweeping the nation" every week. Wine producers in Pennsylvania? Definitely on his list of "Pay no mind."

Minutes passed, and just as Phil was about to ask how much further to the entrance, there was a bend in the road and a mansion came into sight that had been hiding behind the hills of the vineyard entrance. It was a staggering house that made Phil's luxury place on the coast look like a two-star hostel. His jaw nearly hit the seat between his legs. The driver watched from his rearview mirror and smirked. It wasn't often that he drove someone to Benson Vineyards, but the handful he had all had the same look on their face. It didn't matter the wealth or status they may have had getting into the car. It was always slightly diminished by the time they got out of it.

Still bearing his smirk, the driver drove up and into the roundabout driveway to the "main office" entrance of the building. "Mansion" may not be the right word to describe the building. It was a home, sure, but it was also part office, or rather, part office building, given its size. A commercial mansion. An estate of sorts.

"Are we still on track for me to pick you up in two hours?"

Phil was out of the vehicle and looking up at the building. Either the kink in his neck from staring up so high snapped him back to reality or it was the "Sir?" from the driver.

"Yes, that should be more than good enough. This shouldn't take long."

Funnily enough, that's something the driver had heard before too. Again, not that the driver had chauffeured that many people to this place, but the majority come back to his vehicle carrying a bag of tension and disappointment instead of whatever they came here to get.

Phil entered the office entryway. Despite its size, the place flowed, had proper signage, and navigation was intuitive. In other words: beautifully designed on the inside, the same as the outside.

Phil checked in with a receptionist and browsed the family portraits on the walls. Business 101 entails learning what you can about the people you're doing business with. Though, Phil was half following his business protocol and half viewing the place out of pure curiosity and awe. You'd think you were in an art museum, with the museum itself being the art rather than the paintings on the wall. A few of the photos seemed vaguely familiar to Phil, but he chalked it up to the feeling of being somewhere he felt just as important as he. Phil puffed out his chest at the thought, but it deflated a bit once the receptionist called his name.

"Phil. Trace is ready for you."

The receptionist buzzed Phil through a locked door. She didn't need to give Phil any direction. At the end of the long hallway was an open door; along the way there was no shortage of doors, probably leading to testing labs, tasting labs and one lab labeled with "Tartar" on the entry door—this one was transparent glass and what looked like hundreds, if not thousands of barrels stacked behind it. At the end of the hall Phil opened a door, walked in and noticed a desk inside. A person who was undoubtedly Trace sat behind it, and behind him there was a wall of bottles.

Goddamn, the room was glorious. It was clear that 1) Trace spared no expense and 2) It was designed with intention. The shapes were comforting but poised. The colors were energizing, but with flow. Trace was also dressed to impress as if he was to match the room he was in. It's hard to say which was made for who. The room for Trace or Trace for this room. He filled it well.

The only thing off right now was his face. It wasn't entirely off kilter, but it looked like a face that was watching something it didn't expect.

"Phil? Your request?"

Dear reader, Trace wasn't normally this stoic and unemotional. He has had to interact with a few businessmen and women in his time who he needed to treat like he was treating Phil. But it's an exception to the norm, and wasn't how he built his empire. He built it with empathy and kindness. That was one big reason why he didn't distribute outside his home state. He gave too much of a damn about his people. Rather than growing his business outside his state, he used funds to buy properties across the country to lease to people wanting to start up their own dreams. You know, kind-hearted people like Jim. Alas. Trace had a slight look of surprise on his face when Phil walked in because Phil didn't recognize him. Not from his fame or fortune, but from middle school. Trace's facial accent of surprise converted to a look that meant business.

Phil wasn't taken aback much by the forwardness. That's how he preferred to conduct business, anyway, though he couldn't help starting with a compliment. It wasn't to try to gain social capital; Phil actually meant it.

"You clearly have exceptional taste. This place is beyond beautiful."

Phil paused waiting for a response, but there was none.

"Straight to business? That's fair. As I mentioned on the phone, I'm taking over Herough. Or rather, what used to be of it. I've got the perfect concept that is sure to succeed. In case you don't know about me, I've got almost twenty-five different successful restaurants throughout New York, Massachusetts, and Vermont. This concept will be different than Herough, but is sure to be even more successful. Now, I've reviewed the lease terms you had with Jim and I don't see any issues with carrying it over, I'd only like to add a clause about an opportunity to buy the land itself after two years. I'll make sure it's worth it to you."

Phil paused again, this time, waiting for some kind of response from Trace.

Trace kept staring at Phil. It may have only been twenty seconds, but even Phil felt a bit awkward by this interaction so far.

Finally, (*thank God,* Phil thought to himself), Trace broke the silence.

"You clearly don't remember me."

It was more a statement than a question.

"What?"

"You don't remember me, do you?"

This time, it was a question.

Phil started cycling through the Rolodex of people he'd interacted with over the years. Venture capitalists. Lawyers. Chefs. You name it. Phil had a knack for remembering names and faces, but for some reason he couldn't think of a time he had ever interacted with Trace Benson in a business context.

Trace could see the struggle on Phil's face.

"Does Jefferson Middle School ring a bell?" Trace finally asked.

Phil had been thinking of everyone he interacted with in his business life, his adult life, his recent years, not those long behind him. His face scrunched like he was trying to solve a trigonometry problem. (He had failed trigonometry in college...)

Trace gave him a few moments to pull it from the memory banks.

"...Triple Roll Trace?" Phil asked.

Trace's eyebrows angled down. He went to an internal ammunition shop and acquired a deadly grin. His nostrils flared. His ears started to turn a light shade of red at the name, the same as a finger that just got smashed in a door.

ˌIt was the nickname Phil gave him in middle school for the number of belly rolls or leg rolls or chin rolls he had at the time. It rolled off the tongue and all the kids called him it, but none stung like when the originator of it spoke them as he did just now all these years later.

Trace had prepared for this moment. He knew Phil. He knew he hadn't changed since middle school. Still the same bully he was then. For some, time is just a mirror– they grow older, but never different.

Trace leaned forward on the table and didn't give Phil a chance to say another word.

"If you think for even a second I'll lease anything of mine to you, you'd better squash the thought. I'm here try-ing to make this world a better place and you're still picking on others just like you picked on me all those years back. I've read up on you. I don't doubt that you and Jim placed the bet, but you're the last person on Earth I would offer a lease to. I had hoped to discover that you had changed; that this would have been a milestone moment for us; that you'd left your bullyish ways behind, just like I left my unhealthy lifestyle behind. I had hoped to see the improvements we have made in our lives. But apparently not. You can take your request and shove it up your ass, Phil."

Phil was taken aback. Here's the thing about Phil: He couldn't really argue with Trace. He *was* a bully. That's how he got as successful as he was. Not by throwing flowers and compliments, but through manipulation. Phil's brain pro-cessed the scenario quickly and he took a breath to begin defending himself. This was an unexpected obstacle, but he had mastered the art of manipulation and thought he could get himself around this.

"I..."

"Save your breath. I heard enough from you many years ago. Now please leave my property or I'll have you forcefully removed."

With the office door still open, Trace peered behind Phil to indicate with his eyes that he did in fact have force. Not security, per se, but something stronger: family.

Phil coulda blew a house down with how much he huffed as he stood up and walked down the hallway, getting jabbed, poked, and prodded by the eyes of the Benson family. Trace had asked them to come watch as he demonstrated how to handle bullies.

Phil was irate by the time he got outside. There was only one good thing going for him in the moment: the driver was there, though he had a larger smirk on his face than he had when he left, drove to the end of the driveway, and wrapped back around to wait for Phil. The driver never knew what happened within the four walls, but as we said, those he dropped off never stayed for long, so he simply made it a habit to kill the time by waiting right in front.

Fortunately the windows were cracked on the car ride, lest Phil and the driver die from the fumes erupting from Phil's ears.

"How dare he," Phil mumbled.

"What an absolute waste of my time," he spat.

"Whatever," he finally committed himself.

Whatever, indeed. Once Phil was out of the cab and on his way back home, a cooler head prevailed. This was Phil's train of thought.

"It doesn't matter that I can't get a lease or purchase the land or open a new restaurant there. I still have my own place right near Herough. Herough is still gone. And, even better, Trace will look like the bad guy for not letting me rebuild in honor of Jim and his establishment."

Phil's train of thought ended with a smile. Best he let everything about Hereough's go. Choose option C. He had a restaurant group to grow and he wouldn't let this slow him down. "C" it is. Choo. Choo.

≽LVIII≼

From the outside in, it looked like a band of misfits was sitting around Batuk's office table.

There was a pretty, delicate, but fierce-looking woman.

There was a fit hippie who looked like he'd had emotional whiplash.

There was a strapping fella, his naivety showing and his nose scrunched up like he'd smelled things on a different level than the rest of the group.

Then there was a guy who looked half-caff, scarred on the outside and dead on the inside.

Then there was Batuk. Batuk the great. Batuk the mighty. Batuk the man in charge. Batuk looked like his name sounded. Batuk looked like he could make whatever happen in the room with a snap of a finger. From the outside in, that's exactly what you'd see.

Batuk snapped his finger and personnel hastily brought in a makeshift kitchen. They brought in burners and bins of vegetables, tables of meat, and they kept bringing things in, though they did not yet have to move any chairs. It clearly wasn't their first time setting up a pop-up kitchen in the office. Batuk always loved a show, so if business was running long, he'd have chefs perform in the room for him. Again, his way of controlling the situation, environment, emotion, and winning hearts, minds, and, in particular, the stomachs, of the dealmakers he was working with.

No one spoke a word while the room was transformed into a test kitchen. Once the final door and busman left the room, Batuk spoke.

"Jim, if you wouldn't mind. Would you please pull out the bottle and place it on the table?"

Jim thought he was going to have to barter for Nora's life with it, but setting it on the table, still within his reach, seemed harmless. Jim's enhanced senses didn't detect any threatening tone in Batuk's words, either, which was odd. Jim did as was asked.

"Good. Good. It looks like you have a full bottle, which is what I was hoping. Now, I have one more favor to ask."

There wasn't a person at the table who wasn't curious at this point, so they refrained from interrupting, though calling his request a favor was laying it on a bit thick.

"Cook us a meal."

"What?" Jim replied.

"Cook us a meal. It's almost your last one and a full bottle is more than enough for me to analyze and replicate even after you use some. Croy deserves to taste it for a job well done. Shaman Denny deserves it for evading me all of these years. Nora deserves it for the service she provided... up until recently. And Jim, you deserve it for acquiring the last ingredient I need to solidify my empire and finally enter retirement. So, I'll say it once more. Cook us a meal. You should have everything you need."

Jim stood up and grabbed the bottle of Herough sauce from the table.

"You can leave that there and apply it last," Batuk added, pointing to the table space in front of Jim.

Jim released his grip from the bottle, placing it back on the table, though closer to Nora than before even though she was incapable of grabbing it herself.

Jim stood behind the oven and surveyed what he had to work with. After taking a mental inventory, he looked at Batuk.

"Go on," Batuk ordered. This time sounding a bit more impatient than before.

Jim felt in a familiar position of power behind the oven and dared to see just what Batuk could make happen with a snap of his fingers.

"I need music."

"As you wish."

"Cambodian rap, please. Specifically 'Choul Mouy.' On repeat."

Batuk didn't recognize the request, but he was un-phased. He'd dealt with a great number of "artists" in his time and they all had quirks. Batuk was ready for whatever Jim's might be. He snapped his fingers and the song began playing from the speakers that were built into the ceiling.

Jim looked at Nora and smiled. Then he got to work.

Jim started with the meats, grabbing a few varieties and cutting some, chopping another, and tenderizing a third, leaving it as wide as it was when he grabbed it from the cooler. He concocted some relatively simple marinades, knowing the final sauce would be what ultimately set the dishes apart. One was a citrus base, the other a vinaigrette base, and the other a raspberry paste. It took about two sec-onds for Jim to get lost in his muse. Cooking to Choul Mouy was actually invigorating, too. The high-energy rap trans-ferred into the speed and rhythm of Jim's hands at work. Everything was quick and precise. All the elegance of a Michelin star chef and all the speed of a fast-food chain. Jim shifted over to the vegetables and got to work; he made origami with the onion, a paper fortune teller with the spinach, and a sculpture with the water chestnuts. He then moved on to cooking the noodles. After looking at the pa-thetic pasta trying to pass itself off as *lo mein*, he glanced up at Batuk and gave him what no one had given him in over a decade: an order.

"Get me a stand mixer."

Assuming he had given Jim everything he needed, Ba-tuk was more surprised than he was upset by the order. He snapped his fingers. Jim went back to working on the side dishes while he waited for the mixer to arrive. Time was of the essence and Jim realized he needed to build time into the dish so all things would be done at once. The real test for any chef was time management. He fell behind the beat of the subsequent Thai rap songs that played after Choul

Mouy, but he still pressed on, deciding to use the time he would have in some areas to add to their appearance. Like Batuk, Jim was keen on knowing his audience and Batuk clearly wasn't just having him do this for the flavor, he wanted to eat with his eyes, too.

Shaman Denny watched in awe. This was Kar Tresa's Crevice all over again, but this was on a whole different level. *There* Jim had worked with what he had, and a lot of guesswork as to what the unfamiliar, wild ingredients tasted like. *Here* Jim was in his element, at the peak of his powers. And he also had an edge to things: By now he'd gotten very good at using his other senses. There were a few times when he smelled the meat that he thought he tasted it, too. Muscle memory, perhaps.

Time passed and though those around the table remained silent, their stomachs started to speak up. Shaman Denny, who was used to fasting, felt pangs of hunger. Finally relaxed, Croy's cravings caught up to him, too. Though she'd dined well enough during her stay, Nora found herself hungry all over again. And Batuk, well, Batuk wasn't hungry in the traditional sense; he was salivating for the sauce. The dish was simply a vehicle for that. And in his eyes, it was shaping up to be a well-produced Ferrari of a feast.

Once Jim began to cook, boil, and sear the meat, vents in the ceiling and window quietly opened up to allow for airflow. The mixer arrived and he made his own lo mein. Thanks to the architectural setup of the nearby buildings and the wind direction of the day, the aromatics blew down to the street and caused even more people to become piggish, wanting to follow their noses to the source of the smell and roll around in it.

Minutes passed by. Then an hour. Then nearly two, but at about one hour and forty-five minutes into things, Jim was preparing the plates and doing his damnedest not to let any of his sweat droplets fall from his forehead onto the plates. The saltiness of sweat has ruined a few chefs' reputations in the past.

Jim spent the final ten minutes finessing the dishes. Once he was finally satisfied, he looked up at his audience, smirked and said, "Dinner is served."

As a result of that sort of high-intensity muse of an activity, Jim would normally be exhausted, but after placing plates in front of each of those at the table, he sat down in his own seat with a forward lean. He was excited, not by the dish itself, but by the opportunity to get his sense of taste back. This was a dish he'd kill to taste.

Everyone knew better than to splash their forks into their plates like they had fallen off a high diving board. They all looked at Batuk, waiting, hoping, begging for permission with their eyes.

"I'm not uncuffing Nora," Batuk said, breaking the silence but not the bread.

Nora had been so rapt watching the food being prepared that she'd forgotten her hands were even cuffed. Like Denny, she was lost in watching Jim work. Before she could consider if she should just dip her face in the dish and bob for those tidbits of apple she watched Jim cut up, Jim spoke.

"I'll feed you," he reassured Nora.

Certain now that he was not going to get pushback about leaving her cuffed, Batuk gave a nod, which Croy knew was permission to eat. He dove in, and the others followed the second in command.

Jim leaned over to Nora and with one hand, gave her a modest forkful of the dish. While all eyes were focused on the food and interaction, Nora used the opportunity of Jim's body blocking Croy's view to use the bracelet in her hand to cut her cuffs, somewhat like the way it cut through the rock at the Kar's Crevice. Nora was smart enough to keep the ties in her hands and hands behind her back. It also helped that the one person in a room that would have likely detected this ploy was in a state of food bliss. He ate well enough, no doubt, but in his line of work, efficiency was key, and every other trip or so kept him far from a decent meal, so he cherished moments like this. Even a bad person can have good taste.

Shaman Denny took to the meal quickly, too. He'd chalk up his lack of self-control to curiosity and emotional eating. That, and the fact that he figured he was going to die soon, anyway, so why let a wavering appetite control his final minutes on the planet?

Only two people at the table waited to touch their dishes. The first was Jim, as he was feeding Nora. The second was Batuk. He was surveying people's reactions to the food. He deemed that it must be delectable, but Batuk wasn't good enough with good enough.

"Jim. The sauce, if you may. On yours and mine."

Batuk gestured at the bottle to the left of Jim. Jim hesitated. The rest of the room stopped eating for a moment to watch the standoff between the two. They had all but forgotten that the sauce even existed, let alone imagine that it could make this meal taste even greater.

Jim enjoyed having heightened senses. He could feel Batuk's stomach growl, for hell's sake. Though the oven was off and the windows open, he could still smell the food being cooked, not just the finished product in front of him. He could see the cracks and edges of Croy's face smoothening with each bite. Of course, Jim fiercely wanted to regain his sense of taste—he wanted to taste this dish, he wanted to taste Nora's lips, he wanted to taste vengeance. The mental battle was moot, however. Batuk wasn't asking him if he wanted some of the sauce. He was telling him.

"Jim." Batuk nodded at the bottle giving Jim a courtesy he rarely gave anyone: asking them twice.

Everyone at the table set their forks down but continued slowly chewing what they had already stuffed in their mouths. It tasted too good to stop entirely.

Jim grabbed the bottle, opened the flip top stopper and stared at it.

It was colored the green of garden vegetables with streaks of beet skin purple. There were silver speckles throughout—the star dust. Jim's eyes went from awe at the aura of it to a quizzical stare once he realized the sauce had no scent. He moved the bottle closer to his nose and sniffed—nothing. Jim thought it peculiar and began to worry that maybe the sauce hadn't worked out. What if they missed something in the process that the Irishman knew nothing about? What if Jim's base broke it?

Fortunately Jim didn't have the luxury of time to spend with what-ifs. It didn't take a genius super sensor to see Batuk was getting impatient. Alas. Jim let a small number of drops fall like meteorites onto his dish. Having never tasted the sauce before, Jim was unsure how much to add (does he drench the food? Does he make a pool for the food to dip its toes in?), but as Jim tipped the bottle to sprinkle its contents, it was as if the bottle controlled its drops for itself, becoming exceedingly slow to drip out once Jim had sprinkled his food landscape. Each droplet had its acquired target and hit each piece of food precisely on the mark.

Once finished Jim nearly handed it to Nora, who was so enamored by the sauce and its glistening that she nearly reached out and grabbed it before handing it to Batuk.

Catching himself before spoiling the surprise, Jim stood up and walked the bottle over to Batuk, resentfully placing it on the table near his plate before returning to his seat, not taking his eyes off it the whole time.

"Thank you," Batuk said gracefully, if with a bit of grit.

Similar to Jim, Batuk had covered his plate the same way anyone achieves anything of magnitude: drip by drip by drip.

Batuk looked at Jim with a fork in hand.

"I don't know what you were attempting to achieve with this sauce, but I figured that the maker might as well enjoy it before he perishes. Cheers, Jim."

"It's not just any sauce. It's Herough Herough sauce. Cheers," Jim responded. Status. That's all that Batuk really cares about—and if this was the end of Jim's chapter, he'd go out making sure he'd have the last statement, ensuring Batuk would always think of him with whatever *he* had planned for the sauce. Not just magic sauce. Herough Herough sauce.

Batuk and Jim both took a bite of their sauce-speckled dish. It took a few moments, but all of a sudden Jim's taste buds started to tingle. First he felt them. Then. Aha. A taste. Mango. And lemongrass. And, ah, there's the lamb chop. Jim could taste the ameliorative properties of the sauce. What Jim actually tasted was the Seventh Flavor, which was more than a flavor; it was a cycled flavor experience. It was the palate cleanser of flavors, one capable of starting each taste receptor from square one and thus experiencing each flavor as if it were new.

Think about how you can never experience your favorite book again in the same way you did the very first time you read it. Or movie. Or first love. Or first fuck. This sauce allowed your taste buds to read the same book again and again as if it's the first time, but you retain all the memory of having that experience. It's your first theater experience. Your first orgasm. Again and again. That's flavor power. A secret formula. Magic in a bottle. The real Spice of Life. To go at something like it's the first time, every time.

And so Jim chewed and chewed, nearly overwhelmed with the display of genuine pleasure happening in his mouth. Calling the sauce delicious would be an understatement. It was transcendent.

Curiously though, he didn't note a decrease in his other senses. If anything, they, too, felt stronger, as if they had been held back by having something lost. Jim felt invigorated.

Batuk, however, wouldn't have said the same, that is, if he could talk.

No one around the table was watching Jim and the smile on his face as he reacquired his sense of taste *without* the loss of his other heightened senses. They had all stopped chewing altogether, though their mouths remained open, as they watched Batuk.

While Jim was lost in his own sensory world, Batuk was getting annihilated in his.

Combined, both Nora and Croy had seen people die by no fewer than thirteen different edible poisons. Each had a unique effect on the physical nature of the person. There was the classic foaming at the mouth or the convulsing of the body. Some made eyes roll behind the head like they do in movies and others acted in the shadows, with no detectable effect to the outside eye.

Looking at Batuk, you'd guess that he had had all thirteen different poisons in one.

Batuk had saliva bubbles dripping from the crease of his lips. His body turned a deathly shade of purple. His eyes turned a hue of eccentric pink and his irises all but disappeared. His body shook as if being shocked into and out of life—because it was. This was not a painless death.

The group watched, flabbergasted, as Batuk's body and his soul looked like they were the ones doing the eating, of his own essence.

Poison was quickly ruled out in the minds of all those at the table given that Jim was fine. It must have been the sauce each deduced. But how? Why wasn't Jim affected the same way?

In looking at Jim to validate their hypothesis, they discovered the smile. The color of his body was brighter. Jim almost had a sparkle to him.

Truth be told: Batuk's body simply couldn't handle the cleansing effect of the sauce. Moments passed, plants performed photosynthesis outside, and ducks flew backward while those around the table remained paralyzed in disbelief of what had just happened.

Batuk's body fell limp. Mouth with popping bubbles. Eyes rolled back permanently. His fork fell to the floor. His body tapped out.

The group sat and watched for some sign of life from Batuk. All but Croy hoped that there wouldn't be any.

And there wasn't.

If you were to glance at his digital pad on the table, it would indicate only four living bodies in the room.

⇒LIX⇐

Deeper than a dwarven mine, in Croy's mind, he had imagined what it would be like to rule like Batuk. Let's not get Croy wrong here, though: He *loved* what he did, but he'd be lying if he said he didn't think at times of what it would be like to rule from afar, to not go days or sometimes weeks at a time without a damn good meal, and the control one has to feel when things can be done for you with the snap of your fingers.

Croy never actually wanted Batuk's seat, per se. Business acumen wasn't really in his repertoire. He wouldn't have survived as long as he did if that was his true intention, either; Batuk had a way of sniffing out traitors, spies, and those jealous enough to act irrationally on their jealousy.

But the power, control, and authority Batuk held?

Yeah, Croy wanted that.

The thing is, Croy never knew how to get it. He was great at hunting people, but bad about earning respect outside of that skill. Great at trafficking supplies as Batuk requested, but bad at running his own black market.

Here and now, though, Croy knew two things: If he was going to earn the reverence of those who would inevitably watch the footage of Batuk dying (perhaps twice since the first would result in disbelief), he would have to kill the one responsible: Jim. The second is that Croy's vision of rule relied on him leaving the room with Jim's sauce.

Croy's smile at the table nearly matched the size of Jim's with the thought of not only *finally* killing them, but also taking the sauce. A win-win-win scenario, all for Croy.

With his best "what's past is past" attitude, Croy broke the silence both with his voice and the sound of his knife being pulled from its sheath on his waist.

"There's no one to stop me now, Jim. I owe Phil your life, and while I enjoyed the thought of letting you get a head start after Batuk got what he wanted, I've got other plans that letting you live longer would only distract and delay me from. Best I end this now and then take care of Nora and this pathetic excuse for a shaman. Darney, was it?"

Croy launched himself across the table and Jim fell backward on his chair. Croy sat atop Jim's chest with his knife to his neck, not the least bit concerned of Shaman Denny doing anything or Nora with her hands tied. The emotional stress of it all was too much for Denny to think right now, anyway, let alone act in self-defense for a friend who had brought this cruel adventure upon him.

"You're wrong," Jim managed to gurgle out as the weight of Croy's forearm crushed his Adam's apple. Croy was always interested in the final words of the deceased. He considered one day making a book of poetry out of all the final words of his victims. A way to remember the moments, both the heartfelt and the heartless, the threatening and the funny. They always told a lot about the character he was killing.

"What was that, JimBo?" Croy asked, easing the pressure of his knee on Jim's diaphragm ever so slightly to let him speak, though not letting up on the weight of his arm on the throat or the distance of his knife to it.

"You're wrong," Jim squeaked out. "I do have someone to stop you."

Nora knew better than to wait for the punchline of Jim's statement. Croy would have been too quick on his feet for that.

Before Jim finished saying "someone," Nora had let her cut cuffs fall to the floor and kicked Croy off Jim. His knife went flying from his fingers in the opposite direction, but not before nicking Jim's throat slightly enough to draw blood—not so deeply as to result in a fatal injury, luckily.

Nora leap frogged over Jim and flogged Croy in the ribs. Now, in a typical match, as we've seen, Croy would have a slight edge on Nora. But this wasn't a typical 1v1 match.

This truly was life or death to Nora.

This was a threatening-someone-she-loved situation.

This was also a long-time-coming situation.

And to top it off, this was a payback situation for what he had pulled over on her in the mountains.

Nora managed to give Croy a few fresh injuries that would bruise brighter than the one still left on his nose. The pain felt new to Croy, too, who had experienced no shortage of minor scrapes and bumps, but had not gone fisticuffs like this with someone in quite a number of years. He at least always had his knife. Nora kept wailing on Croy, breaking at least one rib, before Croy bit through the pain and bucked Nora off him. He then grabbed her leg and swung her at the glass window, clearly meaning to definitively defenestrate her.

Jim's heart sank, but it quickly bounced back into his chest just as Nora's body bounced off the glass. Batuk knew better than to have anything less than shatterproof glass in this room.

Nora got up and Croy stood in front of her with one arm cradling his ribs.

"Here!"

Jim had grabbed Croy's knife and tossed it to Nora, which she caught in midair by the handle. Elementary lesson for the Tiger Clan, but it's the foundational education of any craft that most often carries one through the toughest of times.

Croy surveyed the room. At this point, even Shaman Denny had stood up, seemingly ready to do whatever Jim or Nora told him to. Nora positioned her body and Croy's knife to attack.

Croy didn't need to be a mathematician to know he was outnumbered. He knew that he only had the space, time, and energy to do one thing. As much as he wanted it to be kill Jim, he instead swiped the bottle of sauce from the table and crashed through the office doors. Nora, Jim, and Shaman Denny, well, they didn't bother to chase him. They had something else immediately to worry about.

"We need to get out of here," Nora said, wishing she could follow it up with a plan of how they would get out of there.

Shaman Denny finally had his moment to shine.

"The stairs," he said.

Nora looked at him quizzically, but Jim had a look of "of course."

Shaman Denny led the way, but was by no means the leader. He was hesitant in exiting the conference room doors for fear Croy was simply waiting on the other side. Perhaps Croy chose to take the stairs and not the elevator, too, and they'd catch up to him if they went too fast. He hoped Croy went up to a helicopter while they went down to the ground floor. The hesitancy quickly faded because exhaustion set in for Shaman Denny.

"Remind me to do some more cardio when we're out of this," he said to Nora and Jim, who, at this point, were pretty much forcing Shaman Denny's legs to keep taking step after step.

Floor.
        After.
                Floor.
                        After.
                                Floor.

The group finally reached the lobby, and they needn't have worried about concealing themselves. The receptionist was used to seeing people exit the stairwell looking like they'd gone six rounds with an ogre. They spilled out onto the stoop of the building, a swath of flesh and sweat.

"Now what?" Shaman Denny asked.

"I've got it from here," Nora said, taking the lead. "Follow me."

A ride was the least the now-deceased Batuk owed Nora. And what would he do about her taking a car, anyway? Nora brought them around the building and walked down a driveway to a parking garage. When you have influence like Batuk, no one even tries to steal from you, and when you believe that speed is the highest of virtues, you make it so your disciples can get to where they need to go with the least amount of resistance.

Nora led Shaman Denny and Jim past a variety of cars. Each one looked as if it was chosen for a specific purpose. A fully armored van in one parking spot. A convertible in another. An Oldsmobile in another. A Corvette in another. A police car in another; authentic, actually. Batuk had an ongoing bribery going to keep it. Nora settled for the one she always asked Batuk for when she was given a new mission. Batuk had always said a different vehicle would be better for off roading or for blending in or simply that she'd get whatever vehicle he had waiting for her at her rendezvous point. What she wanted was an orange, four-seat GT. Designed for high speed and long-distance driving, it may not have been perfect for a group of brutes, but Nora's company this time were slim enough to fit comfortably.

They got in the vehicle and Nora drove out to the intersection.

"Now what?" Shaman Denny asked again.

"Home?" Jim asked.

"To the airport we go, then," Nora said, stepping on the pedal and happily getting lost in the roar of the GT.

⇒LX⇐

Outside an airport is a great place to ruminate on life. Home means a lot of different things to different people. It can mean a place in time, like the present. It could mean the childhood house they grew up in. It could be the company of another.

For Shaman Denny, home was where he could mourn the loss of the Irishman with the only other person in the world that knew him as well, if not better than himself: Siem Reap with Pinmekelah.

Shaman Denny couldn't begin to fathom how to tell her about all that had happened or how she might react when he did, but Shaman Denny at least had a bit of time to think it through. She'd probably respond with something snappy.

"Thank you, Denny. For everything. I have my sense of taste back. I have Nora back."

"I don't know how much there is to thank me for. The Irishman deserves the thanks. I did the worst a human could do. I simply existed."

Nora saw sorrow in Denny's eyes, but before she could say anything in an effort to remove it, Shaman Denny turned his own wipers on.

"But no more. After I reconnect with Queen P, give the Irishman a proper ritual, I'll be off to make the Irishman proud. I don't know what exactly he had hoped for me to do next—go to hell if it's remaking the sauce—but I have an idea that Queen Pinmekelah might be just the person to give me the lead I need to go off of. Star dust might just be scratching the surface of what's available to us. Even the Irishman hinted that there might be other wonders."

Though a shade of hope covered Shaman Denny's face, sorrow remained concealed behind it. Goodbyes are always rollercoasters of emotion that no one can ever get off of.

"I don't suppose I'll see you two again... Be safe. Croy is... a savage."

"That's true about Croy, but you never know about paths crossing," Nora responded with a hopeful smile. "Some of the best people arrive when you least expect them, too," Nora said, looking at Jim. "And the world has a way of dishing out karma. The good, the bad, and, in Batuk's case, the ugly."

Shaman Denny felt like he knew he was on his own from here on out, but allowed himself to believe the lie that Nora's smile offered. It would give him comfort on the inevitable turbulence of the short trip "home."

"Oh, and Denny," Jim hollered as Denny pivoted on his heel and began making his way to his gate. "If you ever find yourself with a little extra well water, have Queen P send it our way. That stuff was magic."

The well. The first time Shaman Denny met the two. You know, maybe, just maybe, that was something Denny could do.

Sayonara, Shaman Denny.

Denny's silhouette faded into the crowd of airport travelers and Nora looked back at Jim. Nora never really knew what home was until now. She thought she knew it with the Tiger Clan, but it was all a guise. Now she knew for sure: Home was and is and always would be wherever Jim was.

And as for Jim, home was New York. Not the Big Apple in its entirety; his slice of neighborhood in particular.

After all that he'd faced, going back to a burnt

restaurant, an apartment he'd likely been evicted from, and a score to settle with Phil seemed like child's play.

"Do you think Croy is going to come for us in New York?" Jim asked Nora.

"I feel like he has other plans right now with the sauce. But yes, I do think he'll come for us before long. We've pissed him off well enough."

As Nora said that, she realized that Croy was actually more likely to make them come to him. A thought she'd put more energy to thinking about down the road. Now wasn't the time to burden Jim with it—and if Croy was going to act quickly, he would have done so already.

Nora placed her hands on Jim's face and held his gaze up to hers.

"But we'll be ready. For now, I think we have some items to sort out back in New York, don't we?"

"I've been thinking about that. I'm not yet ready to see Herough quite yet or face Phil, wherever he is. Let's go to my apartment first and get cleaned up. My feet are killing me."

It was such a nonchalant statement to make after all the recent events, but such is life—a rubber band snapped back to reality.

Jim wanted a shower, sure, and a change of clothes and probably a good shave, but what he really hoped was that Lemon would be there or at least have sent a letter explaining himself. Jim wasn't one to assign blame to things, but if he was going to, things had quite plainly gone to hell when his friend stole the original spice.

"Let's get on our plane, then. I'll admit, I'm looking forward to seeing your place."

Jim had forgotten Nora had never been there. With how close they'd gotten these last weeks, it was as if they'd been together for ages.

Thanks to the size of the airport, Nora, Jim, and Shaman Denny never ran into Croy, who happened to be thinking the same as them: It was time to fly out of Bang-kok. With him he had two important items in his hands: A bottle of Herough Herough Sauce and a plane ticket to Al Alamein, Egypt.

⇒LXI⇐

This flight with Jim was the first flight that Nora took feeling like a normal person without an ulterior motive. She sat cross legged in her seat next to him. Jim was in a daze, trying to replay all of what had happened in such a short time. Nora was in equal awe. She rubbed the now-healed, but scarred spot where she once wore her Tiger Clan tattoo; or rather where the tattoo wore her. Then she moved to the other ankle, which her bracelet once again called home. She felt each of the charms. The tusk. And the newest addition, a small golden money symbol she had taken from one of Batuk's many necklaces. She had yanked it from his deceased body prior to escaping the tower. It served as a reminder of all that she had been through. She didn't want to forget him. What he had done made her who she was today. And for the first time, she was quite content with who that was. She let go of the charms and moved her hand to entwine with Jim's. Home.

⇒LXII⇐

There were a number of letters and packages at the door of Jim's apartment. Most were junk. A couple of threatening eviction letters. Nothing bitter, though. No letter or sign of Lemon.

There were however, two parcels of note.

The first was a letter from Trace Benson. Trace had started the request with insurance for payout on behalf of Jim for the freak fire incident that the police declared a gas leak, lest they be criticized for not discovering the pyromaniac behind it. The return would be beyond what Jim had invested. It was hard for Jim to not immediately imagine the improvements he could make by being able to design the space from scratch, exactly how he'd want it after learning what he did from his first effort. Below the news about Jim's insurance return were a couple of paragraphs about Phil. Here's what it said.

I also heard about your bet with Phil and if he should ever challenge you and claim that the new Herough you build is rightfully his, I'll make sure my best lawyers are by your side to combat it. I doubt he'll be a nuisance to you, however, for two reasons.

The first is that I took the liberty of having the ashes of Herough cleaned up and the land cleared so you have a blank canvas. And while I am sorry to share that there was nothing salvageable in the remains, you'll likely find pleasure in knowing that I had all the ash and rubble placed in a large container and shipped to Phil, noting that a bet was a bet. Herough was his.

Jim gave a hefty Herough laugh out loud to the quizzical but contagiously happy face of Nora who wondered what Jim had read.

The second bit of news is that Phil should be preoccupied with rebuilding his status, anyway. With you nowhere in sight, the media dug deeper to find more dirt on the only person in the public's eye: Phil. He's undoubtedly battling the accusations of bribery from convention judges, verbal threats to other existing and defunct restaurants across the tri-state area, and one horrendous case about a fire at a competing restaurant whose removal accelerated his rise as restaurateur a few years ago; a scenario uncannily similar to yours. Like any good media person, they decided that two ties to fire with Phil was causation, not just correlation. I'm not sure if your absence was part of a grand plan, but if it was, it worked.

Jim couldn't help but think how much Phil deserved all this. His cheating, lying, and bullying finally came around to bite him in the ass.

Anyway, if Phil does ever pop back up as an irritant, let me know. I look forward to swinging by the future Herough. Make it magical.
Blue skies,

—Trace Benson

Jim gave Nora the short version of what the letter meant for them and her excitement was evident.

"I think the real magic that's yet to come is where you decide to go from here," Nora said.

Jim smiled and inspected the final package. There was no return address. He opened the box.

New shoes.

And a note.

You can tell a lot about a person by where they've been, but you can tell even more about who a person is going to become by where they plan to go.—P

After cleaning up and displaying the shoes like a décor piece in Jim's apartment, Jim and Nora wanted to finally rest, but before they could, they needed some food. Well, Nora was hungry. Jim was excited to test out his refreshed taste buds.

Out the door they went.

"Why don't we go see it first?" Nora asked. She wanted to see Herough. Something inside her thought it was important for Jim to see the land. A moment to wrap this adventure up with a bow and ribbon before starting anew. A clean slate to be inspired by. Something new to defend.

Jim was hesitant, but deep down he felt the same as Nora. It was time.

Jim and Nora walked to Herough, where a lot of truth set in.

The truth that the restaurant was completely gone and what lay before them was a completely barren canvas waiting for the artist to show up. From across the street, Jim and Nora could see that Phil's restaurant was closed. It was prime dinner hour, but the lights were off, chairs were stacked on tables, and a thick chain and padlock was wrapped around the handles of the entry doors.

The end of two places, though Jim would make sure the new one would be better than the past. Better for Jim. For the neighborhood. For Shaman Denny. For Pinmekalah and Nora. And especially better for the Irishman. Rest in Irish peace.

As they stood there looking at the empty land and Phil's defunct restaurant across the way, above, the clouds turned an earl grey that steeped too long, and raindrops began to fall. It gave a new meaning to the clean slate in front of them.

"We should probably go before we get really drenched," Nora said.

Instead, Jim took her hand, and walked to the parking lot of Herough where some cars were parked, thinking no harm, no foul since parking was hard to come by in the area. There was a light rumble of thunder, less freaky and more reminiscent of Jim's laugh.

Jim pulled out a small portable music player from his pocket he had picked up while at his apartment earlier. He had added a few songs to it while Nora was in the shower; a slow song playlist in particular. Jim kicked off his shoes so he could feel his way around the asphalt as the night grew darker still. Thunder hiccupped in the background. Rain giggled, too.

"Will you dance with me?" Jim asked, but he didn't need an answer. Nora's shoes were off, too.

Jim took Nora by the waist and she wrapped her arms around his shoulders, hugging him close halfway through the first song. Then, Jim held her at arm's length as he continued to sway. He had to see those Gemini blue eyes in what little light from the nearby light poles glistened off them.

He got lost in them and promised himself he would love this woman forever. He wished that she would do the same for him and he sealed the wish with two kisses on her forehead. Once out of love for her now, and once out of the love for her forever.

Rain pattered down and the thunder turned into a loud, but low purr of satisfaction. Jim lifted the sails up off his lips and let them go with the wind, this time from her forehead to her lips. She held him tighter still, slicing the distance between their bodies by more than half. Jim's tongue found hers and with it the taste of magic. What else could it have ever been?

About the Author

GARTH BEYER is a creative force in the world of storytelling, community building, and craft beer culture. As the owner of Garth's Brew Bar in Madison, Wisconsin, he's known for curating unforgettable experiences that go far beyond the pour.

Garth's passion for connection drives everything he does—from writing metaphysical fiction that explores the weird and wonderful corners of existence, to organizing community events that bring people together in authentic, joy-filled ways.

With a background in marketing and a love for language, Garth bridges worlds: business and art, logic and imagination, local and universal.

You can read more of his riffs at garthbox.com